Hello Faye my wonderful sister

I got this book for you! I hope
See God's love for you as you read through..
It's defo helped me see Him as someone who cares so
much more than I'd ever dare to imagine; God my Lord
Jesus the lover of my soul. I pray this book may bless
you and shift your spiritual vantage point — to know
that Jesus always loved & will alway love you, & I hope
you can yield that truth & walk your life out in
that same love and the boldness from God's love casting
out any last shred of fear.

You are always on HIS mind. May we fix our
eyes and minds on what is true & nobal :)

I love you!
(But will always pale in
comparison to His love for you.)

- Vangie.

The Cord

The Love Story of Salmon and Rahab

CYNTHIA LEAVELLE

Copyright © 2010 by Cynthia Leavelle.
All rights reserved.

Scripture taken from the HOLY BIBLE, NEW INTERNATIONAL VERSION®. Copyright © 1973, 1978, 1984 by International Bible Society. Used by permission of Zondervan. All rights reserved. Quotations marked NIV.

Cover art by Katrina Hamrick © 2010. All rights reserved. Used by permission.

This book is a work of biblically-related fiction.

No part of this book may be reproduced, stored in a retrieval system, or transmitted by any means without the written permission of the author.

First edition published by CrossBooks 2010
Second edition published by Cynthia Leavelle 2015

ISBN-13: 978-1514267158
ISBN-10: 1514267152

Library of Congress Control Number: 2010911549

Printed in the United States of America

To my parents,
Audley and Della Jo Hamrick,
whose lives exemplify
faith and unconditional love

The Cord

*W*hen you go to war against your enemies and the LORD your God delivers them into your hands and you take captives, if you notice among the captives a beautiful woman and are attracted to her, you may take her as your wife. Bring her into your home and have her shave her head, trim her nails and put aside the clothes she was wearing when captured. After she has lived in your house and mourned her father and mother for a full month, then you may go to her and be her husband and she shall be your wife. If you are not pleased with her, let her go wherever she wishes. You must not sell her or treat her as a slave, since you have dishonored her.

Deuteronomy 21:10-14 (NIV)

Contents

Day 1	1
Day 2	9
Day 3	19
Day 4	37
Day 5	47
Day 6	59
Day 7, The First Sabbath	67
Day 8	79
Day 9	87
Day 10	95
Day 11	103
Day 12	115
Day 13	125
Day 14, The Second Sabbath	133
Day 15	143
Day 16	149
Day 17	161
Day 18	169
Day 19	177
Day 20	187
Day 21, The Third Sabbath	195
Day 22	203
Day 23	213
Day 24	221
Day 25	231
Day 26	235
Day 27	241
Day 28, The Fourth Sabbath	247
Day 29	255
Day 30	263
Day 31	271
Epilogue	277

DAY 1

Contentedly grinding barley in the cool of early evening, Rahab looked up when she heard a man approaching, "Salmon." Her voice reflected delight as she rose to greet him.

Unexpectedly, he seized her hand. "Rahab, I've decided to take you into my tent. Come with me."

The cheery greeting died on Rahab's lips. "What do you mean 'take me into your tent'?" she asked, trying to disengage her hand from his grip.

"I'm claiming you."

"Is this part of the law?"

"Yes. Let's go now."

"Do I need to take anything? What about my family?"

Salmon seemed surprised at her questions. "I'll provide everything you need. Your family will be staying here. Come."

Confused, Rahab followed him as he led her out of the alien section. Some of the people they passed watched them curiously, but Rahab barely noticed. Her reeling brain reviewed his words. "What had he meant, 'I'm claiming you.' Claiming me as what—his slave girl, or worse, his concubine?" The idea made Rahab angry. She almost started to turn back, but then she reminded herself, "No, I trust this man, don't I? He's been taking care of us. But what is he doing now?" Unsure of what to think, she kept following.

When they arrived at a circle of tents surrounding a cooking fire, Salmon pointed ahead, "That's my tent." He led her inside and reached for some items. "Here is the knife and the wool garment."

When Rahab hesitated, he said, "I'll leave you alone while you shave your head and pare your nails. Just throw your clothes outside the tent

Day 1

door after you change into the wool. My servants will take care of them." Then he left.

With a shuddering breath, she looked down at the knife in her hand. Finally, she began to cut. The knife was sharp, and she had soon sheared away thick handfuls of hair from her head. Sometimes she nicked her scalp, but each time, she gritted her teeth firmly and continued, her mind whirling all the while with thoughts and questions. "Am I shaking more from fear or anger?" She couldn't tell. "Why did he bring me here into his tent? Why did he tell me to shave my head and pare my nails?"

The tangled pile of dark curls surrounding her represented so much to her—her beauty, yes, but it also had marked her as a Canaanite prostitute. It felt as though her identity had fallen away with the curls. "What strange Israelite custom requires a woman to do these things?" When she finished, her head felt light and a little cool. But the nicked places were beginning to sting, and a trickle of blood ran down her neck from one deep cut.

Her nails had grown long since the end of flax harvest. Using the same knife, she cut each nail, careful not to slice the tips of her slender fingers. Last of all, she removed her delicately woven linen dress and replaced it with the scratchy, shapeless woolen shift that Salmon had given her. For perhaps the first time in her life, Rahab felt ugly as she tossed her discarded clothes outside the tent door. Yet at that moment, she also felt fiercely glad, having no desire to be attractive for anyone, especially not for that man who had brought her here with no warning. "I expected to be free of attention from men here among the Israelites, but obviously that assumption was wrong. On the other hand, he said this was in the law. Yahweh's law wouldn't let him mistreat me, would it?"

"Well, Salmon," she said to the empty tent. "I've done as you asked. What next?" She remembered the first time they had met. Did he really believe what he claimed then, or was he just like all the other men she had known?

That day had been long and hard. Rahab and her family had spent it harvesting her flax fields and hauling the bundles by ropes from outside the city wall to the roof of her inn. Though tired and hungry, she bathed and changed into the provocative clothing she wore in the evening when business was brisk. Her sister, Adah, came into the room while she was still combing out her long curls.

"Two new men are waiting. I've never seen them before."

"Are they from Jericho?"

"I don't recognize their accent. I don't think they're even Canaanite."

Rahab pushed her long brown hair behind her ears, letting her gold earrings dangle freely. "I'll see to them."

Rahab's regular customers had been circulating intriguing rumors about a tribe of strangers on the other side of the Jordan. *Israelites* they were called. Perhaps these men could tell her something new about them.

The strangers were the only ones waiting for her. She felt disappointed but also relieved to see that only two occupied the room. One was a large, imposing man with a full beard and military bearing. The other man was not small, but seemed so next to the larger man. Glancing his way, she found something arresting in the way he was looking at her. Many men had gawked at her before, but this seemed different somehow. Hiding a sigh because she had expected more income from this evening, she beckoned to the men. "Who wants to be first?"

After a moment of hesitation, the shorter and slenderer of the two started toward her. Before he had moved a foot, the larger man grabbed his arm. "No, Salmon, we must not be separated." He turned to her, "Pardon me, but we don't know what you mean."

She spoke sharply. "What are you doing in my inn?"

"Eating and sleeping."

"You didn't come here for me?"

"For you?" The tall man was quizzical. Then understanding dawned on their faces as they took in her hair and clothing.

"No, we don't do that," said the one called Salmon.

"What do you mean you don't do that?" She didn't know whether to laugh or to be offended. "If all you require is a place to sleep, you can find a barn somewhere. I need my rooms for paying customers."

"We'll pay whatever you charge, but we want to stay here."

"Whoever heard of a man who didn't want to lie with any woman who would let him? Truthfully; why are you here?"

Salmon ignored her question. "What we mean is that we don't commit adultery."

"I wouldn't have a business if the men of Jericho acted like you." She looked down pensively at her costume. "Of course, if my husband had believed as you do, I wouldn't have needed a business."

Rahab's mind returned to the present as a sound outside alerted her to the return of Salmon.

Meanwhile, Salmon paced outside the tent for what seemed like hours. He felt the unreality of what he had just done, taking Rahab into his tent to be his wife. Around him, the servants were working industriously—stacking wood, tending the fire, and bringing more water in pots. Their furtive looks told him that they felt as strongly about his bringing Rahab into his tent as his cousin Eleazar had.

"Why do you want to marry her?" Eleazar had protested. "Don't you think you have done enough by rescuing her from Jericho?"

"This isn't a reward for saving my life. I am marrying her because I want to."

"A prostitute, Salmon! What would your parents have said?"

"They would have learned to love her as I have. She's the most genuine person I've ever met."

Eleazar looked unconvinced. "Are you sure her attraction isn't just her beauty?"

"She is beautiful, but I've seen many beautiful women in Israel. Something about her—I think her faith in the Lord—fascinates me."

"What does Joshua say about this plan of yours?"

Salmon smiled. "He didn't seem at all surprised. And he gave his permission."

"Think about her background, her family. What kind of people would allow their daughter to practice prostitution? Why would you want a woman who's known so many men? Have you considered that she isn't likely to remain faithful to you?"

"She would; I know she would."

"Do you really want to be one more in a long line of men?"

Salmon made an impatient motion. "I have made up my mind. I'm telling you, hoping to get your blessing."

Eleazar sighed, "I hope you don't regret your choice."

Remembering this conversation made Salmon restless. Eleazar's questions had occurred to him, too, but something inside resisted facing the truth of Rahab's past. He preferred to focus on what she was now. From the first time he had seen her cascading dark curls and intelligent brown eyes, he had longed to make her his wife. Never had a woman attracted him so much. He was sure that Rahab would soon show any cynics like Eleazar how wrong they were about her.

Glancing up at the setting sun, he moved towards the tent. He hesitated for only an instant before pushing the flap of the tent door aside and entering. In the gloom, he could just make out Rahab huddled on the matting. When she looked up, he could see that she had no hair. He knew that she had been shaving her head, but somehow, he hadn't expected her to look so—plucked. Her expression looked grim.

Fearing to interpret that look, he moved inside. "I see you have done as I said—that's good." Then, following an awkward pause, he pointed to the inner room, which contained supplies and was separated from the main room of the tent by a curtain.. "You will sleep in there, and I will make my bed by the door here."

Rahab stared at him. "I don't understand. Why have you brought me to your tent?"

He turned to her blankly, "Oh, that's right. I forget that you don't know the law. I've asked Joshua to let me claim you as my captive."

When she still looked confused, he continued, "The law says that in that case, I take you into my tent, where you have to shave your head, cut your nails, and change into a woolen garment. After a month of mourning for your family, you can marry me."

"Why should I mourn my family?" Her voice betrayed panic. "You haven't done anything to them, have you?"

"No, I was just stating the law. They're fine. Joshua said we would interpret it that you could not see them for the month. I guess you can mourn not getting to see them."

"What happens here in the meantime?"

"Nothing. I won't lie with you, if that is what you mean. But we can talk."

"Does Joshua's law give the woman any say in this?"

"Joshua didn't make the law. Moses received it on Mount Sinai."

"Well, who gave it to Moses then?"

"The Lord, our God."

"Do you mean Yahweh?"

"Hush; don't say his name!" Hearing the name made him feel a little panicky.

"Why not?"

"Because we're not allowed to use his name flippantly. I don't even say his name at all."

"I wasn't using his name flippantly. I was just asking a question."

"The answer to your question is 'Yes.' He gave us that law, among others."

"What others?" The eagerness of her question surprised him.

"It would take a long time to explain them all."

"But I want to know them all. I want to know everything I can about Yah... I mean, the Lord."

"Maybe I can tell you some more of the law during the next month."

"But if I don't want to stay?"

"Don't you want to?"

"No, I don't."

Salmon stuttered. "But I thought... You seemed so..." Then he fell silent for a moment before stating decisively, "What is done is done."

Day 1

Rahab turned away without responding. She began to clean up the mess that the hair had made on the floor matting. He saw that her hands trembled slightly, and she looked as though she might cry. She moved toward the tent door, but Salmon stopped her. "Where are you going?"

"To throw all this into the fire." She held up the luxurious handfuls of hair that had once graced her head.

"You won't be allowed outside the tent."

"For a whole month, but how will I..."

He answered immediately. "One of my servants will take the chamber pots to the waste burial site."

Rahab threw the hair down again and moved into the inner room where Salmon saw her unroll the bed stored there. She spread out the woven matting and, covering herself with the woolen blanket, lay down with her back to the dismayed Salmon. He thought, "How could I have been so stupid? Why did I think she cared? Because she threw her arms around me that day in Jericho and was glad to see me when I visited her in the alien quarter?"

In all his 41 years, no woman had treated Salmon with anything except admiration, so this situation baffled him. He stooped over to pick up the tangled hair. One of the ringlets curled around his toughened forefinger, and, for just a moment, he sensed something of the pain he had caused Rahab today by dragging her away from her family and requiring her to shave her head.

Salmon heard a quiet voice at the entrance to the tent, so he slipped out, still holding the hair. Othniel stood outside. "How did it go?"

Salmon looked again at the hair and then, carefully retaining the curl that still clung to him, he threw the rest into the fire. Turning to Othniel, he sighed, "I think I've made a big mistake. I thought she would be happy to marry me, but instead, she's angry now and won't speak to me."

"Let's walk away."

They moved down the paths between the tents until they were well out of Rahab's hearing. Othniel said in Canaanite, "What makes you think you've made a mistake? Because she's angry?"

"No, I don't blame her for being angry. I hadn't thought about how she would feel. I just didn't handle this very well. I should have explained before I brought her to my tent." Again, he stroked the curl in his hand with his thumb. "Why are we speaking Canaanite?"

"I have news from Joshua. We are ordered to go to Ai tomorrow early and check its defenses."

Salmon groaned. "Just when I need to be here with Rahab. What else can go wrong! And what will I tell her?"

"Tell her that you are out foraging for food. In a way, that's true." Othniel reached out a reassuring hand to his friend's arm.

"I suppose." Salmon sighed with frustration. "Who knows what will happen now?"

"Don't be too discouraged. You will just have to use these thirty days to try to woo her. We can talk about this more tomorrow."

Salmon returned to his tent. He fumbled in his bag near the door to find a cloth that he kept for wiping his hands and face. Into this cloth, he carefully folded the long curl and returned it to the bag for safekeeping. Then settling himself quietly by the door, he listened for Rahab's breathing, but could hear nothing. He thought how awful it would be if she ran away, but decided that checking on her now would frighten her.

DAY 2

Rahab woke very early the next morning, achy from having fallen asleep tense and emotional. She was afraid to move for fear of drawing Salmon's attention. The wool garment was scratchy, but it was all she had now. Though she had tears in her eyes, she controlled her desire to sob. He would not have the satisfaction of knowing how miserable she felt.

She thought about trying to escape if she could, but rejected the idea. If Salmon brought her there because of Yahweh's law, leaving might displease Yahweh. So many questions waited to be answered, questions about the rules that governed these people and even more about the God who had given the rules. She had staked her life and the lives of her family on her idea that this God of the Israelites was the one true God. But what Salmon had done confused her. Was this part of Yahweh's plan for her? Her thoughts drifted back through her life to the time she first heard the name of Yahweh.

On that day, she was eating with her father, Benne, and her mother, Mora, who had moved from their farm to her inn after the death of Ashtora, the former innkeeper. She had insisted after her father's drunkenness and open purse had squandered all his money. Most of his money had come from the large bride price he had received from Rahab's marriage to Ambaal. He should have saved the money to give back to Rahab when her husband died, but late night drinking binges and gambling parties combined with poor management of his farm to leave nothing. Rahab no longer expected anything from her family. Her mother made it starkly clear shortly before Rahab was married that she was never to come home, even if her husband sent her away.

Day 2

    Mora seemed incapable of dealing with life. She complained endlessly about her husband's alcoholism and the state of their finances, blaming everyone but herself for her difficulties.
    Now her parents and the four children still at home could live in better quarters than the deteriorating farmhouse. With income from the inn and the sale of flax and linen, Rahab could support them all, providing she kept her father from drinking and gambling away her money. Despite their complaints about not having money of their own, they never went hungry as they often had before.
    During their noonday meal that day, Mora was complaining about the large number of sacrifices made to Molech that week.
    "Why so many?" asked Rahab, "I thought we were at peace."
    Benne interjected, "A large group of nomads is approaching. The king thinks they may invade, so he called for the extra sacrifices. He wants Molech on our side in case of war."
    "What have you heard of this group? Are they friendly to Canaan?"
    "Ah," said Benne, "they are a strange group. They worship only one god, and he requires absolute obedience to his laws."
    "What kinds of laws?" Rahab was only half listening. Her mind was occupied with some details of the business, but what he said next grabbed her interest.
    "I have heard that he forbids adultery and child sacrifice."
    "Really," said Rahab leaning forward. "What do you think about that?"
    "Such a god would be against us, our gods, our way of life. They would surely seek to change us, or worse, destroy us."
    "Are they so strong?"
    "They are very large. No one knows how many, but hundreds of thousands were spotted. I heard that their god has given them success in battle. They destroyed the best of Pharaoh's army when they left Egypt, and they have completely defeated Sihon and Og and conquered the Amorite lands. Still, if they came here, we have our fortified walls. I don't see how they could overcome those."
    "And their god forbids adultery?"
    "That's the rumor. I also heard that they have to give their wives a certificate of divorce and can't just drive them away. I tell you, this god seems against men to me."
    Rahab suppressed her rising excitement. "What is their god's name?"
    "Yahweh. It means *I Am*. What a name for a god!"
    What a name indeed!

Peeking quietly around the curtain, she saw that Salmon was not in the tent at all. She was relieved that for one night, at least, he had kept his word about not sleeping with her. But if she knew men, and who better than she, he would not keep his hands off for a month.

She let her gaze wander around the interior of this tent that was to be her home. Like all the other tents in Israel, it had nine poles holding up the dark brown, goat hair fabric. The center pole was so tall that even Salmon could stand inside. The tent had two rooms: a large outer area, and this small inner room where she had slept and where the provisions were kept. But details about the tent indicated to her that the owner had put special care into it. As a weaver herself, she could see that an exceptionally good craftsman had woven the goat hair, one who seemed to have taken special pride in his or her weaving. The rings of the tent were made of metal rather than the carved wood that she had seen on the tents in the alien quarter. Fine palm leaf matting covered the floor, instead of the dirt floors of other tents. She was also surprised at the number of storage jars in the provision room—no shortage of crockery in this tent! Though she had seen much more opulence in homes of the rich in Jericho, she recognized prosperity here, which gave her an uneasy feeling; her only brush with wealth had been her brief and miserable marriage.

Hearing a sound, she adjusted her face to look impassive. Salmon put his head in past the inner curtain and said courteously, "I am going to be gone with another man to forage for food. You may help yourself to anything you need. My servant girl will be in later to take care of things. If you need anything, just tell her. I will probably be gone overnight."

Salmon had come into the tent after checking on his animals hoping to find Rahab more receptive, but after he spoke, her expression didn't change. With a sigh, he turned away, wondering if she would stay in his tent until his return. Just as he had put his head in, he had glimpsed a look on her face that smote his conscience. She seemed so small and forlorn with her shorn head and the lost, even frightened, look in her eyes. It was his decision to bring her here that had given her that look, and he hurt for her. Would she ever learn to care for him? He had waited all these years for just the right woman. He thought it ironic that the right woman should be a Canaanite, when he had always been so careful to follow the law and had looked down on those who did not. Even more ironic, she didn't seem interested in him—one sought after by so many girls and their mothers. Well, he couldn't turn back now and dishonor

Day 2

Rahab. When he thought about it, he realized that he wouldn't ever want to give her up.

Othniel was waiting for him by his own tent in the alien section at the edge of the tribe of Judah. It still irked Salmon that Othniel and the other Kenizzites were treated as lesser people by the Israelites. Hadn't the Kenizzites done as much for Israel as any one else—perhaps more? His mind seemed to be full of questions this morning.

Othniel looked at him curiously, "Well."

"She hasn't spoken to me since last night before you came."

"You can't turn back now, can you?"

"She has already shaved her head. If I sent her away now, it would be a disgrace for her, as if she weren't good enough. No, I'm committed, but I wish I had thought about this some more before I acted so hastily."

"I'm no expert on women, as you know. But I think time could change some things. She can't stay silent forever."

"I hope you're right. I appreciate your encouragement."

He and Othniel had been best friends since they were boys. Othniel had taught him to speak the dialect of Canaanite that had made their job as spies possible. And so far, they had been very successful in bringing back news of the enemy to Joshua.

As if reading his mind, Othniel asked, "What do you know about Ai?"

"I've heard it's a small city, much smaller and less fortified than Jericho. We should have an easy victory, but Joshua wants us to spy it out just the same."

"How far is it from the camp?"

"Only about a half day's walk. We need to keep track of the sun, so we can give an accurate idea of that to Joshua. He wanted to be closer, but not so close that our women and children would be in immediate danger." It touched Salmon to realize that the "women" part of that phrase applied to him now in a more intimate way.

"This is hilly country, isn't it?"

"Yes, a stiff walk for our fighting men."

"But it might work to our advantage in strategy." Othniel always thought in terms of battle plans, one of the reasons he was such a good spy and soldier.

"We should notice any unusual land formations to tell Joshua about, especially closer to Ai." They continued on in companionable silence, stopping at a stream to refresh themselves and observing that it would be a good stopping place for the soldiers as well.

By midday, they could see signs of Ai ahead. The hills around were being quarried. Seeing workmen cutting the stone out of the rocks, they assumed the pose of Canaanite travelers, but were careful to speak to no one. They had found they had better not take chances that their unusual accent might give them away.

As they neared the city, they saw to the north a large plateau separated from the city by a deep valley. In the distance to the west, behind the city, rose several larger hills. The city wall was a flimsy affair compared to the bulwarks of Jericho. Clearly, the people of Ai had counted on Jericho to stand between them and enemies from the east.

Inside Ai, beggars came at the spies at once asking for bread; gangs of boys ran around without supervision, snatching things from vendors. Garbage and filth filled the streets, making the stench almost unbearable. Salmon, disgusted again by what he saw of the Canaanite culture, realized that the Israelite camp was clean. He had taken that for granted. All the laws dealing with waste disposal, which he had always found so burdensome, suddenly made more sense.

In the doorway of one building, several women lounged with uncovered heads. Salmon tried not to make eye contact. He could still be shocked by the idea of prostitution, though it seemed ironic to realize that he now had a Canaanite prostitute living in his tent. "But," he reminded himself, "She's a former prostitute."

Nearer the center of town, they saw evidence of idol worship: a bronze statue of a bull similar to one they had seen in Jericho and a building with a rudely carved statue of an obviously fertile and unclothed woman just inside.

Despite all this, Salmon had not forgotten why he had come there. He saw that there seemed to be little defense except a shoddy city wall with gates of woven branches. The population was not so large either, and they saw fewer military men than they had seen in Jericho. Now, speaking was a risk they had to take. To get more information, they approached a fruit vendor and offered him some Amorite gold for a few figs. Salmon could tell that the man was using unbalanced scales, but to avoid drawing attention, Salmon ignored the cheating and struck up a conversation.

"How is business?"

"Business is terrible, of course. No one will come in from the countryside. They're afraid of being caught here when the Israelites come. We heard what happened at Jericho, and we don't have walls as good as theirs. Our king wants all the men in the area to fight, but he's only been able to muster a couple of thousand. We're doomed unless Baal or Molech deliver us. The priests are making all kinds of sacrifices and promises."

Salmon questioned, as though he didn't know, "What happened at Jericho?"

"You haven't heard? The best defenses in this part of Canaan, double walls of rock, and now the city's gone—burned, and everyone dead."

"How is that possible?" Othniel's face showed horror.

"No one knows for sure 'cause no one survived, you see, but some people thought there might have been an earthquake or something. This god of the Israelites seems pretty powerful. Our men are just shaking in terror."

Salmon nodded sympathetically, but he was thinking that they had picked the right vendor if their goal was to get information. He was a rich source.

Suddenly, the vendor seemed to get suspicious. "Where're you from, anyway?"

"We are Amorites from Bashan," lied Othniel glibly. "We are on our way east from Gibeon toward our land. Are the Israelites close by now?"

"If you're from Bashan, you got no reason to go home. The Israelites killed all your people."

Salmon gasped in pretended shock. "No, surely you are wrong." He looked at Othniel, who gave an imperceptible signal to leave. "We must go at once to see about our families."

"You won't find anyone left," the vendor called after them as they turned and started away. Under cover of their alibi, they moved swiftly toward the gates. No one seemed to take any notice of them, and they were soon out and on their way back toward the Israelites. They had the information they needed. As soon as they were clear of the quarry area, they began to talk.

"So what should our report be?" asked Othniel.

"I don't see any reason to send the whole army up. The defenses are weak, the numbers few, and the potential for strategy is very good."

"I agree. We should be able to take it without much struggle."

"Do you think we will get back to camp tonight?"

"Not if we take a side trip over behind the quarries to see what lies on the other side of those hills."

They headed in that direction as soon as they could do so without attracting attention. Below them lay a country much less populated and rougher than that right around Ai. Salmon noted, "This area might be useful for surprise attacks, but we won't have to worry about that with Ai. Shall we head back?"

Othniel looked at the sun. "I think we should plan on staying overnight at that stream. That will get us in early tomorrow. We have a little of our own food and the figs for which we paid that fruit merchant so dearly."

Salmon smiled wryly. "That kind of cheating would never happen in Israel. We have laws against dishonest scales. Do you believe that the Lord is giving us this land because we deserve it more than the Canaanites?"

Othniel seemed to be thinking hard. "I'm not sure that I can say that exactly. I mean, the land was promised to Abraham long ago, long before any of us were born."

"That's true. But it seems to me that we will make better use of the land than they have."

"I know what you are implying, but isn't the difference that we have the law?"

"Well, I suppose so. But I'm not so sure that the Canaanites would do the right thing even if they had the law."

"Well, you have the perfect test case in your captive. She is Canaanite. See if she is willing to obey the law once she has it."

Salmon was intrigued: Rahab as a test case for the inferiority of Canaanites. Even as he thought about it, he doubted that anyone who had grown up in such conditions as he had seen that day and in Jericho could ever come to obey the law wholeheartedly.

After Salmon left her that morning, Rahab realized that she was alone and probably would be for a day and a night. Instead of being happy about this, Rahab felt angry and out of place in the strange tent. Full of questions, she didn't have anyone to consult and didn't want to start going through his belongings as he had suggested. But she was hungry. Rahab turned toward the various containers behind her and lifted one basket lid tentatively. Inside, she saw some raisins. She took a handful and began to eat when she noticed a large, beautifully carved wooden box underneath the basket. Just when she started to open it, she heard a noise behind her and turned, startled to see that a young woman stood looking at her. Realizing that this must be the servant girl that Salmon had mentioned, Rahab summoned a smile, saying gently, "Hello."

The girl only looked at her guardedly without responding.

Rahab tried again, "Salmon said I could get something out of the stores here. Did he tell you?"

Again, she got no response. The girl seemed to be waiting for her to move, so she did, feeling unwanted and in the way. The girl covered the box up and looked disdainfully at Rahab before going to work. As Rahab settled in the larger room to watch, she realized that the girl was at least eight months pregnant. Rahab wondered if this servant carried

Day 2

Salmon's child. Where had this girl spent the night before? Would she share the tent with them? Was the box hers?

The servant began to make meal preparations, but handled the food awkwardly, almost as though she didn't know what to do with the ingredients. Rahab watched her grind barley into flour and knew that it would make coarse bread. She saw, too, that the girl planned to boil some lentils, but they had not been soaked. "Those will take forever to get soft enough to eat," she said aloud, but the girl only stared back at her blankly.

Then Rahab realized that the girl did not understand what she was saying. She was relieved to know that she wasn't being ignored, but frustrated to encounter one more hurdle in living among the Israelites, a communication hurdle. It hadn't occurred to Rahab before that Salmon's and Othniel's fluency might be unusual among the Israelites. "I wonder how he learned to speak Canaanite so well, but then you can't tell me, can you?"

The girl's continued silence confirmed her suspicions about the language problem. Rahab sighed because she had been hoping to ask the servant the questions that she didn't feel free to ask Salmon. The girl took her food outside to cook on the fire. Rahab wanted very much to go out to watch, if not to help, but she was trapped inside this tent.

At noon, the food was ready, but the taste was unappealing to Rahab, especially when she knew just how she could have improved the flavor of everything. The bread crumbled easily, and the watery, crunchy lentil stew had no seasoning. She ate some to be polite, but even her hunger couldn't make that meal appetizing.

She noticed that the servant had pointedly rolled up Rahab's bed, though Rahab had left it neat enough. She wondered what that was all about. Did the Lord have a rule about beds? After a bit more cleaning up from the noon meal, the servant left, still not speaking at all. Rahab tried to imagine herself in a similar situation and decided that she would have tried to communicate somehow. This servant must have other reasons for silence than just the language barrier. If Salmon was the father of her child, this servant might really resent Rahab's presence.

Quiet filled the tent. Her life here already differed from life in Jericho. She felt grateful for this in many ways. For one thing, she wouldn't miss the noise of the streets. Her inn had been located in the part of town that never slept, where gangs roved about. All night, she had heard loud laughter, screams, children crying. For another, she wouldn't miss the Jericho men, with their leering grins and hot, alcoholic breath. Rahab had learned long before to close her mind to what her business meant.

She had performed a service to make the money that kept her alive and took care of her family.

But all that was going to change now. Salmon said he intended to marry her. What would that mean? Could she ever feel what a woman should feel for her husband? Could he be different from other men? "How can I care for him when he is the kind of man to just steal me this way?" Hearing her own voice speak the words, she sighed to think that she had no one to say this to. Right now, she did not have anyone at all. But had she ever had anyone, really? Her only childhood friend had grown up to betray her. Her sister had been very young when Rahab was married, and her brothers had been just babies. As for her parents, she couldn't seem to forgive them for the marriage that they had arranged for her. She had done a lot of talking in her life as a business owner and the main support for her family, but she had never really had anyone to share her heart with, a person who seemed to care about her as more than a physical commodity.

But then she remembered that she did have someone to talk to now. She spoke tentatively into the silence, "Why am I here? I know that you have been taking care of me so far, but I don't understand this part. Can you show me what to think?"

Just talking to someone else eased her heart a little. She ate a few more raisins before settling down for the night. Surely not every day would be this dull and lonely.

DAY 3

Salmon woke stiff and a little chilled. But as a spy and soldier he had become accustomed to sleeping on the hard ground without a fire. He and Othniel rose and, after washing their faces in the stream, ate a little breakfast. Then they headed back toward the Israelite camp. He was anxious and preoccupied thinking about what he would find in his tent.

He didn't realize that he hadn't spoken for several miles until Othniel asked: "Do you think Joshua will take our recommendation?"

"What's that? Oh, you mean about Ai? I don't know. He surprises me sometimes with the unusual decisions he makes. Who would have thought about marching around the city seven days and seven times on the last day? It was lucky that the earthquake came when it did to destroy the city."

"Do you call it luck?"

"Well, no. I suppose I should say the Lord did it. A coincidence would be harder to believe, but I don't think the Lord would perform a miracle like that for me just because I asked him to."

"You mean a miracle like making Rahab really want to be your wife?"

Salmon looked up into Othniel's smiling eyes and realized that he had been caught. "Is it that obvious?"

"That you are thinking about her all the time instead of about our strategy for conquering Ai? Yes, but I understand. I think more about Acsah than anyone would ever suspect."

"What are your chances for winning her hand?"

"Not very good, unless Uncle Caleb changes his mind. He loves me as his nephew, but he really wants Achan's son to be her husband. Achan's pedigree is flawless." A touch of bitterness tinged his voice.

"Why does that matter to Caleb?"

Day 3

"You don't understand how it feels to be an alien around you full-blooded Israelites. Caleb just wants his grandchildren to be in the tribe of Judah legitimately. I can't really blame him for that, but..."

"But you love Acsah."

"Yes."

Salmon was quiet for a moment. Then he turned to Othniel. "I was thinking about some of the things I said to you yesterday about Canaanites. I wasn't implying that you're inferior. Sometimes I just forget that you aren't Israelite."

"I understand. I'm not offended."

"Do you think Rahab will be treated differently because she's not Hebrew?"

"It will help that she will be your wife, but yes, I don't imagine anyone will ever let her forget that she isn't a descendant of Abraham."

"I wonder if she will have any friends?"

"Besides you?"

"She isn't my friend, yet."

"What about Acsah?"

"As a friend? Do you think she would mind?"

"No, I think that she would be glad to be Rahab's friend. She has asked me a lot of questions about Rahab, especially knowing you wanted to marry her."

"How is it that you get to be with Acsah so much?"

"I know better than to let Uncle Caleb know how I really feel about her, so he lets me be with her as a family member. If he knew the truth, I'd probably never get to see her. I don't want to be cut of from all contact with her."

"Does she know how you feel?"

"I think she may suspect, but that would be bad if she really has to marry someone else."

"So we both have our difficulties with women."

"Yes, we do." Then briskly, "Shouldn't we talk about our report for Joshua?"

They walked on then, discussing Ai.

Joshua's tent stood in the part of camp designated to the tribe of Ephraim. Since Joshua was not a Levite, his place was not as near the tabernacle as Moses' had been. The sides of his tent were up, and a fresh breeze was blowing through. He welcomed Salmon and Othniel, "What do you have for me?"

They described the city and its surroundings and the state of mind of the people of Ai. "You will not need the whole army. The city isn't well constructed, and we saw only a few men there," said Salmon.

"Do you agree, Othniel?" Joshua turned his piercing gaze to the taller man. It occurred to Salmon that agreement between his spies would be important to Joshua.

"Yes, I agree. Three thousand of our troops would be more than enough," answered Othniel.

Joshua hesitated, but then looked up pleasantly and said, "You've been good spies for me. I trust your judgment. The two of you do not need to go. Pick the best units and give detailed instructions to their leaders. They should leave tonight. I know, Salmon, that you need to stay in camp now."

Salmon appreciated this thoughtfulness of Joshua's, but something about his manner made Salmon uneasy. After they had left the tent, he asked Othniel, "Did you notice anything unusual about Joshua?"

"Perhaps a little. Why do you ask?"

"His hesitancy and lack of resolve about the decision were uncharacteristic. Usually he exudes confidence in giving orders. Is it my imagination?"

"No, now that you mention it, he did seem different. Do you think he is ill?"

"I hope not with anything serious. We need Joshua now more than ever."

"Which units shall we send?"

"Let's get the units from Reuben and Gad. They are anxious to finish conquering Canaan, so they can get back to their women and children."

"Yes, they should be willing to fight soon and often."

They headed toward that part of the Israelite camp, where they found the leaders and delivered the order to march toward Ai within the hour. Othniel carefully explained what they knew about the lay of the land and the defenses of the city, and he also mentioned the stopping place to the men who would be leading the assault. In just a few minutes, that part of the camp was moving in the ordered chaos of men being mustered suddenly for battle. Salmon turned away with the feeling that he could set the battle aside and concentrate on the reason he needed to be in camp—Rahab.

She had spent a lonely morning in the tent with nothing to do except watch the silent servant girl move about doing all the work. She saw that the girl was skilled at making goat's cheese. The girl made it in much the same way that Rahab would have—heating the goat's milk before adding a bit of the water from a boiled calf stomach, then straining the

Day 3

milk through a clean cloth before setting it aside in a covered bowl to set. But Rahab thought she would have added a bit of salt to the mixture, too. Rahab was surprised that this girl seemed to know how to make cheese when she didn't know how to make something as basic as bread. She wanted to help, but she couldn't ask in Hebrew, and the servant girl really acted as if she weren't there.

Rahab had not experienced this kind of leisure in a long time, but instead of enjoying it, she found herself restless and miserable. She didn't want the role of pampered concubine. She wondered again why Salmon had left her alone on her first day in his tent. "Perhaps he will have changed his mind and will set me free when he comes back."

Just before noon, Salmon came in, looking tired. She was surprised that he had no food supplies with him. A day-long forage should have yielded something. The servant girl put a meal in front of them: some of the lentil stew and bread left from the day before. The goat cheese would not be ready for several days. If the food had been bad before, it was worse today. Silently, Rahab watched Salmon as he doggedly ate without comment. He caught her glance and grinned at her. "You are wondering why I tolerate such food, but I dare not complain. The Lord has provided this, and we must eat it with thanksgiving."

When she still refused to say anything one way or another, he continued his one-sided conversation. "You probably know that we were in the wilderness for forty years after we had left Egypt." He paused, and, though she gave no indication that she was listening, kept going, "Not long after we came into the desert, people began starving for lack of food. Then a miracle happened; the Lord made a kind of dew fall every night that hardened into small white food pellets. We could gather those together and eat them, so we had plenty to eat for the entire time we were in the wilderness. When we first saw it, everyone said, 'Manna?' which means 'What is it?' so that's what we called it from then on.

"I was just a small boy when I first understood not to complain about the Lord's provision." His eyes stared of as he remembered. "I had finished my chores and sat down near my mother. I asked, 'Mother, will we ever have other things to eat besides manna?'

"She looked at me warily, 'Why do you ask such a question? Don't you get enough?'

"I told her that I had been talking to some of the older boys, who said they wished they could have something different to eat like figs or onions. I was curious to know about what they were saying because I had never had any figs or onions. I was born after we had entered the wilderness.

"My mother told me about what happened to the Israelites at Kibroth-hattaavah. The people had become discontented with only manna and had begun to beg Moses for meat. The Lord sent a cloud of quail. I had to ask what those were. I had never seen quail. The Lord sent so many that people became greedy and killed hundreds of ephahs. But Mother said that when the people started to eat the quail, many of them became sick and died. So many people died in that plague. After telling me all this, she looked at me seriously and said, 'We shouldn't complain, but be grateful for the manna.' That was the first time that I understood that the Lord was very particular about the food we ate and about our attitudes."

"Your god killed people for complaining about the food?" asked Rahab, so surprised that she forgot she wasn't speaking to him.

Smiling, Salmon answered, "We should have been thankful that we had manna, considering that we were traveling in a desert and had no supply of grain available. I like having the variety of foods that we have here in the Promised Land, but of course my generation doesn't know much about cooking with foods other than animal products. I rather miss manna; it had a good flavor. But I'm not complaining," he added hastily. Rahab wanted to smile at his expression, but she steeled herself as she thought again of how he had put her in this position. That reminded her of the servant girl, and her curiosity compelled her to say, "Tell me about your servant girl. Is she a captive of yours, too?"

Though he must have been aware of the bite in her tone, Salmon answered courteously, "Shamar is a young Benjamite who is married to another of my servants, Elon. He works with the animals, and they live in a separate tent. They have been working for me three of the seven years."

"Seven years of...?"

"We cannot keep a male Israelite slave for more than seven years according to the law. I intend to free both Elon and Shamar when the seven years are up and set them up in housekeeping."

"Whereas I, a Canaanite, have a lifetime sentence." Her bitterness was reflected in her voice.

"You're not my slave, Rahab. I want you for my wife, my only wife."

"And meanwhile, we live in the same tent like brother and sister?"

"Yes."

She refused to meet his gaze, but toyed with the bowl, willing herself to eat a bit more of the poorly cooked fare.

"You don't believe me!"

"I don't believe you are lying; I just think you do not know yourself."

"And you think you know me better than I know myself?"

"Yes, I do." She paused and looked into his face. "That makes you angry, doesn't it!"

"I don't see why you are so presumptuous as to think that I'm no different from other men you have known."

Rahab was startled that he had hit so close to the truth. But she just shrugged and said, "We'll see who's right."

Just then, Shamar came and gathered up the food and dishes to take them away. Rahab sighed as she saw even that little bit of work taken from her. Since she had already broken her vow of silence, she decided that the time had come to confront Salmon about how miserable she felt in the situation.

"Salmon, I need to talk to you about something."

"Yes, what is it?"

"I can't live like this. If you won't let me go, at least give me something to do to occupy myself."

"You're bored?"

"Yes, I am."

"Why?'

"Wouldn't you be bored if you had nothing to do all day but sit with no one to talk to?"

"Doesn't Shamar talk to you?"

"She doesn't speak Canaanite."

"I hadn't really thought about that."

"I don't think she wants to try to communicate with me. I think she would prefer I were in the tents with the other aliens, as would I."

"I'll have to have a talk with her. Meanwhile, what is it that you want to do?"

"The things I was doing before. I had an active life before your people came and destroyed my city."

"Are you saying you miss your life as a prostitute?"

"No, of course not. I'm not saying that at all."

"Well, what else did you do that you miss now?"

"I cooked food for the inn, and I farmed my fields and made linen from the flax. The weaving gave me a creative outlet, something to do when business was slow. I don't have anything to do with my hands here, and I miss it."

"I don't know how we could arrange for you to weave. No one has done much weaving in several years since we have been traveling so much. We don't have a lot of cloth making because our clothes don't wear out, so we don't have to replace them. Only when a child outgrows a garment do we make a new one, and besides, most of our clothes are made from wool."

"Your clothes don't wear out? I don't understand."

"My parents told me that clothes get holes and become unwearable in time, but I have trouble imagining that. None of mine ever have."

"That's amazing."

"Yes, I guess so." He looked as though he had never thought of it that way before.

"I suppose I have no reason to weave then, if no one needs new clothes. But you could let me do some of the cooking if you aren't afraid I'd poison you."

This comment seemed to wound him a little, but he replied calmly, "I'll talk to Joshua about this. Meanwhile, I think some of the women might be able to come see you."

"Do any of them speak my language?" she asked rather sarcastically.

"Trust me," he replied shortly before exiting the tent.

After he left, Rahab thought about their exchange. She felt a little guilty that she had been so rude, but didn't he deserve that after what he was doing? Now she was alone again and didn't know for how long.

Salmon first headed toward Caleb's tent. He tried to feel encouraged. Rahab had spoken to him. That was progress, surely. But her attitude made it clear that she didn't have any desire to stay with him. He thought about how her eyes had snapped when she talked. She was the most attractive woman he had ever seen, even bald and angry.

Caleb was sitting next to his fireside on a mat. He greeted Salmon, "What brings you to the alien section? Are you looking for Othniel?"

"Actually, sir, I was hoping to speak to your daughter, if you don't mind."

Caleb beamed at this request. "Acsah, come out here and talk to your cousin's friend."

An attractive girl of about eighteen appeared from the tent behind Caleb. "Hello, Salmon."

Salmon noted that his friend Othniel had good reasons to feel as he did about this girl. "I have a favor to ask of you, Acsah."

"What is that?"

"You have no doubt heard of the woman that we saved from Jericho."

"Rahab? Of course; Othniel told us all about her. She saved your lives when you were spies, right?"

"Yes, well, I've gotten permission from Joshua to claim her as a captive and take her into my tent."

"Oh, I know that law. Then you're going to marry her in a month."

"That is the plan. But I have a problem. She doesn't speak Hebrew, and she is bored sitting in the tent all day."

Day 3

"I would be happy to go over there. Every day if you need me."

Salmon sighed in relief. "Thank you, Acsah."

Caleb entered the conversation. "You've taken a Canaanite into your tent to be your wife?"

"Yes, sir. I have. But she is a believer in the Lord. I am sure about that." He couldn't quite account for the look of disappointment in Caleb's face.

"Father, may I go to see this Rahab now?"

Caleb looked up at his daughter, "Yes, go. Perhaps you will be a good influence on her. Teach her what you can about the law."

"Yes, Father."

Salmon said his goodbyes and made his way over to Joshua's tent, relieved that Acsah had agreed so readily to befriend Rahab. As he walked through the camp of Judah, he nearly ran into a stocky figure who appeared suddenly around the corner of a tent. He looked up to see his cousin Elimelech.

"Salmon! I haven't seen you in days."

"How is your family?"

"We're fine. And we have some good news. Naomi tells me that we are to expect a new addition by the end of the summer."

"Congratulations. I'm glad to hear it."

"I should say the same to you. I understand you've taken the Canaanite woman into your tent. I think you have made a good decision!"

"Well, thank you Elimelech. You must be about the only one who thinks it's good."

"No doubt they object because she's Canaanite. I think it's really broad-minded of you to marry one of the local people."

"Broad-minded?"

"I don't understand this prejudice against the Canaanite culture. It seems to me that we ought to accept people as they are, intermarry, and live together without all this bloodshed."

"But I thought the prohibition was from the Lord because he doesn't want us to follow the local gods."

"We don't know anything about growing crops and living in fertile country. We may need the help of the local gods to be able to prosper here."

"But the law says we aren't supposed to worship any other gods."

"That's true, but if other gods exist, we wouldn't want them to be against us, would we?"

Salmon shook his head. This kind of talk always frustrated him because he had always been so careful to follow the law exactly, and yet some aspects of it seemed unclear to him. He wasn't sure himself why all of the killing was necessary. "What about the plague when the men took the Moabite women?"

"How do we know those two things were related?"

"Moses said so."

"Couldn't Moses be wrong? After all, a man who is trying to stay in power would want to blame any problems on people disagreeing with him."

"Are you saying that you don't believe in the law?"

"I admire many aspects of Moses' law. I just think sometimes we are too submissive. We should use our common sense and not follow blindly."

Salmon tried to think of a courteous way to stop the discussion before it turned into an argument. "I'm sorry to have to interrupt our discussion, but I really need to talk to Joshua about something important."

"Of course, I understand. Just keep what I'm saying in mind. I'm anxious to meet this Rahab. I'm sure she could teach all of us a thing or two."

Salmon nodded before heading off toward Joshua's tent. He tried to push Elimelech's unsettling ideas out of his mind. He thought about Rahab. Would she lead him astray, or was she sincere in her belief in the Lord?

Several people were waiting to see Joshua when he arrived at the tent, so he joined them in line. The others who were there spoke to him with the respect to which he was accustomed. He couldn't help but contrast their attitude to that of the woman in his tent. Yet he still wanted her to be his wife.

Finally, he was able to approach Joshua. Joshua greeted him kindly. "Did the troops get off all right for Ai?"

"Yes, sir. We sent units from Reuben and Gad."

"Good. What is your question?"

"Well, sir, I have a question about the interpretation of the law concerning a captive woman."

Joshua smiled. "Didn't I tell you that she wouldn't be content to sit still all day doing nothing?"

"Yes, sir. You did. How much should she be allowed to do?"

"What does she want to do?"

"She wants to cook and weave."

"Then see what you can do to make that possible. I see no reason that she can't work in and around the tent. The only point I take from the Lord is that she can't see her parents."

"Thank you, sir."

"You're welcome. Are you going to check on her parents?"

Day 3

"Yes, I'm going there next."

"Good."

Salmon knew he had been dismissed. He headed of to see Rahab's parents. They were in a tent that had been provided by Joshua to house them after Jericho. Though not as nice as his, it was just as roomy.

Benne greeted him characteristically. "What have you done with my daughter?"

Salmon clenched his jaw but spoke calmly. "Rahab is living in my tent now."

"You didn't discuss this with me."

"We have a law that allows us to marry a captive woman. Normally, such a woman would not have any parents to ask, so it doesn't give instructions about that."

"Is it against your law to tell a man when his daughter is being abducted?"

Salmon was almost at the end of his patience, so he was glad when Mora interrupted their exchange. But then he saw that she had been crying. "Are you all right?"

She sniffed, "I'm so unhappy. We lost everything we had in Jericho; all our friends are dead; now Rahab is gone. What is going to become of us?"

"I promise that everything will be all right. I'll take care of you."

Mora snorted, "Anything would be better than this tent."

Benne spoke up. "Our farm isn't so far from here. Let us go there now. We can fix it up and live there."

"I'm sorry, but you will not be safe if you are not in company with Israel until the conquest is over. You'll just have to accept that."

Benne looked furious, but before he could respond, Mora spoke, "When will we get to see Rahab again? You've taken her away, and I need her."

"Rahab will be in my tent for thirty days. At the end of that time, I will marry her. She cannot see you until then."

"What is she doing there?"

"Well, starting tomorrow, she is going to do a bit of cooking."

"Oh, could I send her something? I have some things that might be helpful to her."

"Certainly, I'll be happy to deliver those."

Mora disappeared into the tent and reappeared carrying a small cloth sack. "She will know what to do with these." She looked disgruntled. "If Rahab were here, I wouldn't have to divide my supplies like this."

The Cord

Salmon took the sack and used this opportunity to make his escape. "I'll check on you again soon. Let me know if you need anything." With that, he headed back to the tent, leaving Benne glowering behind him.

Meanwhile, Rahab sat alone with only her thoughts for company. Her mind ran over what had happened to her in the last few days. Four days before, the whole nation of Israel had packed up and moved a day's journey west from their camp near Jericho. Salmon had sent servants and pack animals to help her family with the move. At that time, she thought nothing but good of Salmon. He had kept helping them after the battle. Her parents had a difficult transition because they had not known before about the arrangements she had made with Salmon and Othniel. The complete overthrow of Jericho and the loss of all they had ever known were devastating to accept, and they felt like prisoners.

But Rahab had never been so happy. She was finally free of the torment of being married to Ambaal and from the degrading profession of prostitution. She was with people who held values similar to her own, values quite different from those of Canaan. And best of all, she was with the God that she had chosen to believe in from a distance. Now she could know all about him. When Salmon had come that evening two days before, she hadn't been surprised to see him. He had been out to see about them many times and had brought them several necessary items, including food. But this time, his manner had surprised her, especially when he so brazenly took her hand and told her to come with him without explaining why. Her experiences with men had nearly always ended badly, so she had imagined the worst in this case, too. When he handed her the wool garment and knife, her anger had flamed so hot that she still felt it. She had not wanted another husband, but no one had given her a choice. "Well," she thought, "if I have to go through with it, I will, but I don't have to be happy about it."

A soft sound at the tent entrance caused her to look up. A young and very beautiful girl stood there waiting to be admitted. "May I come in?" She spoke softly in Canaanite.

Rahab was so relieved to hear another woman speaking her language that she answered eagerly, "Please, do."

"My name is Acsah. My father is Caleb."

"Welcome, Acsah. Are you here to help me occupy myself?"

Acsah laughed delightedly. "I suppose you could say that."

"You probably know more about me than I do about you."

"Yes, I imagine so, but I want to know more."

"What, for example?"

Day 3

"Is it really true that you are a believer in the Lord even though you are Canaanite?"

"Yes, I believe."

"How could that happen so quickly?"

"If you had seen and lived through what I have, you would be happy to change for a God such as yours."

Acsah looked as if she wanted to ask more questions, but Rahab abruptly changed the subject. "Tell me about yourself. Are you married?"

Acsah flushed, "No, I'm not. But it isn't my fault. My father has very specific requirements for a husband."

"You are too beautiful not to have suitors."

"Yes, well, the man I like the best is not my father's choice."

"I would ask who that is, but I wouldn't know him anyway."

"Actually, you would."

Rahab looked surprised. The only Israelite men she had met were Joshua, Salmon, and the other spy—she looked up—"Othniel!"

"You guessed right. I have loved him since I was very young, but my father wants someone from the direct line of Judah, not a Kenizzite like we are. Othniel is my cousin. We are descended from an Edomite who went with Judah into Egypt."

"So you are Canaanite, too."

"Don't remind me. It has been pushed in our faces all our lives. That's why Father wants a true descendant of Jacob to be my husband and the father of my children."

"But I think I've heard of your father. Isn't he one of the hero patriarchs of the Israelites?"

"Yes, he was the only spy besides Joshua who was not afraid forty years ago to come into the Promised Land. The other ten were afraid and made the Israelite people rebel. The Lord punished all of them by making them wander in the desert for the last forty years. Only Joshua and Father are left of those who escaped Egypt as adults."

"You are so young to have such an aged father."

"I am the child of his old age. He dotes on me, but I'm afraid that if he keeps up his stubbornness, I may die without having the chance to be a wife and mother."

"He is unusual. You have mostly younger people in the Israelite camp."

"It takes young people to survive the rigors of the desert and to conquer a new land."

"I suppose you're right. I think my parents feel a little out of place; so few people are their age."

"I'll ask my father to seek out your father. They would probably enjoy each other's company, and it would give your father an opportunity to see that Canaanites can be happy in Israel."

"Would you do that? That's so kind. I worry about my family. I can't help them from here, and they have been through so many changes."

"I'll do it." She smiled at Rahab, and Rahab realized that she had made a new friend.

"Before you came in, I was just thinking about how I ended up in this situation."

"Do you mean in the camp of Israel or in Salmon's tent?"

"I guess more in Salmon's tent. He hasn't told me why exactly."

"I can tell you a little of what Othniel has told me."

"What did he say?"

"He said that Salmon was really impressed with your faith in the Lord. It amazed him that you would risk your life for him and for Othniel, just because you believe that the Lord is the true God."

"But why does he want to marry me?"

"Let me see, how did Othniel say that? He said that Salmon wanted a soul mate who would care about the things he did and would be interesting to talk to. Salmon obviously thinks you are the one. You didn't know that?"

"No, I just assumed..." What had she assumed? She shook her head as if to clear it. "Acsah, what can you tell me about Salmon?"

"You know that his father was the leader of the tribe of Judah?"

"No, he never told me that either."

"His cousin is the high priest, Eleazar. His father's sister Elisheba married Aaron, so he was kin by marriage to Moses and Aaron."

"I've heard the name Moses, but not Aaron."

"They are the brothers who led our people out of Egypt and gave us the law. Aaron was the first high priest, and Moses was the leader of the people. He appointed Joshua to take his place before he died."

"So you're saying that Salmon was kin to the leader of the whole nation of Israel?"

"Yes; many in the tribe of Judah consider him something of a prince because of his background and connections. He is very rich, but you probably knew that, too."

"No." Rahab was feeling a little bit lightheaded. Why had she not known all of this about Salmon? Why would he want to marry her if he were so prominent?

"What is Salmon like as a person?"

Day 3

"He and Othniel have been best friends since they were boys. Othniel told me he would rather have Salmon by his side than anyone else in a battle. He has always been very careful to follow the law."

"Is that important?"

"Yes, it means he's righteous. Men who aren't careful to do what the Lord says endanger their families as well as themselves. I have heard that all of my life."

"Speaking of the law, what law got me into this tent with my head looking like this and with a man I barely know planning to marry me?" She touched her bald head where a stiff stubble of hair had begun to shadow her head dark again.

Acsah laughed at Rahab's description. "The law goes like this: 'When you go to war against your enemies and the Lord your God delivers them into your hands and you take captives, if you notice among the captives a beautiful woman and are attracted to her, you may take her as your wife. Bring her into your home and have her shave her head, trim her nails and put aside the clothes she was wearing when captured. After she has lived in your house and mourned her father and mother for a full month, then you may go to her and be her husband and she shall be your wife. If you are not pleased with her, let her go wherever she wishes. You must not sell her or treat her as a slave since you have dishonored her'" (Deut. 21:14, NIV).

"You must know the law very well to be able to quote it that way."

"Part of the law commands that we write it on our hearts. We take that to mean that we should memorize the law. I have also memorized some of it in Canaanite. I don't know all of the laws, but I knew that law because I find it so interesting."

"Well, the law explains everything clearly. I didn't know that if I displease him, he can send me away."

"I don't think you are in much danger of that. He seems really attracted to you."

"Perhaps that is the danger."

"Pardon me?"

"Never mind. I noticed that you speak Canaanite very well. Is that from your heritage?"

"Yes, my father wanted us to understand the language of our ancestors. The Kenizzites kept up association with Canaanite traders through the years and maintained their knowledge of the language even in Egypt. He taught the language to me. He is rather inconsistent on that point considering his desire to seem Israelite, but now the ability is rather a blessing."

"Especially to me. What about Othniel and Salmon?"

"Of course, Othniel learned from his parents as I did from mine, but Salmon learned it just because he was interested. When they were youngsters, Salmon begged Othniel to teach him. Othniel says they used it as a secret friendship language when they were boys. I think Salmon must be rather brilliant."

"And, of course, this ability to speak the local language made them better spies."

"Yes, it did. What do you think? Is our dialect close enough?"

"Well, the dialect sounds different from the one around Jericho, but you could pass for a Canaanite. Speaking of language, I suppose now that I am with the Israelites, I should be learning Hebrew."

"The two languages aren't as far apart as you might think. You could pick it up quickly. The words are usually about the same, but we pronounce them differently."

"Could you come sometimes and teach me? I'm sure not many could do it as well as you could."

"I will come as often as I can. Did I answer all of your questions about Salmon?"

"Not all of them, but as many as I can think of now. You make him sound like a nearly perfect man."

"He is very well-thought-of by all of Judah, and really all of Israel. Many have wondered why he didn't marry before. Several young women envy you right now. In fact, if I didn't love Othniel so much, I would consider Salmon, even if he is in his forties."

"Well, that is older than I am, but not as much as it could be."

"How old are you?"

"I am twenty-five."

"I am only eighteen, but that is almost too old to be unmarried in Israel."

"It would be in Jericho, too."

"But you are unmarried, right?"

"I am a widow."

"Of course, you would be, now."

"Yes, my mother is the only married woman left from Jericho."

"Are you sorry about your husband?"

"Would you think me heartless if I said no?"

"I'm sure you have a good reason to feel the way you do."

"I do, but I'm not ready to talk about that."

"I understand, I think." Acsah paused. "Well, I'll leave now."

"Thank you for coming. I'll probably have many more questions to ask you by the time you come again."

"I've enjoyed talking to you."

Day 3

After Acsah left, Rahab sat thinking about what she had learned. If she displeased Salmon, he could let her go. She felt a little more hopeful that he wouldn't keep her forever. Yet she was intrigued by what Acsah had said about his being a prince among the Israelites. Could it be true that he cared about her for more than just her body? That seemed nearly impossible to Rahab. He couldn't know much about her in such a short time. And no man in her experience had ever cared about her for any other reason. Even her father had seen her beauty as a commodity for barter. No, Salmon would end up like all the other men she had known, and she would be just as much alone as she had always been. That thought surprised her. Why did she consider marriage as lonely? What exactly was she looking for?

Before she could pursue that thought, Salmon came in. In her confusion, she stammered out, "Thank you for sending Acsah to visit. She seems like a very kind girl."

Salmon's face reflected his pleasure at being treated with civility. "You're welcome. I thought having some company might help you be less bored."

"It did."

A silence followed, which Salmon broke first. "I wanted to tell you that I talked to Joshua about how much you would be allowed to do. I interpreted the law that you couldn't do anything, but Joshua said that he saw no reason for not letting you cook and do other domestic chores in and around the tent. In fact, he said you could leave the tent some, as long as you do not go to the part of the camp where your parents are staying. That seemed to be clear from the wording."

Rahab nodded. So she would be allowed to cook. That would be better than just sitting.

"You'll need to cover your head. I think I might have something." He began rummaging in the stores, finally opening the carved wooden box that she had noticed on the first day. From it, he produced a piece of blue cloth.

Rahab backed away from the proffered gift, "No, thank you."

Salmon responded insistently, "Don't be stubborn. If you are going out, you must have a head covering."

Rahab didn't want to accept anything else from him, but saw the logic of what he was saying. She took the fine cloth with a sigh of resignation. As she fingered it, she saw that it was an unusually well made blue head covering. It occurred to her that this might be that servant girl Shamar's, and she asked icily, "Where did you get this?" To her surprise, she saw tears in Salmon's eyes.

"It was my mother's."

"Your mother's?"

"Yes." He was quiet.

Rahab's compassionate nature compelled her to say, "Your mother was a fine weaver, wasn't she?"

"Yes, she was."

"Did she make the material for this tent?"

"How did you know?"

"I noticed the fineness of the weave. No one does better work than a woman making something for her home."

"Or in this case, actually making the home. She made it just before I was born in the wilderness."

"Where did she get the goat hair?"

"From our goats."

"You must have quite a few."

"Yes, I do. Speaking of parents, I saw yours today. Your mother sent this to you." Salmon handed Rahab a small skin sack. She looked in it and smiled. Sticks of cinnamon, a small pouch of salt, a smaller bag of cumin, and some dill leaves—just what she needed. He asked, "Where did she get these?"

"I'm not sure. She might have had them with her when we left Jericho. She was always very careful with her spices and herbs."

"Oh, well, when I told your family about your being allowed to cook, she thought these might be useful."

"I'll cook the midday meal tomorrow."

"I will be here just for the pleasure of eating your cooking."

Rahab ignored his attempt at gallantry. "I need to know a little more before I decide what I can cook. Do you have any wheat?"

"I saw some wheat that looked ready while I was out today, but it will take some time to harvest that. I'm not sure how we are going to go about that. The truth is, only Joshua and Caleb have ever planted or harvested crops, and that was in Egypt. None of the rest of us knows how to go about this farming business."

Rahab interjected impatiently, "My father was a farmer. He would know exactly how to harvest that wheat. In fact, those might even be his fields. We are not far from the place where I grew up."

"I thought your family lived in Jericho."

"I lived in Jericho after I was married. But before that, I lived in the country. Besides, a lot of us in Jericho had fields outside the city walls. I have a lot of experience with growing food myself."

"I think I should have another talk with your father. He could teach me something, I believe."

"So what else do you have here that I could use now?"

Day 3

"I think we have some barley. I may be able to capture a bird tomorrow."

"That would be good. Perhaps if you go early in the morning before anyone is up."

"I'll do that." He began to settle his bag and slingshot near his part of the tent.

"Is there anything else I need to know about cooking here?"

"Yes, the cooking fire is in the center of the group of seven tents including this one. All of these share the same fire to conserve fuel. You can use it at any time you want."

"Shouldn't I take my turn with the women from the other tents?"

"Actually, all the people in those tents are servants of mine, so as my soon-to-be wife, you would have first priority."

"All of those tents and the people who live there belong to you? How many servants are there?"

"Four are family tents and two are tents for men only. Altogether I have twelve men and four women. They have ten children among them and another is on the way, as you have observed."

"Why would a single man need so many servants?"

"Most of the men work with my herds, although during battles, they all fight. The wives take care of their families and perform some chores for everyone. Penninah carries water for all the tents from the nearest oasis or spring. Mahlah takes care of all the chamber pots."

"Nice job she has."

"Yes, well, someone has to do it. Serah gathers the fuel for the fire and keeps it going. And you have met Shamar, who used to pick up the manna for everyone, but now does the cooking for me and keeps my tent clean. Your cooking will give her a bit of a break."

"From the look of it, I'd say she could use a break right now. I know how that feels."

"Why? Have you ever been with child?"

"Not that it concerns you, but yes, I have."

"Do you want to tell me about it?"

"No, I don't."

Shamar had left some dried figs and raisins along with the rest of the barley bread for their evening meal. They ate it in silence, then rolled out their bedding in their separate parts of the tent, and lay down for the night. Rahab was thinking about the meal that she was going to fix for the next day. She was surprised at the excitement she felt about cooking to impress this man. She wanted him to know that she had more abilities than just being a prostitute. She didn't stop to analyze why she cared what he thought about her.

DAY 4

Rahab looked over the stores of food in the tent. She found little variety, only the barley that Salmon had mentioned and dried figs, raisins, pickled olives, and the goat cheese that Shamar had made. Just then, she heard Salmon returning from his early morning hunt.

"I snared a bird in the grain field, fat from the harvest."

"Good, I can do something tasty with that."

"I'm going to take care of some business from now until the noon meal."

"Will you be checking on my parents?"

"Yes; I am planning to do that. Do you want to send a message?"

"Thank my mother for the bag of spices. I wish I had something to send to them since you won't let me go myself."

"I will be taking them some goat's milk and fruit."

"Just tell them that I miss them and wish I could be with them."

Salmon sighed. It hurt him that she would rather be with her parents than with him. Gathering his bag and the food, he left Rahab and went straight to her parents' tent. He had not realized how complicated his life was going to get with a woman in his tent. He had to worry not only about her welfare, but about her family's as well. All of this was in addition to managing his servants and flocks. That reminded him that he needed to have a talk with Shamar and find out what was causing her bad attitude toward Rahab. Life seemed very difficult for Salmon at that moment.

When he arrived at Benne's tent, he found Benne hard at work constructing something. "Good morning. What are you making?"

Benne looked up with the special suspicion that he reserved for Salmon. "I am making a loom for weaving some linen. We found some flax near here, and thought we might be able to sell some cloth for

Day 4

money. We have no source of income now that Rahab has been taken from us."

Salmon turned red with anger at all this implied, but still said courteously, "I will be happy to purchase the first piece of linen that you make."

"Oh, I don't make the linen; my wife does. But I can do a little carpentry."

"Do you think you could make a loom similar to that one for me? I would give you a she-goat in exchange for it."

"A she-goat! Well, I suppose I could."

"I think Rahab would enjoy doing some weaving."

"She always was a good weaver. How is the girl?"

"She says to tell you that she is fine and that she misses you."

By this time, Rahab's mother, Mora, had come out of the tent. Salmon handed her the goat's milk and fruit.

Benne turned to his wife, "He says he wants to buy your first piece of linen."

"That's fine, but you know how long it takes me to work without Rahab's help," whined Mora. "I don't understand why she can't come here during the day. You only want her at night, right?"

Salmon patiently explained again, "According to the law, she cannot see you for one month." He quickly turned back toward Benne. "I also wanted to ask if you could help us harvest some of the wheat in this area. Many of our men have never done this kind of work, and we need your expertise."

"You want to use me as a kind of slave?"

"No, not at all. I was planning to pay you. We don't really need you to do the work as much as to show us how to do it."

"Well, I might consider it, if you pay a fair amount. I could have some of the wheat, I suppose?"

"Absolutely. What do you say?"

"All right. When do you want to start?"

"I'll let you know when my men are available. Is there anything I can do for you now?"

"I don't mean to complain. Well, maybe I do, but there doesn't seem to be any wine around here stronger than two-day-old grape juice. Can you get me some that would put some heart into me?"

Salmon said evasively, "I'll inquire about that and let you know later." He changed the subject. "I understand that you've had a visit from Caleb."

"Yes, we have. He seems a nice enough person. At least he speaks Canaanite well. He insists on this one god business though. I have trouble accepting that point of view."

The Cord

"I'm glad you have someone to discuss that with. He is an important man in Israel."

"Is he? Well, perhaps he can use his influence to get us free here. We just want to go back to our farm, since Jericho is gone."

Salmon sighed. Benne just couldn't seem to understand that his family was in danger unless he and all of them stayed with the Israelite camp. "You can talk to Caleb about that if you like, but I know you are safer with us than anywhere else."

"So you say."

He smiled kindly at them, though he was quaking inside. How could he learn to respect his future in-laws? He had trouble understanding how a wonderful woman like Rahab could have grown up with such parentage. "I have to go now to check on my flocks. I'll see you in a day or two."

Rahab's parents nodded without thanking him for the food.

After Salmon left, Rahab decided that rather than making a stew from the bird as she might usually do, she would roast it on a spit and make a sauce for it. She started her preparations by killing the bird, draining its blood into a bowl, and then cleaning and plucking it.

Shamar had come and was watching. She picked up Rahab's bowl of bird blood and started to take it away, but Rahab motioned for her to leave it where it had been. She looked puzzled, but complied.

Rahab made a mixture of cumin, dill weed, and salt, which she rubbed into the skin of the bird. She set the bird aside for later.

Next, she got a clay pot and put in some of the precious water that had been brought for her use. She put some raisins and figs in the water to soak.

Rahab took the grindstones that were part of the supplies and began to grind the barley. Shamar said something and made a motion indicating her willingness to do this, but Rahab stubbornly shook her head. She wanted this meal to be done right in all details. The girl could watch and learn. Indeed the barley was fine flour when she had finished with it. She added water, olive oil, and a small bit of sourdough for leavening. The servant was watching as Rahab kneaded the mixture for a long time before setting it aside to rise.

"Now for the cooking!" she said exuberantly, though she knew she wasn't understood. She covered her head and went out to the fire where several women and a few children, who had obviously been warned about her, stood around. They looked at her curiously as she put the pot of soaked fruit in the hot ashes to boil, adding a bit of her precious

Day 4

cinnamon to it. She contrived a spit on which the bird could be roasted and turned.

Next, she shaped her small loaves of barley bread and let them rise again, while she got a large earthenware bowl and placed it upside down over some of the hot coals. When the bowl was very hot, she placed her barley loaves on the hot surface where they baked quickly and cleanly, sending out a delicious aroma.

Lastly, she took the bowl of blood and added the rest of her cumin, dill, and salt mixture to it, heating it in the hot ashes. Shamar seemed distressed at this and said something excitedly in Hebrew, but she did nothing to stop Rahab.

Rahab's face was flushed under her head covering from the heat of the cooking and the feelings of excitement over her successful endeavors. Salmon would have no reason to complain about this meal. He arrived at that moment and looked admiringly at her. She thought that she would prefer that he looked admiringly at her cooking, but moved quickly to set out the roasted bird, stewed fruit, fresh bread, and sauce in the large room of the tent, which now had the sides raised.

As Salmon reclined on the floor near the food, he looked curiously at the bowl of sauce and asked, "What is this?"

"A special sauce that I make for dipping the meat."

"What ingredients does it have?"

"The main ingredient is blood from the bird. Why do you ask?"

"Quick, take the bowl outside, dig a hole, and pour it into the hole; then cover it up! Perhaps the Lord will forgive us."

"Whatever for? This is a perfectly good sauce that I have had all of my life. It won't hurt you."

"Just do as I say. Now!"

Rahab shrugged, but took the offending bowl out where she dug a hole and poured the blood sauce out, then covered it over with dirt. She noticed that the other women were looking at her with knowing glances. This only increased her frustration.

When she went back to the tent, she saw that Salmon was sitting up straight with a worried expression on his face. She said, "Would you mind telling me what that was all about?"

Salmon quoted in Hebrew, "The Lord said, 'Any Israelite or any alien living among them who eats any blood—I will set my face against that person who eats blood and will cut him off from his people. For the life of a creature is in the blood, and I have given it to you to make atonement for yourselves on the altar; it is the blood that makes atonement for one's life. Therefore I say to the Israelites, none of you may eat blood, nor may any alien living among you eat blood'" (Lev. 17:10-12, NIV).

"Could you say that in Canaanite, please?"

"Oh, I'm sorry. I was just repeating the words of the Lord directly. It says that no one, Israelite or alien, is to eat any blood. He goes on to say that blood must be drained out of the edible animals and covered with dirt. I just hope he will accept what we have done today. You didn't eat any of the sauce, did you?"

"No, I was waiting for you." Rahab felt bruised that after all her careful preparations, his only reaction was negative. "Tell me something, do you really believe it makes any difference what we eat as far as the Lord is concerned?"

"Oh, yes. I know it does. If you had seen what I have, you would understand how important obedience to him is in everything."

One part of Rahab was angry and disappointed with Salmon for not appreciating her hard work, making her want to withdraw inside herself, but the other part of her wanted to know everything she could learn about Israel's God. This would be a good time to ask questions, especially about the law.

While she was thinking this, Salmon bit into a piece of bread that he had picked up. "Mmm, this is really good. You are a good cook!"

For some reason, instead of being pleased, she was irritated at the surprise in his voice. "I suppose not all of my cooking is against the law. Or at least I hope not. How am I supposed to know? Do I have to make mistakes before I find out?"

"I'm going to have to teach you."

"You were saying part of the law just now, right? How did you learn it?"

"My parents quoted it to me on every occasion. Part of the law says that they had to do that."

"Which law is that?"

"The one that says that we are to have the Lord's commandments in our hearts and to teach them to our children when we are at home and when we are walking and when we get up in the morning and when we go to bed at night. We are to have his law before us at all times."

"Say that one in Hebrew."

Salmon repeated that part of the law in Hebrew.

"I can almost understand the words when I know what you are saying. Maybe Hebrew and Canaanite aren't as far apart as I thought at first. Acsah quoted some of the law to me yesterday."

"Which part?"

"The part about a man taking a woman captive in his tent for thirty days and then marrying her."

Day 4

"Oh, I see." An awkward pause followed while both ate more of the good food that she had prepared.

Then Rahab broke the silence. "How did Israel get the law, anyway?"

"I told you that the Lord gave it to Moses."

"Yes, but I want to know how."

"You really do, don't you? All right, I think I should tell you about Moses and how we ended up in the desert first. My father has told me the story so many times that I can remember it exactly as he told it. He said that he and my mother had been married for only a short time. Just as I have, my father waited to marry until he was much older. At that time, they were living as slaves of the Egyptians in the land of Goshen. My father's job was to supervise men who mixed straw into the mud for the bricks that Pharaoh required for building his tomb. The work was really hard, especially because the men were so easily discouraged. Many of them had the attitude that they should act stupid or lazy in order to have less required of them. At the same time, the Egyptians put pressure on my father to produce a certain number of bricks per day. He felt constantly split between his loyalty to his people and his desire to keep his job as supervisor by meeting his quotas.

He said he could still remember the day that Aaron brought Moses in to speak to the leaders of the Israelite people. My father was already considered a leader in the tribe of Judah though he was relatively young. Moses didn't seem very promising then. He didn't speak much at all. He let Aaron do all the talking. Many of the people remembered that Moses had been raised in Pharaoh's palace, and some weren't quite sure they trusted him. But then he did some miracles with his staff, and that convinced the leaders that he was from the Lord."

"What miracles did he do?"

"He changed his rod into a snake, for one thing. And I think he was able to make his hand leprous and then heal it instantly."

"That would be impressive."

"My father said at first everyone was excited and happy that the Lord had remembered them after all those years of slavery. Moses promised to lead them out of slavery to a land of their own."

"You said at first. Did something happen to change their minds?"

"Yes, Moses started by meeting with Pharaoh and demanding that he let Israel go. Instead of letting them go, Pharaoh decided that the Israelites had too much time to think about things other than working for him, so he quit supplying the straw for bricks. That made things much worse for my father because he and his men had to find straw to make the bricks. They had to meet their quotas. My mother said she feared for my father's life at that time; he was so physically exhausted by all the work and so overwrought from worry."

"What did Moses do to help?"

"He kept going back to Pharaoh. Every time he went, a new plague would break out in Egypt."

"What kind of plagues?"

"First, the Nile turned to blood, then God sent frogs, gnats, flies, dead livestock, boils, hail, locusts, and darkness. Last of all he sent the Passover, which finally convinced Pharaoh that he must let the Israelites go."

"What is the Passover?"

"You haven't heard of the Passover?"

"Why would I?"

"True, I'm just not used to someone not knowing these things. Passover happened this way: One evening, the people of Israel ate sacrificial lambs with unleavened bread and bitter herbs. They sprinkled the blood of the lambs above and on the two sides of the doorposts. That night, the angel of death went throughout Egypt and killed the firstborn son of all who did not have the blood sprinkled. Only those who had blood on their doorposts were 'passed over.' The term Passover came from that. Even Pharaoh's son died. When Israel left Egypt, the Egyptian people were glad to see them go. They showered the Israelite people with gifts of gold and silver. The Egyptians gave my father a lot because they respected him."

"Did the Lord order them to sprinkle the blood on the doorposts? I thought he wanted the blood buried and covered with dirt."

"Passover is one exception. The Lord makes it clear that blood represents life. I guess the Passover blood symbolizes the life of the lamb being given in exchange for the life of the firstborn son."

"I think I understand why the Lord requires the blood to be drained out," Rahab observed.

"Why?"

"Sometimes when a man wanted some meat to eat in Jericho, but he didn't want to kill a whole animal, he would just cut off the leg of a living animal. Then he would cauterize the wound and leave the animal maimed until he was ready for the rest of the meat at a later time. I used to be distressed by the bleats of those wounded animals. This law makes that kind of torture of animals impossible. An animal couldn't live without its blood."

"I didn't know anyone could ever think about doing such a barbarous thing."

Day 4

"You wouldn't think anything about it if you didn't have a law forbidding the practice. How do you know how you would act if you had been born in Canaan?"

"You thought it was barbarous, didn't you?"

"Yes, and thinking like that made me different from everyone else." The tone of her voice made Salmon realize how difficult her life must have been in Jericho.

"I'm glad you were different. I like the way you are." This unexpected compliment ended Rahab's defense, and quiet came between them. Rahab got up and began to clear away the food that remained from their meal. Salmon wanted to kick himself for letting the conversation get personal. She obviously wasn't ready for wooing. He sat still, thinking what his next move should be, when Rahab came back and sat down. "You didn't finish telling me the story of how Israel was given the law."

Suppressing a smile of delight, Salmon responded, "Where was I?"

"The Egyptians had just given your father a lot of silver and gold."

"My father said that they packed all the goods they could carry and left in a huge caravan heading east. After several days of going, they suddenly stopped and camped in a place hemmed in by the sea. Then word came that the whole Egyptian army was pursuing them. Clearly, Pharaoh realized the loss of thousands of slaves would be economically disastrous for his country. He wasn't going to let them go without a fight.

My father said the Israelites knew that their armed men couldn't defeat the whole army of Egypt. My father was ready to fight, but even he knew little about warfare.

"My mother told me about that night. They huddled in their tents, terrified. The wind blew fiercely. With everything else, this seemed ominous. What they didn't expect was what they saw the next day. The sea was blown apart, and a wide road opened through it with dry ground to walk on. Moses ordered the people to go through on that road. Dazed by such a miracle, they obeyed. Mother said the walls of water on each side seemed to stand up, and she couldn't help wondering what would happen if they were let go."

"But the walls stayed up?"

"Until every Israelite got across. The Egyptian army came through, pursuing them. The chariots bogged down in the sand because they were so heavy. The Egyptians stopped right in the middle of the sea to try to dig out the chariots. When the last Israelite had set foot on the opposite shore, Mother said she was close enough to see Moses raise his rod. The walls of water crashed down and drowned the Egyptians."

Rahab had sat quietly through all of this, but now she gasped softly. "So he is powerful enough to control nature."

"Who?"

Without thinking she said, "Yahweh."

Salmon decided not to chide her, because nothing could be more worshipful than the way she said it, and he didn't think the Lord would mind.

She shook herself and asked, "So I understand why you didn't try to come north through the Philistine lands to Canaan. Your people weren't ready to fight yet."

"Yes, and the Lord had some things he needed to tell us first."

"The law."

"Correct; we traveled about in the desert where a number of things happened, some good and some not so good, mostly having to do with food and water, but after three months we came to the Desert of Sinai in front of Mount Sinai.

"What happened there?"

"Well, for one thing, I was born there."

"That *was* an important day for Israel."

"Are you being sarcastic?"

Rahab just looked smug and asked, "Why did the Lord take you there?"

"Moses went up on the mountain and the Lord gave him the law."

"Do you mean the law about divorce and adultery and child sacrifice?"

"Among other things."

"I would love to have been there to hear all of it. To really know what the Lord wants would be great. I think if I knew more about what is important to him, I would know him better. How exactly did the Lord do it?"

"Moses brought word from the Lord that he would make them his special people and bless them above all other nations if they would obey his law. My father was in the group of leaders and elders who were allowed to go up close to the mountain to meet with the Lord and hear the law. The leaders agreed for the people that we would do whatever the Lord said."

"What laws did he give?"

"I couldn't tell you all of them now. It would take too long, but the first two were that we should worship only the Lord and we should never make any idols. After that, Moses went up on the mountain by himself. While he was there, the Lord gave him the law, written on tablets of stone. He was gone for forty days and nights.

"My parents said that during that time the people got restless. Many people from the tribe of Judah came to my father, asking him what the plan was from there. They were tired of living in tents in the desert and

Day 4

wanted to return to some of the practices of Egypt. I think my father was appalled that they could promise to obey the Lord and then immediately turn around and start doing the opposite of what he had commanded."

"Why do you think they did that?"

"I don't know. I guess they still didn't realize what the Lord would do to them if they disobeyed. When Moses came down, he found that the people had made a golden calf like those they had seen worshiped in Egypt and were worshiping the calf instead of the Lord. This made Moses so angry that he broke the tablets and called for those who would follow the Lord to fight against those who were breaking the laws. The Levites responded immediately to Moses' call and killed about three thousand of their fellow Israelites that day for engaging in revelry and idol worship. Afterwards, a plague killed many more."

"What do you think about that?"

"I was only a tiny baby. I don't remember any of this."

"I realize that, but I meant what do you think about the Lord killing the ones who did wrong?"

"Well, it probably made people think twice about breaking the laws."

"Had the people heard the law before they did these things?"

"They had heard the part about idol worship and adultery. They really had no excuse for their behavior."

"But Moses had destroyed the tablets with the law. How did he get the law then?"

"He went back up on the mountain, but this time, he took two tablets that he had carved out himself. The Lord gave him the law again."

"Did the people obey this time?"

"What choice did they have? They had seen what happened to their kinsmen who had disobeyed. No one wanted to die by the sword or plague."

Rahab noticed then that a chill had come into the air and that the sun was setting. She assembled a light supper of bread and dried fruits, while Salmon let down the sides of the tent. They ate by the light of a small olive oil lamp. Salmon was smiling as he wished her a good night, as though pleased about something.

Rahab lay down on her pallet thinking about all she had learned that afternoon. This God of Israel could be very severe in his punishments. Still it surprised her that the Israelites were so easily persuaded to worship a golden calf so soon after they had seen the Lord's salvation. She guessed that they were still full of the customs of Egypt and could not easily shake them off. She wondered sleepily if she would make more mistakes because of Canaanite customs that she would not be able to change.

DAY 5

The next day dawned clear and a little cool. Rahab decided to fix something hot for breakfast. She didn't want to disturb Shamar, sensing a definite antagonism from that quarter, so she rose quietly, gathered her supplies, and slipped out past the sleeping Salmon. She had her flint, her jar of meal, and her bag of seasonings. Setting these down by the entrance, she picked up the water jar that she had left out the night before. She found it a wondrous thing to be able to leave things out and not have them stolen, as they would have been in Jericho. Placing the jar on top of her head covering, she headed for the oasis, treading gracefully with the jar balanced with one hand on the covering over her head. Salmon would no doubt have forbidden her from doing this, but she had tasted her freedom now, and, after all, he was asleep.

When she arrived at the oasis, she had to wait for a turn to get at the water. No one spoke to her, but few of them spoke her language. The looks that some of the women gave her made her feel like a misfit. She realized that she had never quite fit in Jericho either. Her ideas of right and wrong didn't match with those of the other women there. She remembered a conversation at the well when she was pregnant.

That day, she had waddled as she steadied the water pot on her way to the city well. It was a hot day in Jericho, too hot for a pregnant woman. With her free hand, she felt her hard, round stomach, touching this part of her that was also someone else. The baby's foot (or was it an arm?) pushed against her hand.

Already Rahab had loved her baby. She knew loving a firstborn child was a mistake. But she didn't want to think about that.

Day 5

She reached the well, already crowded with other women waiting their turn to fill their pots. "When is your time?" asked an older matron.

"Probably one month; it is hard to say."

"You'll be glad enough to be rid of this burden, I should think."

"Carrying a child is no burden."

"Now, Rahab, you know you shouldn't think of it as a child. You mustn't get attached. Maybe later on, you can have that luxury."

"Why do we have to give up any of our babies?"

Another woman spoke up, "Don't let the priests of Molech hear you talking like that. They think it heretical for anyone to question their rites."

Rahab clamped her mouth shut. She did not question outwardly, but inside she felt very rebellious. Taking her turn at the well, she trudged home.

She had never understood how all those women could accept killing innocent little babies just to appease a bronze statue. True, the men felt that the only way to get divine protection in case of war was to have Molech fight for them, but that this god demanded the death of babies seemed wrong to her. Rahab had never met any woman who was happy about giving up the children, yet all accepted it because they felt they had to. Even she, with all her fiery passion about the issue... but she wouldn't let her mind go there. If the women had just joined together and insisted that they would not give up their babies, could they have changed things? She didn't know.

Anyway, all those women were dead now, and all the babies—whether they had been loved or not. It made her a little sad to think about all that death. Jericho was wiped out, and now probably the rest of Canaan would be, too. She accepted that. She knew better than anyone else that the Canaanite men would not have converted to worship of Yahweh. They enjoyed the rites of Ashtoreth too much for that, and Yahweh had made it clear that they could not worship both.

She took a deep breath and enjoyed the fresh morning air. It was a lovely spring day, and she felt good to be out of the tent and doing something.

Back at the tent entrance, she skillfully lit her fire and built it up. Soon she had a cooking pot over the fire with water boiling. To this, she added handfuls of the barley meal, stirring gently with a wooden paddle until the mixture began to thicken. She added a little salt and cinnamon to flavor the porridge and pulled it out of the direct heat. The smell was fragrant in the area, and one by one, the servants came out of their tents and looked her way curiously, as if wondering what brew she was concocting and why she hadn't waited for them to help her.

Suddenly, Salmon pushed back the tent flap and came out to where she was cooking. "I see you are up early. Did Shamar come to help you?"

"She brought the goat's milk just now."

"How did you get the water?"

"I am perfectly capable of carrying water myself. I didn't see any of my family, and I spoke to no one."

Salmon looked a little frustrated at her stubborn independence, but he sat down and quietly accepted the bowl of porridge and cup of goat's milk that she offered him for breakfast.

As he tasted it, he exclaimed, "This is good. I've had porridge made from manna all of my life, but it never tasted like this. What did you put in it?"

"Some salt, cinnamon, and a little honey."

"Honey!" He looked down at the bowl and cup, and smiled. "I guess it is official; I am sitting in the land flowing with milk and honey having some of both."

Rahab said, "Is that significant?"

"The Lord calls the Promised Land that."

"The land flowing with milk and honey?"

"Yes."

Rahab smiled. She felt that her work was well rewarded by his response to the breakfast.

While he was eating, he asked her, "Rahab, the people of Jericho worshiped Molech and Ashtoreth and those other Canaanite gods, too, didn't they?"

"Yes, why do you ask?"

"I've been wondering why you have been able to turn your back so utterly on the Canaanite people. Don't you feel any loyalty to them as your people, your culture?"

"No, I don't."

"Why?"

Rahab thought about how to explain. "What did you see that day you were in Jericho before you came to the inn?"

"Do you mean besides the filth in the streets and the children running wild?"

"Yes."

"Let me think. Of course we were looking at military aspects of the town, but I assume you mean cultural things."

Rahab nodded.

"I remember that we went into the heart of town and saw the tower in the center with the common area in front. On the other side of the

Day 5

common area was a building with stone steps leading up to a large open doorway. Several women stood near the top."

"Those were the priestesses of Ashtoreth. They were waiting for you to come and worship with them. Do you understand what that means?"

"No, should I?"

"They would have lain with you and spilled your seed onto the ground as a fertility rite."

He wrinkled his nose in disgust. "I never realized that before. Your people committed sexual promiscuity in the worship of your gods? That's disgusting." He paused as though remembering something. "Oh, that explains that law that I've always wondered about. Now I understand why the Lord forbids that very action. The worship of Ashtoreth requires it."

"Which action?"

"Spilling the seed."

Rahab nodded, "What else did you see?"

"In the center of the common area was a large bronze statue with an ox head and man's body. Men were gathered around it making a fire in preparation for some ritual."

"They were preparing to sacrifice a baby later that day."

"Was that happening while we were at your inn?"

"Didn't you hear the drums?"

"Yes, I did that night, and also when we were outside the walls later."

"The sound of the drums is the sound of child sacrifice." Rahab stopped speaking and turned away, swallowing hard.

When she looked back, Salmon was looking at her intently. "You really disagreed with your people about this, didn't you?"

"Yes, the attitudes and actions of my people toward babies disgusted me. I had heard that your God forbids child sacrifice. That issue more than any other has made it possible to support your people against my own."

"Can you tell me more about how you were able to come to that conclusion while you were still in that culture?"

Rahab stared at a corner of the tent meditatively then began to tell her own story. "Ever since I was a small child, I have hated the sacrifices to Molech, the god of war. When I was about three, I had a baby brother born that I adored. I helped my mother take care of him. I don't remember everything about that time, but I do remember my parents arguing one night and my mother crying. The next day, they left me with a neighbor and took my brother into Jericho. I never saw him again. My mother has not been the same since that time. Giving up her child seemed to change her personality. Several years passed before my parents had more children. I am so much older than my sister and brothers for that reason."

"That must have had an effect on you, too."

"Especially after I realized what they had done to him. Even now I can remember the first time I witnessed a sacrifice to Molech. I was about nine, and we were in Jericho. My parents had decided that I was old enough to be still. We went to the city's main common area and saw what you saw there. The mouth of the ox's head was wide open, and out of it belched smoke from the fires burning in his red-hot belly. A priest came out and addressed the crowd. He made a noble-sounding speech about the might of Molech, the glory of war, and the beauty of sacrifice. Drums began beating in the background. The priest was joined by another priest carrying a beautiful baby boy, about three months old with sparkling eyes and soft wispy hair curling down the back of his head." She paused—this memory was painful.

"I noticed a young woman with an anguished face starting forward toward the priest, but she was restrained by her husband. With growing horror, I realized what they intended to do.

'No,' I screamed and was instantly grabbed by my father, who clamped his hand over my mouth.

"The priest raised the child into the air before the people, then he turned to thrust that baby into the red hot arms of Molech. As the baby roasted there screaming, the drums rose to a fevered pitch, but they were not quite able to drown the cries of the dying child or the shrieks of his mother.

"I had nightmares for weeks after that."

She looked into Salmon's face, surprised by the look of compassion that she saw there. In all her life, she couldn't remember ever seeing such a look on a man's face toward her. She knew that if she kept talking she was going to lose the careful control that she had developed over her emotions. She wasn't ready for that. "I think you've heard enough of my story to understand why I am on your side and not on the side of the Canaanites."

Salmon nodded, though he looked as though he wanted to ask more questions.

Just then a commotion outside interrupted the intimacy of that moment. People were running in the direction of the tabernacle. They could hear shouts and voices wailing loudly, as if in lament. Salmon said, "Wait here, I will be back as soon as I find out what is happening."

Rahab let down the sides of the tent and moved into the back room, meanwhile listening to the sounds outside. She could tell that whatever had happened was not good news for the Israelites. It made

Day 5

her uncomfortable to think that something had gone badly wrong after all. She wondered about her parents and what was happening to them.

Meanwhile, Salmon hurried with many other men toward the tabernacle. Something about the mood of the people gave him a sense of foreboding. He heard snatches of conversation:

"They say we lost badly, were completely routed."

"How many of our men were killed?"

"I didn't even know we were fighting a battle!"

When they arrived at the tent of meeting, they saw Joshua down on his face before it, crying in agony. Salmon had never seen Joshua like this. It gave him a strange feeling, almost like finding out that his father had died. Now other tribal leaders were tearing their clothes, sprinkling dust on their heads, and collapsing beside Joshua. Salmon felt anguished. Othniel came up beside him and drew him quietly over to the side.

Salmon asked, "What have you found out?"

"We lost the battle of Ai. At least 30 men have been killed, and the men were horribly beaten. Ai is still unconquered."

"I don't understand what happened. You saw the same things that I did. It should have been easy."

"I know, Salmon. I don't know about you, but I intend to keep a low profile."

They slipped quietly away from the tabernacle, but not before they heard murmuring that the Lord had turned his back on them because they had spared the prostitute and her family.

"Othniel, I think I'd better go check on Rahab's family."

"Do you want me to go with you?"

"No, it may be dangerous."

"What about Rahab?"

"I've told her to stay in the tent. I'll get back there as quickly as I can."

"I'm going there."

"Thank you, my friend." Salmon spotted Shamar in the crowd and signaled for her to come to him. "Go to your mistress. Keep her in the tent and help her any way you can. Tell my men to stand guard there until I get back."

"She isn't my mistress."

Startled by this rebellion from his normally compliant servant, Salmon wasn't sure how to react. "Why do you say that?"

"She caused our loss at Ai. I knew all along that she would get you into trouble. We can't have that kind of Canaanite whore here."

Salmon spoke sternly. "You will do as I say and not question my authority. I am still your master. Is that clear?"

Shamar nodded sullenly.

Salmon hurried to the alien quarter with fear in his heart. If his own servant felt that way about Rahab, what would other people be doing? His heart sank further when he got close to Benne's tent and saw a crowd of people standing around it. He pushed his way to the front and turned to face the angry mob.

"Let us have them, Salmon!" yelled one angry man.

"Why do you want these people?" Salmon responded.

"They shouldn't have been allowed to live. We were supposed to kill everyone in Jericho." Other voices joined the man's in assent.

"Wait for Joshua. Don't do anything hasty here." Salmon pleaded with them more calmly than he felt.

"No, we need the Lord on our side again."

The mob pressed closer to Salmon. He tried to hold his ground but had to take a step backwards. Just when he thought they would rush past him into the tent, Othniel called out from the back of the crowd. "Wait, I have news from Joshua."

Salmon had never been so glad to see anyone.

"Joshua says that tomorrow we will have a solemn assembly to determine the Lord's will. He says that all of you should go home and consecrate yourselves."

The crowd muttered, and some still edged forward, but their momentum had been broken. One by one, they moved away until Othniel was by Salmon's side.

"Thank you, Othniel. I don't know what would have happened if you hadn't come."

Othniel said nothing, but reached out to clasp Salmon's shoulder reassuringly.

Salmon wiped the mist from his eyes and said, "I'm going to check on Benne and the rest, and then I'll get back to Rahab. Was everything okay there?"

"Yes, your men were standing guard, and no one seemed interested in challenging them. I heard the news in time to tell them, too."

"What do you think is going to happen?"

"I don't know. We'll just have to wait."

"I'll see you later, and thanks again."

He stepped inside the tent and found Rahab's parents and her brothers and sister huddled in terror in the back room of the tent. He spoke comfortingly to them. "It's Salmon. They have gone away for now. Are you okay?"

Benne rose shakily to his feet and came forward. "What is this all about? I heard screams, and then these people were demanding that we

Day 5

come out of the tent. After what you Israelites did in Jericho, I had no intention of going out."

"In this case, you were wise. I think you should be careful not to go out until I come for you. Tomorrow I will send one of my servants to bring hot food and take care of your chamber pots."

"Can you explain to me what is happening?"

"I'm not sure I understand myself. When I know everything, I will tell you." Salmon thought that Benne didn't seem satisfied with his answer, but he didn't want to say anything to cause panic either. "I will try to come see you sometime tomorrow, or I will send someone to let you know what to do."

After almost an hour of sitting quietly, Rahab roused herself and began fixing some food for that evening and the next day. She sensed that it would be better to work inside the tent as much as possible, surmising that no one else would be thinking about food, and some might be offended at her for cooking.

She had just finished preparing the barley dough for baking when Shamar came into the tent. She looked at Rahab with a look of near hatred. She made a motion and then took the bread from Rahab and went outside. Rahab had known that Shamar wasn't making much of an effort to be friendly, but the animosity now was unmistakable. Perhaps she should speak to Salmon about it. She wished again that he would let her go. This rejection was one more reason that she didn't like being in his tent.

In just a few more minutes, he was there. She started to bring the subject up then, but she really looked at him and saw that he was in anguish. "Salmon, what has happened?"

With a voice that shook, he replied, "We've lost the battle against Ai."

"I'm so sorry. Perhaps you can take more men next time and try again."

"You don't understand. Losing means the Lord has turned his back on us. And the worst part is that it may be my fault. I was the spy that said we could win the battle with only a few thousand men. I was wrong, and the people may blame me for that." He looked away uneasily.

"Salmon, what are you not telling me?"

"I'm afraid some people are saying we lost the battle because we didn't kill everyone at Jericho."

"They want to kill us now." Her voice was flat with resignation.

"Joshua fell on his face before the Lord. He will let us know what is to happen."

The Cord

"Does Shamar think I am the cause of the loss?"

"I'm afraid she might think that, but she will obey me."

"Oh, Salmon, what about my parents? Are they okay?"

"They had a bit of a scare, but I saw them and they will be all right. I'm sending four of my men to watch their tent tonight. The rest will guard here."

The meal of fresh bread, cheese, and fruit was eaten in silence. Shamar served them, but it was clear that she wanted to be somewhere else.

After she left, Salmon said, "Tomorrow there will be a solemn assembly by the tabernacle. Joshua and Eleazar will be offering sacrifices so we can know how to proceed. You will have to attend with everyone else. We are going to have to wash our clothing and take baths before tomorrow."

"What purpose does that serve? Isn't this a strange time for starting a clothes-washing project? The wool will never get dry in time."

"We must do this as part of the consecration ritual. You may bathe in here, and I will bathe with my men."

"What else does consecration include?"

"Well, we abstain from sexual relations, but we have been doing that anyway."

"Is that all? We just wash our clothes and take baths? It seems like as a religious ceremony, there would be more to it."

"Well, I suppose the washing symbolizes that we are clean before the Lord. We are setting ourselves apart."

"Do all of your women think that I am the cause of Israel's trouble?"

"I don't know. Why?"

"I will need someone to help me if I cannot go out, and I don't think Shamar would be a good choice right now."

"I understand. I'll get one of the others."

He left and returned very shortly with a matronly woman whom he introduced as Penninah. She seemed capable and not unfriendly. She shooed Salmon out of the tent after he explained what was needed and brought Rahab a pottery basin filled with water and some clean cloths. She motioned for Rahab to undress and took her shift out of the tent.

Rahab quickly used the cloths to bathe herself. She didn't have to worry about washing her hair because it was still only a short fuzz on her head, too short even to curl. The bath refreshed her, but she was nervous that Salmon would underestimate the time he needed to stay gone. As soon as she had finished bathing, she undid her bedroll and wrapped herself in her blanket. Then she had a lengthy wait. She should

Day 5

have realized that he would take at least as long as she to bathe and might even be waiting for his clothes to dry somewhat. The wait allowed her to dwell on her situation. She might not have escaped the fate of Jericho after all. She felt confused.

Penninah finally came into the tent carrying the cleaned and mostly dry shift. The servants must have used the fire to speed the drying process. Rahab dressed quickly and rolled her blanket back up, and then smiled at Penninah, who returned the smile tentatively and left with the basin of water.

Not too long after, Salmon arrived. His head and beard were still damp, though his clothes, like hers, were somewhat dry. "Are you okay?" he asked her.

"I am all right, but it seems strange to be going through motions of normal behavior when so much depends on what happens tomorrow."

"I know what you mean. I've been thinking about it, and just can't understand what went wrong. I didn't think I'd done anything to break the covenant."

"What covenant are you talking about?"

"In the covenant between Israel and the Lord, we promised to obey him. He promised to give us this land."

"So the failure of the battle at Ai shows that the Lord isn't keeping his part of the covenant, which must mean that someone in the camp has broken the Lord's commands. Is that right?"

"Yes, and since the failure came after winning the battle of Jericho, everyone thinks that the broken command was there."

"What exactly did the Lord command about Jericho?"

"We were to leave no one and nothing alive, and we were to take no booty for ourselves. All precious objects were to be dedicated to the Lord."

"Do you think that the Lord is angry because you did not kill me and my family?"

"I don't know. Joshua was so sure when I explained everything to him. I've never known him to be wrong about what the Lord allowed. He said that we could spare you because you had helped us. But of course, he approved the plan for the battle of Ai, too."

"What will happen to us if...? " Rahab understood the gravity in his face. If Joshua thought that her presence had caused the Israelites to lose in battle, Salmon could be killed, as well. "How do they know that someone's sin caused them to lose the battle? Maybe you were just outmaneuvered this time."

"The Lord promised us success in battle as long as we obeyed his commands. This has happened before."

56

"But is your God so very consistent?"

"We have never failed in battle unless we had violated his commands."

"That wasn't true with Molech. Look at how badly we were beaten by you, and yet the priests of Molech never let the drums cease for days before your attack. How wonderful and yet awful to have a real God who actually does what he says he will do."

"More than you realize."

"Do you want to eat anything else before we go to bed?"

"No, I don't feel very hungry. I don't think my stomach would tolerate any food."

Rahab nodded. She felt a sense of foreboding in all of this. She had heard enough and seen enough to know that tonight might be her last to be alive.

DAY 6

Rahab awoke to the sound of Salmon's voice speaking quietly to someone at the doorway of the tent. Not wanting to antagonize Shamar even more, she quickly rose and rolled up her mat as she had seen Shamar do it. Rahab quietly assembled a breakfast of bread and the goat's cheese, which had cured enough to be eaten as a soft spread. They might not be able to eat lunch if the solemn assembly were very long. Her hand shook a little as she thought about what might happen that day. What would Joshua give as the reason the Lord had turned away from Israel? Did the Lord save her only to punish the people because of it? Then she shook her head. Everything that had happened so far had only confirmed his goodness and love for her. She could trust him with this, too.

Salmon had ceased talking, so she pushed aside the inner curtain and said, "Good morning. Whom were you talking to?"

"I was just finding out from one of my men that your parents spent an uneventful night. You seem so calm, almost cheerful this morning. I'm surprised."

"I was just thinking that I don't have to be afraid because I can trust the Lord. He has been good to me so far." As she said this, she brought the food to him and offered it to him to eat.

As he began to spread the soft goat's cheese on a piece of bread, he stated, "I'm afraid I don't share your opinion in this case. I have seen enough to feel that I must fear him."

"Why?"

"I have several reasons, but I can tell you about one now. Did you know that my Uncle Aaron, my Aunt Elisheba's husband, was chosen by the Lord to be the first high priest?"

Rahab nodded. "Acsah told me."

Day 6

"His sons were chosen to help him. On the very day that the Lord consecrated them to serve in the tabernacle, Nadab and Abihu, my oldest cousins, were helping Uncle Aaron with the burnt offering. They had done everything just the way Moses had said. Moses and Uncle Aaron went in to the Holy of Holies, and when they came out, a roaring fire came out of the Holy of Holies and burned up the offering. My mother told me that it was an incredible thing to see."

"I would imagine so," said Rahab.

"Well, we don't know why Nadab and Abihu did it—maybe they were curious to see God's presence in the Holy Place, or maybe they just wanted to try out their new censers—but they put some fire in their censers that they had gotten from somewhere besides the altar, perhaps a cooking fire. Then they placed incense in the censers and went inside the inner sanctuary. That same fire blazed out, but this time, it killed Abihu and Nadab."

"That must have been dreadful. Especially for your aunt."

"Yes, it was. No one except perhaps Moses believed that the Lord could be so exacting. Mother told me that Moses wouldn't allow Uncle Aaron even to cry for his sons. He had to continue with his duties as though nothing had happened."

"What exactly had they done wrong?"

"The Lord said that only Aaron was to offer incense, and then only in the morning and evening. Only those who are perfectly holy can come into the Lord's presence. Because they weren't supposed to be in there, Abihu and Nadab were breaking the law. People can't be holy if they aren't doing what the Lord says. So he punished them. Although I was only a tiny baby when that happened, my mother told me about it as soon as I was old enough to try to go to the tabernacle by myself. She wanted me to have a healthy fear of the Lord and his law."

"I understand. So you are saying that you may have done something wrong like your cousins and that the Lord is punishing you?"

"I don't know." He put both of his hands on his head in a gesture of confusion. "Joshua gave permission for me to spare your life and the lives of your family."

"Well, it seems to me that this loss is unrelated to your saving me."

"I know what you are trying to do, Rahab, and I appreciate it, but we don't know why the army failed at Ai. We will have to wait and see. I just know that a lot of people are blaming me right now."

"What exactly happened at Ai? I didn't know that anyone from Israel was in battle."

"Neither did most of the Israelites. We sent units from the tribes of Reuben and Gad because their women and children are still on the other side of the Jordan. They wanted to settle in the lands that we took from the Amorites." He sighed, "Thinking about the success of those battles makes this hurt that much more."

"So only a few men went?"

"Yes, at my suggestion. That is why I am at least partially responsible for what happened. As I understand it, the men of Ai routed our men from before their gates and chased them all the way back to the stone quarries a mile or two away from the city. At least 30 of our men were killed."

"How is Joshua reacting?"

"At first, he was really upset, tearing his clothes and heaping dust on his head. But then, he changed. Those who were there say he became very still. Then after a few minutes, he dried his tears, got up, and announced that there would be a solemn assembly today to determine who the guilty party is. He didn't say what the problem was. He simply ordered us to consecrate ourselves and to come to the assembly today when the signal sounds."

Just then they heard the sound of trumpets playing a stirring strain, loud enough for everyone in the nation of Israel to hear it.

"Rahab, it is time."

Rahab covered her fuzzy head with the covering and together with Salmon followed the other people.

As they walked along, they could see hostile stares from other people.

One man openly jeered, "You will be punished, Salmon."

Salmon walked steadily on. Rahab wanted to shrink into nothing. She didn't have to understand Hebrew to know what the intent was. An atmosphere of hatred surrounded them.

When they came into a more open area filled with people already, Rahab could see a long wall of curtains ahead and beyond that, a very large and elaborate tent. A smoky cloud hovered just above the large tent, and she assumed that someone was burning something inside the curtains. "What is this place?"

"It's the tabernacle. You can't go inside because you are a woman and an alien, but I will stay with you out here unless..."

Rahab nodded in understanding.

The high priest Eleazar was standing with Joshua near the entrance to the tabernacle. A bull and two rams were nearby.

"What are the animals for?"

"Eleazar will kill the bull and rams and offer their blood on the altar."

"But why? I don't understand."

Salmon sighed quietly as he tried to think of the best way to explain. "The Lord says that all lawbreaking must be paid for. The price is blood.

Therefore, when we need forgiveness, Eleazar must offer a sacrifice for the people. The blood of the bull will take away the sins of the people and make it possible for God to be with us and be on our side again."

"Oh. What does this have to do with the battle of Ai?"

"Joshua is going to try to understand why the Lord let us lose the battle. He is starting by consecrating the people and sacrificing."

Rahab understood a little, but she didn't see how a bull could take away sins. "Shouldn't just the main lawbreaker be killed?"

"Perhaps the individual who is responsible will be killed, but this is for all of our sins, not just for the one sin that caused the failure at the battle at Ai. This will take care of any unintentional sins in the camp."

"So you are saying that the Lord lets the bull take the place of human sacrifice?"

"Yes, something like that."

Rahab noticed something. "Both Molech and Ashtoreth had forms that included the head of a cow or ox, and both of them required sacrifices or rites which included human beings. How interesting that your god requires the sacrifice of cattle, not of humans, almost as if he is requiring us to sacrifice any other gods to him."

"That's a very astute observation. In fact, the first commandment of the Lord requires that we have no other gods before him. I never thought about that connection." He looked at her in surprise.

When the sacrificing was finished, Joshua and Eleazar moved to where the people were waiting outside the tabernacle. Now Joshua was telling the people that they would pass before him by tribe. From this, he would narrow down until the guilty one was known. Joshua said that person would be destroyed by fire, along with all that belonged to him. "He has violated the covenant of the Lord and has done a disgraceful thing in Israel."

Representatives from each of the tribes went forward and lined up in a row. Then one at a time, each walked in front of Joshua. Joshua had his head up as though he were listening. Rahab wondered what he could hear. Just as the representatives from the tribe of Judah reached Joshua, he stopped them. "Judah has been chosen."

"What does that mean?" whispered Rahab of Salmon.

Salmon clenched his hands uneasily. "It means that the person who is responsible for our defeat at Ai is in the tribe of Judah."

"And your tribe is...?"

"Judah."

Rahab gasped and bit her lip to keep it from trembling. She couldn't believe even now that Salmon might die simply for sparing her life after she had helped him and his fellow spy Othniel to escape from Jericho.

Joshua was calling for all the clan representatives from the tribe of Judah to come forward. Salmon was one of the representatives for the clan of Perez. He moved into his place with the other Perezites to parade in front of Joshua. He smiled faintly back at Rahab where she stood, still stricken with fear of what might happen next. The groups of clan leaders went before Joshua. First the Shelahites went by without incident, then the Perezites. Rahab held her breath, but Joshua did not stop them. Finally the Zerahites came by. Now at last Joshua spoke, "The clan of Zerah has been chosen."

Rahab realized that she had been holding her breath. She took a deep breath now and felt almost giddy with relief. Salmon would not be chosen! It was another man who was responsible for the defeat at Ai. They were safe.

She could watch the rest of the procedure with relief, yet as the family groups of the Zerahites paraded before Joshua and then the individual men from the family of Zimri, she could not help feeling empathy for the wives and daughters of the men of that family. She knew what they were feeling. Had she not felt that way only a few minutes before?

Finally, Achan was chosen. Joshua accosted Achan with these words: "My son, give glory to the Lord, the God of Israel, and give him the praise. Tell me what you have done; do not hide it from me."

Rahab was amazed to hear Achan's answer. "It is true! I have sinned against the Lord, the God of Israel. This is what I have done: When I saw in the plunder a beautiful robe, two hundred shekels of silver, and a wedge of gold weighing fifty shekels, I coveted them and took them. They are hidden in the ground inside my tent, with the silver underneath."

While Joshua sent messengers to check Achan's story, Salmon moved quietly back next to Rahab. She turned to him. "How did Joshua know that Achan was the man out of all these people?"

"The Lord told him."

"How?"

"I think he must hear a voice in his head. He recognizes it to be the Lord and obeys what the voice says. It has never been wrong in my experience. I expect you think that is rather bizarre."

"No, actually, I don't. Perhaps I will tell you why someday."

The messengers had returned and were carrying the silver, robe, and gold just as Achan had described. The objects were spread out before the people. Rahab recognized the robe as one belonging to the dead king of Jericho. He had worn it to her inn one night, proudly boasting that it came as a gift from the king of Babylon. Seeing it there gave her a queer feeling.

Day 6

Then Joshua called for the sons and daughters of Achan to be brought as well as all his possessions including his animals and household goods, even his tent. These were carried in great ceremony to a stony valley to the west of the campsite toward the mountains. All the people followed along in silence. It was about a ten-minute walk, but it took longer because of the thousands of people who were moving there at once.

Rahab surveyed the scene. Achan, his children, animals, and possessions huddled together in the bottom of the narrow valley. Surrounding him on all sides were the hundreds of thousands of his kinsmen, all looking on soberly at this one who had been responsible for their humiliating defeat at Ai, a defeat that cost them the lives of 36 men.

Joshua cried out in a loud voice, which echoed off the hills around into the grim silence, "Why have you brought this trouble on us? The Lord will bring trouble on you today." Then he reached down and picked up a stone from the ground and hurled it at Achan. Immediately, all the men began picking up stones and flinging them at the huddled group. A confusion of bleats, screams, and lowing burst from the throats of people, sheep, goats, and cattle. One by one, Achan and all that had been his fell in a bloody heap.

Then some men brought torches and started a blaze. The fire leaped up and made a bonfire, but this was no celebration. Achan had been well liked. Perhaps each man who had been tempted to take something in Jericho was thinking that this could have been he. When the fire had died down into a smoking mound, everyone began carrying stones to make a memorial pile. Rahab helped carry stones, even as she felt the tears streaming down her face. Joshua said, "Let this pile remind all of the trouble that will come to anyone who breaks covenant against the Lord."

It was evening as Rahab and Salmon walked slowly back to the camp beside many others. The scene she had just witnessed was heavy on Rahab's heart. "Achan deserved what happened to him, didn't he?"

Salmon looked up in surprise, "Yes, we were instructed to devote everything in the city to the Lord. In fact, Joshua specifically told us that anyone who did not keep away from the devoted things would bring about his own destruction. Achan heard that with all the rest of us. Yet he still took those objects. Now he has been punished exactly as was foretold."

Looking at the facts, no one could doubt the justice of what had happened. Rahab felt again her growing awe of this God of the Israelites. When they got back to the tent, they had finished eating their supper before she finally found the courage to ask the many questions in her mind.

"So much has happened today, and I trying to sort it all out in my mind. Everyone thought that we were the cause of the failure of the battle of Ai, but we weren't, Achan was, right?"

"Yes."

"So nothing is wrong with my being in the Israelite camp."

"Nothing whatsoever."

"Yet I have broken more laws than Achan ever thought about breaking. And those are just the ones I know about: adultery, idol worship, breaking the Sabbath, misusing his name, and eating unclean food. I probably have broken others that I haven't even heard about yet. My sin deserves death just as surely as Achan's. I have broken the law and ought to be stoned. And yet I am still alive. I don't understand something here."

"I'm not sure what it means either, but I am grateful and happy that he spared you."

Rahab heard his words but chose not to take them as personally as he might have meant them. She was alive! The Lord had saved her, so that must mean that He did not disapprove of her. She had a right to stay with the Israelites and worship him.

DAY 7
THE FIRST SABBATH

The next day dawned with the sound of steady rain outside. Rahab, who knew that this was the time for the late rains, was surprised only that it had held off for so long. But she had never experienced a rainy day in a tent and had no idea how miserable it could become, especially when water seeped inside and left no dry spots to sit anywhere.

As Rahab set their breakfast out for them, she watched a puddle of water moving from under the edge of the tent toward the middle of the outer room. They could sit on nothing higher than a mat. She had bowls to put the food in to keep it out of the water. For once she was happy to be wearing wool instead of her linen. She was chilled enough in the wool as it became damper against her skin. Breakfast that morning consisted of the bread left from what Rahab had made two days before and some fresh goat's milk that Shamar had brought to them earlier after Elon had milked the herds. Salmon ate the bread with relish, enjoying it after weeks of Shamar's cooking. "I haven't eaten this well since the manna stopped. I'm not blaming Shamar; she has had no experience. Yet I love to have your good cooking."

If the good bread was a treat for Salmon, the goat's milk was for Rahab. Animal products of any kind had been dear in Jericho. Only rich people could afford to have animals. This clear indication of Salmon's status made her uneasy again. She still hoped something would happen to change his mind about marrying her. She didn't want to be a wealthy man's possession again.

Then Salmon smiled at her and announced, "Today is the Sabbath, so I will be staying here in the tent today."

Day 7, The First Sabbath

After complaining about being alone, Rahab should have been happy at this news, but she found that she didn't really want him there. What could they talk about for a whole day?

"I thought we might discuss some of the Lord's laws today. You've been asking me about them."

"Yes, that is a good idea." She was relieved at his choice of topics.

"I should probably start by explaining the Sabbath."

"Please, I've been wondering about that ever since we came into the camp. What is it exactly?"

"When the Lord created the heavens and the earth, he did it in six days, and on the Sabbath he rested."

"Did I understand you right? Did you say that the Lord created the heavens and the earth?"

"Yes, he created everything—plants, animals, people."

"And did he create the stars?"

"Yes, and the sun and rain, too." He grimaced as a drip started just over his head in the tent.

Rahab smiled, but didn't explain what that information meant to her.

"The Sabbath was the seventh day. Because he rested on the seventh day, he gave the law that we do the same. So from sunset on the sixth day of the week until sunset on the seventh day, we can't do any work."

"No work at all?"

"That is what the law says."

"Does that mean we can't cook?"

"Yes, we should probably avoid doing any cooking. Something like this makes a good breakfast because you don't have to make a fire."

"I suppose cheese and fruit would make a good Sabbath meal."

"Yes, that would be acceptable."

"What about my parents? Can they do work since they are not Israelite?"

"No, the law specifically forbids aliens from working."

"The last Sabbath was the day before you came to get me, wasn't it?"

Something about her expression made him ask, "Yes, why? What happened?"

"I was obeying what you told us about the chamber pots—you know, that everyone has to take human waste to the burial site on the outskirts of camp."

"On the Sabbath?"

"Yes, I had to walk through part of the Israelite section to get there, and I got a lot of ugly, pointed looks when I was doing that. Did I do wrong?"

"This is hard to explain, but no one knows exactly what the Lord meant when he said no work on the Sabbath. We've been debating that question for years. Some people want to take a very loose view of it and do just about anything they would normally do. Others are afraid even to walk more than a few feet. We have people in the camp that are at odds on this issue. Probably some of the stricter ones were frowning at you."

"What would you have done if you had been there?"

"I would have waited until after sunset to take the pot."

"Has the Lord given no indication of what he means by no work?"

"Well, when the manna first fell, Moses told people to pick up twice as much on the sixth day, and pick up none on the seventh. Normally, if we picked up more than we needed for a day, it would rot and get worms overnight."

"Ugh."

"Yes, well, the miracle was that the extra picked up on the sixth day for the Sabbath did not rot overnight. It was fresh the next morning. The first Sabbath after the manna fell, a few people went out to look for manna on that day. None had fallen, but Moses told the people that the Lord was very angry that some of them had gone out to look anyway. Another time, a man was caught gathering wood on the Sabbath. He was stoned for it."

"That is serious. What do you think about it?"

"I think that we are supposed to plan our lives so that we don't have to work for our food and shelter. We are supposed to rest. But I don't think that means we should go without food or not take care of our bodily functions. He has never punished us for milking our animals."

"If I understand the command right, it sounds to me like the Lord didn't mean the Sabbath to be a burden, but a blessing. I mean, I worked seven days a week without a break and with no relief in sight for years. What would it have meant to me to have a day off once a week just to rest! I think your people are trying to make this too difficult by making it a chore instead of a break."

"That's an interesting perspective."

"But you don't agree?"

"I don't know what I think for sure. I'll have to think about it some more. Did you have any more questions about the law?"

"I'll have to think about it."

Salmon chuckled.

"Actually, I have been wondering about how my parents are. I haven't been able to see them for many days now. Are they adjusting?"

"They're fine. Othniel told me that Caleb has taken an interest in your father, and they may become good friends."

"And Mother?"

"She cries a lot. I think the shock of everything has been hard on her. She is old to start completely over from nothing, but she understands that she cannot go back."

"Mother has always had a hard time dealing with difficulties." She paused as she thought about all the times her mother had fallen apart, and Rahab herself had been left trying to keep the family going. "What about the others?"

"The little boys are doing very well. They love this nomadic life. They are making friends with some of the others in the outer camp. They seem very adaptable. As for Adah..."

"Yes?"

"She is having the hardest time. She lost not only her friends, but a few admirers as well. She can't seem to find herself in this new world. She spends a lot of time sulking in the tent."

"Salmon, I know I'm not supposed to see them, but ..."

"No, it would not be right for you to go now. But I have an idea. Didn't you say Acsah had been to see you?"

"Yes, Acsah. She would be perfect. She's such a friendly, outgoing person. Do you think she would befriend Adah?"

"I don't see why not. Her father has befriended Benne. By the way, I asked your father to help us to harvest the wheat in the area."

"What did he say?"

"Well, at first, I thought he might refuse because he still sees us as the enemy and himself as a captive, but we talked for a while. I assured him that he was no one's captive, but that we needed his expertise. I told him that he would be well paid for his help and advice."

"You said the right thing, then. He can be very stubborn unless pay is involved." Rahab placed her hand tentatively on his arm. "I want to thank you for taking care of them. I sometimes feel helpless not being able to see to them as I have before."

"You're welcome."

"What other food laws do I need to know?"

"Ah, so you did think of some more questions. Well, you must not cook a young goat in its mother's milk."

"Why not, I wonder?"

"I'm not sure, but the law repeats this often."

"What else?"

"Several categories of foods aren't allowed, especially types of meat." He began to count these on his fingers: "Animals that do not have split hooves and chew the cud; animals killed by wild beasts; animals that die naturally; fish or swimming creatures without scales and fins; birds that eat prey like eagles or vultures; bats; fat or blood from any animal;

insects unless they hop on jointed legs like locusts or grasshoppers; and weasels, rats, lizards, snakes... I think that's about it."

"So you are saying that we cannot eat pigs or rabbits?"

"Right. Even to touch an unclean animal is to be unclean until evening. You would have to take a bath and wait until evening to be clean again."

"Speaking of food, shouldn't I be fixing some for the noon meal?"

"Don't forget that this is the Sabbath."

"I know, but we need to eat." She looked in the stores and saw the goat's cheese. She also pulled out some more raisins and dried figs. "Where did you get your dried fruits and barley if you haven't been in cultivated land for so long. Did you get them from Jericho?"

"No, remember, we weren't allowed to take anything out of Jericho. Everything in Jericho was dedicated to the Lord."

"So our city was a great big sacrifice to your God, is that it?"

"Well, not exactly. More an act of obedience than of sacrifice. But then all sacrifice is obedience."

"And all obedience is sacrifice."

"Perhaps. You know, you make perceptive statements. You give me a lot to think about."

"So, where did you get the food?"

"Right, well, we had some from the plunder of Midian. We got a lot out of those battles. And more recently, we raided the farmhouses in the Jordan River area. All of them were empty. I assume the people had all gone into Jericho for safety. We found quite a bit of grain and dried fruits, but not much else."

"Yes, the barley harvest was just finished, but none of the other vegetables and fruits are ready yet. You probably picked a good time for your invasion if you were looking to find supplies of food. The barley harvest was good, and the wheat harvest promised to be better."

"That would be Joshua's doing."

"How does he decide?"

"He says that he hears from the Lord, and I believe he does, but I commend his humility. He has acted on some brilliant decisions so far."

"I would think that making an earthquake happen just when you sounded trumpets would be a bit more than brilliant, more like miraculous."

"Yes, it was a miracle."

"Here is the food. I was getting hungry."

They ate in a companionable silence, but Salmon couldn't help noticing that Rahab seemed to be shivering slightly.

"Are you cold?"

"I may wrap up in my wool blanket after the meal."

Day 7, The First Sabbath

"Please do, if it will make you more comfortable. We didn't have steady rains like this in the desert."

"Where did you get your water?"

"Usually we would find an oasis. But twice I remember that Moses struck a rock and water just poured out of it."

"More miracles."

"Yes, I see what you are getting at. I just took that kind of thing for granted."

"The Lord was a part of your life so much that miracles were day to day affairs. For me, coming from a culture without the Lord, the purity of the air here, the quiet, and the sense of safety and peace are all miracles."

"I remember what Jericho was like. It was pretty filthy and noisy."

"Do you think that your camp would be clean if it weren't for the laws about waste disposal?"

"We were raised to be clean. We do it because it seems right to us."

"Yes, but it started with the law, didn't it."

"I suppose."

"Tell me more about the law now. You said that eating or touching certain animals would make me unclean. Will other things make us unclean?"

"Yes; I know many other ways. You can be made unclean by touching anything or anyone dead, touching a woman having her period, having sexual relations..."

She gasped a little.

"What is it?"

"Did you say touching a woman having her period would make someone unclean?"

"Yes, why?"

"I'm having my period now."

Salmon had a blank look on his face. "You're having your period. Why didn't you tell me before?"

Rahab felt like crying. It was humiliating enough to have to tell him this without having her ignorance brought up. "I didn't know I needed to, and we aren't married yet. It didn't seem appropriate to..."

Salmon held up his hand. "I have to think. Have you touched me at all?"

"Yes, I touched your arm when you told me about my parents."

"Yes, I remember." His rueful smile seemed to be saying that he had enjoyed that touch, but now he would have to pay for it. "I'm going to have to find a way to take a bath and wash my clothes. And you need to stay on your side of the tent for the next... How many days has it been?"

"One."

"That would make it six more. I'm going to bathe now. Then after sunset, I'll get Acsah to come talk to you about how she copes. I never had this problem before. I don't remember how my parents handled it."

After he had left, she found the wool blanket where it was rolled up into the tight bundle. Rahab still didn't know why Shamar always did that. The blanket wasn't as damp as her shift because it had been in the center of the pallet. She wrapped it around herself and tried to be grateful that she was sitting on a woven mat rather than in the mud. That made her think of her family. How had they fared in this weather? It seemed strange that a man like her father who had been of little consequence in Jericho and the surrounding area should be so important in this nation of Israel because of his skills as a farmer. In some ways the Israelites were very childlike in their dependence. Perhaps that is what the Lord had been trying to accomplish when he took them into the wilderness and then supplied all their needs. Salmon had not appreciated the care that they got from the Lord, but then, she had not appreciated all that her father knew and could do either. She had only noticed his flaws. Thinking of her parents made her sad. She would like to talk to them and see how they were adjusting.

Salmon was bathing in one of the tents of his menservants when word came that he was to meet with Joshua at sunset. This day seemed to be getting worse and worse. He dreaded meeting Joshua now. After his last attempt at spying, he wouldn't be surprised if Joshua removed him from leadership in the army.

The rain had stopped, and the sun sent out glorious rays underneath the clouds just before it slipped below the horizon, ending the Sabbath officially. Salmon watched this brilliant display before sending his servant Elon to Acsah and heading himself toward the tribe of Ephraim. He was the last to slip into Joshua's tent; Othniel was already seated. Salmon was almost afraid to meet Joshua's eyes.

Joshua began the meeting by saying, "We are all assembled. I have heard from the Lord. We are to attack Ai again. The Lord has given me the battle plan as follows: Two divisions will be leaving tonight at midnight to set up an ambush behind Ai. Those men should be able to hide in the many hills that Salmon and Othniel told us about behind the city to the west. These two divisions will remain there quietly without attracting any attention all day tomorrow. The rest of the army and I will leave here in the morning. We will camp northeast of the city on the plateau. The next morning we will advance on the city, and when the men of Ai come out against us, as they did before, we will retreat from them. In this way, we will lure them away from the city. At the same time that we flee from them, I will make a sign by raising my javelin, and the ambush group will move in and take the city. When they have taken the city, they will set it on fire. After that, the ambush group will move out against the army of Ai from the city, and we will turn on them from the east. They will be caught between us."

Salmon was amazed at the brilliant simplicity of the plan. It seemed to him the best use of the land features and the mental state of the enemy, who were no doubt overconfident from the victory of a few days before.

Joshua looked around the group. "I want Salmon and Othniel to lead the ambush force that is leaving tonight. They know the country better than anyone else, and they will be traveling in the dark. Elidad, I want you to muster the three best divisions of your troops now, ready to leave at midnight tonight. You will rendezvous west of camp here by Ephraim. Bring enough food for four days. After you take the city, you will be allowed to keep all the plunder, but as we did at Midian, we will divide everything fairly among all the men who fight and the rest of the camp. We may keep the animals, too. Only the people and the buildings must be destroyed.

He turned to the other men. "Have your divisions ready to leave at daybreak. Are there any questions?" A few men asked him about details of the attack, but, for the most part, it was clear what each division was to do. Salmon felt dazed with relief.

He realized that by putting confidence in his leadership, Joshua was showing that he didn't blame him or Othniel for what had happened at Ai before. He obviously believed that all the blame lay with Achan. Salmon felt a fierce sense of loyalty toward Joshua. He would follow him anywhere.

Having made their plans, the group dispersed. Salmon needed to make arrangements about his stock before he left and make sure that his servants were ready to join their divisions for battle. He also needed to tell Rahab that he was leaving again. Othniel promised to come for him.

Not long after sunset, Acsah came to the tent. "I heard you had a problem. Is there anything I can do?"

"Did Salmon tell you?"

"Not exactly. He sent a servant, but I assumed it was woman problem. Is it your period?"

"Yes. I didn't know until today that I was unclean. How am I supposed to cope? It sounded almost as though I should sit in one place in the tent for seven days and not touch anything or anyone."

"Well, we don't go quite to that extreme, but some things we must do. While it's true that no man can touch you, we don't interpret that to mean that you can't cook. You just can't share bedding at all during that time or else he will have to take a bath and be unclean until the sun sets. Also, don't sit together on the same mat or rock or whatever."

"We can be in the same tent?"

"Sure. You can talk all you want."

"There must be exceptions for children; otherwise, babies would not be cared for."

"Yes, I think the law only applies to everyone over the age of thirteen."

"What about moving about?"

"What have you been using?"

"Rags."

"You can continue doing that, and when the seven days are up, be sure to wash all the bedding, rags, and mats that you have used. I carry my mat with me, so I can limit the number of unclean things I have to deal with after the seven days. Oh, and you also have to take a bath at the end of the seven days."

"Oh, I had to take a bath before the solemn assembly, too. Is that a type of ritual?"

"We have no ritual way to do it, but bathing is mentioned over twenty times in the law as the way to get clean after breaking a law involving cleanliness. The only stipulation is that it has to be in water. For practical reasons, we use a basin of water and rags. You can bathe right here in the tent in the inner room."

"Yes, but what if Salmon were to come in while..."

"Oh, I see your problem. You can tell him that you are going to bathe and ask him to stay away."

"I'm not sure I trust him."

"He didn't invade your privacy that way the other night, did he?"

"No, he got Penninah to help me that time. Do you think Shamar would stand guard for me?"

"She might. Do you want me to ask her?"

"Would you? Or could you teach me how to ask in Hebrew?"

Acsah gave her the phrase that meant, "Would you watch the door when I have to take a bath."

Rahab repeated it several times. "I think I've got that. Let's try it on Shamar."

Acsah called Shamar to come to the tent. She seemed reluctant to come, but complied.

Rahab said haltingly in Hebrew, "Would you watch the door when I have to take a bath." Shamar said something back that Rahab could not understand. "This is so frustrating. I really need to learn her language."

"She said that she wants to know what she is watching for."

"I need her to keep Salmon away."

In the exchange that followed, it was clear to Rahab that Shamar was not agreeable to the proposition. Finally, Acsah sighed and said, "She says that she does not have the authority to forbid her master access to his own tent."

"Acsah, what am I going to do?"

"I'll talk to Salmon and explain everything. You are going to have to trust him, Rahab. He doesn't want to hurt you. I know he doesn't."

"This is all so complicated. I have to admit, this law baffles me. I'm not sure why the Lord has it."

"The women have talked about it a lot and have come up with three reasons."

"What are those?"

"We think the Lord wants us to have a lot of children. The older women told us that men know that women don't easily get pregnant during their period, so some of them want to have sex then to keep from having babies. I'm guessing that babies take the wives' attention away from the men. But the Lord prohibits intercourse during this time, and this law makes the temptation even less for the men."

Acsah continued, "Perhaps the Lord made this law because he understands how uncomfortable we feel during this time. But probably the main thing is that the Lord wants us always to take the handling of blood very seriously, no matter what the source. He emphasizes over and over that blood is the payment for sin and the source of life. We should always treat it with care."

Rahab nodded. She should have known that the Lord would have good reasons for whatever he did. All of his laws she knew about so far seemed designed to make people's lives better in some way, especially the lives of women and children. She had no trouble trusting the Lord. It was Salmon that she wasn't sure about. She would just have to make adjustments.

"You aren't married. Does it make you uncomfortable to talk about such things?"

"Not really."

"I am not sure I feel comfortable talking to Salmon about this."

Acsah smiled in the semi-darkness. "I'd better head back to my tent. Can I answer any other questions?"

"Probably dozens, but not tonight. Thanks for all your help."

Acsah's voice came back to her faintly as she watched her leave the campsite. "You're welcome."

When Salmon came in later, Rahab told him what Acsah had said regarding the cooking and touching. "We just have to be sure to not touch each other at all." She thought that talking about her bodily functions had taken away a certain amount of restraint between them. She wasn't sure how she felt about that. His next words altered her feelings entirely.

"Touching isn't going to be a problem this month anyway. While I was out, I got the word that we are leaving tonight for another attack on Ai. I don't know when I will be back, but Joshua told us to take enough food for four days."

Rahab nodded. It occurred to her that unless the Lord was on the Israelite side, he might never be back at all. The idea caused her a greater pang than she expected. She watched him gather his armor and a sack containing some provisions and a goatskin of water. She wished that the barley bread were fresh, but He could still take some raisins. He seemed very self-sufficient. As he walked away, she wanted to call out to him some word of parting, but she didn't know what was appropriate in the situation. "Oh, Lord, be with him," she whispered.

After he left, Rahab felt bereft. She sat down on the matting that she had decided to use since she found out about her period and looked at her folded hands. She didn't quite know what to do with herself and her emotions. She should be happy, she thought, because Salmon was gone and she didn't have to worry about his bothering her. But somehow, she had come to a point of no longer expecting him to molest her. Still, she held hope that he would get over this desire to marry her and would give her the freedom she wanted. She put her sleeping mat down in the driest place she could find in the tent and wrapped up tightly in the damp wool blanket. It had been a long, emotional day. She was ready to get some rest.

As Othniel and Salmon hurried together toward the rendezvous point on the edge of the camp, Salmon thought about how many interruptions he was having in his wooing of Rahab. At this rate, the month would be up, and she still would not want to marry him. Of course, he could force her to since it was his prerogative as a man, but he would much prefer to have her at least willing, if not eager, to be his wife.

Joshua was waiting at the area where the men were gathering. He began speaking in a clear voice. Salmon noticed that all the confidence and power were back. It gave him some comfort to know that Joshua was sure of the victory this time.

"Listen carefully. Thirty thousand of you are leaving tonight. You are to set an ambush behind the city. You will encounter many hills behind to the west. Salmon and Othniel are with you, and they know the way. After you are set, don't go very far from the city. All of you must be on the alert." He went on to give the details of the battle plan before finishing, "The Lord your God will give it into your hand. When you have taken the city, set it on fire. Do what the Lord has commanded. See to it; you have my orders."

In only a few minutes, the men fell into formation for travel. They were among the most seasoned of the warriors in the army, chosen for this special mission because they could be trusted to follow orders. Moving swiftly on the main road in spite of the dark, they reached the stream a little past midnight and stopped to drink. Then they marched on, this time moving more cautiously and going farther south than the road that went up to Ai.

Salmon found it harder work to get through the countryside in the dark with no clear roads. He felt his responsibility keenly as he and Othniel marched at the front of the divisions. While they marched, Salmon thought about what Rahab had told him about the Canaanites. Her description of child sacrifice seemed to him to be the epitome of evil.

Othniel spoke up. "You seem to have a lot on your mind tonight. Is it Rahab?"

"In a way. Let me tell you what she told me about Canaanite religious practices." He shared what she had said. "I had heard that the Canaanites were wicked, but I guess I thought that they didn't worship the true God because they were confused about whom to worship. I hadn't realized how sinful the actual practices were until I heard her account. No wonder the Lord wants them destroyed."

"I had no idea, either. What you are telling me is disgusting." Salmon could hear the indignation in his voice.

They were going through the unpopulated area that Salmon and Othniel had spied out below the quarries. Salmon was glad now that Othniel had insisted on their coming out of their way to look at it. The way climbed steeply at times, and had it not been for the moon, they might have been lost. Morning was just dawning before they reached the area that was hidden behind high hills, but not too far from Ai west of the city. The men took turns keeping watch. But Salmon didn't sleep at all. He knew that daylight would bring a test of their patience, as they were to stay hidden the entire day and would have to be on alert all that time.

DAY 8

The day before the battle of Ai was indeed one of the longest Salmon could remember. He forbad his men to talk for fear of making too much noise and alerting the enemy. Salmon watched the city from behind well-chosen rocks and promontories. Clearly, the population of the city had swollen. Some of those men must have come from other cities, perhaps Bethel, for he saw many more than he had just a few days before. He wondered if the men of Ai felt overconfident now after their earlier defeat of the Israelites.

As he peered down on the city of Ai, his eyes could pick out some of the sights he had seen when he had visited there only a few days before, but how different his perspective was now from then! Instead of seeing the town center as just an open area with unusual and suggestive statues in and around it, he saw the temple of Ashtoreth and the immoral acts that were performed there in the name of religion. He also saw a gleam of metal and the smoke that marked the statue of Molech. The drums beating meant that even now, some baby was being roasted to death in that barbaric rite. Anger rose inside of him. No god of Canaan would stand against the might of the Lord this time!

He felt the bag hanging on his thigh and took time to open it and take out the cloth containing the single curl he had kept from Rahab's hair. As he stroked the curl with his finger, he thought again of how much he wanted to protect Rahab from evils such as existed in cities like Jericho and Ai. He felt he could give her a good life among the Israelites if he could only get her to trust him.

About mid-afternoon, he could see the army of Israel approaching from the east. They were making no attempt at stealth, but moved through the valley to the plateau across from the city, where they set up camp. The entire army had come to fight this time. No matter how many

Day 8

were in the city, they would definitely be outnumbered! He felt reassured to see them marching in unit after unit.

By the time the last of the main body of the army had arrived and encamped, dusk had set in. From their position, they could see the lights of campfires over on the plateau and the glow of oil lamps shining in Ai. No such comfort was offered to the ambush force. They had to draw their cloaks around themselves more securely and eat cold food in the dark.

Rahab was awakened the next morning by the sound of the silver trumpets that she had heard only once before, the day of the stoning of Achan. She thought at first that some horrible thing had happened to Salmon and the army, and her heart clutched in fear. Just then, Shamar, with tears streaming down her face, put her head into the tent and left the goat's milk, making Rahab rise quickly to find out what was happening. She peeked out of the tent door and saw activity around almost every tent.

She got up, and covering her head, walked in the direction of the sound of the trumpets. As she went, she saw armed men hurrying to the edge of the camp, leaving weeping women behind. Then she understood. The rest of the army must be mobilizing to go to Ai. She followed the men and arrived in time to hear Eleazar give a speech to the men before their departure.

"Hear, O Israel, today you are going into battle against your enemies. Do not be fainthearted or afraid; do not be terrified or give way to panic before them. For the Lord your God is the one who goes with you to fight for you against your enemies to give your victory."

Rahab watched as Eleazar blessed the men and then stepped aside to allow the first of the tribes to go. She recognized Judah because Caleb was in front, and beside him was the standard bearer. Just then, Acsah came up beside her. "This is a sight, isn't it? Over 600,000 men fight in our army."

"I'm overwhelmed to see all of them at the same time. I noticed that your father is the head of Judah."

"Yes, I suppose he will fight. He is so vigorous for an eighty-year-old man. Do you see the standard beside him? That used to be kept in your tent."

"My tent?"

"Yes, the leader of Judah keeps the standard for his tribe. Nahshon lived in Salmon's tent, so the standard was kept there. Now it resides in my tent."

Rahab thought about Salmon living with that always in his tent, reminding him of the importance of his father. It helped her to picture him as a young man and even as a child. She stayed until the last of the men moved away toward the west. Somewhere over in that direction was Salmon. She wondered why he had already left and what he was doing now.

Acsah said, "I'm going to go back to my tent now, but I will come to see you this afternoon if you don't mind."

"I'd like that very much."

Back in the tent Rahab realized that she would be alone for much of this day and probably several more. Because she had things to do now, she wasn't as miserable as she had been before, but she still chafed under the confinement she felt in Salmon's tent. She straightened things up and drank the delicious goat's milk with the last of the barley bread.

She decided to make another batch of bread. She got out the grinding stone and began to grind the fine flour from which she made her bread. The food supplies had gone down quite a bit since she had come into the tent, and she wondered how Salmon planned to replace those. As she worked, she remembered the many times that she had done this in her life. Her mother had given her two tasks to do when she was a girl at home: grinding and weaving. She had enjoyed both of them because she had so much time to think about things when she was doing those fairly mindless tasks. Today she remembered one day in particular when her mind had drifted away from her weaving.

She and her mother were making linen, but because she hadn't perfected her ability to work and think at the same time, her mother had to remind her to get back to work. Each time her mother would catch her daydreaming, Rahab would quickly resume her work, passing the shuttle back and forth and beating the fine linen thread tightly into soft, sturdy cloth. Mora sighed often in frustration. Rahab knew even then that her mother resented all the work that had to be done. She had told Rahab many times that she thought Benne was a rich farmer when she married him. Perhaps his father had been, but the farm's assets had been frittered away. Mora complained endlessly to anyone who would listen about the poverty that they endured because of Benne's drinking. Rahab's hands paused as she meditated on how she hoped for a very different kind of husband than her father had been to her mother.

"Rahab, we have to complete another cubit of linen before the evening meal, or we won't make the sale."

"Sorry, Mother."

Day 8

For a while the shuttle rattled and the wheel spun as they worked together. But Rahab's mind was somewhere else. She often thought about marriage these days. The making of the lovely linen kept her thinking about the bride it was to adorn, her friend Tyra. Tyra's parents had been forced to choose between two potential bridegrooms. One was Ambaal, the rich soldier who had made a handsome offer. The other was Lem, perhaps not as rich, but more responsible and likable, with a farm near her parents.

She had thought then that Tyra's parents had made the right choice when they accepted Lem's offer. Lem struck her as someone who would be easy to live with, and he really did seem to care about Tyra. But Tyra's reaction surprised her. She told Rahab that she thought Lem's hands were clammy and that his constant joking got on her nerves. She didn't openly defy her parents, but she had been rather peevish. Rahab kept thinking that if she were getting married, she would be grateful to her parents for getting her a husband.

Late that same afternoon, the cloth was done, and just in time, for Tyra's mother arrived promptly to buy it. "What a lovely piece of linen! You do such good work, Mora. I tell you, this wedding has me in a state. Oh, before I forget, everyone in your family is invited to the wedding feast."

Rahab somehow sensed a sneer in her voice, as though she thought that the family of Benne would miss no opportunity for free food and drink, but she was kind enough not to say it aloud.

After she left, Mora sighed. Her relief showed as she clutched the precious coins in her palm. "There, that's one job done. Tomorrow we'll get started on that piece for the potter's wife."

Rahab flexed her tired fingers and nodded. Together they tidied up the cramped room, setting the loom out of the way in a corner and putting away the basket of flax fibers and rolls of thread.

Her mother called to her sister Adah to help with the evening meal preparations. She came in breathless from playing a game with the little boys. Rahab placed the raisins, olives, and honey on the table while Adah got the goat cheese and their mother retrieved bread from a basket on the wall. They looked at the meager array of food, which was supposed to feed so many mouths, and then at each other. Always they worried about having enough food. Rahab felt the familiar feelings of wanting to do all she could to help her parents and at the same time wanting to escape. She hoped then that the husband her parents got for her would be able to take care of her and her family.

That very evening, her father came into the house, swaggering with the news he had to tell and the wine that he had consumed that afternoon while making another unnecessary trip to town.

"Rahab, my daughter, you are fortunate indeed. The gods have smiled on you and on all of us."

Rahab looked on in wonder while Mother crossed the room. "What news, my husband?"

"I've had two good offers for Rahab's future today. One is for marriage."

"And the other?'

"Do you know the priest from the temple to Ashtoreth?"

Benne continued speaking in spite of the gasps from both of the women. "We would be exempted from taxes and she would be honored as a priestess to Ashtoreth. We could do far worse," he added as he saw that his news had not been met with the expected enthusiasm.

Rahab's eyes filled with frustrated tears. "Oh, father, you must know that all I've ever wanted is to have a home with a husband and children."

Mora asked, "What of the marriage proposal. Is the offer a good one?"

Benne relaxed a little, "Yes, he made a good offer: ten sheep and a sack of gold coins—by far the best bride price I've heard."

"So why even consider the temple for our daughter?" asked Mora.

"The offer is from Ambaal."

"I see," she paused. "Well, I can understand your hesitation there, but still I would rather see Rahab married than at the temple. And ten sheep..."

Neither parent seemed to notice her during this exchange. At the name of Ambaal she had pulled back into herself. She dared not protest again, but the idea of Ambaal for a husband was almost as horrifying as becoming a temple prostitute. She had never forgotten the day that she was visiting with Tyra in Jericho. On their way to the well, they saw Ambaal whipping a poor old servant woman for dropping and breaking a water pot. The woman's cries for mercy and the cruel sneer on Ambaal's face remained with Rahab. Moreover, he had spoken to them. That in itself was improper, and also his words were suggestive, even lewd. She felt violated, but Tyra laughed at her for being so prudish. Now her own parents were considering him as a husband for her.

After that day, her thoughts as she made the loom clatter were no longer dreamy. She was not looking forward to her marriage.

Rahab sighed, thinking how different her life had been from her dreams as a girl. Then looking down, she smiled at herself. Her hands had finished their work without her awareness, and now several loaves of

Day 8

barley dough sat ready. She went out to the fire to mend it for baking. Soon the smell of bread filled the area with its mouth-watering aroma. Here the good smells were rarely in competition with stench such as the smell of human waste and garbage that pervaded Jericho.

At noon, she ate some of the fresh bread. The afternoon stretched out before her rather empty, when she heard Acsah calling from outside for admittance. "Join me, Acsah," she invited.

Acsah surprised Rahab by pulling a goat hair sack into the tent. When she opened it, a large quantity of wool popped out from where it had been packed in tightly. Rahab said in surprise, "What is this?"

"We have just shorn our sheep, and some of my servants knew how to wash the wool, but no one seems to know how to make anything from it. I heard from Othniel that you were a weaver, and I thought you might be able to make something from this and teach me about weaving at the same time."

"Oh, I would love that, Acsah, but I'm afraid I don't have the equipment I would need. My spindle and loom were burned up in Jericho, and those are hard to replace. I think spindles have to be carved by a master carver. Ours was passed down for several generations." She looked with longing at the wool fibers.

Acsah reached inside the sack and felt around. She pulled out an object shaped somewhat like a child's top, but larger. "This was in my mother's things. I vaguely remember her using it with wool, but I was very young when she died. So I'm not sure."

"Just the thing, a spindle! Now if we only had a comb."

"Would a hair comb work? I've heard of a man in camp who carves those for people in exchange for other things. His wife might sell me one even if he has gone to the battle."

"I think a sturdy hair comb might work. We could try it anyway."

"I'll be right back."

While she was gone, Rahab thought about how little this generation of Israelites knew about domestic work. Their parents had known how to do things, so they had vague notions about weaving and harvesting crops, but they themselves had never done those. If they ever settled down somewhere, she was going to have to teach Salmon how to grow crops. That is, she reminded herself, if she did marry him.

She reached into the sack and pulled out some of the wool and examined it. The curliness of the fibers would make it more difficult to spin into a smooth thread. In fact, she guessed that she would probably have to be satisfied with a thin yarn. "Wouldn't it be nice to make something again," she thought aloud.

She probably should have asked about getting a comb for herself, but then, she realized ruefully, she still didn't need one, and wouldn't for quite a while. Her hair was only about the length of the first joint of her little finger now. The time when she had long hair and some control over her life seemed long ago.

Acsah came back in carrying a large, sturdy comb. "The comb maker told me that some people have noticed that their clothes are starting to show wear, and many are trying to weave again. He has started making the bigger combs that are needed for carding the wool. What do you think?"

"Perfect! And very well made, too."

She began to comb the piece of wool that she held in her hand until it was all lying in roughly the same direction. Then she grasped the top of that set of wool and twisted it around until she had made a tip out of it. She attached this to the top of the spindle and began to turn it, feeding more of the yarn into the line. Gradually the fibers twisted around themselves until they became a long thin thread.

"So that is how it works." Acsah cried in delight. "May I try?"

"Certainly." It took several tries, but Acsah finally was able to make the spindle move as she wanted it to while keeping the fibers steady. "The trick is to keep an even amount of fiber going into the thread at a time. If it varies, the thread will be uneven and the cloth will not be smooth."

Acsah worked with the spindle a few more minutes before passing it back to Rahab. "You go ahead and do this batch. I will come and practice some more with you each day until I learn how to do it better."

Rahab took over the spinning, which went faster and smoother for her than it had for Acsah, but still it wasn't up to Rahab's standards. "Wool is just different," she thought.

"Would you like to have a language lesson?" Acsah invited.

"Yes! How shall we do this?"

"What if I just point to things and call their names in Hebrew?"

"All right."

Acsah began to point to items in the tent: *mat, pole, barley, jar, bowl,* and *cup.* Rahab dutifully repeated the strange sounding words back to her, but as they went on, she began to see patterns and connections between the sounds of her own language and those of Hebrew. "I think I understand." She said a few words in Hebrew that Acsah had not taught her yet to see if she was correct.

"Yes, that is exactly right. You are a quick learner."

Day 8

"Does that mean these words would be like this?" She again said a list of words with similar vowels, but changed the vowel to be like the Hebrew.

"Wonderful! It will take you no time at all to master Hebrew."

"What about sentences? How do you say greetings?"

Acsah demonstrated several common phrases for saying *Hello, How are you today? My name is Rahab. I am Canaanite.* Then she laughed, "I think I will teach you how to say *I love you*. You might need to know that in the near future."

"I need to know how to say it now. I want to tell the Lord how much I love him in his chosen language."

"That is an interesting thing to say. I don't know when I've heard anyone talking about saying, 'I love you' to the Lord. We mostly talk about obeying him or sacrificing to him."

Rahab was surprised. "I understood that the Lord is with your people all the time. How could you help but express love to him?"

"I never really thought about that."

They continued for a little longer, but Acsah said she needed to get back to her tent. "I love the smell of your barley bread. We have been eating mostly porridge with our grain. I know what I am doing with that."

"Here, take some of this with you for your evening meal. Someday soon, I will teach you to make barley bread if you like."

After Acsah had left, Rahab thought gratefully that the Lord had really blessed her by allowing her to have a friend. The afternoon had passed so quickly, and she had learned so much. She couldn't wait to try her Hebrew on Salmon and show him her spinning. This eagerness surprised her. She hadn't intended to care.

She noticed the quiet and thought back again to the days in Jericho when the noise of the streets outside her inn would make her long for her childhood on the farm. Now she was in the midst of a large number of people, much larger than the population of Jericho, but it was peaceful. Was it the presence of their god that made Israelite people so calm? She never heard the arguing and fighting that were so common in the streets of the lower city of Jericho. People seemed to respect each other and each other's property.

She decided to eat a little supper, opting for a piece of bread and some cheese. Though the day had been uneventful, and it was still early, she began to feel drowsy. She fell asleep wondering what was going on at Ai. Would Salmon be in danger? Was he thinking about her?

DAY 9

Salmon rubbed his eyes, gritty and heavy in the very early dawn. One of the few still up watching, he saw the activity in Ai first. The king of Ai clearly intended that any battle should take place away from the city. He was already mustering his troops and moving out to battle lines on the high plains overlooking the valley of the Jordan.

Salmon alerted the waiting ambush force and soon had everyone up and armed for battle, almost silently. In the hush of morning, Salmon spoke briefly, reminding the men of the strategy. They were to give no quarter, but could take the plunder, including the animals. The smiles of the men welcomed this great news. Salmon's food supply wasn't the only one running low. Salmon concluded, "Remember that the Lord has designated us to wipe out this culture of idol worship, adultery, and child sacrifice. He cannot allow such abominations in this Promised Land. It will only be our Promised Land if we conquer it! We can fight confidently, knowing that the Lord is on our side."

After this speech, Salmon turned back to view the valley below. He could just make out the figure of Joshua standing with his javelin in hand. Just a few moments after the trumpet signaled the attack, Joshua raised the javelin into the air, the signal that both parts of the Israelite army anticipated. The main army below made a token stand before beginning to run as if in retreat, while Salmon gave the signal for the ambush to begin.

The men made their way down the hill to the city. That the gates had been left unguarded was a wonder to Salmon, but he was grateful that the defenders obviously had no inkling of the battle strategy.

Once in the city, they spread out, killing anyone who came in their way and gathering the plunder from every house and business. With sufficient manpower, this went very rapidly, but Salmon had a specific goal in mind. He found some metal objects in a metalworker's shop, including a large hammer. He took what was there and then headed for the central common area of the city. There he took that heavy hammer and began to smash it down on the still-hot statue of Molech. The softened metal gave way under his onslaught. Other soldiers joined him in destroying the statue and also the statue of Ashtoreth in the temple doorway, but for Salmon the attack on the statue was personal. His anger and disgust at what Rahab had told him happened in this square gave him vindictive power, and he thought as he smashed the hammer down, "I am doing this for you, Rahab."

When the statue was smashed beyond recognition, he looked around and seemed to come to himself. The men were nearly through taking all that they could from the houses and shops.

"Get the torches, start fires throughout the city. Then regroup at the city gates!" Salmon ordered. Several men found live embers in some of the houses and began lighting torches to start fires throughout the city. Before long, the city blazed.

Outside the walls, the men regrouped to prepare for the real battle to come. They knew that as soon as the men from Ai saw their city on fire, they would turn back to try to save it. They had to be ready to face that army from this side. Salmon chose a few hundred men.

"Elon, take this group to gather the animals from the city and keep watch over them away from the battle lines. Ahira, you and your group guard the city gates. Don't let anyone escape. Nethanel, you take the booty to a safe place." Those groups of men scrambled immediately to do their assigned tasks.

Salmon checked to make sure that his other leaders knew their orders; then he joined Othniel standing at the front of the troops now lined up for battle. Othniel glanced at him, soot already coating his face and blood splattered on his clothes. "So far, so good. Are you ready for this, my friend?"

Salmon responded with a grin, "As I'll ever be. I'd rather be here by you than anywhere else on this field."

Through the smoke they could just make out the figures of men running toward them. With a shout, he and Othniel raced forward and met the enemy. Beside him, Othniel dealt masterful strokes. No one within reach of Othniel's sword got past. Salmon himself dispatched one man after another with his battleaxe. He knew that the enemy was dazed and confused by their strategy.

In less time than seemed possible even with so large a force, the men of Ai were down to a small knot of fighting men. One man called out in terror, "I am the king!" as Othniel knocked his sword out of his hand. Rather than kill him, Salmon and Othniel took him by his arms and led him to Joshua, who was still holding the javelin up. Salmon said, "This is the king of Ai, Joshua. He is the last one to be alive in the army. What would you have us do?"

Joshua lowered the javelin and said calmly, "No one is allowed to live. He must die, too. Get a rope and hang him from a tree."

When that had been done, the Israelites turned back to the city where the last of the inhabitants of Ai were put to the sword and their bodies flung into the fires of the city. The battle of Ai was over before noon. Joshua gave more orders. "Burn all of the bodies from the field of battle, too. But leave the body of the king hanging from the tree until sunset."

Salmon felt adrenalin pumping through his body. He joined in carrying the bodies of the dead soldiers to the city to burn. Having killed many people and handled dead bodies all morning, he was already unclean. Salmon found Joshua and asked him, "Should we send a runner back to the main camp to tell them of our victory?"

"Yes, send the runner to your cousin Eleazar."

Salmon found Elon with the animals. "Did you kill anyone or handle any dead bodies?"

Elon shook his head, "No, master. I handled only animals."

"You will be our messenger to take word back to the camp that we have been victorious. Afterwards, you may stay in the camp since you are not unclean."

"Thank you, master!"

Salmon smiled. He knew that Elon was anxious to be back in the main camp because he was worried about Shamar.

Elon took off running with the energy of youth and anxious love.

At sunset, some of the soldiers cut down the king of Ai's body and flung it in the gateway of the city as Joshua directed. Then the men all brought stones to place over the body. Joshua said to the group, "Let this be a reminder of the Lord's faithfulness to us when we are obedient to him."

After that, the men could settle down around campfires and recount the battle from their individual perspectives. Salmon said to Othniel, "You were great! I don't know when I've seen you fight so well."

"I kept thinking about what Rahab told you about the Canaanites. In some ways, the feelings I have may be stronger because, though the Canaanites are in some sense my people, I want to disown them, for they don't worship the right God."

"Yes, I felt very strongly today that the Lord has given us a mandate to clean out these cities of filth and purify this land for his own people to live in."

"One more city down."

Salmon nodded. He was just beginning to realize that he was physically and emotionally exhausted. He had not slept in two nights and had fought a major battle. "I'm ready to sleep. How about you?"

"I feel the same. I'll see you in the morning." They rolled up in their wool cloaks and were soon sound asleep.

That morning, Shamar had brought the goat's milk early before Rahab was up. Rahab sensed that the earlier feelings of animosity had not dissipated, even after she had been cleared of responsibility for the defeat at Ai earlier. Something else was the matter with Shamar. Rahab sighed. She hadn't asked to be the mistress of servants, and with Salmon away, no one could give orders or try to solve this problem. She was glad to see Acsah when she came earlier than she ever had before.

"How about another language lesson?"

"Wonderful," answered Rahab in Hebrew.

Acsah began by pointing to the items in the tent that she had covered before, excited that Rahab could remember them all. As they continued on to other words, Rahab recognized more similarities and differences in the two languages. She still had a strong Canaanite accent, so she asked Acsah to help her make her sound more authentic.

"Open your mouth a little more for this sound," directed Acsah. Rahab tried again. "Yes, that's better. Now say these words with that sound."

Over and over, they drilled sounds until Rahab felt she could make the sounds correctly most of the time. She knew it would be hard to be consistent with that, but at least she knew what she was trying to do.

"I didn't know anyone could pick up a language so quickly. I think that you do well because you see patterns and apply them."

"The differences in the languages aren't as many as it would seem at first. The pronunciation, not the words or sentences, cause me not to understand. You are a good teacher, Acsah."

Acsah blushed at this praise. "You are easy to teach."

They suddenly became aware that the sounds outside the tent had been increasing. When they went out to look, they heard shouts and saw people pointing at the sky to the west, dark gray though the day was otherwise bright and clear. Acsah said, "Let's go see what we can from that clear spot over there."

The Cord

From the higher, rocky ground nearby, they could make out a tinge of orange on the horizon. Someone shouted, "There's a huge fire in the direction of Ai. Perhaps the city has been defeated."

"Oh, I hope so." Rahab felt excitement at the news. She and the other women with her stayed and watched as the fire became more intense and the smoke began to billow up dark gray and angry.

Acsah said pensively, "I hope that our men are safe." Rahab understood that she meant Othniel particularly.

"When will we know of our loved ones?" asked one woman as Acsah translated.

Rahab thought about that phrase. Was Salmon her loved one? They weren't even married yet, but she was concerned about his welfare. If he died, she could just go back to the tents on the outskirts of the camp and rejoin her family. She missed them, but if something happened to Salmon now, she would miss him. She couldn't define the conflict inside her.

Knowing it would probably be hours before they heard anything new, Acsah headed for her own tent, and Rahab went back to spinning wool. Rahab really enjoyed this kind of work, but she missed her mother. Handwork was more pleasant with someone nearby. She decided to ask Shamar to join her. This would be an opportunity to befriend Shamar. She put down the wool and stepped to the door of the tent, intending to call. Looking out, she saw that Shamar was bent over a pot on the fire.

Something about her posture caught Rahab's attention. Shamar had stopped stirring and was holding her back while still bending over. Rahab had seen enough labor to recognize someone having a contraction. She waited quietly until the contraction eased, wondering whether or not to interfere. Shamar's husband, Elon, was away with Salmon and the other men. She assumed that the other women would help Shamar deliver, but no one else seemed to be around.

Rahab made a decision to help even if Shamar didn't want her. She got a cup from the tent and filled it with some water. Then approaching Shamar quietly, she touched her lightly on the arm. The stark terror in Shamar's eyes startled Rahab. In her broken Hebrew, Rahab said, "Don't be afraid. I will help."

Shamar started to shake her head stubbornly, but another contraction hit her just then, doubling her over in pain. Rahab gently rubbed her back at the point where the ache would be most acute. When the contraction subsided, she gave Shamar a drink of water, then led her to the tent that Shamar shared with Elon. There Rahab arranged the bedding so Shamar could lie in a semi-reclining position. Leaving Shamar, she got a bowl of the porridge and then pulled the pot over into ashes to keep it warm

Day 9

without burning. As an afterthought, she stepped into Salmon's tent and got two lengths of the newly-spun wool thread and the sharp knife she had used to shave her hair.

When she returned to the tent, she found a wild-eyed Shamar, drenched with sweat and shaking with pain and fear. Rahab decided then that she would not leave Shamar again even to alert the other women. She found a cloth and some water in Shamar's tent, and with these began to bathe Shamar's face, softly crooning to her reassuring phrases in a mixture of Hebrew and Canaanite. Between contractions, she fed Shamar bites of the still-hot porridge. Gradually, Shamar calmed some, though the contractions kept coming with ever-increasing frequency and intensity. How long this continued, neither noticed.

No one in Israel knew that Rahab had become something of a midwife to the poor prostitutes of Jericho. She had assisted at the delivery of many babies and knew that Shamar was very close to having hers. She felt in a quandary. She couldn't leave Shamar alone, but she wasn't sure how Shamar would react to her delivering the baby.

A grunting moan from Shamar's lips decided her. Clearly the time for pushing was upon them, and Rahab needed to be able to check the progress of the baby. Shamar seemed too intent on the pushing to notice anyway. In what seemed like hours, but was really only a few minutes, Rahab could see the baby's little head crowning. She encouraged Shamar to push, and indeed Shamar did. With a mighty effort, Shamar expelled the baby's head into the world, and a few seconds later, delivered the torso into Rahab's waiting hands.

Rahab caught the baby's body expertly and removed the mucous from the baby's nose. Instantly, the little girl began to cry lustily. Rahab tied the cord in two places, using the knife to cut the baby loose from her mother. After wiping her off, Rahab put the child on Shamar's heaving chest, where the fascinated mother began to murmur excitedly in Hebrew. Rahab still had to deliver the afterbirth and clean up Shamar. Then she took the baby, and after washing her, wrapped her securely in the swaddling clothes that Shamar pointed out to her. Only then could she tuck the mother and child together under a wool blanket. Shamar looked up from the precious small head before her, and, for the first time, she smiled at Rahab.

As soon as she was sure that both of them were well settled, Rahab went looking for Penninah. She motioned for her to come, which she did, looking curious. Her reaction was complete surprise to find Shamar in her tent holding a newborn. They began to chatter in Hebrew so rapidly that Rahab could tell nothing of what they were saying, though her name seemed to be used at times. She stood back watching for a while, feeling awkward. Finally, she smiled at both women and bowed her way out of the tent. Some porridge had been left in the pot. Though the time for the evening meal had passed, Rahab had not eaten since early morning. She got a bowl of the porridge and took it to Salmon's tent, where she ate with relish. She felt wearied by her ordeal at Shamar's side and wondered what the results would be.

A shout outside alerted Rahab that there was news. In all the excitement over Shamar, she had almost forgotten about Ai. She went out in time to see Elon arrive breathless. He spoke to her, but she couldn't quite understand what he was saying. She knew it had something to do with Ai. She followed him to his tent and so witnessed his excitement and surprise when he found Shamar there holding their newborn. Once again, Rahab had the somewhat frustrating experience of hearing a conversation with her name frequently mentioned without knowing exactly what was being said. After Shamar had talked for several minutes, Elon turned to her and in slow precise Hebrew said, "Thank you very much." That she understood.

She had to wait for Acsah to come again to get the word that the city of Ai and all of its inhabitants had been destroyed. Best of all, not one Hebrew was known to have been killed. This statistic amazed Rahab. The fact that it didn't amaze Acsah made her realize the Israelite history with the Lord. They expected to escape unscathed. And with an emotion somewhat akin to joy, she realized that Salmon would be coming back.

DAY 10

Rahab woke and wondered if Salmon might come back that day. She wanted to tell him about Shamar and her baby, show him how much Hebrew she had learned already, and hear all about the battle. She started planning what foods she could fix that he would like. He was probably tired of stale bread and dried fruit by now.

After rising, rolling up her bed, and eating some breakfast, she started spinning. Before long, Acsah came. Rahab handed the spindle to Acsah, asking, "Do you think the men will come back to camp today?"

Acsah answered in Hebrew, "They may come back to the camp, but not into it."

Responding in Hebrew, Rahab asked, "What do you mean?"

"They will have to stay outside the camp for seven days if they fought as they do in most battles."

"I don't remember this happening after Jericho. At least, Salmon came to see us almost every day right after the battle."

"He and Othniel were clean because their job was to rescue you and your family."

"What difference did that make?"

"It's the law about touching dead bodies. After Midian, Othniel had to stay outside because he had killed people. The priest conducted cleansing ceremonies on the third and seventh days, and they had to wash themselves and their clothes. I thought I would die of impatience."

"Cleansing ceremonies?"

Acsah switched back to Canaanite. "The ritual is complicated; they sacrifice a red heifer outside of the camp and burn it up. Then they take the ashes and put those in water. Everything can be cleansed by being sprinkled with the water from a hyssop branch."

"Can we see the men when they are outside the camp?"

"We are allowed to go there, but we can't touch them. My father forbad me to go out to the edge of camp after Midian because with so many men, it just wouldn't be appropriate."

"But you would go there if your father let you?"

"Probably."

"You aren't anxious, are you?" Rahab teased her.

Acsah blushed, "I worry about him every time he is gone. They nearly always win, but I know that Othniel would be right in the front. If anything did go wrong, he would be the one to be killed."

"But as far as we know, no one was killed this time."

"No, thank the Lord. Aren't you anxious about Salmon?"

Rahab hesitated in her answer, "Of course, I wouldn't want anything to happen to him."

"But you don't love him yet."

"No, I'm not sure I will ever be able to love any man."

"Do you want to tell me why you feel that way?"

"My husband was cruel and unfaithful. He gave me no reason to love him. And as for other men, well, let's just say I knew too many of them."

"Life in Jericho must have been really hard for you."

"It was, more than I can explain. Life in the Israelite camp is like another world, a much better world."

"But Salmon is really different from the men in Jericho, isn't he?"

"He is in some ways." She paused and said, "Still I would rather not be married."

"What are you afraid of?"

Rahab looked at Acsah, startled. She had not thought about her hesitancy as fear. "I guess of being hurt again."

"Rahab, I don't have any idea what you must have been through, and I can certainly understand your feelings, but I don't think Salmon is going to hurt you. I know that he loves you very much. If I were you, I wouldn't dismiss the idea of loving him yet."

Rahab wanted to lash out, to say that Acsah was too young and naive to give advice and didn't know all that had happened to her. But she just kept quiet, hoping that Acsah would drop the subject altogether.

After several minutes of strained silence, Acsah said meekly, "Forgive me for invading your privacy. I'm impulsive."

"I forgive you. You mean well."

"Yes. I want you to have a happy life."

"Having you as my friend makes my life happy."

Acsah smiled, but the smile was tinged with worry.

Rahab decided to change the subject. "I'm hungry. Let's take a break and eat something."

"All right. Do you still have some of that good barley bread you made the other day?"

"Yes, and some goat's cheese. Let me get them."

As they ate the cold food, Acsah drilled Rahab on her Hebrew words, especially those having to do with food and cooking. Just as they were finishing, they looked up in surprise to see Shamar standing just outside the tent holding her baby. She said something in Hebrew that Rahab thought might be "May I come in?"

She answered, "Please come in and sit down."

Acsah smiled delightedly at the success of her pupil. "That was perfect, Rahab."

Rahab held out her hands for Shamar's baby. Shamar surrendered her gladly. Rahab held the tiny child close and felt again the preciousness of a little one. How could anyone want to sacrifice such a treasure? Her heart ached as she was reminded of her loss. Tears pooled in her eyes before she could stop them. In a choking voice, she said to Shamar in Hebrew, "She is beautiful."

Shamar said something then that Rahab couldn't quite understand.

Acsah obligingly translated, "She says she owes her baby to you."

Rahab wiped away her tears and said shakily, "Oh no, you are the one who did all the work. I only helped a little."

Shamar looked uncomfortable and then said, "I don't deserve your kindness, mistress. Please forgive me for the way I have treated you."

Rahab didn't trust her Hebrew to answer something so significant. "Tell her I forgive her. Could she tell me what made her act that way?"

Acsah translated Rahab's words and then listened carefully to Shamar's rather lengthy and emotional answer: "Shamar says she was a servant girl to Salmon's mother, Tarah, who was a kind mistress, a wonderful woman. Shamar almost worshiped her. It has been only a little over a year since Salmon's parents died. Before she died, Tarah shared with Shamar her concern about Salmon's future. She was afraid he would always be alone or that he would choose a wife unworthy of him.

"When Salmon brought you into what had been his parents' tent, Shamar thought that Tarah's worst fears had taken place because you were a Canaanite and former prostitute. She says she also resented your good cooking because it diminished her in her master's eyes."

Rahab nodded. "I can understand how she might feel that way."

Shamar continued, and Acsah translated: "I know now that I was totally mistaken. You are a better person than I am. I think Salmon is getting a good wife, and I think his mother would be very happy. I want to be your servant, if you will have me after the way I have acted."

Day 10

"Of course. All is forgiven. I am glad that we can be friends now." Rahab smiled through her tears.

After a minute, Shamar spoke up again. Acsah started to translate, but Rahab said, "Did she just ask me to help her learn to cook better?"

"She did," said Acsah.

Rahab responded, "I would be happy to teach you all I know about cooking."

Acsah chimed in, "I want to learn, too."

"What would you like to know about first?"

Both of them said at once, "Bread!"

"Didn't you make bread at all in the wilderness?"

Acsah said, "We made cakes out of manna, and they had a delicious nutty flavor. The barley and wheat we have here don't work the same way for some reason."

"Hmm. I have watched you make bread, Shamar, and I think the problem is that you need to grind the grain longer and knead the dough more. Do you add oil or salt to the dough?"

"No, I didn't know we needed to. How much salt and oil do we add?" asked Acsah, who had been translating Rahab's words for Shamar.

Rahab lay the sleeping infant across her lap and cupped her hands to show the amount of flour. "For this much flour, put about as much salt as the last section of your little finger and as much oil as you can hold in your palm. You also must add a bit of dough left over from the last baking that has been allowed to sour. That will be the leavening. When you have mixed the dough together, be sure to knead it for at least forty turns using this motion." Her movement woke the sleeping baby. She handed her over to Shamar who opened a slit in her shift made for the purpose and began to nurse.

When the baby was well settled, Acsah asked if they needed to know anything else to make bread.

"Do you know how to bake it?"

"I think so—small loaves on the bottom of a large earthenware bowl turned over the fire—is that right?"

"Yes, but don't forget to let the dough rise twice before baking. Once let it rise to double in size in the bowl, and once let it rise after you have shaped it into loaves. Then it will bake light."

Shamar sighed and said something in Hebrew that Rahab couldn't catch. Acsah said, "I agree with Shamar."

"What did she say?"

"Oh, just that we should have cooking classes with you. Many women need to know how to cook the foods that we are finding here."

"Perhaps we can. Of course, things will be different when the men get back."

"Yes, but most of the men I know want their women to learn to cook. Can we come tomorrow and learn some more?"

"Certainly. If you come around mid-morning, I will make something for lunch that you want to learn to make."

"Could you show us how you make bean soup?"

"Yes, but only if I remember to put the beans in water tonight before I go to sleep."

"Why?"

"The beans will cook more quickly and cleanly tomorrow if they are soaked all night."

"Oh, I didn't know that."

"I think we just heard the first part of tomorrow's lesson."

Shamar said something that Acsah again had to translate. "You handle the baby so well. Have you ever had one?"

Rahab was quiet for a few seconds and then answered, "Yes, I have."

The silence lasted for an uncomfortable amount of time. Finally, rising to her feet carefully because she was carrying the baby and was still sore from childbirth, Shamar said courteously, "Thank you again for your kindness to me and for delivering our baby. I will go back to my tent now. Do you need anything?"

Rahab caught enough to answer, "No, I am fine, thank you."

After she had left, Acsah asked, "Is there anything I can do for you?" Rahab turned to Acsah, "This idea of a cooking class makes me a little nervous. I'm afraid I don't know the law enough to avoid teaching something I shouldn't."

"I understand your concern, but I'll try to let you know if anything comes up."

"What about the bread? Is there anything I should know about it?"

"I heard nothing wrong with what you said for now, but once a year at Passover, we are forbidden to have any leavening in our houses at all. Our bread must be cooked without leaven for that festival."

"Why is that, do you think?"

"You know the story behind Passover?"

"Yes, Salmon told me."

"When the Israelites ate the original Passover feast, they were instructed to do so standing up with their traveling clothes on and with sandals on their feet. This symbolized their readiness to leave when the Lord changed Pharaoh's mind. Part of that was to have bread that could be fixed quickly."

"And leavened bread takes more time because it has to rise. I see!"

Day 10

"Yes, but the Lord also instructs us to clean our houses before we celebrate Passover, getting rid of any leavening in the house."

"Is leavening considered unclean?"

"Not specifically. We can have it any other time. Moses used to say that leavening symbolizes sin in our lives that must be cleared out before we can be holy enough to worship the Lord."

Rahab sat thinking about this for a minute. Then she burst out, "It all fits together, doesn't it? Some things must be eliminated entirely because their presence in our lives will contaminate everything like leavening affects all the dough."

"Like the sins that we are tempted to do again and again."

"Yes, and like the Canaanites and their culture, which are evil and would infect the whole nation of Israel, causing them to turn away from following the Lord."

They looked at each other for a moment. Then Rahab said, "Why am I still alive, Acsah? I am Canaanite. I could be the leaven that could bring down the Israelites."

"No, Rahab. I don't believe that. Everything you say and do makes me understand the Lord and his law better. You are an influence for good in Israel. We are blessed by your presence."

Rahab's eyes filled with tears, and she started to give Acsah a hug, but remembered in time that she was unclean. "Thank you for your kind words. I wish I were as sure of my worthiness as you seem to be. All I know is that the Lord has been very gracious to me, especially in giving me such a friend."

Acsah returned the smile, then turned to slip out of the tent. "I'll see you tomorrow."

Salmon had awakened that morning on the dewy grass, conscious that Othniel had already risen. He scrambled to his feet and stretched. He felt ravenously hungry; sleeping in the open air always did that to him.

Othniel was over by the fire, cooking something in a pot. Salmon joined him. "What are you making?"

"I'm trying to make porridge, but I guess barley doesn't work quite the same as manna. I'm afraid this won't be very good."

"I'm so hungry it could be dirt, and I'd enjoy it. But I learned something from Rahab the other day that might help."

"What's that?"

"Let's see if we can find some honey somewhere among the men. And let's stop by the herd and help with the milking."

They asked around and finally located a jar of honey in the plunder from Ai. Until after the accounting, the plunder was available as supplies to feed the army. Then they got a pot and went to the herd, where they helped themselves to some of the fresh milk by milking a lowing cow.

Back at their campsite, Salmon added a bit of honey to the pot of porridge which had boiled enough to soften and thicken even the coarsely ground barley that Othniel had used. He offered a portion to Othniel, who tasted it gingerly. "This is even better than I had hoped! Rahab taught you this?"

"Yes, and I told her that now I had enjoyed both the honey and milk of the Promised Land."

"So we have. A land truly flowing with milk and honey. The Lord is delivering on that promise, too, isn't he?"

After breakfast, the men began to pack up their personal gear and help load the plunder on the available carts and beasts of burden. As a leader of ten thousand, Salmon had a distracting number of jobs to do with ten leaders answering directly to him and one hundred leaders below that. He, in turn, answered to his tribal leader, who was Caleb for Judah. The tribal leaders were directly responsible to Joshua, but because Salmon and Othniel were Joshua's chosen spies, they sat in council with the tribal leaders. Salmon was a good leader and well respected. He knew that when he married, he would take a year off from military duty, as the law dictated.

He felt a little uneasy about this because a lot of the conquest of Canaan would happen during that year. He didn't want to shirk doing his part, but he was committed and must obey the law.

By mid-morning, the thousands of men were slowly working their way back down toward the main camp. Moving the plunder was taking so much longer that, clearly, they weren't going to arrive until the following day. Salmon knew that they were in no hurry. Most of them had killed men or handled dead bodies and would not be allowed into camp for seven days. Now that the battle was over, Salmon was anxious as he never had been before to be back in the main camp. He wanted to see Rahab, to tell her about the battle, to have her tell him what the Lord had to do with all of it. Always before, he had enjoyed the life of the military camp and the camaraderie of the campfires, but now he dreaded the time away from her. Perhaps taking a year off just to be with her was a good idea!

They stopped just as the sun was setting. The access to the stream was too small for all the men to fill their water bags at once, but eventually everyone got some fresh water. After another meal of cold food from their bags, making Salmon even more eager to get back to Rahab, they settled down for the night.

DAY 11

Salmon's unit had stopped at a particularly rocky section of the road from Ai to Jericho, so he woke the next morning feeling sore and somewhat bruised. The men around him were in no better shape. He felt his responsibility to maintain morale, so he put on a brave face and urged them to get up and moving.

Soon the whole group was slowly plodding down the road. Ahead, they could occasionally glimpse the main camp in the distance. Salmon realized that he should be grateful that this stretch was all downhill. He found it harder to be as motivated going down as they had been coming up. Finally, the ground leveled off some, and they began to see the cultivated fields of the Jordan valley.

Rahab had gotten up early because of the cooking class. She started grinding grain because she wanted to have plenty ready, all the time wondering if Shamar and Acsah would come alone or would bring some others.

Rahab heard voices outside. When she stepped out of the tent, she saw at least twenty women standing expectantly by her cooking fire. She stopped in surprise, feeling uncertain, but Acsah came forward smiling and said, "Let me introduce you. Most of these women are from the tribe of Judah, although some are servant friends of Shamar's. You know Shamar and Penninah, of course."

Rahab nodded at these and was also formally introduced to Mahlah and Serah, Salmon's other female servants. One young woman was introduced to her as Naomi. Rahab found her infectious smile and good humor attractive. Other women told her their names, but she knew it would take a while before she could remember all of them.

Day 11

Taking a deep breath, she decided to proceed with her lesson. She thought that the best way was just to cook and let the women ask questions. She explained this to Acsah, who passed that information on to the others.

First, she produced her pot of soaked beans and placed them on the fire. Immediately, the questions started. "Those are beans, aren't they? Why do they look different from our beans?"

She answered, "They have been soaked overnight."

"How much water do you need?"

"Twice as much water as the soaked beans."

"What are you adding now?"

"Salt and cumin."

"How much salt?"

"As much as your little finger."

"How long do you cook them?"

"From now until midday."

"What are you doing now?"

Rahab brought out her grinding stones and some more barley. She took the flour she had already done and then demonstrated grinding barley into a fine flour. The women seemed fascinated by what she was doing. As she worked, they sat in a circle surrounding her and the campfire. Some were carrying nursing babies, and a few had to keep watch on toddlers. Older children played nearby, some that Rahab knew were part of her campsite, but she hadn't met them yet. The women chatted among themselves, and Acsah translated.

"My mother told me about bread making, but I couldn't imagine it. I didn't know what barley and wheat looked like."

"My husband brought home a whole sack of things from the battle of Midian that I didn't know how to cook. Now I have a better idea of some of them."

"Manna was so easy. It tasted great just straight, but it made a good porridge and cakes, too."

"I like the fruit here. Have you ever had anything as good as fresh figs?"

"Why does she grind the barley so long? Is there a reason?"

Rahab answered this. "The finer the flour, the finer the texture of the bread. Kneading it for a long time helps too."

"What is kneading?"

Every part of the lesson seemed to interest the women. Rahab made such a large batch of bread that she was able to give each woman a sample of the bread when it was done.

"Delicious."

"I want to make some of this for my family."

Rahab thoughtfully had saved enough of the dough to give each woman a little to take home for souring overnight to leaven tomorrow's bread.

"When can we do this again?"

Rahab replied, "How about tomorrow?"

The women took their dough, and after expressing their thanks, left for their own tents. Rahab looked at Acsah questioningly.

"I think you did a great job. Nothing is better than demonstration for teaching something."

"I never expected so many to come."

"I told you that many women want to learn more about cooking."

"I understood a lot more of what they were saying than I could have before."

"You're doing wonderfully."

"I have so much to learn still."

"You will. I'll see you tomorrow then. Thanks again for doing this for us, Rahab."

Soon, the units of men arrived on the outskirts of camp. Joshua addressed them, "Men, praise the Lord our God; you have won the victory over Ai. I remind you that those of you who have shed blood and killed or handled a dead body must stay outside the camp for five more days to be clean. We will be having the third day cleansing ceremony here in a few minutes. For each group of one hundred, a Levite has water and hyssop branches to use for the cleansing. Stay in your units until everyone has been sprinkled with the water of the red heifer. Those of you who have the plunder must make sure that that is also sprinkled with the water."

As the men remained standing where they were, Levites began to move among them carrying pots of water and hyssop branches. Dipping the branches into the water, they sprinkled the men and their equipment. Salmon stood still while the Levite assigned to his unit came by and sprinkled the water on him. This was another thing that Israelites did that no one else seemed to do. He knew that a red heifer cow had been killed to provide the ashes to make the cleansing water. It seemed like wasted beef to him, but of course he would never say that aloud.

When the ceremony was over, unit commanders counted their men and reported to their superiors. Salmon heard reports from all his leaders that no one had died or was missing of all his 10,000. He found Caleb by looking for the standard of Judah. "None are missing from my men, sir."

Day 11

"Good, all of the reports have come in. Judah has no deaths." Caleb smiled at Salmon. "That kind of news I like to hear." Then he went forward to where Joshua was standing.

Joshua announced that no men were missing from the entire army. "The Lord is with us again. Remember to keep yourselves separate. You may talk to people that come out of the camp to you, but you may not touch them, or they will also be unclean. You yourself may not enter the camp. After the seventh day cleansing ceremony, you must all bathe and wash your clothing. Then you will be clean at sunset and may reenter the camp. If you have any questions, ask your unit leaders."

Then he dismissed everyone to set up outside the main camp. The army spread out and around the main camp so that the soldiers were roughly outside the tribe to which they belonged. Salmon himself was a little south of Judah in an area outside of Issachar because more men from Judah than from Issachar had fought. Salmon was very busy for a couple of hours detailing work, such as where the waste disposal areas were going to be and where food supplies could be accessed. In the shuffle, he came across Elias, Penninah's husband, who, with some of his other menservants, had served in units in the main body of the army, not the ambush group. He hailed him, "Elias, I see you are still in camp. Does that mean you were in the killing action?"

"No, master. I was too far back in the army to be in the action. I have been helping with the animals. But since I am clean, I can go into the camp tonight. I've actually been trying to find you to say that I can run errands back and forth for you or see about your animals."

"I need something done. I commissioned Benne, Rahab's father, to make a loom for Rahab. Could you bring me a she-goat that I can give for the loom and ask Benne to come here to talk to me tomorrow?"

"Certainly, master, I will see to that. I've been over to see about the flocks. They looked fine, but your sheep need shearing. Shall we start doing that today?"

"Yes, go ahead. Do you have enough help?"

"I believe so. Four of us I know are clean."

"Fine. This is a good time. We won't move again soon because of the uncleanness of the army. Try to finish before the Sabbath. Oh, and Elias, take the wool to Serah and Mahlah and ask them to wash it for spinning. I think Rahab would enjoy making something with the wool this year."

"Yes, master."

As soon as he was sure that everything was running smoothly, he took a walk by himself back toward the main camp. He was relieved to be alone after days of giving directions. He felt drawn toward the main camp because his mind was on Rahab, wondering what she was doing this afternoon. Just ahead, he saw a woman bending over, pulling something from the ground. The similarity of her figure to Rahab's startled him. He moved closer.

After the cooking class, Rahab had turned to Salmon's servant girls, "Would you like to eat some of this food for your midday meal? Plenty of food was left."

"Oh, yes, mistress," said Shamar, as the others nodded. She got a bowl of the bean soup and a piece of the bread she had made, and left the rest for them to feed to the members of their families. After she ate her food, she sat down with the spindle and continued spinning the combed wool into the tight thread that she knew would be necessary for making any kind of cloth. She took pleasure in watching the skeins grow larger, but wondered if she had enough wool to make even one item of cloth. She had in mind to make something for Shamar's baby. Delivering a baby was really bonding. That thought made her sad, because nearly all the babies she had delivered had ended up as sacrifices to Molech. The priests of Molech considered prostitutes' babies to be their surplus stock.

She thought about her class for the next day and decided to teach them to make lentil stew. The lentils would have to be soaked overnight like the beans, but the cooking would be fairly easy. She would really like to have something more in the lentil stew than just salt and cumin. Onions would be good, and those should be coming up by now. Perhaps if she were very careful, she could go out into a nearby field and find some.

Rahab put down her spinning and slipped out of the tent. Wanting to avoid the alien section, she threaded her way down and emerged outside the part of camp designated for the tribe of Issachar. The field in front of her contained a few grazing animals, but sticking up in the grass were the spears of new onions. "Perfect," she said, quickly pulling a bunch of the onions and turning to hurry back toward Judah and Salmon's tent. She nearly ran into a man who was standing there. Looking up, Rahab found herself face to face with Salmon. He looked as surprised as she felt.

"What are you doing here?"

"I was just... uh, just going out to look for some onions." She added brightly, "I found some."

Salmon quietly said, "Did you know that I was staying outside this part of the camp?"

Rahab shook her head, trembling slightly at being caught alone away from the tent.

Salmon said simply, "You know not to touch me, of course."

Day 11

"Yes, but will I get in trouble for talking to you?"

"No. The prohibition is on my coming into camp, not your going out of it, though I think you should stay closer to camp for other reasons." He looked meaningfully at her.

For some reason, Rahab had expected a greater rebuke for her escapade. Ambaal might have beaten her for doing something he didn't like. She began to feel that Salmon might be a very different kind of man. Changing the subject, she said, "I see you survived the second battle of Ai."

He started talking immediately, as if everything had been pent up inside him waiting for her. "We were victorious, but you probably knew that. The Lord is with us again. I was a little fearful after the last time. Have you heard much about how the battle went?"

She shook her head.

"I led the group that went up behind the city and hid." He continued telling her all about the surprise ambush on Ai and the ruse that the main army had pulled. She listened with her eyes on his face, noticing how animated he got in describing the battle.

"I assume you killed at least one person since you are outside the camp."

"I did my share of killing. Could you see the smoke from here?"

"Yes; I hoped that meant you had won."

"The city made a huge bonfire. I'm sure it horrified the men of Ai to look back and realize that they had left their women and children completely vulnerable to attack. That must have taken the heart out of them. I would feel awful if a city were on fire, and I knew you were in it."

"Would you really care that much?"

"I would, Rahab."

She had to look away. She didn't feel ready for what she saw in his eyes. The quiet between them seemed charged. Then she remembered something that she wanted to ask him. "I've had something on my mind since a conversation I had with Acsah."

"What is it?"

Rahab hesitated, but then blurted out her question. "Does the Lord always kill those who sin?"

Salmon looked steadily at Rahab. "I have asked myself that question often, but I know this from our history—sin and death are connected." He moved to a nearby rock to sit and motioned for her to sit on another one, but not one too close.

"What in your history makes you know this?"

"We have several stories. Have you ever heard of Sodom and Gomorrah?"

"Yes, I have. Our people tell a story about a terrible natural disaster that happened long ago. No one seems to remember much except that a rain of fire destroyed those two cities. It always seemed sad to me that innocent people would suffer sudden obliteration like that."

"We remember much more of the story than you do because some of our own people escaped from the cities."

"I thought no one had survived."

"No doubt the Canaanites say that. But one man and his daughters lived to tell what happened."

"Tell me the story."

"It really begins with Abraham. He and his nephew Lot were living here in the hill country, but their herdsmen had begun to argue about grazing and water rights. Abraham felt it would be better if the two families separated. He gave Lot the first choice of land."

"Wasn't Abraham the elder? Why didn't he choose first?"

"He wanted to be fair. Abraham was a man who talked to the Lord regularly. It made him different from other people, I guess."

"I think talking to the Lord would make someone different."

"Do you?" He looked at her intently.

"What happened to Lot?"

"Lot looked all over the area and decided to move down into the plains where he could find better pasturage and water. I think he hoped to get rich by trading with the merchants of Sodom and Gomorrah and to enjoy some of the luxuries that city life offered. He did move, and soon he was settled and became quite rich. Unfortunately, he also tolerated some of the practices of people there."

"How bad was it?"

"Well, according to the story, when two angels in the form of men went to the city to determine if anyone there was worth saving, the men of the city demanded the two men from Lot in order to rape them. That seems pretty bad to me. The law forbids any sexual activity between men or between women, for that matter."

"Things like that happened in Jericho, too. I'm surprised you didn't feel threatened by some of the men in the district near my inn. They could be pretty brutal to strangers."

"I did notice some unusual behavior, but I thought I had just imagined things. It didn't seem possible that men would actually ..." He paused and wrinkled his nose as if he were remembering something extremely disturbing.

"Why don't you finish the story." urged Rahab quietly. She knew the kinds of things he must have seen, and now that she was in the Israelite camp, she had a better idea of how that must have seemed to him.

Day 11

"I should have told you that the two angels, with a third person whom some think was the Lord himself, had first appeared to Abraham to tell him what they planned. Abraham knew that Lot was living in Sodom, and he was horrified to think that the Lord would destroy the cities with his nephew inside. He didn't want to argue with the Lord, but he did try to bargain with him that if even as few as ten righteous men were in the cities, the cities would be spared. The Lord promised him that much, but there must have been fewer than ten."

"What happened when the men of Sodom demanded Lot's guests? Didn't he have to honor the code of hospitality and defend them?"

"Lot actually offered to let his two virgin daughters be raped instead of the guests he had taken into his home."

"It seems to me like Lot had compromised with the Sodom way of thinking. I think that when a father uses his children to solve his problems like that, especially his daughters, it is horrible."

"You sound like you have personal experience with this."

"Perhaps I do. What happened after Lot offered his virgin daughters up to the men to rape?"

"The two angels didn't let it happen. They blinded the men of the city and gave Lot just enough time to get his daughters, their intended husbands, and his own wife out before the judgment fell. Lot couldn't get his prospective sons-in-law to leave, and he had trouble getting his wife and daughters to go. In fact, the angels practically had to drag them out of the city to get them away before the rain of fire and sulfur fell. They had told Lot not to look back at the sight, but his wife did look back, and she was instantly turned into a pillar of salt."

"Why do you think she looked back? Was it that she felt sorry for the people in the cities?"

"Or that she disagreed with the Lord's judgment and showed that she cared more for what she was losing than for being saved. The result of their compromise with evil was that Lot lost all that he had gained by moving into Sodom, plus his wife. He must have seen Abraham or some of his people at some time after that, because Abraham eventually knew that Lot, at least, had escaped from the fiery spectacle that could be seen from all the hills in Canaan."

"Lot's story resembles mine. My family and I escaped from the judgment that fell on our city and is falling on all the cities of Canaan. We are just as guilty as the people of Sodom and Gomorrah. Only this time, God used an earthquake and the Israelite army to punish us."

"One major difference between you and Lot is that you wanted to leave it all behind. He didn't."

"I know another difference, too."

"What's that?"

Rahab said playfully, "The two men who rescued me were not angels in disguise."

"How can you be so sure?" he responded in kind.

"Believe me, I know." She twinkled her eyes at him. "But seriously, I doubt if even one righteous person lived in Jericho. I have broken the law, and ought to be stoned. And yet I am still alive. Now that I know more of the law, I feel overwhelmed by my own sin and that of my people."

Salmon hesitated before saying, "Sometimes I wonder if holding you Canaanites responsible for your sins is fair when you have not heard the Lord's law and could not know that you are doing wrong."

Rahab shook her head emphatically. "We knew in our hearts that murder and adultery and stealing are wrong. I know because we didn't like it when someone did those things to us. But we chose to do the wrong things anyway. And if anyone objected or tried to live better than the neighbors, he was called judgmental and proud. I don't think our sins can be justified because of ignorance."

"On the other hand, the Israelites have no excuse at all, not even ignorance."

"Like Achan after Jericho?"

"Yes."

"But what should I do? I am a great sinner, bringing dishonor to the people of Israel by my presence with you."

"You could present a sin offering at the tabernacle."

"That's how our sins are cared for then, by the blood of goats and sheep?"

"It's the only way we have."

"But I can't do even that right. I have no animals of my own."

"I'll provide the lamb for you."

"I know you will, but I feel I should do something myself to pay for my sins."

"That attitude—that God should require you to give up something of great value to you—seems right, but I'm not sure the Lord thinks that way." He paused. "This conversation reminds me of another story about the Lord, a story about child sacrifice, actually."

"I thought the Lord forbids child sacrifice."

"Just hear the story first. The Lord promised Abraham that he would be the father of a great nation."

"Well, that has certainly happened."

"Oddly enough, Abraham had grown very old and still had not had a son of his own. At one point he actually slept with his wife's servant

Day 11

girl to conceive a son, but the son of his concubine was not the son of promise, though he also became the father of a great nation, the Ishmaelites."

"I didn't know the Ishmaelites were descended from a common ancestor with the Israelites!"

"Yes, The Lord always keeps his promises, even when men make mistakes."

"The Ishmaelites would not appreciate being called a mistake."

"Perhaps not, and they have an enmity with Israel that will no doubt cause problems for generations to come."

"Continue with Abraham."

"Abraham's wife did finally conceive a son. His name was Isaac, and Abraham doted on him. He was the son of his own wife and the child of promise. But when Isaac was still young, the Lord told Abraham to sacrifice him."

"Now I'm really confused. Why would the Lord ask him to sacrifice the promised child?"

"It may not have made sense to Abraham either, but he had a habit of obeying the Lord, so he took the boy to Mount Horeb south of here to sacrifice him."

"Did Abraham kill the boy?"

"I'm getting to that. When the boy was tied up and placed on the altar that Abraham had built, Abraham raised his hand with the knife. Before he could bring it down, the Lord stopped him. The Lord was testing his faith. Abraham didn't need to sacrifice Isaac, only to be willing. Immediately, Abraham saw a ram caught in a thicket nearby. He sacrificed the ram instead. He had said that the Lord would provide the needed sacrifice. You could look at this the same way: The Lord has convicted you of your sin by his law, but he has also provided you with a lamb through me to bring forgiveness from your sin. The Lord provides."

"So the answer to my question about sin and death is..."

"Yes, I believe in the connection between sin and death, but the Lord provides a way to be saved from death through the sacrifice of a lamb."

"I am grateful for his mercy. I know that I do not deserve it. But I will love him to my dying day for his goodness to me." This was said with an intensity of emotion that made Salmon almost jealous. Why couldn't she love him like that?

He looked at the sky. "You had better head back now before sunset. I wish I could accompany you to the tent."

"Yes, I'd better go. Is there anything I can do for you? Do you have enough of what you need?"

"Elias has been acting as my go-between. I have everything I need except for one thing."

"What is that?"

"Your companionship."

She blushed and said quietly, "I'll see you later."

"Rahab, much as I love seeing you and talking to you, I don't want you to come out of the camp by yourself again while the military waits out here."

Rahab nodded with understanding and turned to leave.

Salmon watched her go with mixed feelings. He felt elated that he had seen her and talked to her, though she still seemed mostly interested in talking about her relationship to the Lord and not about her relationship with him. But he also felt uneasy about finding her outside of the camp that way. The question of why she was out so close to all those men came into his mind. She wouldn't try to solicit as a prostitute again, would she? The thought disgusted him, and he pushed it away. If no trust was between them, how could they ever be happy in marriage? He knew that he wanted her love more than anything else in his life.

DAY 12

The next morning, Salmon looked up to see Elias coming with the she-goat and Benne not far behind him. Benne greeted him, "You've been out killing more Canaanites, I hear. And I suppose that goat came from the plunder."

Salmon said shortly, "No, I already had this goat. I promised it for the loom. Did you get it finished?"

"Yes."

"Good. Can I get it today?"

"Do you want it here?"

"I'll have Elias come by and get it to take to Rahab later. If you would, please show him your loom, so he can see how to set it up for her."

"I will. So you can't go into the camp. What is all this unclean business? Another of your god's strange rules?"

"Did your gods not demand things from you that you found inconvenient at times?"

"Well, now that you mention it, yes. But sometimes our gods let us have fun, too, if you know what I mean."

Salmon chose to ignore Benne's allusion to Ashtoreth worship. "I need to get back to my men now. If you need anything, tell my manservant when he comes to you." He watched Benne trot away with his goat toward the alien quarter; then after giving directions to Elias about picking up the loom and setting it up for Rahab, he turned back toward his men. A trumpet call alerted him to an officers' meeting about to start. He moved quickly toward the designated area north of the camp.

Joshua gave instructions relative to the plunder. "We will do what we did after Midian, though we don't have as much booty this time. Half of the plunder will go to the camp of Israel to be divided among those without fighting men in their families. The other half will go to the

Day 12

fighting men. One of each five hundred animals will be dedicated to the Lord from the military share. One of each fifty will be dedicated to the Lord from the camp share. The rest of the plunder will be divided evenly. Those in charge of dividing the plunder will grant each unit food from the plunder for the time you are here outside the camp."

Salmon was responsible for the fair division of the animals. He didn't have enough animals to give every family group even one, which made his job difficult. He sometimes looked over at the growing herd that had been designated for the Lord and thought that setting those aside made his job even harder, but he didn't say anything aloud. Had it not been for the leaders of the tens, who knew their men and their needs, dividing equitably would have been impossible. The larger the family group, the more plunder the men were assigned. The process of dividing up the plunder took most of the day, and the soldiers would have grumbled had the officers not reminded them of past suffering that had come for that very sin.

By the time the day was over, Salmon was tired. He headed back to the campfire that he shared with Othniel and some of the other officers. Several of them were sitting by the campfire, oiling the leather of their shields. He sat down near Othniel, who asked him, "What did you get in the booty?"

"I got a large sack of barley, some dried fruit, and some salt."

"I got similar things except I picked a jar of olives instead of fruit, and you gave me an ox. Why didn't you get any animals?'

"I didn't have enough to go around, and I have plenty. Say, I'll trade you some of my fruit for some of your olives."

"All right."

"Oh, and I got this, too. I thought Rahab might like it." He held up a bracelet of beaten gold that gleamed in the firelight.

"Good thinking. I wish I could openly court Acsah the way you are courting Rahab. Do you think you are making any progress with her?"

"I don't know. At first, she didn't seem to want to talk to me at all. Then I discovered that she listens to anything having to do with the Lord and the law. If I talk about those things, she asks questions. But if I try to get too personal, she stays silent. I don't know if she is warming to me or not."

"Well, it sounds like you need to keep talking about the Lord. That may lead to other things eventually."

"I hope so. I have only thirty days to win her. After we are married, it will be harder, I think."

"I don't know. Lots of arranged marriages end up happy."

"That's true, but Rahab has such a history that I think she needs to work through some things before she will be able to be happy in marriage."

"What kinds of things?"

"She keeps alluding to the cruelty of her first husband. I don't know all the particulars, but I know he committed adultery."

"Yes, I remember her saying something about that, the night we were in her inn."

"She has also mentioned that she had a baby, but I see no child. Whatever happened must have been pretty bad because she won't talk about it. And, of course, I have no idea what might have been involved in being a prostitute."

"Don't you?"

"What I mean is that I don't know what effect that had on her emotionally."

"Do you think she is more likely to commit adultery?"

"Perhaps. But I worry more that she will find no pleasure in lying with me."

"So you're saying that you want her to want you physically."

"Yes, exactly, but from love, not from lust."

"Then it sounds like you need to make sure that she really loves you."

"And I'm back where I started. How do I win her love?"

"I see what you mean about history. Tell me again, why do you want to marry this woman?"

"You mean beside the fact that she is the most beautiful woman I've ever seen?"

"I wouldn't go that far. After all, you've seen Acsah."

"I know; I know. But to answer your question seriously, I think her faith is what amazes me. I wish I knew where it originated."

"Perhaps she has more history than just her traumas that she isn't sharing."

Rahab's day had started when the cooking class arrived; only this time forty women, instead of the twenty from the day before, had come. Rahab decided not to worry about the numbers; she would just do her demonstration. Acsah listened for the questions while Rahab worked. The lentils that she had set to soak had swollen to twice their size overnight. She set the pot over a hot spot of the fire to start boiling. She chopped the onions and added them along with some salt to the boiling lentils. Again the women asked questions.

"What is that green stuff you put in?"

Day 12

"Onions."

"Where did you get them?"

"They are growing in the hillside fields near the camp. I think these were near where Issachar is settled."

Later after the stew had simmered for most of the morning and begun to smell good, they asked more questions.

"What makes the stew red?"

"The lentils are that color and cooking them so long brings the color into the water." She was aware that many of the women saw that making lentil stew wasn't that different from making bean soup, but she did want them to know that they had different options. Instead of making barley bread, she made some porridge and showed them how adding honey improved the flavor.

Just as the cooking lesson was over, Rahab noticed Elias putting up a structure right next to her tent entrance that looked vaguely familiar. When she looked closer, she exclaimed, "Oh, a loom! It's already up and staked. How did it come to be here?" She realized that she was speaking Canaanite and that only Acsah could understand her, so she switched to her broken Hebrew. "Did my father make the loom?"

Elias smiled, "Yes, but Salmon bought it from him for one she-goat."

"So much for a loom!"

"I thought so, too. But I think Salmon wanted to make an excuse to help your parents more."

Some of the other women noticed what she was looking at as they were leaving. One of them said, "Is that a loom?"

Rahab answered and Acsah translated. "Yes, I am going to try my hand at weaving this afternoon."

"May I come watch that, too?" asked the exuberant Naomi.

"If you like. I've never woven wool before. I've always made linen. I don't know how this will go, but you are welcome."

After the other women had left, Rahab said to Acsah, "Why don't you stay for lunch with me?"

"I would love to. May I send Serah with a message for my servants?"

"Certainly."

While Acsah sent Serah, Rahab served up bowls of stew and bread for each of them.

Acsah came back and joined her in the opened tent. "I thought the cooking class went very well today."

"Did you? I'm enjoying getting to know some of the women, especially Naomi. Is she a servant?"

"No, actually, she married a relative of Salmon's, Elimelech. Her family's tent isn't far from here. She is delightful, isn't she?"

"Yes, I haven't seen anyone with such high spirits since..." Rahab realized she was thinking about her friend Tyra as she had been in their girlhood. She sighed inwardly and reached for her bowl of stew.

Acsah commented, "I've never had lentil stew, but this reminds me of a story."

"What story is that?"

"It's about Esau and Jacob. I know you've heard about Abraham."

"Yes, and Isaac."

"Isaac had twin sons named Esau and Jacob. Esau was the eldest, but for some reason he despised his heritage as a follower of the Lord and married Canaanite girls against his parent's wishes."

"I don't think I'm going to like this story very much."

"Your situation is different. You despised your Canaanite heritage so much that you are marrying a follower of the Lord."

"Against my parent's wishes?"

Acsah laughed at Rahab's comical expression. "Anyway, one day when Esau was coming home from a long hunting trip, he smelled some lentil stew that Jacob was cooking. Esau was very hungry and demanded some stew, but Jacob was wily. He asked Esau what he would give for the stew. Esau so despised his inheritance from his father that he traded it for the stew, so Jacob got the elder son's inheritance. Later Jacob also tricked his father into giving him the blessing of the eldest instead of Esau."

"So Jacob was the Israelite ancestor and not Esau? He doesn't sound like such a man to be proud of either."

"Actually, Esau was my ancestor. The Kenizzites are descended from his grandson Kenaz."

"So you are descended from Abraham, just not Jacob, right?"

"Yes, but we are still labeled as Canaanite by many Israelites. I think that bothers my father more than it does me."

"I'm sorry, I interrupted your story. What happened to Jacob?"

"Well, right after the incident of the lentil stew, Jacob met the Lord in a special way, and it changed him into a devout follower. Later on, the Lord changed his name from Jacob to Israel."

"Ah, so the name came from him."

"Yes."

"I certainly understand that encountering the Lord would change someone for the better."

"You make it sound like you knew someone that happened to."

"Perhaps I do."

Day 12

    Acsah waited for her to elaborate, but when she didn't, she picked up the conversation again. "By the way, the descendants of Esau are called the Edomites."

    "Is that why their name means 'red,' because of the lentil stew?"

    "Yes."

    After lunch, Rahab was ready to try the new loom. Acsah took the spindle and worked on her spinning as she watched Rahab begin tying the ends of the skeins of yarn she had already spun onto the crossbar at the top of the loom. Each skein dangled down, but she needed something heavier to weight them. "Where could I get some rocks, I wonder."

    "I'll ask Mahlah and Serah. How many do you need?"

    Rahab told her. When Acsah went over to their tents and called them Rahab could hear the conversation. "Rahab needs some rocks about fist size to weight her threads. Could you or your children go gather some?"

    The two of them looked at her with surprised expressions. "Rahab has never given us an order before."

    "Can your boys go?"

    Mahlah answered, "I guess so."

    The two women told their little boys, who soon ran off to get the rocks as though excited about rock collecting. While they were gone, Rahab began setting up the beater bar between the warp threads. The bar was still very loose because she had no weights yet, but that would soon be solved. As she worked, two or three women from her cooking class came and watched her.

    One of the ones who came to watch was Naomi. Rahab smiled at her and said, "Naomi, I understand that you are married to one of Salmon's cousins."

    "Yes, to Elimelech. Salmon's mother was Elimelech's aunt. We're so happy you are going to be a part of our family."

    "Thank you. You are very kind."

    "We are just fascinated by your culture and want to know all about it."

    "You mean the cooking and weaving?"

    "Not just those. Elimelech wants to know all about your gods and the worship of them."

    This startled Rahab. "I have nothing good to say about the gods of Canaan."

    "So is it true that you are a follower of Israel's God?"

    "Yes, I am."

    "Why?"

    Rahab became aware that the other women were listening closely to Acsah's translation of their conversation. "I worship the Lord because he is good, especially to women and children."

"And the Canaanite gods were not?"

"No." She hesitated. Somehow, to speak of the horrible things done in the name of Molech and Ashtoreth seemed too difficult. "If you only understood how wonderful your life is here compared to what it could be."

Just then, Mahlah and Serah's sons came with the rocks. Serah asked, "Why do you need rocks?"

Rahab answered, "To weigh down the warp threads."

"Oh, I didn't realize."

Serah helped her after she understood the purpose of the rocks. Soon Rahab had her warp threads in place and tight. She began to work on the weft threads, which were threaded between the warp threads and then beaten up, with the beater bar. In the three hours that she worked, she was able to do about a hand span of wool cloth. The next hand span would go much faster because the warp was already in place.

As she worked, the women visited. Rahab could understand most of the conversation with Acsah translating, but she realized that she wasn't listening to the Hebrew. She told Acsah in Canaanite to take a break from so much translating, and she would see how much Hebrew she knew. By concentrating, she could get most of what was being said. When she couldn't understand a word, it usually had something to do with Israelite culture. The women were talking about the purification rites for Shamar. "At least she had a girl, so she won't have the circumcision to worry about."

"Yes, but she will need a lamb or at least a pigeon for the sacrifice." Mahlah said.

"Do you think your master will supply that?"

"He may. He is a very generous man."

"Yes, all the other servants are jealous. You have a good life with him."

"Is that going to change with the new mistress?"

"It hasn't so far."

Rahab realized that they didn't know that she could understand so much of what they were saying. She was a little embarrassed to be caught eavesdropping and couldn't decide whether to tell them or not.

She looked at Acsah and caught the twinkle in her eye. In Canaanite, she said, "Should I tell them that I can understand?"

Acsah clearly was enjoying the joke, but before either of them could say anything, Mahlah said, "I was really surprised that after all the chances Salmon had, he picked a Canaanite. But I've never seen a man so smitten. I just hope she appreciates what she is getting."

Now Rahab was caught. She couldn't tell now; it would be too embarrassing for Mahlah and for her. She shook her head slightly at

Day 12

Acsah and kept weaving as if she understood nothing that was going on. She quit trying to understand what they were saying, but her mind could not forget what she had heard.

In a few minutes, she signaled that she was through for the day. She nodded to all the women, and inviting Acsah to stay, slipped into the tent. Acsah followed soon after.

They looked at each other and then burst out laughing. Acsah gasped, "How much did you understand?"

"Enough to know that Salmon's servants think I'm not good enough for him."

"You already had heard that from Shamar."

"Yes, but I guess I thought she was exceptional. What do you think, Acsah?"

"I think that Salmon is getting a wonderful wife, well worthy of him."

Rahab sighed, "Having a real friend encourages me so much! Can you stay for a dinner of leftover porridge? I've made way too much food today."

"Are you sure you aren't tired of having me around?"

"I could just as easily ask if you are tired of being around me. I wouldn't have asked you if I didn't want you."

They settled in sociably over their porridge bowls. Rahab said, "I eat so well here. Except in the inn, I didn't have this much."

"I'm curious about something. I have heard you say that your family was poor. How did you end up owning an inn?"

Rahab hesitated, then plunged into her story. "I have told you that my husband was cruel?" Acsah nodded. "He banished me from our home after I caught him in adultery and objected. I had nowhere to go. I won't bother you with the details, but I was reduced to begging and ended up being taken in by Ashtora, the innkeeper, who made me a part of her business."

If Acsah understood that this meant becoming a prostitute, she didn't betray that by even the batting of an eyelash.

"Ashtora was kind to me in her way, and I think I helped her a lot with her flax field and business concerns, especially as she got older. When she died, she left the inn and her land to me. She had no relatives. This made it possible for me to support my family at a time when my parent's farm wasn't doing so well."

"Were you happy in that life?"

"I was happy that I wasn't hungry anymore and that I could help my family. And I was happy to be independent of my husband. But many aspects of that life were bad—not at all the life I dreamed of as a girl."

"What did you dream about having?"

"I wanted to have a husband and children in a happy home. I dreamed of a husband who would really talk to me and who would work beside me and love me."

"I dream about that now, but my dreams have a human form. Othniel would be just the man to fit all of my dreams, but he seems out of reach as a husband."

"Can you talk to your father about this?"

"No, I know he wouldn't understand. I have tried to discuss it with him in roundabout ways, but he is set on a husband for me from Israel."

"Perhaps time will change his mind."

"It would take a miracle."

"I've seen many miracles in the last few months. I wouldn't put anything beyond the power of the Lord."

DAY 13

Rahab had wanted to get up early so she could weave before the cooking class, but then she remembered that the seven days of her period were up. She needed to get her things cleaned. After bathing herself in the inner room of the tent, she gathered up all of her bedding, soiled rags, and the mat that she had used for so many days and began the task of washing all of these. Then she hung them up to dry from strings attached to the poles and put the sides of the tent up for the day.

She watched other women doing their work beyond the campsite. Now that she was alert to the signs, she realized that a few other women were doing as she was. Every day, a few women had to cleanse themselves and their bedding, except, of course, on the Sabbath. The cooking class had made her feel a comradeship with these other women. Perhaps she would someday begin to think of herself as Israelite instead of Canaanite. Perhaps at a later date still, the other women would forget that she was not one of them.

For this morning's lesson, Rahab had decided to do something different and special. She knew that many of them had access to dried fruits, as she did, so she decided to teach them to make stewed fruit.

That morning, the area around the fire was crowded with women trying to see what Rahab was doing. She wanted to explain herself what she was doing, but realized that trying to cook and speak in Hebrew at the same time was more than she could manage, so Acsah translated again. She showed them how she had allowed the fruit to soak for several hours in the morning, then boiled and simmered it before adding some cinnamon to the mixture. The women who got a taste were amazed at the results.

"This is really good. I would never have thought about cooking fruit."

"The raisins are back to being grapes, and the figs taste almost fresh."

Day 13

"This will be a great dish to serve on cold winter evenings when fresh fruit isn't available."

"I wonder where we can get some of that cinnamon."

This question was a puzzle to Rahab. Cinnamon was something that she had purchased in Jericho, not grown herself. She supposed the only source for it now was in plunder.

In careful Hebrew, she asked them all, "Is this something that you think you could cook at home."

"You can speak Hebrew!"

"I am learning." Rahab looked over and spotted Mahlah in the crowd looking stricken and embarrassed.

After the lesson was over, she came to Rahab. "How much Hebrew do you know?"

"Enough to understand what you said at the weaving lesson yesterday."

"Why didn't you say something then?"

"I didn't want to embarrass you in front of the others."

Mahlah turned red now. "I'm so sorry. If I had known you could understand..."

Rahab understood what Mahlah was saying as much from her expression as her words. "I don't think you should feel sorry, Mahlah. You said the truth, I'm sure. You know your master better than I do. I should be asking you about him."

"He is a wonderful master."

"Why do you say that?"

"He works right alongside the men and doesn't ask them to do more than is fair."

"And you women?"

"He knows that we have children, so he reduces our work, especially when the babies are small."

"But he does make you work?"

"Yes, we expect to. But he treats us as human beings, not possessions. For example, he knew that Shamar's baby was going to come soon, so he made Elon's job at Ai one that wouldn't make him unclean. Then he arranged for Elon to be the messenger back to Eleazar from the battle so he could be home sooner than anyone else. Many masters wouldn't have cared what was going on with their servants' families."

Rahab was pleased that she could follow what Mahlah was saying fairly well. "He does seem very thoughtful. Do you think I am unworthy of him?"

"I might have thought so at first, but I am changing my mind."

"Why is that?"

The Cord

"Because of the way you treated Shamar even though she had been unkind to you. We all knew about that. And also you have been so willing to give the women cooking lessons and weaving lessons. I don't know very many mistresses who would take so much time with their servant girls."

"Perhaps I am learning something about people, too. I've never had so many women treat me with such kindness."

"We have a law about that."

"What is it?"

"He defends the cause of the fatherless and the widow, and loves the alien, giving him food and clothing. And you are to love those who are aliens, for you yourselves were aliens in Egypt" (Deut. 10:18-19, NIV).

Rahab's eyes filled with tears, and at that moment, she worshiped. Yahweh loved her. He said so in his law and commanded his people to love her, too. She said shakily, "Thank you for telling me that, Mahlah. That is beautiful." Then turning, she fled back to her tent, where she wept tears of joy that the Lord God had seen fit to love her.

Salmon rose early. In the night, he had remembered that he asked Benne to help teach the Israelites how to harvest wheat. What better time than this when the men were becoming restless with inactivity and they couldn't go into camp anyway? He found Caleb and asked his opinion. "What do you think about asking Benne to help us harvest some of the wheat in this area? It would give the men something to do and would give us more food for the men. After the plunder at Midian, they seem discontented with the smaller amount from Ai, especially since we got nothing at Jericho."

"I think that is a good idea. Would you like me to ask Benne?"

"Would you? I can have my servant bring him to us. You know something about harvesting crops, too, don't you?"

"Some, but it has been a long time."

Just then, Salmon's servant Elias came to see if he needed anything and to bring him some of the goat's milk from his own herd. "Elias, I want you to go to Benne and ask him to come out to talk to Caleb."

"Yes, master. I thought you might like to know that Rahab was really happy about the loom. She has already woven a hand span of cloth on it." He seemed as proud of this as if he had done the work himself.

"Where did she get wool for weaving?"

"I believe Acsah brought her some."

Salmon smiled. "Thank you for telling me, Elias. How is the shearing coming along?"

Day 13

"We should finish the sheep today as you wished."

"Good. Go ahead and take the first bag to the priests, and then take whatever else you have already to Serah and Mahlah so they can get started with the cleaning."

"I will, master."

Elias left, and with Caleb's consent, Salmon spread the word that any man who wanted to participate in harvesting the wheat crops in the area could keep a share of the wheat for himself.

Before long, Benne had come and, with Caleb's encouragement, was taking the men that Salmon had gathered out into the fields. Some sickles were produced from the plunder of Ai. Benne demonstrated how to cut the grain with the sickle and bundle the grain into sheaves. Then he stood back and supervised as the men began to work. Salmon, looking up at him from his own first attempts at sheaf making, could tell that Benne enjoyed this role. Just then, Caleb hurried up and said, "Don't forget to get the first sheaf and set it aside to give as a grain offering to the Lord."

"Oh, I almost forgot. Thanks for reminding me."

When he went to Benne and explained why he needed the first, Benne sneered, "You people are really under your god's thumb, aren't you?"

Salmon wondered if that wasn't a little too close to blasphemy to be safe, but he decided not to say anything this time. He picked up the sheaf of wheat and put it in a safe place.

When he returned, he saw that Caleb was organizing another group of men to set up a threshing floor on a hill near the wheat field. They were clearing the loose stones and earth off the rock there and sweeping it clear. Soon a cartload of the sheaves was brought, and Caleb showed the men how to beat the wheat with sticks until the grain was loosened from the stalks. A fresh breeze was blowing from the west, perfect for winnowing. The men tossed what they had beaten into the air, and the chaff was blown away. The heavy wheat fell down again on the rock where men were sweeping it aside into piles. All this was fascinating for Salmon, who had never seen a full-scale harvest before. With hundreds of men working and a day perfect for the job, the harvest of the fields nearest the camp was finished before sunset, and each man received a sack of grain for his work. Salmon was exhausted, but he was exhilarated, too.

As they headed back to the temporary camp with Salmon carrying his grain and the first sheaf still unthreshed, Salmon made a point of thanking Benne for helping. "I appreciate your willingness to help teach us to harvest, Sir."

Benne was carrying his reward, a double portion of the wheat. "They could almost do it when we stopped. I think I can make good farmers out of some of those men."

Salmon smiled at his swagger, but then felt his own weariness. The Sabbath rest seemed good to him all at once.

Acsah came to the tent about mid-afternoon. She sat down across from where Rahab was spinning some more wool and reached for the spindle. "Here, I'll spin and you can weave." She began to spin as Rahab moved to the loom. "I saw you talking to Mahlah after the cooking lesson. Did you discuss what happened yesterday?"

"Yes, I think we are going to be friends now. She told me the law about loving aliens."

"I know that command well. I occasionally have to remind someone who treats the Kenizzites unfairly of their obligation to obey that one. I don't know why I hadn't thought to mention it to you before."

"I find it such a beautiful command. The law states clearly that the Lord loves us and provides for us. Doesn't it make you want to love him that much more?"

"It is a great comfort to know that he cares what happens to us. People are so quick to hate anyone different, even people who believe the same things. The aliens usually get blamed for anything that goes wrong in Israel."

"Like after the first battle at Ai?"

"Exactly."

"You know, I'm really relieved that nothing happened to my parents during the panic after that battle."

"Yes, aren't you glad that Salmon and Othniel got there in time."

Rahab looked up shocked. "Got there in time for what?"

"Salmon didn't tell you what happened?"

"He said that they had a bit of a scare. He didn't explain."

"Perhaps I shouldn't tell if Salmon didn't."

"Please tell me. I want to know. Were my parents in danger?"

"Othniel told me that when Salmon arrived at your parents' tent an angry crowd surrounded it, wanting to stone the Canaanites from Jericho because of the defeat at Ai. They were going to drag your family out to the valley at once. They would have carried out their threat if Salmon hadn't come forward and stood in front of them all. They started to move past him, but Othniel came then and the crowd dispersed after he told them what Joshua had promised about seeking the Lord's counsel

Day 13

regarding our loss at Ai. The people are used to obeying Joshua, so it ended without tragedy for you or your family."

Rahab was dumbfounded. "Salmon kept them from being stoned?"

"Yes, the mob would have done it if he hadn't been there."

"I feel like I'm missing something here. How many other things has Salmon done for my family and me that I haven't known about?"

"He loves you, Rahab."

"Let's practice Hebrew now, shall we?"

Acsah looked surprised at the abrupt change in topic, but started drilling Rahab in some more pronunciation points. They had a very productive lesson. The sides of the tent were up, and they could see the servants and their children working and playing around their tents and the campfire. During a lull in the lesson, Rahab couldn't help noticing how happy all the servants seemed to be. They had plenty to eat and good shelters. What Mahlah had told her today about Salmon had impressed her. In that way, he was definitely different from Ambaal. Just then, she realized that Acsah had spoken to her. "Oh, I'm sorry. I was daydreaming."

"Was it a good daydream?"

"No, I was thinking about my husband and how he treated his servants."

"Do you want to talk about it?"

"I couldn't help noticing how happy the servants are here. From what Mahlah told me, Salmon treats his servant girls better than some men treat their wives. Ambaal was not like that at all. The first time I saw him, he was beating an elderly servant for breaking a water pot. That was not unusual. One of the worst aspects of living with Ambaal was watching the way he abused his servants. I tried to make it up to them when I could, but that only made him angry with me. When he beat me, I took some comfort in thinking that I was saving some servant from being beaten."

"Oh, Rahab. I had no idea."

"He is gone now. But I think it is wonderful to see servants being treated as human beings."

"I can imagine so. I don't think you will be surprised to know that we are commanded to do that."

"No, I'm not. It would be like the Lord to think of that, too. He is so good." She sighed with pleasure.

After Acsah went home for the evening, Rahab kept working. Under her fingers, the weaving was progressing, and she knew that every day, her language skills were improving. She felt very content with things at that moment. Yet if she were perfectly honest with herself, she knew that something, or more precisely someone, was wanting. She wasn't ready to admit that she missed Salmon.

DAY 14
THE SECOND SABBATH

Rahab realized as soon as she was conscious that this was the Sabbath. Thinking about the day, she realized that she had little to do, since cooking and weaving weren't allowed. A look in her food supplies satisfied her that she would do very well eating: some bread left from the day before, some fresh fruit, and some cheese, which Shamar continued to make and bring. She supposed it would be best not to go out, but couldn't help sighing while clearing away her bedding and eating a little food from her stock. Acsah's voice outside the tent opening was a welcome sound. "I'm so glad to see you. Can you stay awhile?"

"The men are still outside of the camp, so I thought you might enjoy some company on the Sabbath. I find it such a long, boring day to be alone."

"I'm glad you came. I did feel bored here alone, but I wasn't bored last Sabbath because Salmon was explaining some of the law to me."

"You really like hearing about the law, don't you?"

"Yes. Living here is such an adjustment, and the law often explains the differences for me."

"Differences like the way we treat servants?"

"Yes. But I wonder about other things. For example, people are much quieter here. I don't hear screams and fighting."

"Was there a lot of that in Jericho?"

"All the time. It really wasn't safe to go out of the house in our section of the city, though someone had to go to the well every day, and we had to go out of the city gates to get to our fields. I used ropes to get my harvest to my roof from outside the walls because I didn't want to have to carry them in through the city and have sheaves stolen from me."

Day 14, The Second Sabbath

"Is that what gave you the idea to lower Salmon and Othniel by ropes out of your window."

"Yes. I suppose Othniel told you about that."

"He did. That was quite a story. You saved their lives that night."

"They were on the right side—the side I wanted to be on."

"What other differences have you noticed?"

"I don't hear much discussion of crime here. We used to talk about the latest murder or rape daily, but here that doesn't seem to happen much. Why is that?"

"I can't say that I know of any murders or rapes recently. Even if we had one, we know exactly how that would be handled. Crimes are taken care of in the law."

"What kinds of laws?"

"We have a law that if a woman is raped in the city, but she screams, only the man will be in trouble; if she doesn't scream, they will both be prosecuted."

"What about in the country?"

"She isn't prosecuted because no one could have heard her anyway. Only the man is punished."

"In Jericho, rape happened all the time. Most women had no recourse at all unless they were the virgin daughters of an official or rich man. Then somebody would be punished, whether that person had actually done the crime or not."

"Didn't they have to have witnesses?"

"What do you mean?"

"Here, two witnesses to a crime are required to get a conviction. The testimony of only one witness isn't sufficient."

"This is all so different from what I have known. In Jericho, justice was based on who had the most money. Rich people could get away with anything by paying bribes to the judge. Poor people usually were punished even if they were only accused of a crime. Poor people could never hope to get justice themselves. Once I saw a boy steal an apple from a cart. The vendor killed the boy on the spot; he said he knew the justice system wouldn't do anything."

"Stealing an apple got the death penalty, then," Acsah observed. We have a law that forbids more punishment than fits the crime. It is called 'eye for an eye.' That means that if a man assaults another man and makes him lose his eye, the first man's eye is gouged out, too. If a man murders someone, he is killed."

"Who are the judges here?"

"At first, Moses decided all the cases. You can imagine that he had too many for one man with this many people, so Moses' father-in-law suggested that there be judges over thousands, hundreds, fifties, and tens to settle minor disputes. Only the difficult cases are brought to the leader, Joshua. It works very well. Most problems are solved the same day that someone complains."

"We had judges in Jericho, but most of them were known to be corrupt. A little bribery money would keep them from convicting."

"That's terrible. I can't imagine living where the guilty go free and the innocent are punished. There has to be fairness for the victims and for the accused. Otherwise, people lose faith in the system."

"We had no faith in our system in Jericho."

"I'm beginning to understand why you could turn your back on all of that so easily."

"This is a much better life, but still I have had some adjustments to make."

"What has been the hardest thing for you to adjust to? Following the law?"

"Oh, no. I love knowing and following the law. It reveals the kind of God we worship. Of course, I still don't know all of it yet, but every day I learn more. No, my adjustments have more to do with language and relationships."

"Relationships like the one you have with Salmon?"

"Well, yes, to be frank. I don't quite know how to read him. Though I have been around so many men, I don't think I have ever really known a man as a person. And in many ways he is different."

"Are there other relationships that give you trouble?"

"I worry about my family. I have been the one to be responsible for them over the last few years, and I'm not sure how they are adjusting to not having me around."

"They are doing better than you might imagine."

"Salmon told me that you have been visiting some with my sister, Adah."

"Yes, I have."

"I want you to know how much I appreciate that. She can be a very sweet girl, but she also can be trying."

"We actually have become good friends. I guess I'm just enough younger than you and older than she to be friends with you both."

"I'm glad to hear it. She needs a friend."

"She has been pretty miserable, I have to admit. You probably know that she had at least one man in Jericho who had expressed to her his intention of asking for her hand. She hasn't gotten over the grief of losing all her friends and suitors."

"Have you been able to talk to her about the Lord at all?"

"Yes, we have talked about the law and serving one God. She seems resistant to everything I have to say along that line. I think she really needs to hear from you."

"Why do you say that?"

"I understand about the Lord only as someone who has grown up in Israel and who has known about him and believed in him from my childhood. You have a faith that came about as an adult. And your faith somehow seems more real than mine. I talk about the way she ought to act, not why the Lord is the true God."

"What does the Lord mean for you personally?"

"He is just someone who has always been a part of my life. I know he is real because I have seen the miracles that he has performed, but he seems distant and unknowable at the same time."

"I wish I could give you a sense of the love I have found in the Lord. It has been as real for me as your friendship."

"I love to hear you talk about your experiences with the Lord. It makes me feel better about being a part of Israel."

"But what about your experiences with the Lord?"

"What experiences do I have to talk about?"

"For one thing, he gave you a wonderful father and mother who have loved you and protected you from harm. He has put you in a nation where people believe and obey his law so that your everyday life is good. He has given you the love of a good man and hope for a happy future. All of that is from him, isn't it?"

"Yes, I guess you are right. I just hadn't thought about it before."

"Perhaps only when we have really bad experiences can we recognize what is good, especially what is good about what the Lord does."

"Talking to you always makes me see the Lord differently than I ever have before. That's why I think you need to talk to Adah."

"But I can't until the end of the month, can I?"

"No, I'll do the best I can with her until then."

"One relationship has been only a blessing to me. I'm not sure that I have ever really had a friend before. I thought I did once, but I was wrong. Your friendship means so much."

"I'm the blessed one. You have supplied something for me that I didn't know I was missing."

"What is that?"

"A woman's nurture. I can't remember my own mother very well. My father is a great man, and he has many female servants who care for me, but I haven't had this kind of relationship with a woman before."

Rahab reached out and gave Acsah a hug. "This is for your mother. She would want you to have that."

Acsah had tears in her eyes as she left the tent.

Talking about friendship with Acsah reminded Rahab of her childhood and her one friend, Tyra. Tyra had lived on a farm not too far from Rahab's family; unlike Benne, Tyra's father had been hardworking and steady, with Tyra's older brothers to help him, so they were fairly prosperous. Tyra, as the youngest and only girl, had pretty much whatever she wanted. This was fascinating for Rahab, who, although more stunning than Tyra, did not have her vivacity and daring. Rahab's few times of getting in trouble as a child usually stemmed from Tyra's suggestions that they somersault in the flax field or spend all day in the hills without telling their parents where they were going.

After both of them were married, Tyra's determination to have her own way revealed itself when she had an affair. Unfortunately for Rahab, the man Tyra chose was Rahab's husband, Ambaal.

The real irony was that after she had been driven out by Ambaal and Tyra and had become the most successful prostitute in town, Ambaal became obsessed with her, especially since he was the one man in the city she refused to serve. This obsession made Tyra insanely jealous. She sought ways to get revenge, including telling the king what she knew about the spies in Rahab's inn. How Tyra got that information, Rahab never knew. But she knew it had to have been Tyra because of what Ambaal was yelling outside her door the day the walls came down. He said, "I know you have something to do with the Israelites, Rahab. Tyra told me about your spies."

Rahab had been unfortunate in Jericho in both friendship and marriage. Now she was in the camp of Israel being offered both again. Could she trust the offers? She wasn't sure, at least about marriage.

Salmon was bored. He had been bored on Sabbaths before. Why was this one worse? His sigh of frustration got Othniel's attention. He said, "Nothing much happens outside the camp on the Sabbath, does it?"

"No, but that's true inside the camp on the Sabbath, too."

"I guess you're right. I used to hate it when I was a boy."

"Same here. I would say, 'Mother, please can't I go play with Othniel.' And she would give me her patient look and say, 'No, son, the Sabbath is a day of rest.'"

"My father used to drill me on the law. It seemed to me that learning the law was more like work than picking up manna."

"It's funny. I felt the same way; yet last week when I was in the tent with Rahab and all she wanted to talk about was the law, I wasn't bored at all."

Day 14, The Second Sabbath

"What are you saying?"

"I'm not sure. I don't know if I felt that way because I was with her or because seeing the law through her eyes made it more interesting for me."

"What kinds of questions did she ask?"

"She wanted to know what honoring the Sabbath meant exactly. I tried to explain about all the controversy surrounding the interpretation of that law. Do you know what she said?"

"What?"

"She said that we seem to be trying too hard to figure out exactly what we could or couldn't do. She said we ought to be happy to have a day of rest once a week. The Canaanites don't ever have a day off."

"I never thought about that before. I always took having a day off from work for granted. It would be tough to work seven days a week without a break."

"She also said she thought the Lord wants us to use the time to get to know him better."

"She says really interesting things, doesn't she?"

"Yes." He paused. "You know, I really miss her."

"I understand. I really miss Acsah, too."

They sat quietly then, looking at the cold campfire. Then a man approached them from one of the other campsites. Salmon looked up to see who was coming.

"Hello, Salmon. I came to see how you and Othniel are dealing with this Sabbath away from our families. Are you as bored as I am?"

"Join us, Elimelech." Salmon motioned to a place near the fire.

Elimelech sat down. "Well, we've destroyed another Canaanite city. No one left alive, and all those buildings ruined for habitation. What kind of reputation do you think we are getting in Canaan?"

Othniel said quietly, "It won't much matter when everyone is dead, will it? Aren't we supposed to kill everyone?"

Elimelech's breath went out with a whoosh, "I know of one Canaanite who is still very much alive, and so is her family. How does she feel about all this killing, Salmon?"

Salmon had the uncomfortable feeling he had felt lately with Elimelech. What was it about Elimelech that threatened him? "Rahab is satisfied that we must do what the Lord commands."

"Do you really expect me to believe that she thinks we should destroy her own people? She isn't telling you everything, I'm sure."

"How is Naomi feeling these days?"

Laughing, Elimelech replied, "You're funny, Salmon. You obey the law better than any other Israelite I know, but then you choose to marry a Canaanite. And I know you have as many questions in your mind about this strategy of Joshua's as I do, but you refuse to discuss it openly." He leaned forward and jabbed a finger in Salmon's direction. "You can try to hold on to open-mindedness and blind faith at the same time if you like, but I know what I think."

"Do you? I don't see you taking a stand against Joshua."

"What would be the point now. I'll just bide my time. After we are settled, then we shall see." Elimelech rose to his feet and left them sitting quietly before the fire.

Salmon said wryly, "He never did answer my question about Naomi."

Othniel shook his head, "I had no idea that Elimelech was so rebellious in his thinking about Joshua and the law. What exactly does he think we should be doing?"

"I'm not sure, but I think he believes that we can just peacefully move in here next to the Canaanites and be their neighbors and friends, sharing women and land and gods with no problems."

"That could never happen. The Canaanites will fight us every inch of the way before they will let us have any of this land."

"I agree, but still..."

"You don't like all the killing, do you?"

"I wonder if that is the reason we are sitting here outside the camp—to contemplate the seriousness of taking human life."

"We did it because we were ordered to by Joshua, who heard it straight from the Lord."

"Yes, I know. Knowing God ordered it is probably the only time we should kill. Otherwise, we would be breaking one of the ten."

"You shall not commit murder?"

"Yes."

"From what you have told me, I think Elimelech would be really surprised to know what Rahab thinks."

"I think Rahab would be really surprised to know that any Israelite would question the Lord and his law."

"Do you think this kind of thinking is widespread?"

"You mean pretending that they are in unity with Joshua's orders while trying to undermine his leadership? I hope not."

They sat quietly looking at the fire pit, deep in thought. Then Othniel spoke, "Are you hungry?"

"Yes, let's see what we can have."

The only food to eat was the cold food that had been given to them the day before. Salmon would be so glad when tomorrow was over and he could return to the main camp, to his own tent, and to Rahab!

Day 14, The Second Sabbath

After sunset, which marked the end of the Sabbath, Salmon went out to check on the animals. He was coming back into camp in the dark when he overheard a conversation around one of the campfires.

"So Salmon is going to marry the Canaanite prostitute."

"What do you bet he isn't waiting for the wedding to sleep with her?"

"A prostitute. That sounds like a luscious treat." The man who said this followed it with something that made Salmon almost sick with fury. How dare they speak of Rahab in that way! He stepped into the circle of firelight and stared around at the faces, some embarrassed, some fearful, a few defiant. Then without a word, he moved on to his own campfire, still seething inside.

When he got to the campfire, he sat down by Othniel. "You look upset. What happened?" asked his friend.

Salmon told him what he had heard. "If I hadn't been unwilling to lower myself to their animal level, I would have called them out and challenged them for that."

"You know men talk about such things when they are away from their women."

"I know, but I never realized before how I would feel about having my own woman discussed in that way."

"She was a prostitute."

"I know; I know!" He put his head in his hands. "Why does everyone keep reminding me of that fact."

Othniel kept quiet. Salmon sat moodily for a long time before he said, "She was a prostitute. Men had her before me. Probably a lot of men."

"Would it help if you knew why she became a prostitute in the first place?"

"Knowing might help, or it might make me feel worse."

"You are really upset by this, aren't you?"

"I am. I guess that even though I knew she was a prostitute, I have been ignoring that, imagining her as pure. She seems so naive to me. But hearing those men talk about her made me realize what she has been doing." He sat moodily contemplating his situation. "I can't change my mind now, and I won't." His voice took on resolution. "I am committed, and I'll see this through. I just wish I understood why she would do such a thing."

"Could you ask her?"

"I should. Not now, but later when the time seems right." He shook his head. "This makes me want to keep Rahab in the tent and never let her out."

"Do you think she would accept that?"

"No, she wouldn't. She is rather stubborn on that point."

"Then you have a dilemma, my friend. She may have to deal with her reputation herself over time." They sat musing in silence for a few minutes before Othniel added, "Loving a woman is a great responsibility, isn't it?"

"Yes. And I feel really helpless out here while she sits inside going through who knows what, adjusting to the servants and living in a tent and being away from her family. Sometimes I doubt God's timing for the way things happen."

"I suppose real faith comes in there—trusting God's timing when it doesn't make sense to us."

DAY 15

The women had agreed that they would not have cooking class on this day because their men would probably be coming in, and they wanted time to prepare. Rahab was looking at the skeins of wool that she had spun. They were beginning to run low as she used them in the weaving, and she didn't want to ask Acsah for more raw wool when she had already been so generous. She looked at the weaving she had done to see if what she had would be long enough for a baby blanket.

As she stood outside the tent, she saw that Serah and Mahlah seemed to be working very hard on a project over by their tents. Curiosity overcame her shyness, and she walked over to see what they were doing. They had several large baskets, which were full of something white and soggy. As she watched, they took some of the mass out of the basket and began to spread it on the outside of the tent. Then she realized what it was—wet wool that they were trying to dry.

"Where did you get it?" she asked carefully in Hebrew.

"It is our master's wool. We are drying it out now. Earlier, we took it to the stream and washed it there."

"What does he plan to do with it?"

They looked at each other questioningly, and then Serah blurted out, "The wool is for you, a surprise from our master."

Rahab was taken off-balance. To have this brought right now, just after she was wishing for wool, was like a miracle to her. "Can I help you prepare it?"

"Have you ever worked with wool before?"

"Not much, but I have done a lot of work with flax. I'm sure they are similar. I can help comb it anyway." She raced back to the tent, where she got the comb she had been using with the wool. When she showed

Day 15

it to them, they smiled. Mahlah confessed, "We actually haven't worked with wool much. We would welcome any help you could give us."

Rahab immediately went to work, helping wring out the soggy wool and spreading it out. In a couple of hours, the hot arid air had dried the wool thoroughly, and she was able to start combing it. She could see that there would be enough wool for any weaving of that kind that she might want to do for the year. Such bounty seemed overwhelming to her. Before long, she was spinning more skeins to finish the baby blanket.

As she sat at work, she thought that the time for being alone like this was almost over. Soon Salmon would be back in the tent. Try as she might, she could not be sorry that he was coming. She had loved getting to know Acsah better and establishing relationships with all the women that had been coming to her, but she preferred Salmon's company to any of theirs. Something inside of her wanted to reject that thought, but she had to admit that he was a good person to have around—thoughtful, intelligent, and sometimes funny. No, she couldn't be sorry that he was coming back.

She stopped to eat a light meal, knowing that tonight she would fix a good meal for Salmon.

Acsah came by to give her a last language lesson. They tried conversing entirely in Hebrew, and found that Rahab could understand better than ever. "You've made so much progress in only a little over a week. I am just amazed."

"You have helped me do it. I can't thank you enough for taking the time to work with me on this."

"It has been a pleasure. What are you going to fix for dinner?"

"Stewed fruit, barley bread, and porridge."

"All three? I was going to make barley bread and lentil stew, but I forgot to put my lentils on to soak. I may make the stewed fruit, too."

"Do you need some cinnamon?"

"Do you have some to spare?"

"I have enough for my good friend."

"I wonder where we can get more cinnamon?"

"Perhaps in the plunder."

"I wonder if the men will know that it's valuable when they see it?"

"Let's hope someone did. We'll have to show them what to look for in future raids."

Rahab could see that Acsah was restless. She felt a little bit that way herself. "Why don't you go home earlier so you will have plenty of time to work on the supper."

"I am a little nervous about it."

"You'll do fine. I'm sure both your father and a certain cousin will notice the difference and be impressed."

"Thank you for all your help. I owe you so much."

"If we had to keep a record of debt, I would owe you much more than you owe me."

"Let's not keep a record then."

Salmon found himself standing with the men of his unit waiting again for the Levites to finish the cleansing ceremony. He was so tense with the anticipation of seeing Rahab that he felt like a bowstring that had been strung too tight. Looking around him, he could see other men who looked in much the same condition. Many of them were married men who weren't used to being away from their wives for so long. He still had sixteen more days before he could marry Rahab. He thought being away from her would make the time go faster, but being around the men and their bawdy comments had only whetted his appetite further. At times like this, he almost wished he could be Canaanite and have no conscience about taking Rahab tonight if he wanted. Something warned him that he was treading on dangerous ground in his thoughts.

He tried to concentrate on the Levite who stood in front of him sprinkling water on him. He knew the principle behind the cleansing ceremony and would not have disobeyed, but he couldn't help wondering what good it did to put the men through this. If Rahab were here, she would think of a way to explain it that made the Lord's law seem logical and good. The thought surprised him. He hadn't realized before that she nearly always did that.

That made him wonder what the Lord did intend by having them go through this ceremony. He knew the basic idea had to do with not touching blood or dead bodies, and that the Lord always had major restrictions about cleanliness whenever either of those was involved. That must mean that the Lord didn't want them to take the shedding of blood lightly, that death was something to reject as the opposite of God. In his present situation, he had been killing human beings, at the Lord's command, but still he was not to think lightly about killing. For the first time, Salmon began to understand a little of how Rahab's mind worked when it came to the Lord.

She always assumed that the Lord was good and right in his commands; if she didn't understand, she thought about what the Lord was trying to teach through the law or situation. Her faith in the Lord's goodness still amazed him. Where had she learned to think like that?

Day 15

At last, the Levites finished the mass sprinkling, and the men were dismissed to bathe and wash their clothing. By the time the clothes were dry where they had been spread over rocks and bushes, it was nearly sunset. Salmon gathered together his personal possessions and his share of the plunder. With the other men, he watched until the sun dipped below the horizon. Then with a shout, the men began moving as one body toward the main camp and their beloved families.

Just as Acsah was leaving, Penninah came up and told them, "Word has come that the army will be allowed back into camp this evening."

Acsah beamed excitedly and hurried away home to prepare herself for Caleb's and Othniel's homecoming.

Rahab went right to work and fixed the fresh bread. She also made the stewed fruit that she knew he liked and some porridge, which she left in the ashes to stay warm. The barley was almost gone, but she didn't want to stint on his homecoming supper.

The food was ready, and she had become impatient before she heard the sound of people talking excitedly. She started to go out when suddenly the tent flap moved and Salmon was there! Seeing him this way in the lamplight made her feel like she was dreaming. She had a need to touch him, so she started helping him take off his armor.

"I'm glad to be back here. I thought the seven days would never be over."

Rahab brought water for him to wash his hands, feet, and face, though if she had thought about it, she would have known that he had bathed that day. But for some reason, she wasn't thinking clearly. She murmured interestedly as he talked.

"I guess you know this, but one thing was different from Jericho. The Lord gave permission for us to take the plunder and livestock. I got this sack of barley and this fruit and salt. I traded some of the fruit with Othniel to get some olives and oil."

"Wonderful. I was just wondering where you would get more grain. The Lord provides so well, doesn't he?"

"Yes, I suppose so." Salmon sounded disappointed in her response. "And this sack of wheat I helped harvest two days ago with the help of your father."

"Father helped you? I'm so glad. Was he much help?"

"Absolutely; he taught at least two hundred men how to cut wheat and put it into sheaves, and Caleb organized the winnowing."

"Two hundred!"

"Yes, we harvested enough wheat for all of us to have this much to take home. Your father got a double portion. We couldn't have done it without his help. I wish you could have seen all of us out there working." He was almost boyish in his enthusiasm.

"I think perhaps you might learn to like farming."

"After that experience, I think you may be right." He smiled at her. "Oh, I just remembered, "Here, I brought you this." He handed her the gold bracelet.

Rahab exclaimed, "Oh, how lovely. Thank you for thinking about me at such a time."

Salmon turned red at the praise. "I thought it would look nice on your wrist."

Rahab regarded him quietly, and he looked back. The atmosphere in the tent was different than before the battle. "I was afraid for you," she admitted.

"Were you? I appreciate that."

Rahab took a deep breath and moved away to get the food. "Are you hungry?"

"Starved."

While he was eating, he said, "I know I told you a little bit about the battle, but one thing I wanted you to know that I did in Ai, because I did it for you."

"What was that?" She turned to look him in the face.

"I destroyed the statue of Molech with a hammer. No more babies will die in that statue's arms."

She looked at him in understanding and gratitude. "You've done what I've dreamed about doing for years, but I didn't have the strength or opportunity." She was quiet in her praise, but she felt deeply what his action meant.

"I did it because of what you had told me."

She nodded, "I'm glad you understand what I was trying to express about the wickedness of Canaanite culture."

"I do understand." He handed her his dish. "Thank you for the excellent meal. I missed your cooking."

"Oh, that reminds me. Did anyone tell you about our cooking classes?"

"Cooking classes?"

"Yes, I hope you don't mind, but I've been teaching some of the women how to cook with the vegetables and fruits here."

"Who came besides Acsah?"

"About sixty women came the last day."

He looked dumbfounded. "Perhaps you are mistaken."

"No, I'm sure sixty came."

Day 15

"How could you teach them when you don't speak Hebrew?"

"Acsah translated for me, but I've gotten to the point of being able to understand quite bit of Hebrew now."

He said in Hebrew, "Do you have any idea how beautiful you are?"

Rahab responded, "No, I don't."

"Ah! So you do understand."

Embarrassed, she suddenly remembered that she needed to put some beans into water for the next day. While she was doing that, she said, "Elon got back with the news about the battle. He was able to see his new daughter only a day old."

"I had heard that Shamar had her baby."

"Yes, a little girl."

"Will she let you near the child?"

Rahab looked surprised and then started laughing to realize how much things had changed in just the few days that he had been gone. "I was the first to hold the baby."

"What?"

"I delivered her."

Salmon's mouth dropped open. "How did that happen?"

She told him of the birth of Shamar's baby. He shook his head in disbelief. "So you worked as a midwife, too. Weaver, cooking teacher, midwife, linguist, philosopher—you are an amazing person, Rahab."

Rahab didn't miss the fact that he had left prostitute off his list of occupations at which she was skilled. She was glad he wasn't thinking about that, or if he was, he wasn't talking about it. "Are you ready to rest? I am."

"Yes, I could use a good night's sleep in a real shelter. I'm glad to be here."

She wasn't ready to say it, but she also was glad he was back in the tent.

DAY 16

When Salmon woke, he saw Rahab peeking through the curtain dividing her little room from the room where he had been sleeping.

"Good morning," she said softly.

She looked very beautiful to him in the dim light of the tent. Her hair was a curly dark halo and her eyes were large as she tried to see him in the darkness. "Did you sleep well?" he asked.

"Yes, I did. Did you?"

He couldn't tell her that his sleep had been troubled by dreams about her, so he answered simply, "Fine, thank you."

"I wanted to thank you for my loom and the wool."

"Is that working out for you?"

"Yes, it gives me another way to make connections with the other women."

"You are doing a good job of making friends here. I was worried about you, but I shouldn't have been."

"The Lord has been looking out for me. He has provided me with opportunities for meeting other people and learning the language. Acsah has been a great help, too."

As they quietly ate breakfast, Salmon searched for a way to stimulate conversation. He felt that their relationship had become warmer since the beginning, but after two weeks, he still couldn't think of any topic she would be interested in besides the Lord. He wondered how long it would take for her to become interested in him. "Would you like to talk some more about the law?"

"Yes, I would like that a lot."

Salmon was amused at her enthusiasm. "We've discussed some about food and cleanliness issues. Let me think of other topics." He paused to think.

Day 16

She interrupted his musings with a question. "I have noticed that your servant girls leave cooking pots and other items outside their tents sometimes overnight, but the next day everything is still there."

"Yes, why does that surprise you?"

"In Jericho, we could not leave anything outside for any length of time, much less overnight. Sometimes people broke into the inn to take things. I had to keep my money with me or hidden in secret places, even from my parents. My father would have taken it to buy wine and to gamble. I just thought there might be a law about this."

"Yes, you're right. In fact it is one of the first ten, which are the important ones to remember."

"Can you let my father know this law? I worry that he might break a major law without knowing any better."

"Caleb has been talking to him a lot about the Lord. I will ask Caleb to mention this one in particular. You are right when you say that your family needs to know the law."

"So do I. I'm not even sure about all of the first ten yet. I know not to misuse his name; to keep the Sabbath; not to commit adultery, and now not to steal, but that isn't ten. What are the others?"

Salmon laughed out loud. "I'm sorry. I just can't get over your enthusiasm for learning about the law."

"Aren't you excited about knowing what the Lord wants?"

"Well, I wouldn't say excited. But I agree with you that learning them is important. Here are some you missed: honor your father and mother; don't murder; don't give false testimony; and don't covet anything or anyone that belongs to your neighbor. That isn't every word of what the written form of the law says, but it covers the basic ideas."

"I'm worse than I thought. I think I have broken every one of the laws. What does he mean by false testimony?"

"Well, it could mean in a trial, but some people think it means that we are not supposed to lie."

"It is worded very carefully. If he had meant don't lie, he would have said that. Do you think he knew that in some situations we shouldn't tell everything that we know or think? I mean, what if I hadn't lied when you were in Jericho?"

"Sometimes you say things that I find amazing. Where do you get these ideas?"

"I'm not sure. I just think a lot, especially about the Lord and who He is. Don't you do that?"

"I do think often, but I'm not sure that I spend much time thinking about who the Lord is. He is just God, the only one."

"What do you think about?"

"Lately, I've been thinking a lot about you."

Rahab became very quiet. Salmon watched her face furtively to see if she was any more responsive to these kinds of comments than she had been. He did not feel encouraged by what he saw. Several minutes passed before she spoke again. "I still have questions about the law. That last one, not to covet, isn't an action exactly, is it?"

"Well, no, I guess not."

"Does the Lord see into our minds?"

"I never thought about that before. I guess he must if he can speak to men in their minds." Salmon mused, "I never tried to keep that one about coveting, particularly, because I thought no one would ever know whether I was coveting or not."

"A God who reads my mind! That means He really does know me." Rahab was quiet for several minutes.

"You are thinking again," teased Salmon gently.

"Yes, I just realized that I have always thought that if someone really knew me, knew me inside, I mean, that would be the end. He or she wouldn't care about me anymore. So I have always held back from letting anyone know the real me, even though I felt alone. Now I see that the Lord knows me and still wants to have a relationship with me. I don't have to be alone or feel unlovable again." Her face glowed with the thought.

Salmon moved uneasily. "Is the Lord the only one you plan to show the real you?"

Rahab looked surprised. "I hadn't gotten that far in my thinking. Why do you ask?"

"I just think that a husband and wife ought to be close to each other. I wouldn't want to be shut out."

"Are you willing to be completely real with me?"

Now Salmon looked surprised. "I guess wanting you to be open with me is unfair if I'm not willing to be open with you. I think conversations like this one are a good start."

She abruptly resumed the former topic. "I need to think some more about these laws. Do you have any other aspects of the law you can tell me about?"

"A lot of the law had to do with setting up the tabernacle."

"What did he say to do?"

"He gave very detailed instructions about the dimensions, how things were to be made, what objects to include."

"What kinds of objects?"

Day 16

"An altar for the offerings, and another smaller tent that contains the holy place and the holy of holies. In that tent are the golden candlesticks, a table, washing bowls for the priests, and, of course, the ark."

"What is the ark?"

"The ark is a large box overlaid with gold that contains the stone tablets of the law as well as a jar of manna and Uncle Aaron's staff. The only person allowed in the Holy Place is my cousin Eleazar. Before Uncle Aaron died, only he could go in."

"I remember you telling me that when we talked about Nadab and Abihu." She was remembering what she saw of the tabernacle the day of the solemn assembly. "I noticed the bases of the tent posts the other day. Are they made of silver?"

"Yes, they are."

"How did they get so much gold and silver in the wilderness?"

"Remember, the Egyptians gave us rich gifts including silver and gold when we left Egypt. Moses asked for an offering from the people to make the tabernacle, and everyone gave generously." He glanced at the angle of the sun shining into the tent. "I hadn't realized that we had been talking for so long. Are you hungry?"

Rahab reluctantly got up to fix the lunch. While she was fixing it, Salmon sat quietly thinking about their conversation and how it reminded him of his talk with Elimelech.

He sat so long that Rahab finally spoke, "What are you thinking about?"

"I had a conversation with my cousin Elimelech the other day."

"Is he the one married to Naomi?"

"Yes, did you meet her?"

"She came to some of the cooking classes."

"Did she tell you that she and Elimelech are expecting a child?"

"No, she didn't mention that. Is that what you were talking to him about?"

"We were talking about the Canaanite gods. He seems ready to embrace them as well as the Lord. Some of the things he said are clearly against the law, and yet when he is talking, I can't help being confused about what is right."

"What, for example?"

"I get the impression that he thinks we should respect, maybe even accept, the local gods of the Canaanites if we think it will be good for growing crops. He pointed out that the Canaanite gods demand much more substantial offerings than our God. His assumption seems to be that a god who demands so little of his people must not be much of a god."

"My father has said things like that to me, too."

"What do you think about that?"

"You know I think what Molech demands of people is evil. It is wrong to kill babies."

"I am having trouble understanding how a nation of people could reach a point of not only killing children and engaging in immoral acts, but of thinking that those are good things to do. Do you think you could help me to understand?"

Rahab sighed, "I know that at some level, my people believed that they had to participate in the child sacrifices to Molech to win wars and in temple prostitution to have fertile crops and animals. A lot of pressure came from those in power to conform."

"From the king?"

"More so from the priests. They ruled even the king when it came to idol worship. I always felt that they were using temple prostitution to get more riches for themselves."

"How?"

"They reserved the best prostitutes for those who made the biggest offerings at the temple. In that sense, I guess the worship of Ashtoreth did increase fertility, because some of the men worked harder in their fields in order to have more to give. But I don't believe that fertility came from Ashtoreth directly. As for the sacrifices to Molech, my father used to say that any god worth worshiping required the blood of firstborn sons."

"I suppose it seemed like such a simple solution. A man sacrifices his firstborn son, and all his sins are taken care of for life."

"I don't think the sacrifices to Molech had anything to do with sin. At least, I don't remember the priests ever talking about it that way."

"Why did you make sacrifices then?"

"To win the favor of the gods in battle or to get fertility for the land."

"Did it work? Did they give you what you wanted?"

"Well, you saw how well Jericho fared against Israel. As for Ashtoreth or Baal, the rains seemed to come and go with little connection to anything we did. Some years when we had done everything the priests demanded, there would be droughts. The priests always claimed we had displeased the gods in some way, but I couldn't see it. I decided that the gods were capricious and demanding."

"The crops this year seem to be good."

"Yes, ironic isn't it? None of the people of Jericho will enjoy the fruits of their labors or worship."

Day 16

"Actually, we were promised this crop. The Lord said we would reap what we had not sown and that we would enjoy the bounty of the land."

"So the Lord is stronger than Baal and Ashtoreth. I knew he would be. He is good, and they are not."

"How could they be stronger when they are nothing but statues of stone or metal?"

"What's the Lord, then? I thought he was a gold box. Isn't the ark your holy object to worship?"

"No, the ark isn't our god; it is only a place put on earth to be kept as holy and sacred where the Lord's presence can rest. He is not an object or contained in an object. We are forbidden to worship any man-made object."

"Where does the Lord live, then?"

"When he chooses, his presence hovers over the ark in the holy place, but sometimes his presence fills the whole tabernacle."

"I envy you the opportunities you have had to see the presence of the Lord. Is it awe-inspiring? I mean, he doesn't strike you as being a gimmick produced by the priests like the Canaanite gods, does he?"

"No man could do what happens when the Lord makes himself known."

"So what is he?"

"You still don't understand, do you? The Lord is hard to describe. He is above us all and yet speaks inside of some. He can be seen in fire and cloud or heard in a voice. You seem to think that he is only one of many gods, but he isn't just the greatest god; he is the only God."

"The only God." She stopped and seemed to be reflecting on his words. "Yes, I see that. When you say it, I know that He is. The others are just man-made idols."

"I don't think I realized that I hadn't told you that."

"Is this part of the law, too?"

"Yes, the first two commandments and the most important: 'You shall have no other gods before me. You shall not make for yourself an idol in the form of anything in heaven above or on the earth beneath or in the waters below. You shall not bow down to them or worship them; for I, the Lord your God, am a jealous God, punishing the children for the sin of the fathers to the third and fourth generation of those who hate me, but showing love to a thousand generations of those who love me and keep my commandments'" (Ex. 20:3-6, NIV).

"If the Lord is the only God, why would Elimelech talk about worshiping the Canaanite gods?"

"That is what I find so distressing. He seems to think they are real somehow and have power in this land. I didn't realize before that any Israelite could feel that way after all that we have seen."

"What do you mean?"

"You said that the Canaanite gods were capricious, but the Lord isn't. When he promises something, it always happens. Sometimes I have prayed for something I wanted, and the prayer wasn't granted, but anything that has been written in the law or said by Moses or Joshua has come true."

"Yes, like the situation with Achan and the battles of Ai."

"Exactly. I hadn't really thought much about this before. But talking to Elimelech has me worried that this attitude is widespread."

"I don't understand how anyone with a God as wonderful as the Lord would be attracted to gods like the Canaanite gods. Don't they know about the awful things that are demanded in the name of those gods?"

"Perhaps the idea of making a single lifetime sacrifice to a god and being done with it has an appeal. I admit that having to think about every action all day long in relation to the law gets tedious at times."

Rahab didn't respond. She seemed to be thinking very hard about what he had just said. After a few minutes of silence he prompted, "Rahab?"

"I'm just trying to think this one out. Something about this baffles me."

"I'm not sure I understand either. I just know that I can't agree with anyone who wants to break a commandment so directly as Elimelech."

"Was that all that you talked about with him?"

"No, he was also questioning me about the Israelite strategy of killing everyone in Canaan."

"I see."

"He thinks we shouldn't kill everyone. On that point, I almost see what he means. Do we have the right to march into a land and just decimate it in this way, killing everyone and destroying the cities and villages as we are?"

"Why do you kill everyone?

"Joshua says the Lord commands it."

"Do you believe that Joshua speaks for the Lord?"

"Yes, I do."

"Then it seems to me the only reason you have. You believe it is what the Lord wants you to do, so you do it. Why don't people like Elimelech really believe?"

"I suppose they are blind in at least some ways. They see miracles, but because they don't want to believe that the Lord is who he says he is, they try to explain those miracles away. They see the results of

Day 16

worshiping other gods, but because they don't want to obey the Lord, they say he isn't there for the worshiping."

Rahab sat quietly looking at him. The ideas they were discussing seemed otherworldly in the context of the bowls of food before them and the breeze that was blowing through the opened tent. The God of the Israelites was someone so much more than she had anticipated, but she felt unworthy to approach him. Her feelings of inadequacy had only been sharpened by their discussion of the law. She had kept none of the ones she had heard so far. She deserved to die by their law.

He looked at her quizzically, "Did you have any more questions about the tabernacle?"

"What happens at the tabernacle?"

"Sacrifices."

"Are they sacrificing today?"

"Yes, the priests sacrifice nearly every day for people who want to offer a sin offering."

She looked at him meaningfully.

"I haven't forgotten. I have a lamb ready. How would you like to go to the tabernacle?"

"Could we? I would like to offer the sin offering, but I don't know how."

"I will do it for you."

After Salmon had gone to get the lamb, he came back for Rahab. They walked quickly through the tents of Judah and Levi until they reached the cleared central area in the middle. Salmon pointed out his cousin's tent, which was the nearest to the tabernacle entrance. Rahab could hear the bleating of other animals and see smoke rising from inside the large rectangular cloth wall before her.

They were close enough now to see the tabernacle clearly. "Is that the smoke hovering just above the tabernacle?"

"No, that is the presence of the angel of the Lord."

"He is actually there in that cloud?"

"Yes, I believe so."

"I didn't realize that when we came here before. How amazing! I am actually here in his presence." She felt she should fall down and worship. "I am not worthy to be in such a holy place."

"You are bringing a sin offering. That should make you acceptable before him." He pointed to the southern curtains. "Let's go to the front to make the offering."

Just when they got to the front of the tabernacle, a tall man in his mid-fifties came out wearing the garb of the high priest. Rahab was a bit overawed by the presence of this obviously holy man, but Salmon greeted him familiarly, "Eleazar, I want you to meet my intended. This is Rahab."

Eleazar nodded coldly to Rahab and turned to Salmon with a questioning look.

Salmon explained, "Rahab would like to offer a sin offering today to cover the unintentional sins she committed before she knew the law."

Eleazar seemed startled by this request and motioned to Salmon that he wanted to speak privately. That he didn't lower his voice made Rahab realize that he didn't think she could understand what he was saying.

"What is this all about, Salmon?"

"I just told you. She is sorry for her sins and wants to offer a sin..."

"I heard what you said, but I don't understand. Is this your idea?"

"No, she really wants to do this."

"Does she understand what sin is? I mean the prostitution and the idol worship."

Salmon hissed, "Lower your voice, she can understand you."

They turned away then and Rahab couldn't hear what else was said between them. After several moments, Eleazar turned toward Rahab with piercing eyes. "I have heard much of you from Joshua and from Salmon. Is it true, my child, that you want to believe in the Lord God."

Rahab responded softly, "I do believe, sir. I love your God very much."

"Then he is your God, too."

"Yes, he is."

Eleazar smiled, "I would consider it a privilege to accept the offering on behalf of the Lord. What have you brought?"

"A lamb."

"Let us proceed."

The two men went into the courtyard of the tabernacle, leaving her outside while Salmon performed the sacrifice. She felt a little left out of the ceremony but thought about what it all meant, that the lamb was paying for her sins by giving its life. She understood that blood was the price for sin and that someone or something had to pay. She was sorry for the lamb but grateful that the Lord had provided some way to make her clean before him so she could be a worthy worshiper, too. It made her realize that she never wanted to sin again if every time she did, a lamb had to die for her.

Surprised to realize that Salmon and Eleazar had come out again, she struggled to say something to let them know that she understood fully the significance of what had just happened, but she could think of nothing.

Day 16

Eleazar said, "I will go into my tent and get those for you if you are willing to wait a few minutes."

"What is he going to get?"

"A surprise for you. Something I think you will like."

Rahab couldn't imagine what that could be, but in a moment Eleazar emerged carrying a large cylinder of cloth. "Here it is. You may keep it for as long as you want. If I need it, I will come and get it."

"Are you ready to go back to the tent?" Salmon said to her after accepting the object from Eleazar.

"Yes; thank you for bringing me and for sacrificing for me." She smiled at Eleazar. "I'm happy to meet you."

"I hope to see you here again at the end of the month for another ceremony."

Walking back to the tent, Rahab wondered what was in the package and tried to absorb all that had happened to her already that day. It had been a day full of new ideas that required reflection.

They were back at the tent before Salmon revealed what he was carrying. "These are some scrolls with the history of our people and the laws as they were given to Moses. They are in Hebrew, and I thought we might use them to teach you more Hebrew."

"And to know the law better. How wonderful!"

While they were eating their supper of goat's cheese and bread, Rahab asked Salmon, "Were you and Eleazar talking about the scrolls before you went in for the sacrifice?"

"Yes, among other things."

"He didn't approve of me before, did he?"

"What makes you say that?"

"I heard what he said about the prostitution. If your relatives are opposed to our marriage, I could just go back to the tents of the aliens. Then you wouldn't have to disappoint them by marrying me."

"He doesn't disapprove now. I think you made a very good impression on him today."

Rahab wasn't sure whether to be happy or sorry that his relatives would no longer provide a reason for changing his mind. She was glad to have the scrolls, though. Reverently, she picked up the scrolls and handed them to him. "Please read some tonight."

He began with these words: "'See, I have taught you decrees and laws as the Lord my God commanded me, so that you may follow them in the land you are entering to take possession of it. Observe them carefully, for this will show your wisdom and understanding to the nations, who will hear about all these decrees and say, 'Surely this great nation is a wise and understanding people. What nation is so great as to have their gods near them the way the Lord our God is near us whenever we pray to him? And what other nation is so great as to have such righteous decrees and laws as this body of laws I am setting before you today?"'" (Deut. 4:5-8, NIV).

"That is exactly what I have been thinking!"

He continued, "'Only be careful and watch yourselves closely so that you do not forget the things your eyes have seen or let them slip from your heart as long as you live. Teach them to your children and to their children after them.'"

"Who was saying all that?"

"Moses. He gave us a review of all the commandments before he left us."

"You were there when he said these words?"

"Yes, I was."

"That must have been wonderful."

"Actually, I remember getting rather warm standing in the sun."

"Still, I would love to have been there to hear all the law at once. I wish that my people had had good laws like these to live by."

"Do you think they would have lived by them if they had?"

"I don't know. We will never know about the people of Jericho. They are gone. But I want to obey all of the law."

"Why? Why do you think the law is such a wonderful thing?"

"I guess because it tells me more about the kind of God that the Lord is."

"And that's important to you."

"The most important thing to me."

"Why?"

"Because I love him." A silence fell between them for several moments. Then she said, "Keep reading." So he did.

DAY 17

As he did every morning, Salmon looked over automatically in the direction of the tabernacle. What he saw startled him into action.

The cloud was up; it was time to move. He began rousing his servants, giving orders that sent them scurrying about in rehearsed activity, each knowing exactly what to do; they had done this so many times before. Some of the men went immediately to gather the pack animals while others went to organize the rest of the herds. Women rolled up the sides of tents and wrapped crockery and cooking pots in cloths so they could be loaded on the animals as soon as they appeared. Bedrolls were placed near the pots for loading also.

Salmon realized suddenly that he should check on Rahab's parents. He quickly ordered Penninah and Shamar to come with him and Elon to follow afterwards with pack animals, not noticing that his own tent stood quietly unmoved.

When he arrived at his future in-law's tent, he found Benne standing outside, looking around at the activity, but not moving himself.

"Forgive me, sir. We must move our camp to another location."

"Are you saying that we have to move, too?" asked Benne with a raised eyebrow.

"I'm afraid so. I have brought some of my servants to help you."

Benne answered belligerently, "What right do you have to tell me and my family what to do? I don't want to leave this area!"

Salmon reminded himself to remain calm and speak courteously to this man, though he felt like ordering him to do as he was told. "I understand how you feel, sir. But for your own protection and care, I am asking you to continue with our people. I promise that as soon as we are ready to settle, I'll find a good situation for you, much better than you have had in the past."

Day 17

Benne looked unconvinced and would have said something else if, at that moment, Mora had not come out of the tent and said, "Benne, I think we'd better do as he says. Everything we had was destroyed in Jericho, and everything we have now he gave us. We can assert our independence later."

With a sigh, Benne said, "I don't like this."

"I know, but I don't think we have much choice. Rahab will be going, right?"

Salmon smiled gratefully at Mora and said, "Yes, of course, she would want you to come with us. My maidservants will help you pack up your household supplies and bedding. When Elon comes, he will help load everything on the animals. I must return to see about my campsite."

He stayed long enough to see that Mora and Adah were cooperating with Penninah and Shamar before he headed back to his own tent. He hoped his servants could be diplomatic enough to get everything done without any delays.

Salmon came into the tent and was startled that Rahab wasn't packing up their bedding and cooking tools. "Why aren't you ready to go? We are ready to strike the tent now."

Rahab looked up coldly. "I have no idea what is going on."

"We are moving the camp to another location."

"Why are we moving so quickly? Can't we take a day to prepare to leave?"

"The Lord commanded us to be ready to leave at any moment. I hadn't considered that you wouldn't know."

"But how did you know so quickly?"

"The cloud lifted."

"What cloud?"

Salmon realized his mistake. "The cloud of the presence of the Lord, which hovers over the tent of meeting. When it lifts, we all know that we must leave. No one has to tell us."

"Well, someone needs to tell me," Rahab said pointedly. "Unlike you, I have not lived all my life in constant readiness for this type of move. Moreover, I'll be packing someone else's belongings, not my own. Where have you been?"

"I was helping your parents."

"Where is Shamar?"

"She is helping your parents, too. Look, I'll help you get everything together."

"No, that's all right. Just tell me how you keep the cooking pots from breaking."

Just then they heard the blast of the silver trumpets sounding. "That's the signal for Judah to start the procession. We should be ready to go."

Rahab felt exasperated, but with a little coaching from Salmon, she soon had everything packed for a move. She was embarrassed to face the servants when she emerged from the tent. Most of the tents were already being loaded on the pack animals. Quickly they got their things together and set off walking with the tribe of Judah toward the northwest. Rahab was still feeling miffed that Salmon wasn't helping her more by anticipating what she would need to know to make it in this culture. He seemed to take it for granted that everyone lived the same way, so she should know what to do.

The journey was hot and dusty. Though the grazing animals traveled in back, the pack animals and people kicked up enough dust to make a choking cloud. Rahab felt that she was the only one feeling displaced. Everyone else seemed to take the rigors of travel for granted.

Suddenly, Salmon, who was walking nearby, exclaimed, "Oh, my sandal strap broke."

Rahab said, "Do you have another pair?"

"No, I have worn this pair since I was sixteen years old, and this is the first time they have broken."

"How could you have been wearing the same pair of sandals for all these years, and with traveling, too?"

"Everyone is wearing the same shoes we have always had. Isn't that normal?"

"Not at all. I have had a new pair of sandals every two years or so since I was a child."

"Why would you need that many pairs?"

"Because the old ones wear out or break, and they have to be replaced."

"Oh, this must be like the manna. The Lord made the shoes last as long as we were on the other side of the Jordan, but now that we are in the Promised Land, our shoes will wear out and will need to be replaced."

"Another miracle, then."

"Yes. This having things wear out is going to be troublesome."

"Let me have the sandal. I can probably fix it somewhat. Later, I will repair it."

When they stopped a while later, Rahab was able to fix the sandal, but she was less successful at providing a good meal. She tried to find something in her disorganized packing that they could eat without cooking. "How did your women cope with the inconvenience of never knowing when they would have to move?"

Day 17

"The manna made it easy, because it could be eaten without cooking. I suppose now they are trying to have extra fruit and perhaps some bread— though to be truthful, I'm not sure how they're coping now either. I am envied by many of the men because you know how to cook the local foods."

"What was the reaction when the manna stopped?"

"Well, it happened the day after we had celebrated Passover."

"When was that?"

"I see I need to explain a lot of things. It's time to get moving again. I'll tell you about everything as we walk along."

Together they reloaded the pack animals and started walking with the group. He began by saying, "Let me tell you about what happened after we left your house that night in Jericho. You remember that you sent us into the hills north of Jericho after you let us down from the window?"

"Yes; did you go?"

"We did. You gave good advice. We could hide where few people lived, and we could watch the movements of your soldiers. That also gave us an excellent overview of the countryside, so we had more information to give Joshua."

"When did you go back to the camp?"

"After three days. We could see from where we were hiding that the soldiers had returned to the city."

"Was it hard hiding in the hills?"

"Your gift of food made it easier. Remember, we have been traveling all our lives, and many times we have been away from the camp overnight. We are used to sleeping outside."

"Still, I imagine you were anxious to get back to your camp safely."

"We were. But I was thinking a lot about you."

"About me?"

"Yes; your faith in the Lord really surprised me. I did not expect to find a follower of the Lord anywhere in Canaan."

"I did not know his name until we got word about your successes in battle. What happened after you got back to the camp?"

"We were anxious to report to Joshua, so we went immediately to his tent though we were still dripping wet from swimming across the Jordan."

"What did he say?"

"He didn't notice. He was interested in our report. We told him how your king was preparing for a siege, but that your people's hearts were failing with fear because our reputation had gone ahead of us. We told him about the walls of the city and how they were situated, how the fighting men mostly kept to the tops of the walls, and how you saved our lives and helped us to escape. He agreed then that we could save you and the lives of your family, provided the scarlet cord was tied in your window."

"Did he object at all to saving us?"

"No, he acted like he was almost expecting something like that to happen."

"Then what?"

"We got up the next morning and began moving the whole camp from Shittim to the Jordan. We felt uneasy when we saw the Jordan at flood stage. After waiting there for three days, some of the men went to Joshua and told him that we couldn't cross at that season of the year."

"How did he respond?"

"He told them to tell the people to prepare to move the next day. He said, 'When you see the ark of the covenant of the Lord your God, and the priests, who are Levites, carrying it, you are to move out from your positions and follow it. Then you will know which way to go, since you have never been this way before. But keep a distance of about a thousand yards between you and the ark; do not go near it' (Josh. 3:3-4, NIV). He also told us to consecrate ourselves, so we would be ready to see the Lord do amazing things the next day."

"Why do you think you had to keep your distance?"

"The ark is holy. Only the Levites are allowed to carry it. You remember what I told you about my cousins? People who have tried to go near the ark have had terrible things happen to them. We have no trouble obeying that kind of command. We fear the ark."

"What happened next?"

"Joshua told the Levites who were carrying the ark to go right into the river."

"Into a flooded river? Why?"

"We were surprised, too. But then Joshua explained. He said that the Lord was going to prove himself to us by causing the river to quit flowing. None of us except Caleb and Joshua had been adults at the crossing of the Red Sea out of Egypt, so we had a hard time picturing that kind of miracle. Anyway, we broke camp. The Levites started forward with the ark and the people fell in behind them at the prescribed distance. None of us dared do anything except exactly what Joshua had said."

"What happened to the ark?"

"I was standing near the front and could see what happened. I was amazed. As soon as the Levites' feet touched the water, the flow of water stopped. I can't explain at all what happened—as if a huge pitcher upstream, which had been pouring water, was suddenly tipped back

Day 17

up again. Because the riverbed was rock and sand, we could walk on it. The ark moved to the center and stopped. Then tribe-by-tribe, we all marched across. It took hours to get everyone across. All the time I was wondering what had happened to the water that should have been coming downstream."

Rahab spoke up, "Adam, a town north of there, was flooded. Some of their people escaped with their lives to Jericho and told us about it, though they didn't know what caused the flooding. But of course that was going from one disaster to another."

"I suppose all of them were killed in Jericho then." Salmon mused. "The Lord destroyed one town without any help at all from us. After we had all crossed the Jordan, Joshua sent twelve men that had been chosen, including Othniel, to pick up twelve big stones from the center of the river bed where the ark was."

"Was the ark still there?"

"Yes, the Levites stood all that time holding it. We knew from experience that the Lord would quit blessing if we quit obeying. They stayed, and the water was held back. The men brought out the twelve stones."

"What were the stones for?"

"To build a marker to remember what the Lord did that day. It actually was built at Gilgal."

"Gilgal? Where is that?"

"We named the camp where we stayed during our assault on Jericho that. You may have seen the pile there after we brought you into camp."

"Yes, I did. Those stones were huge! Each was carried by one man all the way from the Jordan?"

"Yes, Othniel is a mighty man when he has to be."

"He seemed quiet and gentle to me."

"Sometimes the quiet ones are the scariest in battle."

"Yes, I remember that the men in the inn who boasted the loudest about their battles were the ones who generally lost to the quiet ones in the fist fights that would break out. What happened to the Jordan River?"

"As soon as we were well out of its path, Joshua told the Levites carrying the ark to come out of the riverbed. Just as they were safely up and out, we heard a great roaring sound. A huge wall of water came down the riverbed and for some distance on either side. We stood open-mouthed to see the might of that water. If that had let loose while we had been in the middle... well, let's just say it made me think. It took a while before the river returned to its normal flood size. Meanwhile, Joshua urged us to keep moving until we reached the plains of Jericho so we could make camp there.

The first thing we did there was to have the twelve men set up those stones in a marker. Joshua made a speech. He said that in the future, our descendants would see those stones and ask what they were about, and we are to tell them that these stones mark the day in which the Lord stopped the waters of the Jordan so we could cross over on dry land. He said that people all over the earth would hear about what happened that day."

"I don't know about all over the earth, but everyone on our side of the Jordan was talking about it. If our hearts were melting with fear before, we were almost paralyzed with fear after that. I heard some of the men saying that even the kings from the coast were afraid now to unite against your god. They believed him to be unbeatable."

"So do I now. This event solidified Joshua's position as leader. No one could doubt that the Lord had chosen him as the successor to Moses. That support made what he did next possible. Otherwise, I think there might have been a rebellion."

"What was that?"

"He told us that all the men who had been born in the wilderness would have to be circumcised.

"Ouch!"

"Truly. All the men who had been born in Egypt had been circumcised as babies, but none of us who were born later had been. Circumcision was part of the covenant that the Lord made with Abraham. He was circumcised with every male in his house. Joshua made it clear that our victory in Canaan depended on our having this done. We weren't too happy about it, I assure you."

"Just think; if we had known that, we could have attacked you and probably defeated you during that time."

"We thought about that, too. It took tremendous faith that Joshua knew what the Lord wanted for us to let him do it."

"Is that why several weeks passed from the time you crossed the Jordan until you lay siege to Jericho?"

"We waited long enough for our wounds to heal. We celebrated the Passover while we were there."

"So that was when you did that. What does that involve?"

"The Lord specified that every year we have a commemoration of the Passover. He was very clear in his requirements for celebration. We eat bread made without yeast for seven days."

"I heard about that part from Acsah."

"We hold a solemn assembly on the first and last days of the seven. We do not work at all for seven days except to prepare food. On the

Day 17

seventh day, we eat a Passover lamb and recount all that happened in Egypt. We remember all that the Lord has done for us at that time."

"Do you know what I like best about the Lord?"

"What?"

"When we talk about him, we are talking about what he has actually done. That was never really true for the Canaanite gods."

"Yes, I've been thinking about that since we talked about it yesterday."

"And..."

"I'm glad I have the God I do, but I do get tired of constantly having to be obedient."

"Do you mind obeying Joshua?"

"Not at all. He is a great leader. He has never led us wrong in anything he has told us. I trust him with my life."

"Do you trust the Lord?"

"What choice do I have? I am Israelite. How did we begin this conversation anyway?"

"We were talking about food."

"Oh, right. I said all of that to say that the day after the Passover supper, we foraged in some of the fields outside of Jericho. We found some fruit and barley because the barley harvest was just ending. Also, we found some things in farmhouses that had been abandoned by people going into Jericho. Most of us had never eaten that kind of food. The next morning, no manna fell. We were shocked after always being able to count on that source of food. We realized that we had to conquer the land so we wouldn't starve."

"Oh, look. Something is happening up ahead. Are we stopping for the night?"

"It looks like it. I'll help you unpack, and then I'll go see about the animals."

"I'll try to have something better to eat tonight than we had at lunch."

"Thanks, and Rahab?"

"Yes."

"I just wanted you to know that I enjoyed talking as we walked. It made the time go faster."

"You're welcome. And I appreciate the information. It helps to know more about your people."

He smiled at her before turning to undo the knots on the packs.

DAY 18

"Rahab, wake up. The cloud has lifted; we must go."

"This early? The sun isn't even graying the sky yet." She felt stiff from the unusual amount of exercise the day before. "What could Joshua be thinking," she grumbled.

"It isn't Joshua who decides when we go."

"The Lord?"

"Yes. Do you need help?"

"No, I can manage today."

Soon Rahab was walking along with the rest of the tribe of Judah. She noticed that several people were looking at her as if she had deformities. She didn't know whether to be amused or insulted. Though no longer a cause for animosity, she sensed a lot of curiosity about her. She was glad when Salmon caught up with her after helping the herders get the animals rounded up and started in the back.

"Have you noticed how much people stare at me?"

"Yes, I suppose they do."

"Why is that do you think?"

"I have overheard some of them wondering how you have broken so many of the Lord's laws and yet he seems to favor you."

"Well, as soon as I know what all the laws are, I'll do my best to obey them."

Salmon looked sideways at her. She hoped he could tell that this was a sore subject with her. He said, "I'm sorry I can't tell you everything at once, but I try to tell you things as they come up."

"I know you do, but it would be nice to find out before I make a mistake and not afterward."

"Are you saying that you would like me to teach you all of the law?"

"Oh, yes."

Day 18

After the noon break, Rahab asked, "How long will this journey last?"

"We have no idea. We just follow the cloud until it stops. We could settle somewhere tonight or travel several more days."

"All the walking is uphill."

"Well, it would be from the valley of the Jordan. And this area is quite mountainous."

"I'm not sure if I'll ever get over the soreness of so much walking."

"Actually, if we keep this up, you will adjust and feel stronger for it."

"That's easy for you to say. You've been doing this all your life."

"Wasn't farming hard work, too?"

"Yes, but we used different muscles for that."

Salmon laughed. "I told you yesterday about what was happening to us after we left Jericho. What about for you? What was it like in the city?"

Rahab looked at him. She sensed his genuine interest in what she had to say. This still amazed her, because she had never really had a man to talk to like this. "Well, as soon as you had left, I tied the scarlet cord in the window. I told you the other day about how the king sent soldiers to question me; I pretended not to know much except that two strangers had come. I sent them off on that fruitless search up and down the roads between Jericho and the Jordan River. At first they doubted my word, but I was so nonchalant, that they eventually gave up asking me."

"You are good at hiding things, then."

"Yes, that was important in my business."

"Because of spying?"

"Because of jealous wives. Anyway, after that, there really wasn't much to do except to wait. I listened carefully to what my customers had to say about the Israelites and their movements. Everything I heard convinced me that I had done the right thing. Of course, I could tell no one, not even my family, what I had done. Once my sister saw the scarlet cord and started to take it down from the window. I told her that it was a talisman against evil spirits. She left it alone, but she looked at me strangely. I wasn't usually very interested in the religious taboos of our people."

"Are you interested in ours?"

"Very." She glanced at him and saw a slight smile on his face. "Anyway, the day your people started marching around the city was almost a relief. The city had been shut up tight ever since you had crossed the Jordan safely and was full of people, not just the refugees from Adam, but also all the farmers in the surrounding country. I had a lot of business selling food and drink, but I had stopped doing the prostitute work after your visit."

"Why?"

"I thought the Lord probably wouldn't approve of what I had been doing, and well, I guess I thought you wouldn't approve either."

"Did my approval matter to you?"

"It did." She was surprised to realize that his approval still mattered. "Are you glad to know that I stopped being a prostitute right after I met you?"

"I'm glad."

She noticed that he started to say more, but she went on with her story, "We watched the ranks of people marching around the city. We thought you would stop and begin attacking at any moment. Our soldiers were on alert all along the walls with their weapons ready. But instead of attacking, you just marched around the city and then away again."

"Believe me, we were as confused about the orders as you were. But that was what Joshua had said to do, so we obeyed him."

"And he said to march around the city."

"Yes, once, with the sound of the trumpets."

"It felt eerie watching you march—no sounds except for the sound of the trumpets and the tramping of feet. I wondered where you were in that massive number of people. All the time we expected something to happen, but nothing did."

"What were you doing?"

"I had a bit of trouble keeping my family indoors. We had shut our doors to customers, and I went out myself only once a day to get some water from the well."

"Were you frightened?"

"I had less reason to be than anyone else, but yes, I was sometimes afraid that you would not honor your word. I prayed to the Lord that you would remember me when the time came for attack."

"I would not have broken my word."

"I know that now."

"So what about the soldiers?"

"At first I heard a lot of talk about what strategy you were using. They were a little unnerved. But after about the third or fourth day, they relaxed, and even began to joke, thinking that the Israelites were afraid to attack or couldn't figure out how they could possibly defeat such a strong walled city. Some said you would give up and move on."

"It must have been part of the Lord's plan to break down the preparedness of the people so that what happened was more shocking and devastating."

"No doubt. Anyway, the seventh day came. I was looking out my windows at the flax field when you came into sight again. I wondered how many more days this would happen. My sister Adah was anxious

Day 18

to get out of the house. She begged to go to the well for water. I incautiously let her go, thinking nothing would happen that day either. I told her to hurry, but she found some friends, and stayed gone a long time. Before long, I realized that you weren't leaving, that you were going around again. As you went around again and then again, I became more concerned that Adah was not back yet and finally went looking for her myself."

"That was really dangerous."

"Yes, I know, but I couldn't let my sister be killed, could I?"

Salmon shook his head, but still looked concerned.

"When I finally found her, she was gossiping with her friends and hadn't even gotten the water yet. With a lot of persuasion on my part, I finally hurried her back to the inn. When we got inside and shut the door, my father told me that the Israelites had been around for the sixth time and were on the seventh pass. We had not been back inside very long when I heard a pounding on the door. I called out, 'Who's there?' It was Ambaal. He told me that he knew that I had harbored the spies from Israel and that he had come to take me to the king to tell what I knew about this battle strategy. I refused to open the door, telling him to leave me alone. I was really scared that Ambaal would manage to open the door and drag me out of the house. He was never an easy person to dissuade. Just when I thought he would break through the door, I heard the trumpets and then a mighty roar."

Salmon interjected, "Thousands of voices all shouting at once make an incredible din. How did the earthquake affect you?"

"I thought I was going crazy; the walls of the house seemed to be moving; the floor felt unstable. Pots fell off shelves. Tables and benches moved across the floor on their own. I couldn't keep my balance, but there was nothing stable to grasp. I can't describe what it felt like, but I was terribly frightened. I could hear a rumbling sound as if the very foundations of the buildings were crumbling. Finally, we heard a terrific crashing noise, and then dust rose all around outside and began to come in the lattice of the window. What did you see from outside?"

"As you said, we marched around seven times on that seventh day."

"The number seven seems terribly important to the Lord."

"More than you know. Othniel and I had begun the day in a position so that every time the trumpets sounded we were on the north side of the city across from your window. So when the trumpets sounded the seventh time, and we all shouted according to Joshua's instructions, I had a clear view of your window. I could just make out the scarlet cord from the distance at which we were standing. First came a pause, and then we, too, felt the ground moving beneath our feet. Standing up was hard, but as we were on open ground, our only danger was from falling down ourselves. What we saw were the walls just slipping down as though they were loose rocks in a rockslide. Men were falling with the walls; people were screaming and shouting from inside the city, and we heard the same deep rumbling sound. For just an instant I thought I saw that your house was still standing while all around the walls had collapsed, but then the dust from the crash rose and obscured everything.

"All our soldiers immediately made a dash for the city. The walls had fallen so that everyone could climb the rubble straight up into the city. Joshua told Othniel and me that our first concern was to get into the city and see that you and your family were safe. So he and I ran, too, trying to get to your house before anyone else could. I was hoping that you had closed up your house as I had told you. When we reached the place, we could see that your house was all that was left standing of the whole outer wall. All around us, our men were killing what was left of the people, who put up no resistance at all in their state of shock. I can't say that I enjoyed all that slaughter, but the Lord commanded that."

"Yes, I know."

"How were you during the battle?"

"When the shock of the collapsing walls ended, my family started wailing, 'We're all going to die. Let's get out and run away.' I had to tell them then that if we stayed put, we would be saved, but if we left that house, we would be killed. They could see the soldiers run up the rubble outside our window with swords and battleaxes flashing. I had a very hard time convincing them that the inn was the safest place to be. Meanwhile, Ambaal, who must have survived the fall of the walls because he was so close to the house, was shaking the door again, this time to get in. Somehow he knew that the fact that our house had survived the collapse was a sign that it was protected. I had a few difficult moments trying to hold the door shut to keep Ambaal out and my family in. They were all against me.

"Then Ambaal quit yelling, and I heard the sound of swords clashing just outside my door. I was terrified that someone besides you would get to us first. I tensed for the assault on the door, but then I heard the most wonderful words I've ever heard: 'Rahab, it's Salmon. You're safe now.'"

"You certainly gave me a warm welcome."

Rahab blushed as she remembered that she had opened the door and flung her arms around Salmon's neck. "You can't imagine what a relief I felt seeing you."

Day 18

"I think perhaps I can. I was relieved to see you as well. I was afraid something might have happened in spite of our precautions. But there you were, safe."

"I felt so emotional at the time. I look back now and realize that I wasn't as ready for all the changes as I thought. We left everything and everyone we had ever known on that day."

"Was it hard to leave your possessions?"

"Not so much, but I did get one thing before I left the house."

"What was that?"

"The scarlet cord from the window."

"You got it? I didn't know. I haven't told you before, but that cord was my mother's. She told me that it represented the Lord's presence to her because it was scarlet like the blood of the lamb at Passover time that saved our lives."

Rahab reached inside of her loose wool garment and pulled out the cord from around her neck like a necklace. "Here, take it back. I was going to keep it as a reminder of the Lord's salvation that day, but you have a longer association with it than I do. I think you should have it."

"No, you keep it for both of us. We will be together and remember the Lord's care for both of us when we see it."

Rahab fingered the scarlet cord, which was a precious object to her now for all it meant to them. "So were you the one I heard fighting outside our door?"

"No, but I remember that one of your soldiers was fighting very fiercely with one of our men just in front of your house. He seemed very arrogant for someone whose city wall had just fallen down."

"That was probably Ambaal. I think I saw his body on the ground as we went out with you." She paused as she remembered the carnage that she and her family had witnessed as they had been escorted out of the house. There had been bodies of soldiers, yes, but also women, animals, and children.

"We guided you out of the city, because your family seemed really disoriented."

"Yes, I remember that Mother was weeping loudly."

"How did you feel?"

"I just remember thinking that he had kept his promise to keep me alive. I was awed that my faith in him had been so rewarded."

"He being…"

"The Lord."

"Of course."

"Then you took me to Joshua."

"Yes, I wanted him to see that we had kept our word and saved only you and your family."

"He was very kind to me. He thanked me for saving the lives of his two best spies."

"Yes, and made arrangements for you to have a tent and provisions on the edge of the camp."

"I appreciated having a place to stay right away like that. I know I felt completely spent by all that had happened. My parents were almost catatonic."

"Look, the cloud has descended again. We are stopping."

"I wonder where we are exactly. It seems like the middle of nowhere."

"I see several taller mountains here. I wonder if that is significant."

"Why do you say that?"

"Well, when Moses was recounting the law, he told us to go a certain mountain in the Promised Land. I wonder if this could be the place."

"Do we have enough provisions?

"After Ai, we have enough for a long time. Let's get unpacked and get our tent up. I'm ready to eat and sleep."

DAY 19

Rahab heard rain when she woke and looked through the opening of the inner room across the tent at the sleeping Salmon. He looked almost child-like in his repose. He was a handsome man, maybe even more so than Ambaal. At least he had a kind face; Ambaal always seemed to be frowning and had a pettish, spoiled attitude that took away from his good looks. Well, Ambaal was gone now, and here she was with a different set of people, with a man whom she was just getting to know. Yet, in some ways she already felt closer to Salmon than she ever had to Ambaal. What made the difference?

Just then Salmon opened his eyes and met her gaze. "Good morning. What are you thinking about?"

"I was just thinking about my dead husband."

"Oh." He looked uncomfortable. "I'm sorry for your loss."

"Don't be. He was cruel and unfaithful. If anyone deserved to die in Jericho, Ambaal did. He would impregnate young girls and then claim their babies as sacrifices to Molech for his own credit. He married me, but drove me out of the house when I was pregnant with our first child." She stopped and turned away.

"Actually, you told me a little about this that evening in Jericho when you hid us from the king."

"Did I?"

"I will never forget what happened then."

"How did you end up in my inn anyway?"

Salmon smiled at her curiosity. "If this rain keeps up, we have all day. Let me start at the beginning. Joshua called Othniel and me to a secret council not long after the encampment on the other side of the Jordan River. He had a special assignment for us to go into the land to spy, especially in and around Jericho."

Day 19

"He must consider the two of you to be especially trustworthy."

"I believe he does. He told us that no one was to know that we were from Israel. While there, we were to gather as much information as possible. In particular, he wanted to know the mood of your people. Were you concerned about our coming, or did you believe that you could withstand a siege? What were your defenses? He wanted us to get into the king of Jericho's mind if we could. I thought what he was asking was impossible. I had no way of knowing that I was going to meet someone who had access to the king's mind and the willingness to tell what she knew."

"I'm glad I could help in that way," said Rahab.

"Joshua was really worried that we would be tempted to sin by the women of Jericho the way the Moabite women seduced our men. We lost 24,000 people in the plague that resulted from that. I didn't think that would be a problem for me until I saw you."

"Saw me? What difference did that make?"

"Let's just say I had never understood before what caused men to want to break the Lord's law against adultery." He looked at Rahab with a smile on his face, then continued, "Before we left Joshua's tent, he gave us some Amorite coins to use for expenses."

"I remember being surprised when I first saw those coins. I knew that the Amorites of Bashan had all been destroyed by the Israelites, so how could there be Amorites in Jericho? That probably helped me guess who you were."

"They were the only coins we had, but we probably shouldn't have used them. They called too much attention to us."

"Go on with your story."

"We left that night right after evening prayers. We had to cross the Jordan River, which as you know, was at flood stage. The crossing was very difficult even for two grown men. I wondered then how the Lord planned to get the women, children, animals, and supplies across. Of course, I didn't know what would happen later. We had to fight the current in the dark; it threatened to carry us way downstream. But eventually, we both reached the far side. Jericho was a relatively short walk, but we decided to enter it in the morning when the city gates were open and our clothing had dried completely—no need to excite suspicion by having the look of men who had just swum a river. We were going to pretend to be merchants, find a noisy inn with a lot of unguarded conversation, and try to find out what Joshua wanted to know.

The next morning, we entered the town and walked around at first, just to get an idea of the relative placement of buildings and defenses.

Most of the defense was on the inner wall. The garrisons were billeted there, and soldiers stood all along its top."

"Yes, that's why bringing down the wall was so devastating. Almost all of our fighting men had been killed before you even started into the city."

"We also went into the town and saw the tower in the center with the common area in front containing that large bronze statue of Molech. Men were gathered around it making a fire."

"Many babies died because of fear of your coming." said Rahab.

"The thought sickens me. All that death, and Molech failed you anyway, didn't he?"

"I didn't expect anything from Molech, even then."

"Well, you are different from most Canaanites." He smiled again and then continued, "We saw a contingent of soldiers at the doorway of the king's palace. They looked hard at us, as though they recognized from our behavior that we were outsiders and curious, too curious. No one else was in the square itself but a young woman just about your age and an older man."

"What did the young woman look like?"

"She had on a head covering, so I didn't really look at her face."

"Did she have a lot of gold jewelry?"

"Yes, I did notice that. She had several bracelets and prominent earrings."

"I think that was Tyra, the woman who betrayed me with my husband. That would explain how she might have known about you two."

"What are you saying?"

"Ambaal said something the day of the earthquake that made me think Tyra was the one who informed the king that spies were in my inn. What could she have overheard to make her think that?"

"I suggested to Othniel that we find an inn. We asked the older man sitting at the edge of the common area where we could find an inn that would provide a room and food. The man looked knowingly at us and said, 'You want Rahab's place, built into the outer city wall on the north side. A lot of the soldiers frequent it. I think you'll find it to your liking.' We thanked him, but I wondered what that look was about. I was afraid it might mean he suspected us."

"He was probably assuming you meant that you wanted a prostitute. Most of the inns in Jericho had that service. That might have been enough information for Tyra to guess that you were spies. She was always very sharp, and she was looking for a way to get me into trouble. Well, it doesn't matter now, does it? I mean, she and Ambaal are both dead now."

Day 19

"Were there several places the older man could have named? Why do you think he recommended your inn?"

"Well," Rahab in obvious discomfort, "I suppose because I was the best in town, at least for that kind of thing."

Salmon looked bemused. "I could pursue that topic of conversation, but I think I'll wait until I know you better, or at least until nearer the end of the month."

"Why don't you just finish your story?"

"When we reached the northern side of the city, we found a crowded area between the inner and outer walls, full of beggars—even children—in shabby garments with arms outstretched for handouts. We also saw thieves and drunkards. I had not been much in cities, but we had seen enough of Jericho that day to know that this was not the prosperous section of town. I suppose the rich wanted to have two walls between them and the enemy."

"Yes, property was much cheaper in that area. I guess that is why a lot of inns and shops opened there."

"We asked until someone directed us to the doorway of your house. We could hear many voices coming from inside. An attractive young girl, who listened to our requests and took us to the eating room, met us—Adah, I believe. Was she a prostitute, too?"

"No," Rahab sounded agitated, "I did not want her to go through what I had been through. I needed help with other areas of the inn, but I wouldn't let any of my family do that part of the business."

"I noticed that the men in the eating area were rather free in their comments to her."

"Yes, and I hated that for her, but I did the best that I could to protect and yet still support my family."

"She kept bringing in food to various men, so we looked at it and asked for things that we were sure were not against the law. Fruit and barley bread seemed relatively safe. When we paid with Amorite gold, some of the men were looking at us. One said, 'If you are an Amorite, you are lucky to be alive.' As we ate, we heard the conversations around us without appearing to do so. From these, we gathered a little. Most of the men seemed to think that the Israelites camped across the Jordan were a danger; others thought that the flooded Jordan and city wall provided all the protection that was needed, but I got the impression that those men were the blusterers. When we had finished eating, we told Adah that we needed a place to stay. She showed us to a room on the second floor for what we thought was sleeping. But then you came in."

"I'm embarrassed now to think about how I must have appeared to you then."

"Do you want to know the truth?"

"Yes, I think so."

"I had never seen a woman who attracted me so much. When you asked who would go with you, I was ready to go. Othniel had the presence of mind to keep me from the temptation."

"You were attracted to me?"

"I still am, even if you don't have a full head of hair."

Rahab self-consciously touched her head, which now was in short curls. "I was really surprised when you said that you didn't come to the inn for a woman. I couldn't make sense of it until you told me about your God."

"Your behavior surprised me, too. You seemed so interested in our laws. When you told me that you were married and that your husband was still alive, I was dumbfounded. Such a thing could never happen in Israel."

"No, you're right. But in Jericho, all the men seemed to think about was satisfying themselves without thought for the consequences to others, especially women and children. That's why I asked so many questions. I was sure that your god was the true God."

"We were both surprised by the questions you asked. I wanted to know how you had heard about Israel's God. That information was just the sort of thing we had come to find out,"

"I had access to a lot of the men of the city, including the king, and they told me more than they probably should have. The king told me himself that if you were able to cross the Jordan and breach the walls, there would be nothing we could do to stop you. He told about how the Lord dried up an ocean, and defeated Sihon and Og, the Amorite kings. The men of the city didn't like Israel's God, but to me he seemed good and just. I could see that his laws protect the helpless and innocent, unlike those of the gods of Canaan."

Salmon heard the vehemence in her voice and knew that there must be more behind it, but experience had taught him not to pursue that for fear that she would clam up altogether. He said simply, "Your faith amazed me. All you had to go on were rumors, yet that alone made you renounce the old gods and turn to the Lord."

"Yes, but I had good reasons." She got quiet for a moment. Then she said, "So that's how you ended up at my inn."

"Yes, I'm inclined to think that the Lord had something to do with it all."

"I believe so, too." They had been talking for a long time and hadn't even eaten yet. "Are you hungry?"

Day 19

Salmon was surprised. "I am, but I wasn't really thinking about it. I guess we should get up and act like normal people. But I do enjoy talking to you."

"You can keep talking while I fix some food."

"Back to that day in Jericho, what did Adah say to you when she knocked on the door while we were talking in the upstairs room?"

"She told me that some soldiers had come and wanted to talk to me. I told her to keep them occupied until I could go down."

"Is that when you made the decision to trust us?"

"Yes, I was convinced that you were Israelite, and I was willing to do anything for those who followed the Israelite God. I decided the right thing to do was to get you up on the roof to hide."

"All that flax nearly covered the roof. That made a perfect hiding place."

Rahab put the food in front of him, and they ate while the conversation continued. "We had harvested it earlier that day. I had to hope you would stay still under the flax while I got rid of them. What were you thinking while I was gone?"

"I was wondering if I could trust you or if you would betray us. I prayed silently that the Lord would get us out of that situation and that your faith was indeed genuine, because it seemed important to me that you be a believer in the Lord. The waiting seemed to last forever; I was trying not to notice the cramp that was starting in one of my calves or the tingling in my arms, which were going to sleep. Once I thought I heard the sound of several people walking quietly about on the roof, looking around, but I dared not move."

"Yes, they wanted to check everything. I didn't protest at all because I was afraid they would suspect more if I denied them access. I just hoped you were well covered. It took a while to get rid of them, even though I said that you had been there, but had already left. I sent them in the direction of the Jordan. They told me that they would shut up the city to keep you from escaping. Did you think I would never come back?"

"We were contemplating how we might escape if it took much longer."

"With the city gates shut, they probably thought there would be no escape. But since my house was part of the outer city wall, I could use my flax ropes to let you down from the window; no one would see us after dark."

"I was impressed with how well you handled everything. To me, you were not only beautiful and fascinating, but also resourceful."

Rahab felt a bit nonplussed by this comment, but continued, "I knew that very few people lived in the hills north of town so that would be

The Cord

the best direction for you to get away. But I assumed that you would need some provisions."

"You were right about that. We really appreciated your thoughtfulness."

"I wanted to help you, but I was also terrified that you would give no quarter, not even to me. Do you remember that before I let you down, I made you swear to me that you would show kindness to my family?"

"We pledged our lives for yours because you had already proven to us that you could be trusted."

"And I trusted you, too. Somehow, I knew that you were sincere. Otherwise, I never could have waited those weeks while more and more stories came back to us about what the Lord was doing."

"I remember when we went down to the second floor, I wasn't sure Othniel would fit through that little window."

"Yes, it took our combined strength to let him down the wall and to the lower level below the wall. It hadn't occurred to me that I would have to let you down by myself until then, but you were strong enough to let yourself down without my help." She looked admiringly at him.

"Othniel could have, too, only we didn't think of that with him. I almost left without realizing that we had to have some way of communicating. I'm glad I remembered to give you that scarlet cord."

"And it helped you find our house later, didn't it?"

"Absolutely. You have no idea how all those windows looked the same when we were marching around, except for yours with the scarlet cord. The reason I made you promise to bring your family into your house was that my experience in battle said that you would be killed if you weren't inside. I needed that barred door to give me time to get there before someone else could get to you."

Rahab shuddered as she remembered the day of the defeat of Jericho. What if he hadn't gotten there first? "I'm so glad everything worked so well. So many things could have gone wrong in the chaos."

"Yes, the Lord was with us in that, wasn't he?"

She nodded. "Before you went out the window that night, you looked like you were about to say something, but I hurried you on. What was it?"

"I'm not sure I know even now. All I know is that it was very hard to leave you. I wanted to promise something, more than just safety."

"What?"

"Would it sound strange if I told you that I wanted to promise that I would take care of you after the battle was over?"

"Did you really feel so much for me that soon?"

"I did."

Rahab turned away in confusion. Going over the story of that time with him made her remember how she had felt about him then. If she

Day 19

were perfectly honest, she would have to say that he had attracted her. She had never met men who were such gentlemen. Now she felt what? She couldn't say.

"The rain has stopped."

"Yes, it has. I guess we can get up and start finding out what is going on."

He went out but was back in just a few minutes, "Joshua has asked for volunteers to build something for him here. I don't know when I will be back. You might not want to wait supper for me."

Rahab decided while he was gone that they needed more bread. It had been several days since they had any bread. She remembered with pleasure that they now had some wheat, and she couldn't remember when she had tasted wheat bread. She began grinding the wheat to have the bread ready for a late supper.

Salmon knew that it was already later than he had told Rahab he would return, but he had news that he needed to tell Benne and Mora before the next day. He approached their tent with trepidation. Anytime he tried to communicate something to Benne about the Lord, he got a negative reaction. Benne came out when he called. "Are we going to stay here for a while, do you think?"

"Yes, I think so. At least I know we will stay here for two days, because we have some ceremonies over the next two days which will keep us here."

"Ceremonies? What kind of ceremonies?"

"Well, the first day we will have fellowship offering sacrifices on Mount Ebal."

"Do we have to go to this ceremony?"

"Yes, I'm afraid you do. But we have one compensation. The fellowship offering is an unblemished lamb, and we get to have the major part of it to make a feast for ourselves afterward. I am planning to provide a lamb for you and your family so you can have a feast, too. I thought you might want to invite Caleb to join you. Most groups will have invited guests."

"A feast, huh? Well that doesn't sound so bad. What about the second day?"

"Joshua will be reading the law out to us from Mount Ebal."

"More about your god. And I suppose you expect us to go to that, too."

"Yes, everyone must attend."

"I don't suppose you have a feast with that one."

"No sir, but I do recommend that you take a cold lunch with you. The ceremony will last most of the day."

"Well, we'll be there. It might be interesting to see how you Israelites worship your god."

"Thank you, sir. I will bring the lamb after the ceremony tomorrow." He hurried away to his own tent, where he found Rahab setting out their supper, including the freshly baked wheat bread. She looked at him expectantly, and he quickly explained, "I've been helping to construct a wall and altar on Mount Ebal. We were able to put it together quickly with so many men working. Joshua has called for a solemn assembly tomorrow."

"A what?"

"We had one before when he picked out Achan as the cause of our defeat at Ai."

"Salmon, you don't think that I've done anything to bring the Lord's displeasure, do you?"

"No, nothing like that. This fulfills the command that Moses made to us before he died, to come to Mount Ebal and Mount Gerizim. I had almost forgotten about that. Joshua said that he is going to be offering burnt and fellowship offerings. If we had sin in the camp, he would be offering a sin offering. I am going to get a lamb to offer as a fellowship offering."

As he was talking, he sat down and began eating the good food. His first bite of the wheat bread caused his eyebrows to rise in appreciation. "Is this made from the wheat?"

"Yes, do you like it?"

"Very much."

"You were telling me about the ceremony tomorrow. What is a fellowship offering?"

"An offering to the Lord that shows a right relationship between the giver and the Lord. We can give thanks for his divine help and blessing. I thought you might approve considering all that has happened lately."

"Definitely; I'm pleased that he would accept an offering that shows how much we appreciate all he has done. May I pick out the lamb?"

"Yes, I'll take you there in the morning on our way. We have to be sure to get one without any kind of blemish. The law requires that."

"I'll be sure to get a good one."

"You know what the best part of a fellowship offering is?"

"What's that?"

"We get the lamb for a feast afterwards, except for the breast and right thigh. Those go to the priests."

"What does the Lord get?"

Day 19

"He gets the fat portions and kidneys."

"I'll plan a good dinner for tomorrow. I'm so glad I will have some bread ready."

DAY 20

Though this was the day of the fellowship offerings, things needed to be done. Rahab fixed a quick breakfast of bread and cheese. Both she and Salmon went to get the lamb from his flock. Instead of getting only one lamb, Salmon chose a second one.

"Why are you taking two?"

"I am getting one for your parents to have a fellowship feast, too."

"Oh, Salmon. They will enjoy that so much."

"I told them that they could invite Caleb to their dinner, but I'm going to invite Acsah and Othniel to ours. Is that all right with you?"

"I would have suggested it if I'd known we could." Together they started out to the place of assembly.

When they arrived, leading the bleating lambs by ropes, they stood with the rest of the tribe of Judah and five other tribes on Mount Gerizim. The other six tribes were across the valley on Mount Ebal. Joshua stood with the Levites who were holding a large box covered with golden artwork. "Is that the Ark of the Covenant?" Rahab asked Salmon.

"Yes."

"How beautiful." Her eyes rested on this symbol of the presence of the Lord. Then she looked around some more. Up on the Mount Ebal side, Rahab could see the altar built of uncut stones resting on a ledge made by a wall also made of uncut stones. "Is that what you were helping to build last night?"

"Yes."

"It's huge! There must have been many of you working together to put it up so quickly."

"Probably three hundred men helped set it up. Do you see that section just below the altar? I helped build that."

"Is the altar where the sacrifices will take place?"

Day 20

"Yes, I'll take the lamb up to him when he announces the fellowship offerings."

Rahab watched the procedure as Joshua brought the burnt offering himself.

Salmon said, "That is Joshua's own bull, a valuable animal." Joshua presented it and then slaughtered it. He cut it into pieces while Phinehas, Eleazar's son, arranged the fire and then placed all the pieces of meat on the altar. The smell of cooking meat filled the air.

"What does the burnt offering mean?"

"It means that the giver pledges total surrender to the Lord. The bull takes Joshua's place on the altar."

"Do you mean that the bull dies literally, but Joshua is dying to his own plans and wishes symbolically?"

"I hadn't thought of it that way, but yes, something like that."

"That seems like a big step to me, but I can see how someone who has been through what Joshua has would want to be totally surrendered to the Lord." She was quiet for several minutes, and then suddenly turned to Salmon and whispered excitedly, "I think I understand now."

"What's that?"

"Do you remember the conversation we had about the other gods' demanding more than the Lord because they ask for the death of a firstborn son? I just realized that although the Lord doesn't require child sacrifice, he wants something even more costly from his followers."

"What do you mean? What could be more costly than the death of a child?"

"The life of the person."

"God doesn't allow human sacrifice."

"I didn't say the death of the person; I said the life of the person. I think some people are more willing to sacrifice their children than to have to give up their lives, every waking breath and decision in obedience to the Lord's commands."

"I think I understand what you are saying. The Canaanites prefer the child sacrifices because, although it hurts dreadfully to give up a child, they feel they have appeased their god and can live their lives as they choose."

"Whereas the Lord wants us to follow him every day, in everything that we do."

Salmon looked thoughtful. When the burnt offering was finished, he joined several others waiting in line to present fellowship offerings. Rahab watched him, happy to be included in the worship of the Lord with his people. As Salmon slaughtered each lamb and separated out the parts for the offering, the priests, and their feast, she thought about all that the Lord had done for her in the last few weeks. She had been saved from death in Jericho; she had been saved from death after the first battle of Ai; she had been given friends, and not least of all, she had seen the Lord's promise to her of love and protection fulfilled.

Her heart swelled in emotion as the parts of lambs began to burn, and the smell of cooking meat and fat filled the air. "Oh, Lord," she prayed in her heart, "please accept my gratitude for all you have done for me. I know this isn't a burnt offering, but I want to be surrendered to you, just like Joshua." Tears ran down her face, as she looked up into heaven. She didn't know exactly where the Lord resided, but she felt that only the heavens were big enough to hold a God as marvelous as he. She lost all track of time, and was surprised when Salmon returned to her side.

As the last of the fellowship offerings were given, Joshua turned to the people. "The Lord made plans for us to hear the book of the law again. You will remember that Moses arranged all of this before he left us. Some of you have never heard the law, and even those of you who have may have forgotten parts or have gotten lax in obeying it to the letter. So tomorrow, I am going to copy the Ten, the Decalogue, here, with all of you watching to see that I do this exactly right. You will be my witnesses. Then I am going to read out the law as Moses gave it to us for all of you to hear: men, women, children, aliens, everyone. You will stand and listen to the whole of the law that the Lord gave to Moses. If we are going to conquer this land, we need to have his law always fresh in our minds, so we will not be tempted to conform to the sinful practices of Canaan."

Rahab listened with open mouth. She said excitedly, "The Lord knew about my need to hear all of the law and is providing this for me. I am going to hear the law, just as Moses told it. I need never be ignorant again. How did the Lord know? But then he knows everything, doesn't he?"

Salmon nodded. "You amaze me, Rahab. I was just thinking what a boring day tomorrow would be listening to Joshua read all of that, and you are excited about it. I feel ashamed that I don't see things with your eyes. But right now, we can return to our tents and prepare the fellowship feast with the lambs that have been slaughtered today. I will take the lamb I slaughtered for your parents to them and explain."

"And I will begin cooking."

Salmon went back to the alien section carrying the lamb meat. He gave it to Benne and Mora, who said, "I have an idea of how to fix it that will be very tasty."

Day 20

"If you are as good a cook as your daughter, it will be wonderful, I'm sure." Salmon was glad he had already drained out all the blood. Mora might not know to do that. "Is Caleb coming?"

"Yes, he said he would be honored. He is a good man," replied Benne.

Mora spoke up, "His daughter is lovely. She has been by talking to our Adah, and she tells us a lot about how Rahab is doing."

He quickly said his good-byes and headed toward his own tent. As he walked, he wondered what Acsah had told them about Rahab. What had Rahab told Acsah about him? He realized that he had no idea what she might say to a woman that she wouldn't say to him. For some reason, this disturbed him.

All things considered, Rahab thought she had outdone herself with the feast. She had put the piece of lamb into a large stew, which simmered over the cooking fire. Penninah had gathered and shared some fresh leeks; Rahab had the wheat bread, fresh figs and grapes. The eating of fresh meat was still a rare pleasure for Rahab; they had not often had meat in Jericho.

Othniel and Acsah both planned to come, though Acsah hadn't been sure if Caleb would agree to let her. Rahab was delighted when they both arrived and greeted them with a feeling of deep joy. She sat everyone in the outer room of the tent with the sides up, while the servants sat in their own tents nearby enjoying their share of the feast. Lambs or goats were cooking at fires throughout the camp as family and friends gathered in smaller groups to share the feast of the fellowship offering.

Othniel said, "Rahab, this is a wonderful meal. Salmon has been bragging about how well you cook."

Rahab looked at Salmon. "You have never bragged to me about how I cook."

Salmon grinned, "Yes, I have. You just don't remember."

She couldn't help smiling back. The mood of playful banter was a release after the solemnity of the day's ceremonies, and yet how she had enjoyed that, too.

As host, Salmon reminded them of the purpose of the feast, to declare their right relationship with the Lord and thank him for all his blessings to them. "Remember that anyone unclean may not eat the fellowship offering lamb."

Each person was asked to mention something for which he or she was grateful to the Lord. Rahab's face glowed with pleasure as she said, "I am so grateful to the Lord for saving my life and the lives of my family, and that he has allowed me to be a part of his people."

As they began to eat the feast, Acsah said, "Rahab, your sincerity shames me. I was just going through the motions of the ceremonial part of the feast, but you really felt it, didn't you?"

Rahab was surprised. "Yes, I cannot help it. The Lord has been so good to me. He anticipates my needs. I have been wanting to know more of the law, and tomorrow I am going to get to hear all of it. What could be better than that?"

Othniel and Acsah exchanged glances. He said, "Do you know how long it takes to hear the entire law read?"

"Salmon said it would take nearly all day. Is that right?"

"Probably. Be sure to take some food and water with you."

"Aren't you excited about hearing the law again?"

"I'm sure we should be, but we've heard some or all of it regularly all of our lives, and frankly, we are a little bored with it."

Rahab felt confused, as though they thought her naive for her enthusiasm for the Lord and his law. Was there something wrong with her?

Just then Othniel interrupted her thoughts by asking how she was adjusting to life in the Israelite camp. His asking made her realize that she hadn't really seen him much since the battle of Jericho.

"Some things have been confusing, but I'm very happy to be with the Lord and with his people. I think that Salmon's servants have begun to accept me in spite of my heritage and former occupation."

Acsah looked mischievously at Salmon. "Has Salmon told you that he has a prostitute in his lineage already?"

Rahab looked keenly at Salmon, who held up his hand in protest. "She wasn't really a prostitute."

Acsah's eyes twinkled, "Then why did she dress like one and go soliciting?"

Rahab said, "This sounds interesting. Tell me the story."

Salmon jumped in, "I'll tell the story. I don't trust Acsah to get it right."

Acsah laughed while Salmon began. "My ancestor, as you know, was Judah. He had three sons by his wife, a Canaanite named Shua."

"Was she the prostitute?"

"No, I'm getting to that part. Judah arranged a marriage for his eldest son, Er, to a girl name Tamar. Soon after that, Er died."

"Because he was wicked," inserted Acsah.

"Are you going to let me tell this story?" Salmon shook his head in mock outrage. "Actually, you are right. He died because he was wicked. So Judah gave Tamar to his second son, Onan."

"So she could have sons for Er through the brother? We have that law in Canaan," said Rahab.

"Yes, Hebrew law says that, too. But Onan didn't want to have sons that were called his brother's, so he refused to get her pregnant. He died, too. Judah sent her home to live with her parents until his youngest son, Shua, grew up."

"Did she get to marry Shua?"

"No, Judah was afraid all of his sons would be dead, so he neglected to arrange for that."

"I would be angry if I were Tamar."

"She was. One day when she heard that Judah was going to be near her home, she dressed up like a prostitute and sat by the city entrance. When Judah saw her, he asked her to sleep with him."

"This is where the prostitute part comes in."

"Hush, Acsah. She agreed to sleep with him on condition that he leave his seal, cord, and staff with her as surety for his payment to her of one goat. He met her demands and slept with her. From that, she became pregnant."

"Did Judah know she was his daughter-in-law?"

"No; somehow she kept her face covered. When he tried to send the goat later, she could not be found. Later word came to Judah that Tamar was pregnant and had been prostituting herself. He was angry and demanded that she be burned to death."

"Did she still have his seal, cord, and staff?"

"Yes, she sent word as she was about to be burned that the man who owned those was the father of her child—well, children, as it turned out."

"So did Judah admit that he had done wrong?"

"Yes, he said that she was more righteous than he, because he had promised her a husband but had not kept his promise. She was allowed to live, but he did not sleep with her after that. She had two boys named Perez and Zerah."

"Twins run in the family, don't they. Wasn't Jacob a twin?"

"Yes."

"And you are descended from Perez."

"How did you know?"

"I'll never forget the day the Perezites paraded in front of Joshua. Zerah was picked that day."

"So, Rahab," asked Acsah, "was she a prostitute or not?"

"Based on Salmon's story, I would say she was the only one who did the right thing. She knew the law, and she fulfilled it. That she did it in the garb of a prostitute didn't make it less righteous."

Acsah nodded her head, "I do think it isn't fair that she was the one who was going to be burned for prostitution, but Judah had nothing to fear except being laughed at."

Othniel chimed in, "That is one aspect of Israel's law that differs. It states that when adultery occurs, both the man and the woman must be put to death, not just the woman."

Rahab looked up at this. "Equal treatment for men and women. That is wonderful. The Lord is so good!" The others murmured in assent.

"He was certainly good in letting us win the battle of Ai," said Salmon. "I wish you could have seen Othniel in battle. He fought marvelously. You wouldn't think so to look at him, but he is a fierce warrior."

Rahab saw the look of adoration that Acsah was giving Othniel as he blushed at the praise and shrugged as if what he had done was not important. Rahab saw what they could not see. She was excited about what the Lord had done for her because she loved the Lord with the same kind of adoration that Acsah felt for Othniel. "If they felt love for the Lord, they would be as enthusiastic about worshiping him and hearing his words as I am," she thought. Looking again at Acsah and Othniel, she wondered if their love for each other would grow stale over time, like their love for the Lord. Were strong feelings of love only sustainable for a short time at the beginning of a relationship, but then they faded later? She was thinking about that when she caught Salmon looking at her.

"You are awfully quiet. Do you want to share your thoughts?

"I was just thinking about love."

His gaze grew more intense. "Please do share."

"I was just wondering if all married love becomes stale and boring with time. Can couples do something to keep it fresh and ardent all their married lives?"

Salmon responded, "My parents did."

"What do you think made the difference?"

He thought for a minute before saying, "They were always very polite to each other. I don't remember hearing my mother criticize my father ever. And he was thoughtful of her needs. He would think of things to do for her that he knew she would like. He treated her as a person, not a servant. They talked about everything that mattered to them. And inside the tent they were always very physically affectionate, even in front of me."

Acsah spoke up, "Do you think their actions kept the love fresh, or that their love kept their actions loving?"

Rahab said quietly, "If just going through the actions of love made people feel love, then all of you would love the Lord more than I do. You have been with him doing what he requires much longer than I have. There has to be something more than just doing the right thing for love

Day 20

to stay alive and grow. I think maybe it has to do with a dying to self-love in order to feel love for the other."

Othniel shook his head, "That's a bit deep for me."

Rahab became more animated as the idea took form in her brain. "I think what I am trying to say is that only when we are willing to give without a selfish motive do we feel real love. If the only reason a man loves a woman is that he wants his sexual appetites satisfied, then he is not really loving her, but himself." She happened to glance at Salmon as she said this and saw that he was staring fixedly at her. "In the same way, I think that if the only reason we serve the Lord is so he will fulfill his part of his promises, then we aren't really loving him, only ourselves. When we sacrifice to him because of who he is and focus on his greatness and his goodness without reference to ourselves, we truly begin to love and can keep on doing it."

Everyone was silent for a while after that. Rahab felt that she had quashed the lively conversation that had been going on, but the ideas that she had voiced lingered in her mind for long afterward. Where had such thoughts come from?

DAY 21
THE THIRD SABBATH

The next day had a feeling of holiday to Rahab. She was so excited about finally hearing all of the law. She and Salmon went early to get a place where they would be able to see clearly what was happening. On Mount Ebal across from where they stood on Mount Gerizim, they could see that several men were working now, putting a thick coating of plaster on the outside of the wall of stones that Salmon had helped set up like a large retaining wall below the altar. "I wonder what that is going to be used for," she wondered aloud.

Salmon responded, "Didn't Joshua say that he was going to write the law for all to see?"

"So he is going to write the law into the plaster."

"I believe that is the idea."

"I wish I could read."

"I will tell you what he writes."

"How did you learn to read?"

"I was taught by my father."

"You are blessed to have had such a father."

"I know that."

Before long, all the people had assembled. They arranged themselves as they had the day before. Joshua stood before them, ready to write. As he wrote in large letters that could be read even across the valley, Salmon said them aloud for Rahab's benefit:

"I am the Lord your God who brought you out of Egypt, out of the land of slavery. You shall have no other gods before me" (Ex. 20:2-3, NIV).

Rahab thought again that she would be happy to have only the Lord as her God. She didn't want any other god. They had not been good gods to her.

"You shall not make for yourself an idol in the form of anything in heaven above or on the earth beneath or in the water below. You shall not bow down to them or worship them; for I, the Lord, am a jealous God, punishing the children for the sin of the fathers to the third and fourth generation of those who hate me, but showing love to a thousand generations of those who love me and keep my commandments" (vv. 4-6).

"I wonder if the Lord means more than just wooden and golden idols. Do you think he might mean anything that we rely on for happiness?"

Salmon said impatiently, "Why wouldn't you want to keep it simple. Not making or worshiping idols is enough."

"Perhaps you are right." Rahab decided not to comment again, but she couldn't help thinking that the Lord probably meant that He should be the most important thing in a believer's life.

"You shall not misuse the name of the Lord, for he will not hold anyone guiltless who misuses his name" (v. 7).

"Remember the Sabbath day to keep it holy. Six days you shall labor and do all your work, but the seventh day is a Sabbath to the Lord. On it you shall not do any work, neither you, nor your son or daughter, nor your manservant or maidservant, nor your animals, nor the alien within your gates. For in six days the Lord made the heavens and the earth, the sea, and all that is in them, but he rested on the seventh day. Therefore, the Lord blessed the Sabbath day and made it holy" (vv. 8-11).

"Honor your father and mother, so that you may live long in the land the Lord is giving you" (v. 12).

"You shall not murder" (v. 13).

"You shall not commit adultery" (v. 14).

She looked at Salmon and wondered if it could be true that she was about to marry a man who believed in this law.

"You shall not steal" (v. 15).

"You shall not give false witness against your neighbor" (v. 16).

"You shall not covet your neighbor's house. You shall not covet your neighbor's wife, or his manservant or maidservant, his ox or donkey, or anything that belongs to your neighbor" (v. 17).

Salmon said, "Joshua has finished writing The Ten."

Rahab looked at the shining white wall of words, drying fast into a monument to the Lord and to his law. Joshua turned and looked over the host of people standing there. "I am going to read all that Moses has written to all of you. You may sit on the ground now." Rahab sat down on the ground.

Salmon leaned over and said, "Be prepared. The last time this happened it took nearly the whole day."

"Shhh," said Rahab. "I want to hear every word."

Joshua's first words sent a thrill through her. "These are the words Moses spoke to all Israel in the desert east of the Jordan..." (Deut. 1:1). This was the speech that Moses had made just a year or so before. Salmon had been there when this speech was made. Now she would get to hear it, too.

The first part of the reading recounted the history of the people from the time that they were at Mount Horeb until the defeat of the Amorites just before this speech. It spanned forty plus years of time and included all the major events of the people in the desert. Because Salmon had read the first part of this to her, Rahab was able to follow fairly well. She was struck again with how frustrating the Israelite people must have been to Moses and to the Lord with their grumbling and disobedience. She wondered if she would have been one of the grumblers had she been with the Israelites then.

Even when Joshua got beyond the part she had already heard, the repetition in the language was enough that Rahab could catch the principle ideas. She understood that Moses was warning the people over and over not to be stiff-necked and stubborn about obeying the law. She caught phrases that sent a thrill through her, "...you will find him if you look for him with all your heart and with all your soul" (Deut. 4:29); "The Lord is God; besides him there is no other" (v. 35); "Keep his decrees and commands, which I am giving you today, so that it may go well with you and your children after you..." (v. 40).

She recognized the Ten, the Decalogue. Not long after that, she heard these words, "Love the Lord your God with all your heart and with all your soul and with all your strength" (Deut. 6:5, NIV). Right after that was the law about impressing all the commandments on children that Salmon had told her about, but for some reason, he had never mentioned the commandment about loving the Lord. She wondered why.

Rahab looked over at Salmon when she heard the part about smashing and burning the idols of the land, thinking he would be glad that he had just done that in Ai, but he didn't seem to be listening all that closely. She found this disturbing, and she almost said something, but didn't.

With a sigh, she focused her attention again. Joshua was reading something that answered the question that she had discussed with both Salmon and Acsah. "After the Lord your God has driven them out before

Day 21, The Third Sabbath

you, do not say to yourself, 'The Lord has brought me here to take possession of this land because of my righteousness' (Deut. 9:4, NIV). No, it is on account of the wickedness of these nations that the Lord is going to drive them out before you." It went on to explain, as though the Lord knew people would ask why the Canaanites had to be completely destroyed.

Following the summary of the law was more about the history of the Israelites right after the law had been given. In that part she heard the verse that Mahlah had told her about how the Lord loves aliens. She felt her tears well up again. What a precious promise! Now that her ears were sharpened to it, she heard the words, "Love the Lord your God" repeated again and again at different times. She was amazed that such an important command wasn't discussed more.

One section was mostly on laws concerning the tithe and leaving grain for widows and orphans to glean. She couldn't remember any of the laws of the Canaanite gods that even considered the plight of the poor and needy. It made her aware again of how good the Lord was.

One whole section dealt with the justice system—many of the things Acsah had told her on the Sabbath when Salmon was gone. Then she heard the law concerning taking a captive woman as a wife. All her situation was there—the shaved head and nails, the mourning for parents, and the abstaining from sexual relations. It seemed strange to hear her situation described in front of all these people. It made her self-conscious, especially when people turned and looked at her.

Joshua called for a break so everyone could have a bite to eat. Rahab gratefully opened the goatskin of water and fruit and bread she had brought. She and Salmon shared their food. "You are really excited about all of this, aren't you?"

Rahab nodded her head. She was still a little in awe of all she had heard. She wanted to remember everything.

Before long, Joshua resumed his reading. Rahab caught at phrases and sentences as they went by, trying to understand and retain everything. Her questions began to grow as the words went on. She and Salmon had a lot of talking to do.

Then she heard something interesting. He read the part in which Moses commanded Israel to do just what they were doing. They were to go to Mount Ebal and offer fellowship offerings. Suddenly the whole body of people rose to their feet as though they had been rehearsed. The Levites down by Moses began to shout the curses, "Cursed is the man who carves an image or casts an idol—a thing detestable to the Lord, the work of the craftsman's hands—and sets it up in secret" (Deut. 27:15, NIV).

Then everyone shouted together, "Amen!"

"Cursed is the man who dishonors his father or his mother" (v. 16). "Amen."

This continued for twelve curses altogether. Then, still standing, the people heard more blessings and curses read by Joshua. She saw this as a significant time, for it brought out all that had been read that day in capsule form, and emphasized the importance of obedience. Then at the end of the reading of the blessings and the curses, Joshua and the Levites began to sing a song:

> Listen, O heavens, and I will speak;
>   hear, O earth, the words of my mouth.
> Let my teaching fall like rain
>   and my words descend like dew,
> Like showers on new grass,
>   like abundant rain on tender plants.
>
> I will proclaim the name of the Lord.
>   Oh, praise the greatness of our God!
> He is the Rock; his works are perfect,
>   and all his ways are just.
> A faithful God who does no wrong,
>   upright and just is he.
>   Deuteronomy 32:1-3, NIV

The wonder of the moment overcame Rahab, and she listened intently as the song continued. The song clearly pictured the people becoming crooked and depraved. The words described the people's disobedience and the Lord's heartbroken, but necessary, punishment: the people being turned over to their enemies. Rahab wondered if this was something that had happened in the past or was going to happen in the future. The song was sad, but all the people seemed to know it. Rahab could not imagine that the Israelite people, having heard all that they had that day, and knowing that song, could ever turn away from the Lord. She felt it would have to be many generations before all this could come to pass.

Joshua finished the story of Moses, and dismissed the people to go back to their tents. Rahab was very thoughtful as they walked back. She had a lot of answers, but she had a lot of new questions, too.

Salmon looked at her inquiringly, "Do you want to talk about it?"

"I do have some questions. But I want to think about this some more first."

※

After they had eaten their Sabbath evening meal, Rahab finally spoke up. "I've been thinking about that commandment, honor your father and mother. I'm not sure I know how to obey that one. What are your thoughts on it?"

Salmon was very quiet.

"I'm sorry; I didn't mean to bring up anything unpleasant for you."

He shook his head, "No, no, I'm all right. I just have so much emotion when I think about that commandment. You can't possibly understand until your parents have died, as mine have."

"Truly, I am sorry."

"I want to talk about it, if you don't mind listening to me."

"I would like to know."

"I just wish I had realized while they were still alive how special and precious they were. I obeyed fairly well, and I really admired them both; yet when they died, I realized that they were so closely intertwined with my life that they could not leave me without tearing me up inside. Both my parents died on the same day. I guess for them going together was a blessing, not having to mourn the other, but I was devastated."

"How did they die?"

"They died in the plague over the Moabite seduction. Some of our men were seduced by Moabite women and began to worship Baal Peor. A plague broke out in the camp. My parents were among the 24,000 that died. Not everyone that died was guilty of the sin, but I think the Lord was so incensed at the deliberate disobedience that he was willing to wipe out the whole nation. I had just come weeping to the tabernacle to tell about their deaths when the Simeonite clan leader Zimri strolled by with his lover, Cozbi. I think my parent's deaths may have been the breaking point for my younger cousin Phinehas. He killed Zimri and Cozbi by sending a spear through both of their bodies in their tent after they blatantly flaunted their relationship in front of the whole assembly like that. His action saved the nation, for the plague stopped spreading then. Phinehas loved my parents. A lot of people did."

"You obviously have no trouble obeying this commandment to honor your parents. I have never heard you say anything but praise of them."

"That is the horrible thing. I didn't praise and honor them when they were alive. As they got older, they made more mistakes, and that caused me to think less of them sometimes. I kept thinking that they ought to be perfect, but how could they be? Not that I said anything dishonoring aloud—I knew better than that—but I didn't recognize all they had done right." He showed her a ring that he wore on his little finger. "This was my mother's ring. It reminds me of them and how much I owe them."

Rahab reached over and gently touched his shoulder in a comforting motion. He looked up in gratitude and continued, "Sometimes we expect too much of our parents and don't realize that they are human beings. Yet they deserve the honor of their children, for their children owe them their very lives. I'm not explaining this very well, but I think that I didn't begin to grow up myself until I accepted my parents' humanity and then gave them credit for doing so much right in spite of that humanity. I only wish I had understood all this while they were still alive and could have told them myself how much I admired them, how much I loved..." His tears were choking him. Rahab wanted to wrap her arms around him to comfort him. Instead, she moved a little closer and put her hands on his, letting her tears flow, too.

That night as she lay on her pallet, she thought about that conversation. Though her parents weren't the outstanding people that Salmon's had been, given her parents' backgrounds and their culture, they had been good to her. Many parents in Jericho did much worse. And she believed that her parents had always cared about her. She recognized that until she could forgive her parents for their failures toward her and begin to show them respect, she would not have complete peace with the Lord. "Salmon, are you asleep?" she whispered softly.

"No, I'm still awake."

"You go visit my parents often, don't you."

"Yes, I do. Why?"

"The next time you go, would you tell my parents that I'm sorry for all I've done to cause them grief through the years and that I appreciate the sacrifices they've made for me?"

"I'll be glad to carry that message." Rahab thought she could hear a smile in his voice.

DAY 22

The cloud had not moved the next day. It appeared that they might settle here near Mount Ebal for some time. Salmon and Rahab ate a leisurely breakfast and just talked.

"Listening to you tell about your parents yesterday made me curious about your life as a child. What was it like growing up in a camp in the desert?"

"Very much like this camp. As a child, I found it fascinating. I was interested in every aspect of the camp—the animal pens on the outskirts, the women with their water pots heading to and from the oasis, the small cooking fires—but most of all, I was fascinated by the tabernacle. Something was always happening at the tabernacle. At night it glowed with the fiery presence of the Lord, and in the daytime, a cloud covered it. Levites moved about, and animals made sounds."

"What did you do as a child?"

"Even when I was only a little boy, I had to take care of my own sleeping mat every day by straightening and rolling it into a tight roll. We kept them that way during the daytime because everything in the tent was stored to be ready for travel at a moment's notice.

"Oh, so that explains it."

"Explains what?"

"Why you always roll up your bedding that way every morning."

"Another mystery solved!" He chuckled. "I also had to pick up manna. I hurried every morning to get my basket to go out to gather the daily supply. Many others would be there already, bent over picking up the tiny white pieces. Mother helped me, as soon as she returned with water from the oasis. We had servants, but my mother was a firm believer in work as a way of building character. Together we would finish gathering the three omers of manna, which made the right amount for our family.

Day 22

We would then return to our tent to begin preparing the morning meal. Mother crushed the manna with a mortar to form flour."

"What kinds of foods did she make from it?"

"Mostly, we had manna porridge, though some people made a kind of flat cake from the manna. We could eat the manna straight, too. Because we had animals, I usually had goat's milk and cheese. But we rarely ever had fruits or vegetables of any kind."

"But you didn't know anything different."

"Right. Anyway, Father soon would join us for breakfast. Then I watched the phenomenon that I never tired of seeing, the manna evaporating off the ground as the sun rose higher in the sky." He stopped. "Am I including too much detail?"

"No, I like knowing what your life was like then."

"I'm glad you care."

"What kind of child were you?"

"I imagine I was fairly normal. When my mother scolded me for not doing my chores before I wandered off, I would start to protest, but then she gave me the look which meant I was about to hear what the Lord had to say about disobedient children, so I did what she said. Although I acted submissive, I did not feel that way."

"You were a typical boy, then. My little brothers are just like that sometimes."

"Were you a good girl?"

"Of course, always." This she said primly, but with a twinkle in her eye. "So you had a fairly happy childhood, then."

"Yes, a lot of love filled our tent. But some things happened to all of Israel during my growing up years that have affected me deeply. Some I will never forget."

"What, for example?"

"The most dramatic one was the Kohathite revolt."

"I'm not sure I've heard about this. Could you tell me the story?"

"The first day started rather normally. My mother was looking for me to remind me to do my chores. That day, she found me looking with rapt attention at the Levite workmen as they assembled the outer court framework of the tent of meeting. She had to walk all the way from our tent with the tribe of Judah through the Levite camp, which lay west of us, to my Uncle Aaron's tent where I was standing and holding the hand of Aunt Elisheba.

"She hurried up to us and started to apologize for letting me get in the way, but Aunt Elisheba just smiled. 'It has been a long time since my

The Cord

own sons would let me hold their hands,' she said. A look of sadness crossed her face."

"She was remembering the death of your cousins, wasn't she?"

"I would imagine so. Aunt Elisheba was devout, but she seemed to worry a lot, especially when Uncle Aaron and my cousins Eleazar and Ithamar were doing their duties in the tabernacle.

"I followed my mother back to our tent, but as soon as I finished doing my chores, I begged to go back to the tabernacle, and my mother said I could. Something was always happening at the tabernacle. But that day, what was happening was ugly. As I drew nearer to it, I heard the sound of angry men.

"Father was there by my Aunt Elisheba's tent. I told you that they were brother and sister?"

Rahab nodded, not wanting to interrupt the flow of the story again.

"I walked quickly until I was even with the tent where Aunt Elisheba still stood facing the tabernacle and wringing her hands. "I said, 'Aunt Elisheba, what is happening?'

"'I do not know for sure, but Korah came a few minutes ago leading a lot of men with him. I have been trying to hear, but I can't. Oh, Nahshon, I'm so worried, you know...'

"Father wouldn't let me stay. He told Aunt Elisheba to take me back to my mother. 'I will find out what is going on, and I will come and tell you. I promise.'

"I didn't want to leave, and I could tell that Aunt Elisheba didn't want to take me, but both of us knew we had no choice when Father spoke to us like that.

"We reluctantly made our way back to the tent where Mother still worked, unconscious of the crisis. She looked up with concern as we came into the tent. 'Is something the matter?'

"Aunt Elisheba told her about Korah. She started crying and said, 'Oh, Tarah, I am so afraid. What if Aaron or my two boys are in danger?'

"Mother took her into her arms and tried to comfort her as if she were a child.

"I sat wide-eyed and watched the two women. When Aunt Elisheba was calmer, she told what Father had said. Mother said briskly, 'Well, meanwhile let's have some food and wait for Nahshon to come.' She moved outside to the boiling pot and after stirring it, moved it off of the fire. She dipped out bowls of manna porridge for the three of us. I ate hungrily and drank the goat's milk. Then without being told, I moved into inner room of the tent and spread out my pallet for my afternoon nap. I was just about to drift off to sleep when I heard my father talking quietly to the women in the outer room.

Day 22

"'Yes, Korah is the ringleader. He, On, and the Reubenites Dathan and Abiram have incited a rebellion against Moses and Aaron among 250 of the assembly leaders.'

"'Oh, no,' gasped Aunt Elisheba. 'How can Aaron and Moses maintain control against so many?'

"'Not so fast. Moses said that he is going to let the Lord himself choose who is holy enough to come near him. He called for Dathan and Abiram to come to the assembly, but they refused. Moses was very angry. He told Korah and the other Kohathites to come tomorrow to the tabernacle with censer and incense. Aaron is to appear, too.'

"Aunt Elisheba began to moan softly and rock back and forth. 'Oh, God of our fathers, Miriam is dead, and you have taken away two of my sons. Must you take my other sons and my husband, too.'

"Father interposed, 'Aaron has done nothing wrong. He need not fear if he is innocent of disobedience. You know how the Lord has blessed and proven his choosing over and over. We just need to trust in the Lord's justice.'

"Gradually Aunt Elisheba calmed down some. She rose and said, 'I must return home now. Aaron will be wanting his midday meal. Please come to our tent for the evening meal. We would like to have you near us.'

"Father agreed and Mother said, 'I will bring the rest of our manna and a jar of water.'

"'Thank you; we will see you then.' Quickly she slipped away.

"After that, I fell asleep. When I awoke, it was nearly time for the evening meal. I quickly rose and rolled up my pallet again. Then I went outside to look for my mother. She was just returning from the oasis with a pot of water on her head.

"She told me that we had been invited to Uncle Aaron and Aunt Elisheba's tent for evening meal. When I told her that I knew, she wanted to know what else I had overheard.

"I told her that I had heard my father tell about Moses and the men and Uncle Aaron, but I didn't really understand.

"'I'm not sure I understand either, son,' she sighed.

"Then I asked her about the reason that Aunt Elisheba was like she was, always nervous and afraid. Mother hesitated, then plunged in and explained about Nadab and Abihu. My mother seemed to want me to know this because she had always been worried when I got too close to the tabernacle. I think she thought my curiosity would get me killed."

"Any mother would who had seen what she had," Rahab said.

"That night our family took our evening meal with Uncle Aaron's family. Uncle Aaron was solemn as he raised his hands in blessing over the manna. Everyone ate quietly. Finally, Father ventured, 'What do you think will be the outcome of tomorrow's assembly?'

"Uncle Aaron reassured all of us that he had examined his conscience thoroughly and could not see that he had intentionally sinned against the Lord or against those who had accused him. He was trusting in the Lord for justice. But he mourned that again our people had rebelled against the Lord. Every time the people rebelled, a plague or fire broke out and hundreds or thousands were killed. He said, 'I do not understand why they keep testing the Lord. This time it appears to be jealousy.'"

Rahab asked, "Why were they jealous?"

"The Kohathites are also Levites, but they are not eligible to be high priests according to the Lord's instructions. They thought they should have the chance to be high priests as well," Salmon explained and then continued, "My father said, 'No doubt tomorrow we will see a sign from the Lord.'"

"Did you?"

"Yes, I will never forget what I saw. I woke early the next morning with an uneasy sense of anticipation and yet dread. I gathered manna quickly, keeping an eye out for any excitement that might come along.

"Suddenly we heard the sound we had been listening for and dreading—a single trumpet blast calling the leaders to assemble.

"Father turned toward the tabernacle. Mother caught his hand and said, 'Do be careful.'

"He replied, 'I will, my love.' I remember that scene even now as the way married couples ought to treat each other. My parents really cared about each other."

"You were blessed to have so wonderful an example of marriage in front of you all those years."

"Yes, I was. I hated to see my father go that day. After hearing about Abihu and Nadab, I was no longer as confident that our family had some special protection that kept us from losing anyone. I begged to go closer so we could see what would happen.

"I think my mother wanted to see, too. She said we could go as far as Aunt Elisheba's tent again. But she insisted that I stay right beside her, which was a good thing. Anyone wandering loose that day was not safe. Together we made our way through the camp of the Levites. Around us we could hear people complaining:

'Who do Moses and Aaron think they are, anyway?'

'Why should they always tell us what to do?'

'I'll go back to Egypt before I'll follow them one more day.'

"I was shocked at the sound of the angry voices.

Day 22

"Aunt Elisheba stood by her tent and barely acknowledged our presence. She was staring intently at the entrance to the tabernacle where 250 men stood holding incense censers in their hands. Moses and Aaron stood together flanked by Eleazar and Ithamar. Aaron also held a censer.

"Suddenly blinding light blazed from the tabernacle. We heard a roaring sound that sounded almost like a human voice. As we watched, Moses and Aaron fell face down before the tabernacle crying out. At first I thought they had died, but then their voices could be heard pleading for mercy for the Israelite people.

"Moses jumped up, all at once, and walked quickly south from the tabernacle entrance. As he went, we could hear him shouting, 'Move away from the tents of Korah, Abiram and Dathan; don't even touch anything of theirs or you will be swept away.'

"I could see all the families of Abiram and Dathan gathering outside the tents. They hadn't come to the assembly because they were protesting Moses.

"Moses shouted out, 'This is how you will know that the Lord has sent me to do all these things and that it was not my idea. If these men die a natural death and experience only what usually happens to men, then the Lord has not sent me. But if the Lord brings about something totally new, and the earth opens its mouth and swallows them, with everything that belongs to them, and they go down alive into the grave, then you will know that these men have treated the Lord with contempt'" (Num. 16:28-30, NIV).

"What happened?"

"As soon as he finished speaking, the ground began to shake and a loud rumbling burst out as the earth split open directly beneath the tents of Dathan, Abiram, and Korah. You have been in a similar experience when Jericho's walls fell. It felt like that to us, but for those tents, it was worse. Women and children screamed and clutched for handholds that were not there. The goat hair tents collapsed, and pots broke as everything and everyone in that part of camp tumbled into the fissure. But as suddenly as it had opened, the earth closed back, burying them alive. I was flabbergasted. I had wanted to see the glory of the Lord, but this was terrifying to a small boy, especially when other people were running by saying we would all be buried alive.

"Then in the midst of the panic came another sound, even more terrifying than the earthquake."

"What was it?"

"An intense light, brighter than lightning, flashed from the inner sanctuary with a thunderous clap. When my dazzled eyes adjusted, I saw before me the charred bodies of the 250 leaders holding their censers."

"What about your uncle and cousins?"

"I'm sure Aunt Elisheba was wondering that, too. But Mother quickly said, 'No, look, Aaron and Eleazar and Ithamar are still standing over there.' She pointed to the tabernacle entrance.

"Aunt Elisheba's knees gave way beneath her even as she cried out, 'Oh, praise the Lord!'

"I was trembling beside my mother, watching for what would happen next. Moses moved back over to Uncle Aaron and quietly gave an order. We watched as Eleazar began to move among the charred remains of all those leaders of Israel, picking up the hot censers without touching the bodies, and taking the censers out of the camp.

"Aunt Elisheba told me that he was recovering the censers for tabernacle use, but he could not touch any dead bodies, for he must not defile himself.

"Then Moses explained this to all the people and told them that they could claim their dead. I hoped that people would quit rebelling so there wouldn't be any more death like that, but I could hear deep mourning all around me. The 250 men were well loved. I also heard muttering about how Moses and Aaron had killed the Lord's people, and this confused me. It seemed to me that Moses and Uncle Aaron hadn't killed anyone.

"The next day, the muttering had grown to defiance. Again the whole assembly gathered outside the tent of meeting. The cloud settled over the tent and Aaron and Moses moved in front—seemingly alone against all this anger and hatred.

"Then, suddenly again, Moses and Uncle Aaron fell on their faces as they had the day before. I thought that after what had happened when they did that the day before, I should prepare for something extraordinary."

"Was it fire or earthquake again?"

"No, this time it started slowly. As we waited, a woman screamed that her baby had died in her arms. Nearby an older man toppled over. People around him checked and saw that he, too, was dead. Men clutched their throats, and glassy-eyed, they crashed to the ground. This was happening so fast that people stood immobilized in shock and fear, wondering who would be next.

"Uncle Aaron jumped up and ran into the tabernacle. He returned shortly carrying a censer, the same as he had carried the day before with the sweet smell of burning incense in it. He dashed through the crowd calling out, 'Lord, please forgive the people for their rebellion.' He headed straight for the place where people were falling dead and ordered the living people to move aside as he ran between them and the dead bodies with his censer. Wherever he went, the dying stopped, but it

Day 22

took thirty minutes for him to reach the edge of the crowd. By that time, the number of dead people lying about was tremendous.

"Uncle Aaron looked sad to me as he made his way back to where Moses stood at the tabernacle entrance. Moses began talking to the people. 'This is a terrible tragedy. My heart aches for you. But it all could have been avoided if you had just acknowledged that the Lord has chosen Aaron to be your priest. I know that you are disappointed about not getting to the Promised Land, but that, too, is a consequence of your choices. The Lord wants to bless you, but he will do it on his terms, not yours. Now, the Lord has instructed me to collect a staff from each of the twelve tribal leaders. Bring them to me here with your name carved on them. The staff that sprouts overnight will belong to the man God has chosen to lead Israel.'

"I saw my father looking down at his walking staff. He had had it for twenty years, and it was a good sturdy one. Slowly he took out a flint knife and began carving his name in the side as I watched. Then with other leaders, he took the staff up to Moses. Moses waited until he had all twelve, including Aaron's. Then he went into the tabernacle and laid them inside.

"The next day, the trumpet sounded twice for an assembly of all the people. The people came slowly. Most of them had spent the night helping to prepare graves for the nearly 15,000 people who had perished over the two days. Many were in deep mourning, for very few families had been spared a death.

"I was heavy-hearted. Two of Father's closest friends had died. Again I was aware that I was not protected from the Lord's wrath if he decided to act.

"As we approached the tabernacle, Father moved on ahead to the front of the assembly. There stood Moses holding the twelve staves in his hands. One by one he called out the names on each staff, and the leader came forward to claim his.

"When he said, 'Nahshon,' Father went forward and claimed his staff, which was still in the same condition as before. As he backed away, I noticed a small tree behind Moses and wondered about it.

"Then Moses reached behind him, grasped the little rootless tree in his hands, and brought it forward. "Aaron," he read.

"Uncle Aaron stepped forward, but Moses did not give the staff to him. Instead, he said, 'Look at this staff. It has not only sprouted, it has budded, leafed, blossomed, and produced some almonds overnight before the Lord. This is the Lord's sign that Aaron is his chosen priest. This staff will remain in the sanctuary as a reminder to the rebellious.'

"Then beginning with my father and the other twelve leaders, everyone fell on his or her knees before Aaron and Moses, begging them for protection against the wrath of the Lord. I don't think I have ever been the same after those four days. I had learned that seeing the glory and power of the Lord might be dreadful as well as amazing."

As he stopped speaking, Salmon looked at Rahab and was surprised to see tears running down her cheeks. "What's this? Are you okay?"

Rahab dabbed at her tears with her hands. "I'm sorry. I just can't stop picturing a little boy watching all this horror and trying to make sense of it."

"It means a lot to me that you care," Salmon said warmly.

Suddenly they both realized that they were still sitting over the remains of breakfast, and noon was past. As Rahab cleared away and Salmon went out to check with his men about the animals, he reflected that her tears were a promising sign in their relationship. It still amazed him how much she enjoyed hearing about the Lord and his people.

Later that evening after dinner, she said, "It seems sad to me that you spent all the best years of your youth wandering around in the desert when you could have already been in Canaan."

"Yes, I have felt that way many times, but lately I have changed my mind."

"Really, why?"

"If we had come into Canaan forty years ago, we would have destroyed Jericho without your help. You would never have been born, and I would have grown up and never known you. For me the forty years of wandering are worth it if I get to have you in the end."

Rahab ignored the personal message in this and pounced on the idea behind it. "Are you saying that God chose to delay your entrance into Canaan just so I might be saved from death in Jericho?"

Salmon seemed to be considering this idea. "Not exactly. I think he delayed because our people sinned by not following Moses and trusting God, but he must have known even then that you would be born, and he had all this planned."

"That idea is almost too big for me to comprehend. I mean it seems to imply that God gives us the choice to do the wrong thing, but he uses the results of that to accomplish his purposes anyway."

"Well, he is God, isn't he?"

"Yes, he is."

DAY 23

Over breakfast the next morning, Rahab said, "You told me once that the Lord created the earth and sky. Did he create people, too?"

"Yes, but in this order: The first day, he created light and day and night. The second day, he created the sky and something that is hard to describe—an expanse of water with land beneath it. On the third day, he gathered the waters into seas and made dry ground. On the same day he made vegetation. The fourth day, he formed the sun, moon, and stars and started them marking days and seasons. On the fifth day, fish and birds were created. On the sixth day, he made the land animals, and then finally man."

"On the seventh day, he rested?"

"Yes, you remembered."

"When he created man did he create woman, too?"

"He created woman, but not out of the dust as he did man."

"How did he create woman?"

"Well, after he had created man and named him Adam, he looked about and decided that it wasn't right for the man to be alone." At this statement, Salmon looked meaningfully at Rahab.

Ignoring his look, she said composedly, "So how did he make her?"

"He made Adam fall into a deep sleep. While he was asleep, the Lord took one of Adam's ribs and formed the woman out of that. When the Lord brought the woman, Eve, to him, Adam was delighted. He said, 'This is bone of my bone and flesh of my flesh' (Gen. 2:23, NIV). The law includes a statement that is one of the first commandments in the law and explains why the Lord hates adultery."

"What are the Lord's words?" Rahab eyes sparkled while she leaned forward in eagerness.

Day 23

"'For this reason a man will leave his father and mother and be united to his wife, and they will become one flesh' (v. 24). I think God is saying marriage should be permanent and the start of a new family."

"Yes, the Lord would have a perfect vision of how life ought to be. That is what I wanted when I was a girl. I wish... but why wish. I cannot change my past."

Salmon jumped at this chink in her armor. "No, you cannot change your past, but you have the opportunity for a fresh start as though none of that happened. Rahab, I desire to be your husband exclusively for the rest of my life."

She looked at him, but said nothing.

"I know you think I want you only for your body. I do believe that becoming one flesh is a very important part of marriage, but I really want your companionship. It isn't right that I should be alone, and the Lord has brought you to me."

"Is there no chance that you might change your mind?"

"No, of course not. Why would you ask that question?"

"I just know that the law about marrying a captive says you can send her away if you are displeased with her."

Salmon stared for an instant. "No, I will never send you away! How can I give you confidence that this relationship is permanent?" His voice betrayed his frustration.

When she didn't respond at all to what he had said, Salmon became discouraged. With a sigh, he went out to help his men with the animals. Rahab spent the rest of the morning spinning more wool. Several days had passed since she had had a chance, and she wanted to finish the blanket for Shamar's baby before the little girl was grown. She avoided thinking about Salmon and his desire to marry her by concentrating on what he had said about Adam and Eve that morning. She had many questions as a result of that conversation.

When he came in at noon, she had prepared a good dinner for him. As he ate the leek soup and bread, she asked, "Do you remember the talk we had about Adam and Eve earlier today?"

"Yes," he looked at her intently. "Why do you ask?"

"I was thinking about another time when we talked about how people seem bent on disobeying God's laws, even though their lives are better when they do obey. How about Adam and Eve? If God created people, why would he make us naturally bad?"

"Actually, they were good when they were created; the Lord said that his creation of man was 'very good'" (Gen. 1:31, NIV).

"So what happened to people?"

"Did I tell you that he set them into a beautiful garden called Eden?"

"I don't remember that."

"Well, in that garden was a tree called the knowledge of good and evil. The Lord forbad them to eat its fruit. He allowed them any other fruit in the garden. And at first, they were very careful about not going near the tree."

"But only at first?"

"Another character comes in here. The wicked one came to Eve in the form of a serpent and tempted her to eat the fruit by saying that it would make her like God. Eve listened to the evil one and ate the fruit. She got Adam to eat some, too."

"That was the first act of disobedience."

"Right, and for that they were given the sentence of death. They did not die immediately, but before that time, they weren't going to die at all. They also were removed from the garden and given the task of earning their bread through hard work."

"So from the very beginning, the result of disobedience to the Lord is death."

"Yes, and the curse that resulted from that first disobedience has been on man ever since. Man is like Adam and Eve, easily persuaded to do the wrong thing even when it is not in his best interest."

"Or hers. So I guess that means that all the bad things that happen are a result of sin?"

"I'm not so sure about that connection. What about the death of my parents? They were righteous people."

"Yes, I see that, but the curse made it so that everyone dies eventually, right?"

"Yes, that is the hardest aspect of God's justice for me to accept."

"Death?"

"Yes."

"Is it not something that God addresses in his law?"

"Well, I know that God never dies. And when someone righteous died, like Abraham or Isaac, the law says he was 'gathered to his people' (Gen. 25:8, NIV). That seems to indicate some kind of reunion with loved ones."

"So you may be reunited with your parents someday?"

"Yes, if I am righteous enough."

"Perhaps death is not a bad thing to someone on the other side of it."

"What do you mean?"

"Death seems horrible to us because we see it from this side. We see the pain and suffering, the terror and decay. We feel the separation from loved ones deeply. But God seems to be beyond death. So when we get to the other side of death with him, we may see death differently."

Day 23

"Perhaps you are right. I'll think about it anyway. I am going back to the fields again. Several lambs are being born right now."

"Salmon, before you go, I have a question for you." He turned to her, smiling openly. "Yes?"

"Could you ask Elias to put up the loom for me here? I want to work on the blanket some more."

"I will do that." He started out the doorway of the tent, then he turned and said, "Thank you for asking me, Rahab." Something about the gentleness of his tone made her sorry that she had ever doubted his generosity.

She had just gotten to the loom again when Acsah came. She said in Hebrew, "I thought we might have another language lesson. Let's speak only Hebrew. If you don't understand something, I will explain. If I have trouble understanding you, we will work on your pronunciation."

"That would be great. You see that I have my loom up now. Would you like to practice your spinning while we visit?"

"I will." She picked up the spindle and began working the wool, while Rahab continued her weaving on the loom, which was just outside the opened tent.

Acsah said, "I've noticed that my clothes are starting to look different, more used. I think that the Lord is allowing our clothes to wear out. I will need to know how to weave if we have to replace our clothing now."

"That makes sense. Salmon's sandal broke on our walk here. He said that was the first time he had had any problems with them."

"I'm afraid we got rather spoiled in the desert."

"What word did you just use?"

"*Spoiled?*" She explained the meaning in Canaanite and had Rahab repeat it. "I wonder if I'll ever become skilled at making cloth."

"You will. I enjoy weaving and making things."

"Say *weaving* this way." She said the word and had Rahab repeat it several times. "You are right about wanting to make things. When I was little, I liked to make children from sticks and vines. I would sometimes dress those with rags from our tent. I always wanted to have the chance to have real children and make clothes for them." She looked down then with a sigh.

"Are you discouraged about Othniel?"

"Yes, I know my father would banish him from my sight if he knew how I felt. But I must be patient."

"Perhaps the Lord will grant you this desire. He has met so many of my needs and wants that I'm sure he would do this for you, too."

"Rahab, I've been thinking about our conversation the other night. What you said about love—that we would not find sacrificing and obeying the law tedious if we really loved the Lord—made a lot of sense to me. You keep talking about love in relationship to God. Do you really think that we have to love him? Isn't it enough if we do what he says?"

"I'm sorry; I am having trouble following you, and I think this is very important."

Acsah repeated all she had said in Canaanite.

Rahab looked thoughtful for a moment. Was it enough to simply obey, or did the Lord want more than that? Something stirred in the back of her brain. "Didn't Joshua say a commandment about loving the Lord? I thought I heard something like 'Love the Lord with all of your being.'"

"Hear O Israel... the Lord is one. Love the Lord your God with all your heart and with all your soul and with all your strength" (Deut. 6:4-5, NIV). Acsah quoted almost mechanically, as though she had been drilled in this verse many times. "Why didn't I see that myself? I know the law, but not how to love the Lord like you do. I mean, I've always tried to follow the laws carefully, and, in my mind, the Lord is the true God and worthy—but I don't know how to feel love for him."

"How did you fall in love with Othniel?"

"I noticed his kindness. As I grew up, we started talking to each other a lot. I started thinking about him when we weren't together. Later, I could see how much other people admired him, which made me admire him more. Then others told me all the stories of what he did in battles and as a spy. I don't know exactly; it just grew the more I knew him and thought about him."

"I think the answer to your question about loving God is in there somewhere. You try to know the Lord better every day. If you know him better, you will learn to love him more."

"How do I know him better?"

"Well, knowing his law and meditating on it is a good starting point. I believe that's the purpose of the Sabbath—to give us time off to really concentrate on knowing him. Think about all he has done for you as a people. You can see his care over and over in your people's history—like the manna and shoes. But for me, all he has done for me personally helps me to love him. Since I decided to have faith in him, he has changed my whole life for the better. The more I think about that, the more I love him. And every day, he gives me new reasons to know and love him."

"That makes sense, I think."

They continued to work for a while longer, but both were deep in thought, so the language lesson suffered. Acsah said quietly, "I'd better go now. I will think more about what you have said."

Day 23

"I have faith that the Lord wants you to know him better and love him more."

Later when Salmon came in from working with his animals, he found a very pensive Rahab. "You seem to have a lot on your mind."

"Yes, Acsah was here for a while, and we had a very unsettling conversation."

"Unsettling in what way?"

"We were talking about the law."

"Oh."

"It sometimes seems to me that you Israelites pick and choose which commands to obey."

"What do you mean?"

"Everyone would notice if you worked on the Sabbath or stole something or made an idol, so you are very careful about obeying those, but you seem somewhat more careless with ones that have to do with the mind or emotions."

"Which laws are you thinking of?"

"Well, you admitted yourself to me once that you've never been careful about the law about coveting. And I know from my own experience that Israelites are not always kind to aliens."

"True. I see what you mean. But to be honest, the law states no penalties for breaking one of those laws. They would be very hard to enforce."

"Doesn't the Lord know when they are broken?"

"Well, yes, he does." He paused a minute before saying somewhat testily, "Are there any others that you want to point out?"

"Yes, the command, 'Love the Lord your God with all your heart and with all your soul and with all your strength' (Deut. 6:4-5, NIV). Why have you never quoted that one to me? It seems terribly important."

"Well, it doesn't seem to come up in everyday living very much. And besides, how can a person be commanded to love someone? Love isn't something that you can just decide to do, is it?"

"No, it isn't."

The silence between them was eloquent.

Rahab moved to put out a simple supper for them of wheat bread and cheese. After a few minutes, she spoke into the charged atmosphere, "What I don't understand is how you could have been traveling in the presence of the Lord all these years and not love him just from being with him."

"I think you are very unfeeling about the things I have experienced. If you knew all that I had seen and felt, you would doubt God's goodness, too." There, he had said what he never meant to say.

"Do you really doubt that he is good?"

"Oh, I suppose not, but sometimes his judgments are so harsh. I have always been terribly afraid of the Lord and what he would do to me if I didn't obey."

"Why?"

"Well, you know part of it. I've had my cousins struck down for using unholy fire in their incense burners; I've seen men swallowed up by the earth for rebellion and disobedience. I've seen plagues wipe out thousands because they complained. My father's generation did not get to come into the Promised Land at all because they failed to enter it when God told them to." He stopped, lost in thought.

Rahab murmured, "Tell me more about your father."

"My father was a great man. He was strong and intelligent, a mighty leader. He could also be so gentle and kind. He noticed everything that concerned my mother and me, even though he was busy with all his responsibilities.

"I remember when he came to the tent one morning when we had settled after a journey of several days. He had been organizing the animals and seeing to the comfort of the widows. He asked if I would like to go with him for an inspection tour of the camp. Of course, I was thrilled, and, in a way, I think my mother was, too. I was quite a handful at that time. So he made both of us happy because she got a break from me, and I got a chance to be with my father. He took me up on his broad shoulders, and we started out.

"Slowly, we worked our way up and down the rows of brown goat hair tents speaking to this man or that, listening to complaints and checking on conditions. From the top of my father's shoulders, I could see above the tents in many directions, but beyond them were more tents. As you know, it takes a lot of tents to house more than 600,000 men and their families.

"I was thrilled to be seen with my father. He was 51—a little old to have a firstborn son of 5, but young for the responsibilities that were his. As head of the tribe of Judah, he was leading what was by far the largest of the 12 tribes. Judah's job was to lead all the other tribes when traveling, even ahead of the Levites. Father was responsible for the 74 judges within the tribe who mediated conflicts and settled disputes. The people of Judah looked up to him, especially since his sister was married to the high priest. But no one admired him more than I did." Tears sprang into his eyes, "I miss him."

Day 23

"Did you obey your father?"

"Of course, I did. Whatever he said, I did without question."

"Why?"

"Because he was my father, because I loved him, because I believed he knew what was best for me. Why are you asking me these questions?"

"Were you afraid of your father?"

"No, not really. I mean, I might have been when I was younger, before I understood why he told me to do certain things and before I knew that he loved me."

Rahab stopped asking questions and sat quietly looking at Salmon, and as she sat, a light began to dawn in his face.

"You think that the Lord is like my father, don't you?"

She nodded.

"But Rahab, how could the Lord be like my father? My father punished me, yes, but he also loved me and took care of me and spent time with me and gave me everything I needed."

"And the Lord has not done those things for you? What about the Red Sea and manna and the pillar of fire and cloud? What about clothes and shoes that didn't wear out and the defeat of all your enemies?"

"I never thought of all that as coming from love. I only thought of it as an agreement. We did our part and he did his."

"So you thought of it almost like an alliance rather than a relationship?"

"I wouldn't have said it quite that way, but I suppose so."

"I think that is sad."

"Why?"

"Because you are missing the best part of having the Lord as your God."

"Perhaps I am."

The quiet between them lasted for a long time as Rahab cleared away the supper things and spun some more wool by the lamplight. Salmon sighed deeply, and said, "I think I'll go on to sleep."

Rahab nodded and put away the spinning before moving silently into the inner room.

DAY 24

Salmon woke the next morning knowing something about the conversation from the day before had disturbed him, and he thought about how testy Rahab had been. Just when he thought she was getting closer to him, something came up about the law that seemed to distract her away from his desire for her—to fall in love with him. He realized that time was getting short before the wedding date, and he didn't want her to enter marriage indifferent to him. Part of that fear was his feeling that he didn't know what being a prostitute had done to her. If he knew why she had become one and how that affected how she thought, maybe he could reach her heart. So he decided to dedicate the morning to finding out what he could. He broached the subject abruptly at breakfast. "I know this is a touchy subject, but I've wanted to ask you more about how you became a prostitute. Do you mind telling more about that?"

She hesitated. "You have a right to know, but the story is a hard one to tell." She stopped and seemed to be considering how to begin. "In Jericho, prostitution was common. As I've told you before, Ashtoreth actually required temple prostitution as part of the ceremonies for fertility, but I was not one of those women. I was just a common prostitute, despised by all women in the city."

"Did your parents choose that for you?"

"No, not exactly. Let me see. I guess I should start at the beginning. I was only 15 when I was married. I had thought before that I would be grateful to my parents for getting me a husband and that I would be happy and excited about that."

"Are you happy and excited now?" interrupted Salmon.

"Not in the same way that I would have been as a young girl. Why do you ask?"

"I'm sorry. Continue with your story."

Day 24

"I knew that Mother was concerned about my future. I had been causing too much comment for this to be a simple matter. As a child I had attracted attention from the men of Jericho. And at 15 even the loose shifts I wore could not conceal the fact that I was becoming a young woman."

"Nor the rough woolen garment I have supplied for you, in spite of the Lord's intention."

"Hush, I'm not finished with my story. Anyway, we lived so far out on our small farm that none of us went into Jericho very often. That was good because, although my father was a fairly good father and husband at home, when he went into town, he would often be tempted into drinking too much. Then he would waste what would have provided us with a better living.

"After I reached my 15th birthday, my father could scarcely walk down a street in Jericho without being offered a drink and the possibility of negotiations over bride prices. For a man addicted to the wineskins, this was a heady time, and he had put off many different men hoping that the drinks would keep coming and the price go higher. We were always so poor that my desire was to have a husband who would be rich enough to make me secure and also generous enough to help my family."

"Well, haven't I?"

"Haven't you what?"

"Haven't I made you secure and helped your family."

Rahab smiled at his comical look. "We aren't even married yet."

"No, but we will be soon, and I want to meet all your requirements for a husband."

"Are you going to let me tell this story?"

He hung his head in mock shame, and she smiled again. "Well, the husband my father accepted was rich enough, but he didn't meet any other requirements as far as I was concerned. I was not at all happy with my father's choice. I still remember when he told me about it. He had two good offers. One offer was that I could be a temple prostitute."

"Your own father would be willing to make you a prostitute?"

"Well, he would have been exempted from temple taxes, and would have had a certain amount of prestige in the community."

"Our law forbids fathers from letting their daughters become prostitutes."

"I think that is a marvelous law. No man should allow his daughter to become a prostitute."

"What was the other offer?

"I could marry a rich man named Ambaal. I already knew that Ambaal was a cruel, self-centered man, but I had always wanted to be someone's wife, not a prostitute. The marriage feast took place only a week or two after I first heard about it. I spent the last few days working hard to finish the linen for my own wedding garment. Ambaal came to our house when our betrothal was announced, but his eyes on me were those of a man looking over a new purchase with a possessive air. I don't think he saw me as a fellow human being—more like a new cow or wineskin from which he anticipated pleasure, but for which he felt nothing.

"My mother tried to give me advice. She told me to let him do whatever he wanted in bed. 'Men will keep you if they feel that you are always available to them. And don't expect him to be faithful; most men want to have freedom to do as they choose. He will probably feel an obligation to visit the temple of Ashtoreth some. And don't get too attached to your firstborn son. It will be wanted for sacrifice to Molech. Work hard, and don't look at other men. If you are sent away, don't try to come home. We might have to pay back the bride price, and we couldn't manage that.' My mind swirled with this advice. None of it seemed at all what I had imagined marriage to be."

"What had you imagined?"

"I had pictured a dreamy scene in which my, as yet unmet, husband and I lived in bliss, talking about love and life and everything while we worked side by side, and then lying together at night, whispering our thoughts to each other in the dark."

Salmon smiled at her, "Perhaps this husband you've dreamed of is no longer unmet."

Rahab looked startled. When she didn't say anything for a long time, Salmon asked her, "What are you thinking about?"

"I just realized how much I had lost sight of my original dreams of marriage until now. I guess I've given up hope of ever having that kind of marriage after all that has happened to me."

"What has happened to make you feel that way?"

"I think realizing that I never had seen that kind of marriage myself. I asked my mother once if Father ever showed her any affection. She said he did sometimes, but that I shouldn't count on that in my own marriage. Most of the marriages in Jericho had little to do with love or affection. She said it would cause me problems if I expected that from my husband, that I would be better off assuming that he wouldn't care very much. Men think much more about themselves than anyone else."

"Israel has many happy marriages."

"I believe you, but I am not Israelite."

"That shouldn't make any difference, should it?" Salmon pleaded. "I believe that our marriage will be different from those you have seen or experienced."

Day 24

"I am not the same girl who dreamed those dreams. So much has happened to me, starting with that wedding night."

"Was it bad?"

"So bad. When it arrived, Ambaal came to take me to his home. He had been drinking freely of the wineskins already and didn't hesitate to have some of his new in-laws' offerings, though he looked about the crowded room and less than bountiful tables with something like disdain. With me, he was a little more satisfied.

"The marriage bed was a nightmare that I would prefer to forget. As for his subsequent behavior, I knew that he was participating in the temple rites and even going to common prostitutes on a regular basis. That was bad enough, but what ruined our marriage was what I discovered when I was about eight months pregnant with our firstborn."

"What happened?"

"I had been to the well to get a jar of water. I entered the house expecting Ambaal to be out. I heard a sound and discovered Ambaal and my best friend Tyra together. I asked them what they were doing, and they didn't even have the decency to be ashamed. Tyra said she and Ambaal had always loved each other, and she hated her parents for making her marry Lem instead. Ambaal didn't deny any of this. I asked Ambaal, 'Why did you marry me if you were in love with Tyra?'

"He replied that he needed some kind of wife, and as I was the most sought-after girl in town, he had to have me. I was just something else to brag about to his friends. Meanwhile, he intended to keep up his relationship with Tyra.

"I told them that I would not accept that situation. Ambaal would have to choose between Tyra and me. As soon as I said it, I knew I had made a mistake. Ambaal simply shrugged and said, 'Tyra, of course, even if she is married to someone else. You can gather your things and go, but if you go home, I'll demand the bride price from your father. I'm sure he'll be happy to repay that.'

"I was so shocked by this turn of events that I could only go numbly to gather the few possessions I had that were really mine. I did not have much, and I couldn't have carried much even if I had. I wandered through the streets of Jericho, sick at heart. Not only had I lost my husband, I had lost my best friend as well—and I couldn't go home. I ended up in the part of the city that you said was not prosperous. There I tried to sell some things for food to an old crone, who told me that I wouldn't get much for them. She guessed my situation and suggested that my best option was to become a prostitute in her inn. I told her I would rather die. She laughed at me and told me that dying was definitely one of the options available. I sold her some of my things for a few shekels. Before I left, she said the offer was open to me at any time.

"I tried to make it on my own, but I was young and naive. For several days, I wandered about, sleeping in corners and eating sparingly. Finally one night, some thugs assaulted me. They gang-raped me and stole what was left of my things. The shock sent me into early labor. I crawled down the street until I was on the doorstep of Ashtora, the innkeeper, all my dignity and self-respect gone."

Rahab had told all of this matter-of-factly, but when she looked up at Salmon, she saw that he was stricken by what she had said. "I had no idea," he said choking. "Rahab, you don't have to live in your past anymore. That is all over now. You are among good people who will not harm you or allow harm to come to you."

"I know that. But nevertheless that past is what it is."

"Do you understand that I love you?"

She turned on him angrily. "I don't want you to love me."

"Nevertheless, I do. My love is there for the taking. Why do you resist it?"

Rahab bit her lower lip. "It's complicated. I'm not sure I understand myself."

"Can you try to understand?"

She closed her eyes then and a silence fell between them. Several minutes passed before she began to speak softly. "I am unworthy of being loved. I have been a prostitute and an idol worshiper. You should be disgusted with me and reject me."

"I love you anyway. But you know that. You have something more that you don't want to tell me."

"If I accept that you love me, I will feel that I have to give you something in return. I don't want to be indebted to anyone."

"True, I want you to love me in return, but you don't have to love me to have my love. I give it freely."

"I don't know. It would be so much simpler if I didn't have to deal with this."

Salmon didn't press her. Yet something about her demeanor gave him hope.

After lunch, he decided to check on Rahab's parents. He kept doing this from a sense of duty rather from a desire to spend time with them. He wondered as he walked if he would ever learn to like Benne, especially after what Rahab had told him that morning.

As he approached the tent, he could see that Benne had a guest. He started to turn back, but then saw that the guest was Caleb. Caleb saw him and motioned for him to join them in the large room of the tent, which was opened to the breeze.

Caleb said, "I was just telling Benne what a wonderful man your father was in Israel—a great leader of Judah."

Salmon smiled at Caleb and looked at Benne, who seemed to be studying him narrowly. "So you are some kind of prince or nobleman, is that right?" asked Benne.

"Not really, sir. We do not have that kind of hereditary system in Israel."

"But you are rich?"

"I can provide very well for your daughter."

"What I want to know is what you are going to provide for me. As her father, I think I am entitled to some kind of bride price since you have taken her away, especially since she was such a good source of income to me before."

Caleb interrupted at this point. "Benne, I have told you before, prostitution is not allowed by our law. Rahab could not practice that trade here even if Salmon were not marrying her."

Benne muttered something under his breath. Clearly, he didn't think much of such a law.

Salmon kept quiet. Caleb spoke up, "Since I am here, will you let me act as arbitrator for the two of you on this issue?"

Salmon agreed readily, but Benne hesitated. "Do we have to use the laws of Israel for deciding this?"

"We can use the Canaanite laws. I know of no specific laws for bride prices in Israel for this situation. Now, my understanding of the Canaanite law is that you receive a bride price from the bridegroom, to be saved for the bride on the death of her parents or first husband to give her something to offer her second husband. Do you still have the bride price for Rahab to give Salmon now?"

Benne began to splutter, "No, of course not. Everything was destroyed; you know that!"

"I see. I also understand that the father in Canaan is required to give a dowry to the bridegroom of property, animals or gold. Are you prepared to give a dowry?"

By now, Benne was nearly purple with rage. At this point, Salmon said quietly, "Perhaps Benne would prefer the Israelite laws concerning dowries better. The only law regards virgins. As this doesn't apply in Rahab's case, I require no dowry. However, as I value her as highly as if she were a virgin, I am willing to pay Benne a bride price for her hand of ten oxen, sixty sheep, and two sacks of Amorite gold. Will he be satisfied with that?"

The Cord

Benne gasped.

Caleb said, "I advise you to take it, Benne. You will not see so generous an offer again in Israel or Canaan for any woman from any man."

"I accept." His manner toward Salmon was already perceptibly more respectful.

Caleb then turned to Salmon and asked quietly, "Why so generous, Salmon?"

"Because Rahab is worth it."

Rahab seemed to have a lot on her mind that evening and was very quiet. After asking her so many questions about her past in the morning, Salmon felt he should leave her alone, so he didn't talk much either. He decided not to tell her about the bride price. She might not understand what motivated him. Not long after their evening meal, which was wheat bread and goat's cheese with olives, Rahab said she was tired, and she went to bed earlier than usual. Salmon followed her example soon after. He lay thinking about what Rahab had told him about her life. What horrible experiences! No wonder she had become a prostitute. And yet he sensed more that she hadn't told him. He fell asleep pondering what that might be.

The banging on the door was so violent that Rahab saw that it would not hold. Ambaal was shouting, "I'm going to get you, Rahab—you and our baby. You won't get away from me this time." The floor was shaking. She could hardly hold on to her baby and keep standing. All at once the door came crashing down. Ambaal grabbed her and the baby and started to haul them both away. She was crying, screaming, begging him to let them go. "Leave us alone..."

"Rahab, darling, it's okay." She was confused. Who was holding her? The emotions were all so real to her that she started to fight her way out of the arms that held her.

"It's me, Salmon. You are safe. I won't let anyone hurt you."

"Salmon?" She'd had a dream. It was all over. She quit fighting and began to cry. "He got through the door like I was afraid he would do that day when the walls came down, only my baby was there, and he got us, and I was terrified." Her tears became great wrenching sobs that shook her body as Salmon held her close in his arms, one hand cradling her head against his shoulder.

"There now. It's okay. I won't let anyone treat you like that ever again."

"But my baby, my precious baby."

He continued to hold her even after her sobs subsided somewhat. "Do you want to talk about it?"

Her breath still came in little gasps as she hesitated. "It's a long story."

"I want to hear anything you will tell me."

"Do you remember that I told you about going to the innkeeper Ashtora when I was in labor with my baby?"

He murmured, "Yes," squeezing her a little tighter.

"I had a healthy baby boy, in spite of all that had happened to me. Ashtora was not really such a bad person. She let me wait to start in the business until I was well-recovered from childbirth. That was kind of her, considering that she had me to board during that time, and I ate a lot to provide the rich milk that I wanted my baby to have. But in the end, I turned out to be a good investment for her. The first few months of being a prostitute were better than what I had just been through. I had my baby, a place to stay, and food—and no contact with Ambaal. I actually was pretty good at what I did."

"You said that before."

"Yes, the credit must go to Ashtora. She was experienced and gave me a lot of pointers about how to make men happy. What she told me was to make every man feel that he was the only important person at that moment. In my own mind, I would simply pretend that every man was the husband I had dreamed of and treat him accordingly. Many of the men said that if their wives were as good to them as I was, they wouldn't be coming to the north side of the city. It made me sad to think that every woman has the power to make her husband happy if she were just willing to care and make the effort."

Salmon stirred as though that thought held significance for him.

"I would not have chosen that life for myself. If only my baby could have been born into a happy, secure marriage among a people like the Israelites! But I was happy that the baby was still alive.

"One day Ashtora told me something that made me almost desperate. She said that she hadn't wanted to mention this before, but the reason that she had no children of her own in spite of her long profession was that the priests took all of her boy babies for sacrifices and none of the girls survived. She said that she had given birth to 10 children in her life. When I asked how they could justify taking children who were not firstborn, she said the priests claimed that all harlots' children are probably the firstborn by her for some man. If we tried to resist, they would threaten to ban our business, saying it competed with the temple prostitution.

"Of course, I was devastated, because that would make it nearly impossible for me to keep my baby. But I must have had some lingering hope because I was not prepared for what happened then. A loud knocking at the door interrupted our talk. I snatched up my precious six-month-old and hurried out, mentally trying to get into the role that was required of me—the voluptuous seductress—but my whole being was in an agony of protest.

"Standing at the door when Ashtora opened it was a tall man in military garb. 'I heard that you had a new girl here, really good-looking. If you'll let me examine the product, I might be interested.'

"I could hear him from the next room and froze. Ambaal! Now what could I do? If only Ashtora could get rid of him without my having to be seen.

"'I'll go get her for you. Just a moment.' Ashtora came into the back room and motioned for me to go up front.

'I can't,' I whispered. 'It's Ambaal.'

"She said, 'If I send him away, he'll just be back.'

"I knew I would have to face him sooner or later, so I handed her the baby, squared my shoulders and marched out to him with a look that was anything but seductive. He was eager until he saw who I was. He adjusted quickly and demanded to know what I had done with his firstborn. I lied, telling him that the baby had died, but he seemed to doubt my word. He wanted the baby for Molech because the king had been pressing for a sacrifice."

"What did he do next?"

"He said I had no rights because I was still his wife, so he could have me any time he wanted and without having to pay either. But I refused to give in to him. Five months of dealing with men had given me a poise that surprised even Ambaal. I simply refused to continue the conversation and walked out. But after that I was really afraid for my baby.

"I should not have been surprised when a few days later, he returned with a priest of Molech and several of his soldier friends. He demanded the child. I tried to protest, but one of the soldiers had seen the child one night and had told about it. They searched the house and found the baby."

Rahab stopped talking as her emotions started to overwhelm her again. After a minute, she gained control and could finish the story. "I tried to keep them from taking the baby; I really did! I cried and struggled, but the priest took him away, sneering at me for thinking that a common prostitute could keep a child while people in respectable homes were willing to give up their children for Molech. I would have followed, but Ambaal held me by the arms. Then he slapped me and said that I was going to stop being hysterical and attend the ceremony as the mother of the child."

"The beast."

"Yes, I thought so, too. He would not rule me any longer. Wrenching my arm free of his grasp, I ran out the door, eluding the surprised soldiers. I should have followed the priest and tried to get the baby then, but I was panicked by everything that had happened. I have never forgiven myself for not going back."

"You couldn't have stopped them, Rahab. Don't keep feeling guilty about what was outside your power."

"My head knows that I couldn't, but my heart says I should have tried. I kept running through the city gates and away until I was sure I had not been followed. I found myself in the flax field. When I stopped to catch my breath, I thought my heart would never stop pounding in my ears. Then I realized that the sound was not my heart, but the distant drums from the city beating relentlessly louder and louder. I covered my ears and shrieked aloud, 'No, no, my baby, my baby—forgive me for not saving you.' Then the drums stopped, and I knew it was all over. I must have fainted, because I don't remember what happened next."

Salmon spoke softly to her. "I'm so sorry that this has happened to you. I thought something like that must have from other things you have said, but I had no idea how horrifying it was for you."

"The guilt of it all has weighed on me ever since. I have broken all of the commandments, even 'Do not murder.'"

"Ambaal and those priests did the murdering, not you. You must forgive yourself for what happened. How I wish I could take away some of the pain you are feeling!"

"I believe you. You have comforted me, and I am grateful. But I did so want to be a mother, and now..."

"Now you will soon be married to a man who has always wanted to be a father."

She peered at him in the dark. This idea had not occurred to her yet. Then she realized that Salmon was still holding her in his arms. Instead of moving away, she nestled against his strong chest. Now that she had told him the worst, she felt different, as though some barrier had come down between them.

After a few minutes, she came to herself and pulled away from him. But she did not want to leave his arms. It took a great effort to say, "I'll be all right now. You can get back to sleep. Thank you."

Salmon slowly moved away to his side of the tent.

DAY 25

Salmon woke first. He lay on his back, staring up at the ceiling of the tent, remembering the late hours when he had comforted Rahab in her nightmare. For twenty-four days, he had been thinking and dreaming of being her husband, but now he understood the delight of having her in his arms. The longing to hold her again was so great that he almost slipped back into her part of the tent. "No," he said to himself. "I must wait another five days." The time seemed too long to endure at that moment. Impulsively, he arose and gathered his bag and equipment for hunting.

If he stayed away today, perhaps these feelings would pass, and he would have more self-control. He exited the tent and stopped Shamar as she came toward him carrying that day's fresh goat's milk. "I am going hunting. When your mistress awakes, tell her where I am and that I won't be here for most of today."

Shamar looked surprised but only nodded. She offered him some of the goat's milk, which he drank thankfully.

After he left the tent, Salmon found Othniel. "What are you doing today?"

"Nothing in particular, why do you ask?"

"It has been a while since we went hunting. Would you like to go with me?"

"Sure. But I'm surprised you feel you can leave Rahab for that long."

"I'll tell you about it later."

They spent most of the morning tramping far enough from camp to find a quiet area that looked likely for birds. Then they lay quietly in the field, waiting for the opportunity to snare or slingshot a bird. By mid-afternoon, they had four apiece. Salmon observed, "We'd better stop now and head back for camp."

Day 25

"Let's drain the blood and prepare the birds before we go. I thought you were going to tell me about you and Rahab."

"She woke up in the middle of the night with a nightmare, and I comforted her. She told me a lot more about her life, things that I suspected but didn't know for sure had happened to her. She showed more emotion last night than I have ever seen from her before."

Othniel looked up from the bird he was plucking. "How do you think this will affect your relationship?"

"I don't know exactly. She has been more open with me lately, sharing parts of her past that explain so much about who she is. She has had an awful life before now. I really understand more why she has such faith in the Lord. The contrast between life in our camp and her life in Jericho is just like day and night."

"So why did you think that this would be a good time to stay away?"

"The truth is that I am a coward. I couldn't face her after last night. My feelings are so powerful right now that I don't trust myself. I don't know how I am going to last for five more days."

"You may have a problem if she doesn't understand your need to be away."

"I know you are probably right. But you don't understand how powerful the temptation is for me right now."

"I understand more than you may think."

"I sorry, my friend. I know my situation is far better than yours. I will marry her in a few days, but you have little hope of having Acsah. Has Caleb said anything recently?"

"Two days ago, I was with him for a meal. He started talking about how disappointed he was that Achan's son was killed with Achan after the first battle of Ai. He had really hoped to arrange that marriage. He said his second choice would have been you, but that you had put yourself out of consideration by taking the prostitute into your tent. Now he says he will wait until he knows what part of the land will be allotted to him and choose then. He says he doesn't want to put any more fighting men out of commission right now. I was tempted to speak up then and ask him to consider me when the time came, but I don't want to take a chance on being banished from Acsah altogether."

"I am sorry for Achan's son, but for your sake, I'm glad that he is gone. You may still have a chance eventually."

"Perhaps. I appreciate your encouragement. I try to be patient, but like you, I feel the waiting is torture."

The Cord

They packed up their birds then, and headed back to camp, each deep in thought.

—◆—

Rahab stirred when she heard Shamar enter the tent. "Good morning," she said to Shamar cheerfully in Hebrew. She was anxious to see Salmon, unsure of how things stood between them after last night.

Shamar said, "Good morning, mistress. My master wants me to tell you that he will be away most of the day hunting. He drank some goat's milk for his breakfast."

Rahab tried not to look surprised at this news, but she felt keen disappointment. She had told him so much about her life in the middle of the night and felt vulnerable. What did his absence mean? It had not been his habit lately to go anywhere without talking to her first. She wanted to see if the closeness she had felt to him last night would hold up in the light of day. Clearly, the experience had not meant as much to him as it had to her. She would have to adjust her thinking again. He wasn't as different from other men toward her as she had hoped if he could have an experience that intense with her and then go off hunting as if nothing important had happened.

With a sigh, she decided to go about her business. If it meant so little to him, she wouldn't let it mean anything to her either. She had several projects to work on. The weaving would soon be done. She already had about two cubits of wool cloth that would be suitable for the blanket for Shamar's baby girl.

At noon, she took a break to eat some cheese and bread, then continued with her work. She was really pleased when she had reached the length she had planned and could tie off the ends of the weft threads, forming the single piece of material. When Shamar came in with a pot of bean soup and fresh bread for supper, Rahab said, "I want you to have this for your little Tirzah."

"Oh, mistress, I am so touched. Your first piece of wool weaving for us? It is too much."

"I made it for her. May it keep her warm in the cool nights and remind her of how much the Lord loves her."

"May the Lord bless you." Shamar had tears in her eyes as she took the blanket from Rahab and exited the tent.

Rahab decided not to wait for Salmon. She had no idea how long he would be gone. She ate the good food, much improved by the cooking lessons Shamar had attended. Afterwards Rahab spun more wool into thread, wondering what she would make next, perhaps another baby blanket?

Day 25

    She thought about what Salmon had said about wanting to be a father. When he had said it, she had been thrilled, but just now, she was having trouble believing in anything he had said in the night. She felt hurt and a little angry. He hadn't treated her with such indifference since her first day in the tent, and that had been the time he was out spying on Ai. What reason might he have now?

    Just when she had decided to put the spinning away and go to bed, she heard him outside. The sound of his voice stirred her strangely. It reminded her again of how she had felt the night before. She quickly rolled out her bed and lay down with the wool blanket over her. She didn't feel like talking to him right now. Her feelings were too bruised by his neglect.

    Salmon came into the tent and saw that some food had been left for him, but Rahab was not to be seen. Did she leave him? No, he saw that she was already asleep. He was a little surprised since it wasn't that late, but he assumed that the nightmare had made her weary. He was actually glad. Not seeing her tonight would make it easier to avoid temptation.

DAY 26

Salmon left right after breakfast the next morning, saying as he left, "I may not be in much today. Several more ewes have had lambs, and the work is more than my men can handle alone."

Rahab nodded without giving him any indication of her mood.

Salmon paused to look over the fluffy white hillside where his animals grazed. Getting closer, he found that his flocks were doing better than he expected. He counted 30 new lambs just since the battle of Ai. He now had several hundred sheep and goats as well as nearly a hundred oxen and donkeys. His men were skilled shepherds, fiercely loyal to their master, and very careful of his stock. Elias, the head shepherd, approached Salmon now, carrying a bleating lamb. "This one's mother rejected her. She will die unless we hand feed her."

"You tried her with other ewes?"

"Yes, not one would accept her."

"I'll take her with me now. Perhaps one of the women can save her. How are the rest?"

"All the births have been relatively easy. We had to help ewes a couple of times."

"Good. No stillbirths?"

"None, master."

"I'm glad. We have been blessed this year." He reached for the lamb. "I'll be back later."

Rahab had just settled in with some spinning when she was surprised to see Salmon coming back to the tent carrying a tiny lamb, bleating piteously. "Oh, the poor dear!" She was already heading for a bowl of goat's milk and a soft cloth.

Day 26

"Her mother rejected her, and we haven't been able to get any of the other ewes to serve as surrogate," he said, gladly surrendering the lamb to Rahab's outstretched arms.

She wound the cloth into a nipple shape and dipped it into the milk before offering it to the lamb to suckle. It latched on desperately. "Poor thing, it must have been starving."

"Probably so, but I wasn't expecting you to do this. I could ask Mahlah or Serah."

"I don't mind. You could have your midday meal from the bread and cheese back in the inner room."

"Do you want some?"

"Not right now. I'll take care of the lamb while you eat."

"You look very natural with a baby."

Rahab hesitated only for an instant before saying, "I enjoy caring for little ones."

"I hope we can have several together."

His casual taking up of the intimate conversation they had shared two nights before confused Rahab after his absence the day before. She decided to act nonchalant. "Several lambs?"

"No, I meant children of our own, Rahab."

"I see." She felt a desperate need to change the conversation to something less personal. "Don't you have to go back now to the other sheep?"

Salmon was watching her closely. "No, things are better than I expected. This lamb was the main difficulty, and you have solved that problem for now. I can stay here with you."

"Then why don't you read to me from the scrolls." She tried to hide the near panic in her voice.

Salmon retrieved the scroll and opened it. He began reading the account of the creation of Adam and Eve, putting special emphasis on the words, "So God created man in his own image,/ in the image of God he created him;/ male and female he created them. God blessed them and said to them, 'Be fruitful and increase in number; fill the earth and subdue it'" (Gen. 1:27-28, NIV). He kept reading and again emphasized, "It is not good for the man to be alone. I will make a helper suitable for him" (Gen. 2:18, NIV). And "For this reason a man will leave his father and mother and be united to his wife, and they will become one flesh" (v. 24).

"We've already talked about those verses. Can you read something else?"

"What would you like me to read?" Again, he seemed to be watching her carefully.

Rahab had never felt so uncomfortable with Salmon. She sensed that something was on his mind, but she really didn't want to know what. With great relief, she saw Acsah coming into their campsite through the opened doorway. "Acsah, look what I have."

When Acsah came over, Salmon excused himself, saying he would be back before supper.

Acsah cooed over the baby lamb and even took her turn at feeding it.

Rahab waited until she was sure Salmon was gone before asking, "Do you have any idea why Salmon has behaved so strangely around me yesterday and today?"

"What do you mean?"

"Two nights ago, I woke with a nightmare, and he came into the back room of the tent to comfort me. We had a long talk, and I told him a lot about my life—parts I had not wanted to share before. I don't know how I expected him to act the next day, but he just disappeared. He went hunting."

"Yes, I know. He took Othniel with him."

"Then today, he came into the tent with this lamb and just sat looking at me. When I asked him to read the scroll, he wanted to read only passages about Adam and Eve in the garden."

"Hmm... I don't know for sure, but your hair has grown back a lot. You are looking more attractive every day."

Rahab sighed in exasperation. "I liked it better when he just talked about the law and neutral subjects."

"It's only a few more days until your wedding. Are you ready to be his wife?"

"I'm still hoping he will let me go. Right now I feel very uncomfortable with him. I can't figure out what he is thinking."

"Would you like me to talk to him or ask Othniel to?"

"No, I think it would only make things worse. I'm sorry to bother you with my troubles."

"I don't mind. I see you have taken the blanket off the loom."

"Yes, I gave it to Shamar for baby Tirzah."

"What are you going to make next?"

"I haven't decided. What about you? Are you going to get a loom and start weaving?"

"I need to. I'm sure that now our clothes are going to fall apart all at once. I need to know how to make more."

"You can do it. I need to get a spindle of my own so you can start using this one for yourself."

"I heard that a man in the tribe of Dan makes spindles now. Perhaps you can ask Salmon about that."

Day 26

"Well, not tonight anyway."

"I understand. Don't look now, but Salmon is coming back again."

"Don't leave me, Acsah."

"I think I'd better, Rahab. You two need to work this out, whatever the problem is."

Salmon had been out with the sheep and goats again, working with his men to shepherd them to a nearby spring. While he worked he thought that he just wanted to feel as close to Rahab as they had been the other night. She had been so open to him that night. He felt that his leaving the day before to go hunting had been a mistake. She seemed more distant than ever. But how could he get close again? He felt that he really did understand her problems now. She just needed the tender love of a good man who cared about her. But he wasn't sure how to communicate that to her. With sudden decision, he told his men that he was going back to the camp.

When he went into the tent, he was surprised and pleased to see that Acsah had already gone. Rahab was busy fussing over the lamb, not looking at him at all.

"How's our baby?"

"She's fine. She has a full tummy now and I think will soon fall asleep, if she has peace enough." She said the last with an asperity that only amused the enamored Salmon. He was on a mission.

"May I sit by you?"

"If you must."

"Are you afraid of me, Rahab?" He sat down much closer to her than he ever had before.

She angled her body away from him. "Why would you ask a question like that?"

"You seem to be avoiding me today."

"I wasn't the one who went away all day yesterday."

"I'm sorry I left you. I should have stayed here. I know that now."

She didn't reply to this but continued petting the lamb.

"Are you very angry?"

"Why should I be angry? You have a right to go hunting or anywhere else you want without deference to me."

"But I have made you unhappy and that disturbs me."

"Look, you don't owe me anything. Feel free to do as you please. I have some things that I can work on here as soon as this lamb goes to sleep."

"What I please is to sit by you and talk to you."

"All right. What do you want to talk about?"

There was nothing inviting in her manner at all, but he persisted doggedly. "I want to talk about our marriage less than a week away."

"I don't need to talk about marriage. I've been married before."

"Yes, but this will be totally different."

"How do you know? I have no reason to think that marriage to you will be different from marriage to any other man."

Smiling to hide his disappointment he said, "Hasn't anything that has happened in this last three weeks meant anything to you? It has meant a lot to me."

"Just what are you getting at, Salmon?" She turned back and nearly bumped into him because he had moved so close to her.

"What I am 'getting at' is that I love you." He looked deeply into her eyes hoping to find some kind of response there, but they were veiled. Still, her nearness filled his senses.

As if by instinct, Rahab bolted, upsetting the lamb, which started bawling. She moved toward the doorway of the tent. "I find it hot in here. I'm going out to see if I can help Shamar make bread. Why don't you take the lamb to Penninah or Mahlah? I don't think I am doing much good for it." Then she was gone.

Salmon didn't see Rahab again until suppertime. By now he felt almost desperate to break through her defenses, but she gave him no opening at all. They ate the fresh bread and lentil stew in silence and ended up retiring early. Rahab fell asleep immediately, but Salmon lay awake for a long time wondering what he was going to do next. When he finally did drift off, he had vivid dreams from which he kept waking.

"Rahab, are you awake?"

"What? Who?"

"It's Salmon. I can't stand it any longer; I love you so much, and I want to hold you in my arms and..."

Rahab came fully awake as she realized that it was the middle of the night and Salmon had moved into her part of the tent. "Salmon, what are you doing?"

"I want you." He reached for her in the dark and pulled her close to his wildly beating heart.

"Salmon, we mustn't do this. The month isn't up, and we aren't married yet."

"I am going to marry you. Please don't make me wait any longer."

"If we do this thing, you will despise me in the morning. I know." By this time she had moved herself out of his grasp and away from him.

Day 26

"I could never despise you. I tell you I love you with all my heart. Don't you care about me at all? I thought you did, but I must have been wrong," he added with a bitter tone.

Rahab sighed, "Salmon, I..."

"I will not tell. No one else will know."

"The Lord will know."

"Doesn't the Lord realize how hard it is for a man to live with a beautiful woman and never get to lie with her. How can he be so cruel? I am tired of these laws that keep me from doing what I want."

"How can you call him cruel after all he has done for you? He is good."

"I don't understand his goodness when it tortures a man like this."

Rahab burst out passionately, "You don't understand the Lord's goodness because you are surrounded by it. His law is his goodness. Don't you see, if you had lived as I have where laws are devised by men with no higher motive than looking out for themselves, you would understand. His goodness keeps your marriages together, your children safe, your disputes settled fairly, your poor provided for, and your focus on something—Someone—higher than yourselves. I don't claim to know the why of every little bit of his law, but I know it is good. You are so immersed in his goodness that you think it comes from you."

Salmon was quiet now in the dark. Rahab could not tell how he felt about what she had said. Finally he said, "I won't bother you again. You can go to sleep without worrying about me."

Rahab felt her way back to her bed, assured that he had returned to the doorway. She lay quietly, but wide-awake for a long time. Then in the darkness she could hear the sound of a man's deep sobs. Her heart nearly broke, but she decided to wait to speak until morning.

DAY 27

When Rahab awoke, she sensed that something was different. Then, with a sinking feeling, she remembered what had happened. Had Salmon really tried to seduce her in the middle of the night? How would he act today after what she had said to him? She wanted to lie still and not face this day. "Oh, Lord," she prayed. "Help us to get through this. I have been through much worse things in my life, but this feels worse. Give me wisdom to know what to say to this man."

At last, she propped up on one elbow and looked around the partition across the tent, but Salmon was gone. She felt fearful at this. Would he leave her without saying goodbye? With an effort, she rose and began to roll up the beds and to prepare a morning meal. She didn't even know if he would be there to eat with her, but she had to act like things were normal.

Just when she had the barley cakes and the fruit arranged, he came in. His face looked haggard from lack of sleep and from worry. She looked calmly at him and indicated the food. Without a word, he sat down and picked up a piece of bread. She was afraid to break the silence. She wondered how long the awkwardness would last.

Finally, after they had both made a token effort at eating, he looked up and spoke. "I despise myself this morning."

Rahab didn't know what to say for a moment. She asked, "Why do you say that?"

"Why wouldn't I say that? I've been so proud of myself and of my ability to keep the law, and now I've tried deliberately to break the rules for a situation that I voluntarily entered. I've ruined everything."

Rahab wanted to smile at the woebegone look on his face. He seemed like a little boy. "Why do you think that?"

"I know you must hate me for what I tried to do."

Day 27

"No, Salmon. I don't hate you."

"I wanted so much to convince you that I was different from all those other men you have known, and instead I have acted just as much like an animal toward you as they did."

Rahab felt compassion for him. "Salmon, you cannot help being a man. You would be different indeed if you did not have desires." She paused. "You have convinced me that you are different from the men I have known."

Salmon looked up, surprised. "I don't know how."

"When I asked you to stop, you did. That has never happened before. All the men that I have known have taken me with or without my permission. That counts for something."

He was silent for several minutes. He seemed to want to say something but was hesitant. "Do you remember the day we heard the law?"

"Yes, of course. Why do you ask?"

"Do you remember that when Joshua was writing up the second law about not having any idols, you said something about it."

"Yes, I remember that you seemed irritated by my talking so much."

"I was irritated, but not for the reason you think. What you were saying made me realize something that I wasn't ready to face then. You said that an idol could be anything that we relied on for happiness besides the Lord."

"And you said that I shouldn't read more into the law than was said."

"Yes, but the reason I didn't like what you said was that I knew even then that I was making an idol out of you. You have become more important to me than anything or anyone else."

"Oh, Salmon. I don't know what to say."

"Let me finish. There was something you said a few nights before that, which also has been bothering me, and I finally put the two thoughts together in my mind last night."

"What was the other thing I said?"

"You said that a man who wants a woman only because she can satisfy him sexually doesn't really love her, but himself." He paused and looked down at the uneaten bread in his hands. "Those words have been like torture to me. Then last night you said some more things that I am still trying to understand. What did you mean when you said that I'm so surrounded by the Lord's goodness that I think it comes from me?"

She hesitated but then said, "I've noticed that you, and really nearly all of you Israelites, compare your behavior to that of the Canaanites or Egyptians or whomever, and you feel that you are superior. All I was saying was that your righteous behavior isn't a result of your being superior, but of your having a superior god. I think that if you ever quit trying to obey him, you will be just as evil as the Canaanites."

"After what happened last night, I am in no position to argue with you. I have treated both you and the Lord badly. I think the only god I have is myself."

"Perhaps the Lord knows that we are all going to fail him, but he still gives us the chance to ask his forgiveness and offer sacrifices to atone for that. Being able to get his forgiveness is one of the greatest things about your, I mean, our religion."

"I always wanted to try to be so good that I wouldn't need to make a sin offering."

"I don't think any of us can do that. I think the Lord wants us to come with humble hearts, ready to confess that we are sinners and need his forgiveness."

"You have done that. I need to, also. I am going to ask Eleazar to offer a sin offering for me today."

"That is a good idea."

He still looked very sad. Rahab thought something more was bothering him. "Are you going to be all right?"

He dropped his head then and sighed heavily, "Rahab, I don't want to say this, but I feel this would be fair to you in light of what has happened. I am releasing you from your obligation to marry me. You do not have to go through with it."

Rahab was startled. For nearly a month, she had hoped this would happen. Her desire for so long had been to be free of men, to live alone or with her family. She never believed he would ever give her a choice in the matter. But now that the release had come, she didn't feel as elated as she had expected.

She looked around the tent that had been her home. What should she take and what leave behind? So many of the things she had used were his. She saw the cooking pots in which she had prepared the meals that he had liked so much, the precious scrolls, the rolled up mats where they had rested separately, talking about life and the Lord. She would miss those conversations.

When she came to this tent, she had brought only the linen clothes on her back, and she knew these were gone. The only other thing was... She hesitated as she touched the knot of the scarlet cord, which she still wore around her neck. This was his, not hers. She reached in her wool shift and pulled it out and over her head. As she looked at it—the symbol of his saving her from Jericho, of his mother's faith, of the blood that paid for their sins, of their joined lives—she realized that she could not leave him without feeling torn apart.

Day 27

Rahab looked at Salmon's bowed head, and feelings of such tenderness overwhelmed her that she could hardly keep from throwing herself into his arms. Quietly she said, "Salmon, I don't want to leave. I love you. I want to marry you."

"Do you mean it?" He looked up into her eyes. "Oh, Rahab, I..." Sobs began to shake his body. "I am unworthy."

"So am I." She reached across to him now and laid her hand on his. He gathered her hand into both of his and kissed it gently. They sat thus for several minutes, overwhelmed by emotion.

Salmon was the first to stir. He kissed her hand again, then reached up and cupped her face, looking deeply into her eyes. "I love you, so much."

"I believe you, now." She returned his look without fear and with a growing awareness that this was a precious gift—this ability to love and be loved by another human being in this way. She felt that her heart would burst with the happiness of that moment, and she worshiped Yahweh for giving this to her.

Salmon didn't want to leave her side that day, and she didn't want him to. "Will you go with me to take the sacrifice to the tabernacle?"

"Yes, I want to."

Together they went to the flock to pick out a female goat. Rahab asked, "Why do you take a goat? When we took an offering for me, we took a lamb."

"This sin offering is for me. Leaders must sacrifice a goat as a sin offering. Members of the community offer lambs."

When they got to the tabernacle with the goat, Salmon stopped by his cousin Eleazar's tent to see if he were available to make the sacrifice. He came out in surprise. "You were just here a couple of weeks ago. Why are you offering another sin offering?"

Salmon said sheepishly, "This sin offering is for me. I have become aware of my own need for forgiveness."

Eleazar looked at him steadily. "If you need to offer a sin offering, then I don't know anyone who doesn't need to."

"I can only attest to my own need. I can't judge anyone else's."

Eleazar nodded his head as if in understanding. "Let's go then."

Once again Rahab was left outside the curtains of the tent while Eleazar and Salmon went inside to make the sacrifice. She prayed to the Lord, whom she knew very well could hear the thoughts of her heart, "Thank you, Lord, for this way of getting forgiveness for our sins. Thank you that Salmon understands now. And thank you for the love that you have given to me for him. He is much more than I had ever dreamed of.

But you knew just what I needed and wanted, even when I didn't know myself, didn't you?"

She turned as Salmon and Eleazar came out of the tabernacle again. She looked up into Salmon's eyes and recognized there a peace that had been missing. They thanked Eleazar and headed to the tent.

When they got back, she put out the bread and cheese for a light supper. Then she sat across from him and smiled at him. "You look much happier than you have."

"I guess I'm still dazed. One instant I was giving you up forever, and the next you were offering me what I've been longing for since I met you."

"That was the Lord's doing. He gave me this love I have for you."

"Then he has my gratitude."

"And mine."

DAY 28
THE FOURTH SABBATH

Salmon came into the tent excitedly. "Rahab, Joshua is coming here for a midday meal. He sent word that he will be here in a short time. What can you prepare quickly?"

Rahab had never seen Salmon so agitated. She answered him calmly, "We are having goat's cheese and wheat bread. Do we need more than that?"

"Do we have anything special? Some fruit or meat or something?"

"It's the Sabbath. I can't cook anything, but I will put some fresh fruit with it. Why are you so upset?"

"I don't know how to explain. When the leader of the whole nation comes to visit, he could say anything."

Rahab began putting fruit out even as she considered his words. "I do see your point, but I suppose Joshua is a human being just like we are, isn't he?" She was surprised to see his intensity of emotion. She had served the king and all the high officials of Jericho at one time or another in her inn and was keenly aware that position did not make men superior beings. Though she had no reason to think ill of Joshua, she also didn't think he was anything but another man. Salmon was displaying for Joshua the kind of excitement that she had felt about seeing the presence of the Lord at the tabernacle the first time.

The food was prepared and attractively displayed by the time Joshua came. Salmon seated his guest while Rahab retreated into the back room of the tent to give them freedom to talk about business, though she could still hear their conversation.

Joshua said as he ate the food, "I had heard that you were eating well, but I wanted to see for myself."

"Is that why you have come to visit, sir?"

Day 28, The Fourth Sabbath

"That was one reason. I also wanted to remind you that you will not be serving in the military for the year after you are married. I appreciate all that you have done for the nation; your leadership will be missed. But that is the law."

"Yes, sir." He hesitated. "Was there anything else?"

"Yes. I have heard from Eleazar as well as from you and Othniel, that this Rahab seems to have an unusually strong faith in the Lord. Do you think I could question her about that?"

If Salmon was surprised at this request, he hid it. Calling Rahab from the back room, he sat watching them as they conversed.

Joshua looked at Rahab speculatively, then he began speaking in fluent Canaanite. "Young lady, I have heard much about your faith. You are becoming somewhat legendary among the people of Israel in the short time you have been with us. I have a number of questions I would like to ask you. You had never had personal contact with Israelites before Salmon and Othniel came to your inn that night, isn't that right?"

"Yes, that's right."

"So what happened to make you so ready to accept the Lord as your God?"

She looked a long time up at the roof of the tent and began to tell him her story. "I was married to a most evil kind of Canaanite man. After he had sent me away from his house, I gave birth to his child, but he came with priests and took the child to sacrifice to Molech. He tried to force me to watch the sacrifice, but I could not. I ran into the fields outside Jericho to escape him. There I passed out from the grief and lay in that field for hours.

"I awoke bewildered, with a heaviness in my heart that soon turned to agony as I remembered where I was and what had happened. Rising at last, I felt the ache of grief even in my muscles and began to walk about the fields thinking. I thought about my life: how I had been given to the bridegroom with the highest bride price though he was a known womanizer and abuser; how I had been thrown out of the house after I objected to his affairs; how I had wandered pregnant in the streets where I was robbed and raped before I was finally reduced to earning my living as a common prostitute. Now my child had been taken from me and offered up to Molech."

Salmon made a sound of distress as if this rehearsal of her life pained him. Joshua looked at both of them with something like compassion in his gaze.

Rahab continued, "Don't fret. I can talk about it now. Anyway, while I walked I kept asking myself questions about life and religion. What had the gods of my fathers done that was so great? Ashtoreth had enticed the men in the city to focus on their sexuality so much that they weren't satisfied with their wives, and none of them knew how to love anyone but themselves. Molech sent them off to wars that left widows and orphans behind, and worse, he ate our children with a voracious appetite. And the other gods, what about them? Baal, Asherah, all of them were bloody, murderous, vindictive gods. None of them were worthy of worship; none of them were worthy of all they took.

"The agony of my grief overcame me, and I threw myself on the ground, wanting to die. I began to sob, crying for what seemed like hours. The pain was like a knot inside of me that no quantity of tears could dissolve.

"Much later, a stillness came over me like that after a storm. Night had fallen by then, and the sky was ablaze with millions of stars. I looked up and was struck by the immensity of the night sky. As my breathing became less ragged, I allowed myself to take it in—so many stars, so far away. Then sounds penetrated my consciousness, crickets chirping, a light breeze. I thought to myself, 'Someone created all of this. Whoever made this was not cruel and murderous, but one who loves beauty and peace, one who is much, much bigger than a clay figurine or bronze statue.'"

Joshua nodded his head. He was following her closely.

"I said aloud, 'Who are you?' The sound of my voice startled me, and I wondered what was inside me that felt the need to address this creator god. I asked him, 'Did you create me? Why am I alive? Why did my baby have to die? Will I ever know love?'

"Again I sat silent, listening, soaking in the night. Then thoughts came to me that were in my mind yet seemed to come from somewhere else: 'I love you. I am coming. Wait and watch for me.'

"'Is it you? Did you speak?' The silence was still there, and I felt him waiting—waiting for me to decide something. I asked myself if I believed in this voice in my head, and whether it would make any difference if I believed.

"Somehow, I knew. Believing would make all the difference in the world. I said aloud, 'Yes, I believe in you. I will wait.'

"A warmth crept into my chilled body from my fingertips up my arms and into the empty spaces inside of me that I hadn't known were there. I felt full of something that I couldn't name. But I knew this: I was loved." She paused then, but her eyes were shining as she remembered. "Strange that I could look back to a moment that happened on the worst night of my life and remember it as one of the best because I met the Lord then." Joshua seemed at a loss for words. After a few moments of

Day 28, The Fourth Sabbath

quiet, he said, "So you trusted in this voice inside of your mind and were just waiting for him to have a name."

"Yes. Later, the things we heard about the God of Israel and what Othniel and Salmon said about him that night in my inn convinced me that he was the God I was waiting for, the one who loved me. Since then, he has proven over and over to be the one."

"I understand what you heard. I, myself, have had similar experiences."

"Oh, tell me about them! What did he say to you?"

"When Moses died, and I knew I was to take over the reigns of power, I was terrified."

Salmon gasped, but Rahab nodded in understanding. "But he spoke to you?"

"Yes, like you, I heard his voice in my head. He said, 'Be strong and courageous.' He promised to be with me as I led the people. He reminded me to know and obey the law. I was transformed by the encounter. His message made a great difference in my ability to lead the people."

"He doesn't have to say very much to change a person's life completely, does he?"

"No, he doesn't. I sometimes think that those moments when he speaks directly are the only moments in life that have real value."

"Yes! By comparison, other events and relationships in life seem relatively unimportant." She glanced over at the stricken Salmon. "But having said that, he has given me friendships and love, too, that I know to be gifts from him, and so for me, they are part of my relationship with him."

"Relationships like marriage to Salmon?"

"Yes, I believe that Salmon is a gift from the Lord far beyond what I had ever hoped for."

Joshua now turned to Salmon who was sitting, listening to them discuss him as though he were not present. "Salmon, you have a gift here in this woman of inestimable value. I hope you cherish her all of her days. She will bless you and all of Israel beyond all reckoning."

"Thank you, sir. I know that I am not worthy of her, but I will do my best to be worthy."

"I believe you. The Lord bless you both, my children."

With that, Joshua rose to his feet with surprisingly agile grace for a man in his eighties and headed out of the tent, but he turned back to say with a twinkle in his eye, "Her ability to cook is not the least of her gifts." Then he was gone.

The tent was very quiet after Joshua left. Finally, Salmon spoke softly. "Why have you never told me that story before?"

Rahab paused before answering carefully, "Early in our relationship here, I was angry with you, and I didn't want to share so deeply of myself. Later, it never seemed like the right time. Had you asked me directly as Joshua did, I would have told you."

"I knew there had to be something more that caused you to have such a passion for the Lord, but I guess I was afraid to know what it was."

"Why were you afraid?"

"I think I was afraid of admitting how far short I fall from having real faith in the Lord and of admitting that a Canaanite woman has more faith than an Israelite man."

"How do you feel now?"

"I envy you."

"Envy me?"

"Yes. I have a lifelong knowledge of the Lord and his law, but I don't have the surety of faith that you have. You have met him as a person, not just an idea."

"Haven't you ever thought that the Lord might be speaking to you?"

"No... well, maybe I have, but I didn't want to believe it because he seemed to be telling me to do something that I didn't want to do."

"So did you just ignore the voice in your head?"

"Yes, I felt my only obligation was to obey the law, no more. But now I am beginning to think that there might be more to knowing the Lord. Does he talk to you now?"

"Not often. I am learning to know him now by learning about his history with the Israelites and by studying his law. Every story you have told me tells me more of his character. He is always good in every story. The stories of the Canaanite gods are about lust and deceit and killing. They were not very good role models to build a life on."

"I hadn't really thought about how good the Lord is."

"I think you do know the Lord. How could you help it when you are so surrounded by him, but I think you have come to take him and all he has brought to your people for granted."

"That is easier to do than you realize when we haven't known any other way of life. Besides, the freedom that the Canaanites have to indulge desires appears tempting. Our life seems dull by comparison."

"Do you think you would be happier living as the Canaanites do?"

"Well, no, at least I don't think so."

"I wish I knew how to communicate to you what I feel in the Israelite camp compared to Jericho. We were so bound by the whims of our gods, and what they asked did not make our lives better. Everything the Lord requires makes our lives better in some way, makes us better people."

"Even sacrifice?"

"Yes, I think so, because sacrificing to him reminds us of our need for forgiveness, and it allows us to give up something in gratitude and worship to him. What he asks for is not too much. The sacrifices we made to Molech only made us into murderers and left us bereft."

"I want to know the Lord the way you do."

"You have already made a start by wanting it. I think perhaps that is the first step."

"Does the next step involve listening to the voice in my head?"

"I don't think I can answer that question for anyone but myself. I didn't have the law or the tabernacle or the history to help me know him. Maybe he only talks to those who need that to get started because they have nothing else. But whatever you need in order to know him, I think the Lord will provide it. I would trust that he wants you to know him and just seek him in every way you can." She smiled as she rose to clean up the dishes from lunch.

As she did that, Salmon said, "I need to go out some later. I'll be back for supper after dark."

"All right."

After sunset, Salmon retrieved two bags of gold from the place where he kept his treasure and headed off to the alien section. As he approached Benne and Mora's tent once again, he wondered how he would be treated this time. Then he remembered that he had promised to deliver Rahab's message about honoring her parents to them, and he hadn't done that yet. That made things even more complicated.

Benne came out to meet Salmon and beamed on him with more cordiality than he had ever shown before. Clearly having a rich and dutiful son-in-law appealed to him. "How are you this fine day?"

"I am well, sir. I have brought the two sacks of gold that I promised, and I have made arrangements for you to look at the oxen and sheep tomorrow morning to see if they are acceptable."

"Fine, fine. Come in and have some grape juice. I wish I could offer you something more substantial."

Salmon entered the tent and sat down, where he was offered a cup of drink. He gasped, "This is substantial enough for me, sir," after a swig of the strongest wine available in Israel. He sat the cup down and began, "I have a message for you and your wife from Rahab. Is your wife nearby?"

"Mora, come out here," commanded Benne.

Mora appeared from the back room and stood as Salmon cleared his throat and delivered the message. "Rahab said to tell you that she is sorry for the trouble and disrespect she has given you through the years. She wants you to know that she loves you and appreciates all that you have done for her."

Benne and Mora looked amazed at this speech. "Did Rahab really say that?" asked Benne.

"Yes, sir. I am just delivering her message."

Mora began to weep softly, "That is the most wonderful message I've ever received. What has entered her head to make her say that?"

"She actually told me this on the day we heard the law read. She and I talked a lot about what the Lord God meant when he said 'Honor your father and mother.'"

"And your God's command has had this effect on our daughter?" Benne seemed genuinely at a loss over this information. "Perhaps the laws of this god are worth knowing more about."

"I hope you will learn about them, sir."

"I'll talk to Caleb about this some more."

Later that evening, Salmon told Rahab of her parents' reaction. "They were really moved by what I told them. I haven't seen your father so open to the law of the Lord before."

Rahab's eyes shone in the lamplight. "I have so desired that my parents would begin to understand the ways of the Lord and want to know him, too. But it seemed impossible to me for my father to change."

"I have felt the same way. I was afraid he might do something that would get him in trouble."

"The Lord always blesses obedience, doesn't he?"

"He definitely has in this case." Salmon looked at Rahab with that look of tenderness that moved her deeply and made her change the subject for fear she would forget herself. She asked, "Are you ready for sleep?"

Salmon nodded, but she sensed that he understood.

DAY 29

At breakfast the next morning, Rahab remembered that she needed to talk to Salmon about the spindle. "Acsah was in here a few days ago. She mentioned that people are beginning to weave again because clothes are wearing out."

"Yes, I noticed a worn place on the hem of my coat."

"Acsah will need her spindle back if she is going to do her own weaving."

"Are you saying that the spindle you have been using is Acsah's?"

"Yes, I thought you knew that."

"I assumed you were using the spindle from Mother's box."

"You have a spindle?"

Salmon went to the same box from which he had removed the blue head covering that he had given to Rahab earlier. He sat for a minute looking quietly at the contents. Then he turned to Rahab with a look of sadness and yet peace. "You should take over the contents of this box to use for yourself."

Rahab moved closer and looked into the box. Inside were possessions that any woman would prize: carved sewing needles of various sizes, a fine weaver's comb, the spindle, a delicate shell comb, and some beautiful gold and silver jewelry. "I can't use your mother's things, Salmon."

"Why not? Mother is gone, and you are my wife, or soon will be. Why should these things stay in this box when they could be used by you?" He looked steadily into her eyes. "Mother would have wanted you to have these."

Rahab reverently picked up the shell comb and realized that she had enough hair now that she actually could comb it. Holding it, she felt a kinship with the woman who had raised Salmon. "Thank you, Salmon."

"For what?"

Day 29

"For trusting me with your mother's possessions."

After breakfast Salmon left to see her parents and check on the animals.

Before he left she asked him, "How is the lamb I cared for?"

"I'll check with Elias. I know that Penninah was feeding it, and that it was getting stronger."

"Will you be back for lunch?"

"I want to be." He stooped over and whispered in her ear, "I'll miss you until then."

She smiled up at him.

She made herself busy with the chores of the tent, humming the tune from the song she had heard at the reading of the law to herself. She couldn't remember when she had felt so content with life. And even better, Acsah came for a visit.

"Look what Salmon has given to me." She showed Acsah the open box.

"What is all this?"

"Tarah's box of personal items—her jewelry and handwork. And see, here is her spindle. Now I can give yours back."

"That's wonderful. I am looking forward to weaving wool myself."

"Thank you for letting me borrow it for so long. You might have been using it."

"I had to learn how first. Watching you spin has been the best way to learn to do it myself." She placed a mat on the floor of the tent before she sat down.

"Your period?" Rahab guessed.

"Yes." She smiled brightly, "Do you want to practice Hebrew?"

Rahab answered in Hebrew, "Yes, but I also have another favor. Tell me about any laws related to marriage."

"Most of them you know already like not lying with your husband during your period and what to do when marrying a captive woman. Quite a few deal with who may not marry—brothers to sisters or children to parents, for example."

Rahab nodded. She didn't think it worthwhile to point out that in Canaan and in Egypt, brothers did marry sisters sometimes. "What about bride prices and dowries?"

"I don't know of any laws about those. But we do have them. I think we mostly follow the practices that are similar to those in Canaan, because I know that our ancestors did the same things when they lived here."

"Which ancestors?"

"Have you heard the story of Jacob and Rachel?"

"I've heard of Jacob."

"That's right. I told you about Jacob and Esau myself."

"And the lentil stew?"

"Yes. If you remember, Jacob cheated Esau out of his birthright and blessing. Their mother, Rebekah, was afraid that Esau would kill Jacob, so she begged Isaac, their father, to send Jacob back to her people to find a wife. She really didn't like Esau's Canaanite wives, so she had a good reason to give Isaac."

"Did Isaac agree to let him go?"

"Yes. On the way there, Jacob encountered the Lord in a dream about a stairway to heaven. He was changed by that experience. After that the Lord was with him."

"Did he find a wife?"

"Almost at once, in a way. When he got to the country where his mother's people lived, he met a beautiful girl next to a well and immediately fell in love with her. She turned out to be his cousin. Her father, Laban, was Rebekah's brother."

"You must like this part of the story—the part about marrying cousins."

Acsah smiled at her before continuing. "He didn't get to marry her immediately. Laban agreed to let him marry Rachel, but only after he paid a bride price of seven years of labor."

"Seven years?"

"Yes, but the story says he loved her so much that it seemed like nothing to him."

"Then what happened."

"Laban tricked him. He had another, older daughter named Leah, who wasn't as beautiful and had weak eyes. By custom, he needed to find a husband for her first. He must have been having trouble. So on the wedding night, he waited until Jacob was drunk, then covered Leah up with veils and sent her in to be the bride instead of Rachel. You can imagine how angry Jacob was at being tricked."

"Yes, but I can also imagine that he had more sympathy for Esau's feelings after that."

"I think maybe he did."

"What did Jacob do about it?"

"Laban let him marry Rachel a week later, but he had to work another seven years to pay for her."

"Another seven years? That meant he essentially worked fourteen years for the woman he loved. That was a fabulous bride price."

"Yes, almost as good as the one Salmon paid for you."

"What?"

"You didn't know about the bride price?"

Day 29

"What are you talking about?"

Acsah looked surprised, "My father acted as arbitrator for your father and Salmon about a dowry and bride price. He had planned to convince your father to be reasonable by pointing out that according to Canaanite law, he really owed the bride price from your first marriage to Salmon as well as a dowry."

"Father could never repay the bride price. He was paid ten cows and a sack of gold. Those things were gone long before the end of my first year of marriage."

"My father said he knew that Benne would be unwilling to pay that or the dowry. But what Salmon did was unexpected. He not only waived his right to a dowry, he paid your father a new bride price, as though you had never been married before."

"He didn't have to do that, did he?"

"No, and what is really astonishing is the amount. He paid ten oxen, sixty sheep, and two sacks of gold."

Rahab sat back stunned. "I had no idea!" She sat at a loss for words, trying to take in all that Acsah had told her.

"If I were guessing, I would say that Salmon likes you a little bit," Acsah teased, but then noticed that Rahab had tears running down her face. "I'm sorry, I didn't mean to make light of something so meaningful."

"That's okay. I'm just so overwhelmed. Do other people know this besides my parents and your father?"

"Oh, yes. All over the camp people are discussing this. Such a bride price has never been paid in Israel before."

"He wants everyone to know that he values me."

"Yes, I think you are right."

"Acsah, I've never shared this with you before, but I have difficulty accepting that anyone could love me for myself. I always assume that the person wants me for selfish reasons. I think you were the first besides the Lord that I felt liked me as a real person. I have appreciated your friendship so much. It has made such a difference. Now I really believe that Salmon loves me, too. Can you understand what I mean?"

"I haven't had your exact experience, but I understand what you are saying. Does this mean you have changed your mind about being turned out by Salmon?"

"Yes. I didn't think this possible until a few days ago, but I have learned to love Salmon in a way that fulfills all my girlhood dreams."

Acsah smiled at her. "I hoped you would fall in love with him. He really is a great man." She glanced out at the sun. "Oh, it's almost noon. I'd better go see about Father's food."

"Thank you for coming by. Do you realize that you didn't have to correct my pronunciation once?"

Acsah laughed, "That's because you let me do most of the talking." Rahab realized that she had not fixed anything for the noon meal, but just then, Shamar came in carrying a pot of porridge and some goat's milk. Rahab smiled at her, "Thank you, Shamar. I wasn't paying attention to the time at all."

"I am so much stronger now than I was right after the baby came. I can do this for you. It really is my job, and I know more about how to do it now, thanks to you."

"May I see little Tirzah?" She stood up so she could look at the baby, who was riding comfortably on her mother's back. "She is so beautiful, Shamar. And so content."

Shamar beamed with motherly pride. "She sleeps under the blanket you made. I will always keep that blanket for her."

"What a kind thing to say!"

Shamar ducked her head in embarrassment, then exited the tent just as Salmon walked in.

Rahab felt her heart leap at the sight of his beloved face. Being in love was so different from any feeling she had felt before in her life. She wanted so much to touch him, but she knew that would not be wise. Instead she said, "I heard what you did for my parents with the bride price, Salmon. How can I find adequate words to tell you what that means to me?"

He said, "I'll let you show me in a couple of days."

Rahab responded in kind, "I will."

Their words were light, but the desire between them was so strong.

With an effort Rahab asked, "Are you ready to eat?"

"Yes, I'm starved." He sat down and began eating the porridge. "This is good. Did you make it?"

"No, Shamar did. I spent the morning with Acsah. She took her spindle back, so she can begin spinning and weaving in her own tent now. She will need a loom, too."

"I'll see if Caleb wants to ask your father to make one for her."

"I really appreciate your having him make this one for me. I know how much you paid for it. But I'm afraid Elias has too much trouble taking it down and putting it up so much. I wonder how much longer the camp of Israel will travel together."

"That is a difficult question to answer. The Lord will tell us through Joshua. If we follow the pattern we've started, we will conquer areas and set up cities for some of our non-combatants to live in to care for the

Day 29

land and occupy it, but the army will stay together and keep going until everyone has received an allotment of land."

"It will be good to have our own home together, won't it? But I think I couldn't be happier there than I am right now with you."

"I am very happy, too. But not for the reasons I thought would make me happy."

"What do you mean?"

"For forty years, we wandered in the wilderness. We were looking for a place we could call our own, a place where we could build permanent homes and cultivate food, a place where we would not have to move at a moment's notice."

"So you thought that just having a nice home and all that goes with that would satisfy the longing that drove you in the desert?"

"Yes." He paused for a moment. "But now I know it would take more than that. I would not have been happy in a permanent home by myself."

"I've been waiting, too. But I wasn't waiting for a permanent home. I had a home in my inn in Jericho. I was prosperous there with plenty to eat and drink; my clothing was the best in town, for I wove it myself from the linen that I grew. But I was not happy there. Having my physical desires met wasn't enough. I wanted love, not just appreciation or admiration or lust, but real love. The Lord offered that to me after my baby's death. Once I received that, I felt that it was what I had been waiting for all of my life. You have asked me where my faith came from. I knew nothing of your laws, of obedience or punishment or even might in battle. My faith began because when I cried out from a broken and empty heart for help, I was met by love." Her voice dropped to a whisper as she said these words.

Salmon looked at her with those feelings of tenderness that her avowals of faith always stirred in him.

Rahab responded to his look with a question, "Salmon, I've been wondering something."

"What's that, dearest?"

"I don't understand why you care about me like this. I have never regarded myself as worth much to others except for what I could do for them. Doesn't it bother you that I was a prostitute, hated by every woman and exploited by every man in Jericho?"

"I think perhaps there was a time when I would have thought myself too holy and important to have a prostitute for a wife." He looked away as he thought. "I knew when I saw you in Jericho that you were the most attractive woman I had ever seen. We hadn't been with you long before I realized that you were a prostitute, but at the same time, I saw your faith, your intelligence, and your personality." He paused as though considering his words carefully. "When we were out in the hills waiting for the time to go back to Gilgal, I thought a lot. I tried to forget you—I don't mean that we wouldn't have kept our oath—I mean that I tried not to feel anything for you. I kept reminding myself that you were a sinner. I told myself that I was only enamored because you were a prostitute and knew how to be attractive for men; but I have been around attractive women before, and none of them have had this effect on me. Then I thought I wouldn't think about you until we saw if Joshua would even allow us to save you and your family. But the idea of killing you in Jericho made me ill."

Rahab was looking intently at him as he told his story.

"After the battle of Jericho, I kept coming out to your tent to see if anything you would say or do would make me change my mind, but being with you only increased my desire to make you my wife. Finally, one night I acknowledged to myself the truth. I was in love with the person that you are, and nothing, not even the knowledge of your past, would change that for me."

Rahab nodded her head with tears streaming down her face, but said nothing.

"I know now that I should have wooed you and not just taken you as I did. But once I knew that I wouldn't change my mind, I wanted to have you near me. Can you ever forgive me for my haste?"

"I already have forgiven you."

Salmon smiled. "When I look at you, I don't see a former prostitute. I see you, Rahab—a beautiful, intelligent woman with utter faith in God and insatiable curiosity about his law; with strength of will and spirit, and with the most beautiful brown eyes God ever put in a woman's face. If you can put your past behind you, so can I."

Rahab sighed with pleasure, "Having you love me has done more to show me what the Lord is like than anything else that has happened to me."

DAY 30

Salmon went out early in the morning to personally invite Caleb, Othniel, Joshua, and Eleazar to come to his wedding and the feast. He also made a special trip to Benne's tent. "I am inviting you to come to our wedding tomorrow morning. This will be your first opportunity to see Rahab again."

"When should we come and where?"

"It will be mid-morning at the entrance to the tabernacle. Then in the evening after sundown, we will have a feast near my tent. You are invited to that as well."

"We look forward to both."

Salmon thought as he moved away that Benne could be quite charming when he tried.

When he got back to the tent for the noon meal, he saw the delight in Rahab's face as he stepped into the outer room. What a gift her love was! And tomorrow she would be his wife. Thinking about that made him wonder if he were ready to be her husband. Would he make more mistakes like the day he had gone hunting? He was prompted to ask, "I've been curious about why you were so upset with me the other day after I went hunting."

Rahab put the food in front of him. "After opening up so much to you the night before, I was feeling vulnerable. It really hurt me that you had gone, because I thought it meant that what had happened between us meant nothing to you."

"Quite the opposite, believe me."

"So why did you go hunting?"

"Truthfully, after having you in my arms, I was just too tempted by your presence; I was afraid I might do something rash. But as a woman, you probably don't understand what I'm saying."

Day 30

"I am probably tempted as much or more than you are. But why did you think that running away was a good idea?"

"A story I was told in my childhood about one of our ancestors."

"Could you tell it to me now?"

"The story is rather long, but you probably would enjoy it. The Lord plays a prominent part in it."

"Then I know I will enjoy it."

"This story is about Joseph, one of Jacob's twelve. Did I tell you that Jacob's children were born of four different mothers?"

"No, I don't think I knew that. You aren't planning to do something like that to me, are you?"

"Never. You are woman enough for me. Actually, there was one woman who would have been enough for Jacob, too, if he had been allowed to marry her first."

"Is this the story of Leah and Rachel? Acsah told me about them. Where do the other two women come in?"

"They were Leah's and Rachel's servant girls. They became Jacob's concubines. I don't really have to start at the beginning, then. I can just tell you that Joseph was Rachel's firstborn. That should tell you a lot of the story right there."

"Jacob favored Joseph over his other sons, didn't he?"

"Yes, and as a result, his brothers caught him in a remote area where they were shepherding, took the coat that his father had given him away, and sold him into slavery. Then they smeared blood on the coat and claimed a wild animal had eaten Joseph."

"How awful for Jacob!"

"Yes, it was."

"So what happened to Joseph?"

"He was taken to Egypt. He worked for a man named Potiphar, who had a beautiful wife. This is where the story gave me the idea to run away from temptation.

"Potiphar's wife lusted after Joseph, who was such a good slave that Potiphar had made him steward of his household. She tried to seduce Joseph. One time, she had him cornered, but he ran away, leaving his coat behind him."

"He had trouble keeping coats, didn't he."

"I hadn't thought of that, but you're right. Anyway, the running away kept him from the temptation to commit adultery; but she used the coat to accuse him of attempted rape, and he ended up in prison."

"I assume he got out of prison eventually."

"Yes, because the Lord intervened. He gave Joseph the ability to interpret dreams. In short, he was taken out of prison to interpret one of Pharaoh's dreams, and as a result, was made second in command to Pharaoh in Egypt. What he had predicted from the dream was a famine throughout this part of the world. Joseph helped Egypt be so prepared for the famine that they could sell grain to people from other countries."

"Let me guess. His own family came to buy food."

"Exactly right."

"Did he get his revenge on them?"

"He tested them some to see if their hearts were changed before he revealed who he was. But then he arranged to have everyone including Jacob move down to Egypt to live."

"Is that how the Israelites came to be in Egypt?"

"Yes."

"Why isn't there a tribe of Joseph?"

"Jacob adopted Joseph's two sons and they became tribes themselves, although we sometimes call them half-tribes—Ephraim and Manasseh."

"So Joshua descended from Joseph."

"Yes."

"Did Joseph ever forgive his brothers for what they did?"

"That is probably the most inspiring part of the story. He said that though they meant to do him harm, God had planned all that happened to him to save the family during the famine. God brought good out of evil."

"That is what he does best, I think. Isn't that what we were talking about the other day when you said that the Lord punished the Israelites, but the good that came out of that for you was that you could meet and marry me?"

"Yes, I see a similarity. God brings good out of man's evil."

"I love that story. Thanks for telling me."

"You're welcome."

Then he looked up with a twinkle in his eye. "Did you mean it when you said that you are tempted as much or more than I am?"

Rahab blushed in confusion. This was a direction to the conversation that she would prefer not to follow, but she could not bear false witness. "Yes, I meant it, of course."

"Would you like to elaborate?"

"Not right now." She quickly changed the subject. "I heard Joshua say that you would be exempted from military duty for one year. I guess I didn't catch that when I heard it before. Is it true?"

"Yes, the law requires that for newly married men."

"Do you find that upsetting?"

"That I will be able to be with you every day, all day long for a whole year? Not at all."

Day 30

Rahab looked at him bemused. Every day, all day long with this man—the idea seemed attractive to her now. How much had changed! "Why do you think the Lord has this law?"

"Well, I think it ensures better marriages and fewer young widows. But it also increases the chances of children being born to every marriage."

"How strange and wonderful to think that I might be a mother again with no fear that my child will be sacrificed."

"And I will have the chance to be a father."

"I think you will be a very good father."

"Why do you say that?"

"For several reasons. First, you had a very good father yourself."

"True."

"Second, you are a very patient man. I have seen that in the way you have treated me while I had so much to learn during the past month. And you are a great master to your servants."

"What makes you say that?"

"I think what you did for Shamar and Elon was really wonderful."

"What did I do?"

"Didn't you deliberately assign Elon to tasks that wouldn't involve killing at the Battle of Ai so he could be the runner back to camp and not have to wait outside the camp while Shamar was having her baby?"

Salmon grinned at her, "Maybe I did. How did you find out about that?"

"Mahlah told me. She said other things that made me see what a kind master you are. I realized then that you would be different as a husband because you were so different from Ambaal as a master. So I think you will be a good father, too."

Salmon looked tenderly in her eyes and said, "You don't know how much those words mean to me."

"Why is that? You knew you were a good master, didn't you?"

"Hearing those words from your lips is what make them valuable to me." He paused then. "Anything else?"

"I remember what you said about teaching children the law in the morning, during the day, and at night. You have done that for me, and I know you will do that for our children."

"You know I had ulterior motives, don't you?"

"What do you mean?"

"I wanted to talk to you, but the only way I could get you interested was to talk about the law or the Lord."

"I guess I was pretty closed to you, wasn't I?"

"Yes, you were. Can you tell me now what you were thinking and feeling then?"

"I was afraid to trust any man at that time. I've never had a relationship like this one before."

"What do you mean?"

"All my relationships with men have been based on their desire for my body, either through marriage or as customers. I never felt that any of them saw me as a person."

"So you thought that was the only reason I wanted you, too?"

"Yes, but I am convinced now that you care about me for who I really am."

"Believe me when I say that I am well aware of your body. But I do see you as a person. Spending this month with you has been invaluable, because now I feel we are friends. I see a lot of the men with their wives, and they don't really seem to know each other. They share a tent, children, everything but themselves. I don't think they even realize what they are missing."

"What makes the difference?"

"We have had to be together; we had no choice, but since we couldn't have intimate relations, we have had nothing to do but talk. Actually, this is really what I've always longed for, but didn't think I could have." He laughed gently.

"What?"

"Oh, I was just remembering a conversation I had with Othniel when we were in the mountains after you helped us escape from Jericho."

"Tell me about it."

"We were sitting in a valley between the hills where we thought we could risk a small fire in the cold that night. Othniel asked me why I had never married. Of course, I asked him the same question, but he had a ready answer. He will not marry unless he can have Acsah."

Rahab smiled, "Poor Othniel. What are the chances that Caleb will relent?"

"Better than they used to be. The situation with Achan really disturbed Caleb. He might be more likely to accept Othniel for Acsah now."

"Why is that?"

"Caleb wanted Acsah to marry Achan's son. But now that is out of the question."

"I don't think Acsah knew that."

"It is probably better that she not know it."

"Othniel is by far the best choice in camp for her. I wonder that Caleb refuses to see that."

"That's my question, too. They could have married years ago if he didn't insist on a descendant of Jacob. Anyway, Othniel kept pressing me to answer his question about why I never married."

Day 30

"What did you say? I've been curious about that myself."

"I just said that unlike him, I had never seen anyone I wanted to marry. He was surprised and started to say that many young maidens would be happy to sleep in my tent with me."

"Really, I hadn't noticed."

"Are you being sarcastic?"

"A little. Actually, I think I am the envy of quite a few girls in the camp, but don't let that make you proud."

"I'll try not to, but when the men ask me how I was able to get the most beautiful woman any of them have ever seen as my betrothed, I am tempted to be proud."

They smiled at each other before Rahab said, "Finish telling about Othniel."

"I just told him that I didn't want a young girl. They are all so much the same—naive girls with no thought except getting a husband. I wanted more than that."

"What did you tell him you wanted?"

"I said that I wanted someone who knew as much of the pain and difficulty of life as I did and who could help me understand it better, maybe ease it some."

Rahab nodded. "I understand what you are saying."

"Othniel didn't at first. He said it sounded like I wanted my mother. But I insisted that wasn't true either; I told him that I wanted a woman to hold in my arms and to fulfill me as a man."

What did he say then?"

"That he did understand, that deep down all men want a true soul mate."

"Do you think so, too?"

"Yes, I do. Men don't talk about that much, so we give each other the impression that all we care about is physical desire. Perhaps some even believe that, but I think any man would prefer a woman who is both his lover and his best friend."

"That sounds beautiful to me. Like everything I ever dreamed about in a relationship."

"I feel the same." They smiled at each other again before Salmon continued. "After he said that, Othniel was silent for a moment, then he burst out laughing. When I asked him what was so funny, he said he was thinking that I should marry the prostitute back in Jericho because she had certainly experienced a lot."

"So Othniel thought you should marry me?"

"So did I, but I was serious." His eyes looked deeply into hers. "Do you have any idea how attractive you are to me at this moment?"

268

Rahab trembled before the intensity she saw in his eyes, not with fear, but with an excitement and anticipation that she had never felt before.

"I have something to show you." Salmon reached for his bag.

"What is it?"

"This." He opened the bag and took out a rag. Inside the rag was a single brown curl, long and dark. Rahab looked at it for a moment before she recognized its import.

"You saved one of my curls from that first day."

"Yes, it has been a symbol for me throughout these days of waiting. It reminded me that I had put you in a position you didn't want, and it reminded me of your vulnerability. Remembering those things helped me to be more patient and self-controlled than I might have been otherwise."

Rahab smiled as she thought about the journey their relationship had made in the last month. He had loved her from the beginning. She knew that now and loved him, too.

DAY 31

Rahab woke with a feeling of great joy. Today she would be married to Salmon! It surprised her to realize that only a month before, she was sure she did not want to be married to this man. Now she could hardly wait. What had made the change?

She heard a sound at the tent doorway. Salmon had already left. They had agreed to meet at the tent of meeting. "Who is it?"

"Acsah. I have something for you."

"Come in Acsah."

Acsah came in with shining eyes. She was carrying a bundle, which she handed to Rahab. Rahab unrolled it with surprise. "A new linen garment—where did you get this?"

"Your mother made it, and Salmon bought it from her for you to wear today. We kept the secret from you. Your mother has been making linen again. She and your father harvested what was left of the flax in the fields near Jericho before we left the area. Your father made her a new loom and she has been working at that, making extra income for your family. She has been happier since she could weave again and is looking forward to having you join her now that you will be free to do so."

Rahab's eyes filled with happy tears. "Everyone has been so kind to me and to my family—especially you, Acsah. I appreciate your friendship so much. I don't believe I have ever had a true friend before, and you have been one to me."

Acsah smiled at her. "You have taught me so much about loving the Lord. I am happy to call you my friend. But today I am envious of you. Perhaps soon I will have the chance to wear a piece of white linen that you have made for me for my own wedding day."

"I want that for you, too."

Day 31

Rahab put on the white linen garment and felt her curly hair, which had grown a lot in one month. She no longer looked like a little boy. Carefully they lifted her head covering over her head. "Rahab, you look radiant."

Together, she and Acsah made their way toward the tent of meeting. All along the way, people stopped what they were doing to look at her and smile. She had many friends now in Israel. Word of her devotion to the Lord had spread, and many of the women had benefited from her unselfish sharing of herself already. As they neared the tabernacle, she felt surprised to see her family standing nearby. For some reason, she had not expected them to be at her wedding. She turned and saw Salmon, smiling and waiting for her at the entrance to the tabernacle. Their eyes met, and she saw the look that stirred her so deeply. Standing near him holding the wedding canopy were Joshua, Caleb, Othniel, and Eleazar. She moved forward as if in a dream and joined him under the canopy.

Then in front of all those present, he declared his intention of taking the Canaanite Rahab as his wife. He gave her the ring from his little finger that she knew had been his mother's. Tears welled up in her eyes as she realized the meaning in the gift.

So they were married, and Salmon took her officially into his tent. She stood looking at him with her smooth linen dress defining her figure and the dark ringlets on her head setting off the deep brown of her eyes.

"The month is finally over. It has been a hard test of my self-control," said Salmon.

"I think God did his best to help you out by making me ugly with my shaved head and shapeless wool shift."

"You were beautiful to me even then, but now, you ravish me."

An embarrassment came into their manners. "I guess we can put the beds together now, can't we?" said Rahab to break the awkward silence.

They began to move their bedding toward a point in the middle. Their hands touched, and Rahab turned to look in his eyes. "You don't have to be afraid of me. I'm the same person I was yesterday and the day before."

"Yes, I know, but I've never done this before. And I'm not sure how to get started."

Then Rahab reached up and pulled his head toward her and surprised him with a gentle kiss. "Salmon, I want you to know that I love you as I have never loved any man before."

His arms went around her and held her tightly. She could hear his heart beating and feel that he was trembling. "Oh, my precious Rahab." Their lips met again in what became a passionate, electric kiss. "Oh, my.

I had no idea it could be like...!" She stopped his mouth with another kiss, and they were swept up in the joy of finally acting on the passions simmering for so long between them.

Later, as she lay in his arms at rest, he spoke softly. "So this is the becoming one flesh that Moses wrote about in his book of beginnings. I think our enjoyment must be even greater because nothing is between our souls and spirits either. I feel that I know you so well after spending this month talking."

"I agree, but Salmon, I've been wondering about something."

"What's that?"

"Didn't the Lord warn the Israelites not to marry Canaanite women for fear they would turn the men away from the Lord to idol worship?"

"Yes, he did."

"Yet he has a law that says if a man takes a woman captive and wants to marry her, she should live with him for a month as I have been doing. Why would he make such a law if you aren't supposed to marry us?"

"That's a very good question. I believe the Lord has made it clear that he wanted me to marry you. I suppose the difference has to do with your willingness to turn from idols to worship of the Lord."

"Does that happen very often?"

"No, it doesn't, and some of the men have been fooled into thinking their wives have changed when they really haven't."

"I feel strange about this—almost as if the Lord had us in mind when he made that law."

"Perhaps he did. Anyway, I can say now that it is a good law, though at times, as you know, I wanted the waiting to be over. You are the wife and companion that I have been looking for all of my life."

"And you are my gift from the Lord to seal his promise to love me and take care of me. I had hoped only to be allowed to survive and have a God worth worshiping. He has given me that and so much more." She kissed him again and put her head on his chest with a sigh of deep contentment. They lay like that for several minutes before Salmon said, "Did you know that we are unclean now?"

"Are we?"

"Yes, we have to take a bath because we have to be clean this evening."

"Why is that?"

"Because we are having guests."

"What? Who?" Her head came up in confusion.

"I am giving a grand feast in honor of my new bride."

Day 31

"Oh, Salmon!" He couldn't tell if she was overcome with joy or consternation.

She needn't have worried. The servants had taken care of everything. She saw that Salmon had provided several sheep for the event as well as many baskets of grapes, figs, and pomegranates and bowls full of goat cheese. The extravagance of it convinced her again that he wanted all Israel to know she was a bride that he prized, though she was Canaanite and a former prostitute. The grace of these expressions of his love stirred her. How she loved him!

Among the first guests to arrive were her family members. Her mother came to her, and Rahab saw that she was crying. "I am so glad I'll be able to see you again. It has been so hard to manage without you." Then in surprise she noticed, "You look happy. I thought you would be pining away for us."

Rahab smiled at her mother. "I have missed you, Mother. I'll come to see you often now and help you all I can. We can make linen together again."

Mora said in an undertone, "Did you really send a message by Salmon saying you appreciate all we've done for you?"

"Yes, Mother. I did send that message and meant every word."

"You've changed, Rahab. I'm not sure how exactly, but I think I like it."

Rahab also hugged her father. Benne choked a little as he said, "Rahab, I don't know when you have looked so happy. I see now that this Salmon of yours is a real gentleman, and he's even richer than Ambaal. Do your best to hold on to him."

Rahab smiled and said, "I will, Father."

She also hugged her little brothers and her sister. She could see that Adah seemed a little happier than she had the month before. She brightened perceptibly when Acsah walked up with Othniel and Caleb. Clearly, she and Acsah had bonded.

Just then Salmon came over to her, with Eleazar beside him. Eleazar laid one hand on Rahab's head and another on Salmon's and said, "The Lord bless you and keep you; the Lord make his face to shine upon you and be gracious to you; the Lord turn his face toward you and give you peace" (Num. 6:24-26, NIV). Tears were in Rahab's eyes as she thanked her high priest and now, cousin.

Salmon whispered in her ear, "That is the blessing that Moses gave to my Uncle Aaron to use in blessing the people. Not many brides in Israel get to have it given directly to them."

"I am indeed blessed already, my husband."

For a second he looked a little startled by the title. Then a broad smile lit his face. "I am blessed, too, my wife." Then quietly, "My precious Rahab."

EPILOGUE

Boaz spoke to his servant. "Who is that young woman gleaning in the barley field?"

"That is the Moabitess, Ruth, who accompanied her mother-in-law Naomi back to Bethlehem after Elimelech's death. She asked if she could glean here. I gave her permission, and she has worked steadily all day, except for one short rest. I have heard that she has become a believer in the Lord."

"Yes, I have heard of her. You say she believes in the Lord? She's very beautiful, isn't she?"

"Almost as beautiful as your mother, may the Lord rest her soul. Rahab was the most beautiful woman I ever saw."

"She was beautiful on the inside, too. I never knew any person with greater faith in the Lord. She obeyed him without question. And yet she was not a descendant of Abraham."

"No, but the Lord accepts those who will follow him, even if they are aliens."

Boaz laughed, "That reminds me. My mother's favorite command was that we should treat aliens with kindness. I think I'll obey that command right now." He walked away across the grain field toward Ruth.

CPSIA information can be obtained
at www.ICGtesting.com
Printed in the USA
BVHW091856060522
636357BV00008B/203